THE PRINCE AND THE WEDDING PLANNER

JENNIFER FAYE

A PROMISE TO KEEP

ALLISON LEIGH

First Published in Great Britain 2020
by Mills & Boon, an imprint of HarperCollinsPublishers,
1 London Bridge Street, London, SE1 9GF

The Prince and the Wedding Planner © 2020 Jennifer F. Stroka
A Promise to Keep © 2020 Allison Lee Johnson

ISBN: 978-0-263-27870-5

0320

MIX
Paper from
responsible sources
FSC™ C007454

This book is produced from independently certified FSC™
paper to ensure responsible forest management.

For more information visit: www.harpercollins.co.uk/green

Printed and bound in Spain
by CPI, Barcelona

THE PRINCE AND THE WEDDING PLANNER

JENNIFER FAYE

PROLOGUE

February, Tuscany, Italy

THIS WAS A living nightmare.

Bianca creaked open the door to her parents' bedroom. She peered inside, just like she used to do when she was a little girl. She paused as though waiting to be bid entrance. That would never happen.

Bianca tentatively stepped into the room, her gaze hungrily taking in her surroundings. The bed was made just as her mother left it each morning. There was still an indentation on her father's pillow as though his head had just been there—as though he would return to it that evening.

But that wasn't to be the case.

Her parents had died. The acknowledgment made her heart clench. One minute they'd been vibrant and active. In the next moment, they'd died in a horrific vehicle accident.

They hadn't been going anywhere special. It hadn't been a special day. It had been a perfectly ordinary day on a perfectly ordinary ride to the city to do some ordinary shopping. And yet it had ended with extraordinarily horrific results.

The backs of Bianca's eyes burned with unshed tears. She blinked repeatedly and sniffled. She had to pull herself together. Falling apart now wouldn't help anyone.

The funeral had just concluded and the will was to be read shortly. Everything was being pushed into fast forward as the vineyard had to be maintained. Springtime would soon be here and work would kick into high gear. Without someone in charge, the Barto Vineyard would suffer—her father's legacy would languish. His precious prize-winning grapes would wither on the vine.

The family's attorney thought with the vineyard at stake, it was reason enough to push her and her two siblings to read the will today of all days—while she was still wearing her black dress from the funeral, while the estate was still filled with mourners that had come to pay their respects.

All Bianca wanted to do that day was remember her parents—to bask in the love that lived within the walls of this vast villa. She pushed the door closed before stepping further into the bedroom. It was here, within her parents' suite of rooms, she felt closest to them.

It was here that her mother showed her how to put on makeup for the first time. It was here that her father had told her she could go away to university in the UK. Bianca walked around the spacious room, running her fingers over her mother's elaborately carved dresser with the huge mirror suspended above it.

She picked up her mother's silver hairbrush and noticed the few long dark strands of hair tangled around the bristles. The last of her mother. Tears clouded Bianca's vision as she thought of never seeing her parents ever again. It still seemed so utterly inconceivable.

She kept walking around the room, her fingers tracing over all the things, that until just days ago, her parents had touched—had used. The thought tugged on her heart strings. How could they be here one moment and then gone the next?

Bianca pressed a shaky hand to her mouth, holding back a wave of emotion that threatened to drown her in unbearable sorrow. She struggled to make sense of it. Why had they been stolen away when they were still so vital—still so needed? When she still didn't have their approval—their blessing for the choice she'd made about her path in life.

Knock. Knock.

"Bianca, are you in there?" It was her brother's voice.

"Yes." She'd been found too soon.

The door creaked open and Enzo's somber face met hers. Thankfully, he didn't ask what she was doing in their parents' room. She didn't want to explain how she was grasping at anything that would make her feel close to them once more.

"Everyone is waiting for us downstairs in father's study."

The moment was at hand. Her parents' final wishes would be known. And then the estate would be divvied up between her, her older brother and her younger sister. It would be so—so final. Her parents' absence from their lives would be undeniable.

"I... I'll be there." She turned her back to him, not wanting him to see the unshed tears shimmering in her eyes. She could be strong like him. She could get through this agonizing day without crumbling into a million pieces.

She needed to think about anything but the hollow spot in her heart. She lifted her head and her gaze came to land on the old photos on the wall. It was a collage of her grandparents, her parents' wedding and herself and her two siblings. They'd all looked so happy—

"Bianca, they loved you." And then her brother exited the room, closing the door softly.

It was like her brother to cut through everything to get to the heart of the problem. Did her parents love her like they'd loved her siblings? She had her doubts.

Bianca paused next to her mother's nightstand. It was there that she noticed her mother's journal. She recalled coming across it as a child and her mother shooing her away. She'd asked her mother what she wrote in her journal and her mother said it was a way to vent or a chance to mark something memorable. Her mother didn't write in it often. Her mother had said she liked to reflect upon where she'd come from, so she knew where she was going.

As a teenager, Bianca had tried keeping a journal of her own, but with two nosey siblings close to her own age, it didn't go well. And when her little sister announced one evening at dinner that Alfio Costa had kissed Bianca after school, she had burned her journal and vowed never to write in one again.

She so desperately longed to hear the gentle lilt of her mother's voice but she couldn't recall it. It was like her mind had erased the memory. How could that be? If she was already forgetting her mother's voice, how soon until she forgot what she looked like and their moments together?

She knew that she was being overly dramatic, but her emotions at the moment felt amplified. She didn't know how to calm them. She picked up her mother's journal. Her fingers traced over the buttery soft binding. Inside were her mother's final words.

Her fingertip traced down over the gold gilded pages. Part of her wanted to open the cover and let her mother's voice speak to her. And another part of her said not to do it. Whatever was written within those pages was none of her business. The struggle raged within her.

At last, she convinced herself a fair compromise was just to read a little bit. Just enough to hear her mother's voice once more. One page. That was all. And then she'd put it away.

She let the book fall open to a random page. There was her mother's very distinctive handwriting. Bianca would recognize it anywhere.

Her gaze hungrily took in every word. Once more, she could hear the lilt of her mother's voice. It was as though she were there in the room with her. Her mother was speaking about her upcoming wedding anniversary. There was mention of a gap growing between Bianca's parents and how her mother wanted to do something that would draw them back together again.

Bianca read the last lines of the page.

Has the past come back to haunt us? Has he truly forgiven me? Or does he blame me and my child...

Blame her? And one of her children? For what?

Not even pausing to consider the right and the wrong of it, Bianca flipped the page.

...for the affair.

Bianca's breath lodged in her throat. Her mother had had an affair? How could that be? Her parents always seemed so much in love. How could this have happened?

Bianca dropped onto the edge of the bed, her legs no longer able to hold her up. Her mind grappled to understand the ramifications of this.

Knock. Knock.

The door opened and her younger sister stepped inside. "Hey, Enzo said you were up here. Everyone is waiting for you. The attorney is looking a bit impatient...okay, a lot impatient."

Bianca didn't care about the attorney. This news altered everything she thought she knew about her parents—everything she believed about them—everything about her not living up to their expectations.

"Bianca, what is it?" Her sister moved across the room, stopping in front of her. "I know this is hard for you. It's hard on all of us—"

"It's not that." She didn't know if she should say something to her sister about the affair. Maybe it was best she just left it alone. Was that even possible? This was a bombshell. And it would blow apart her family—

"Hey," Gia grabbed the journal out of her hands, "this is Mamma's journal. What are you doing with it?"

Guilt washed over Bianca. "I… I just needed to hear her voice—to feel like she was still here."

"And so you thought you'd read her private thoughts."

"It was only one page and then…" Bianca stopped herself. Should she share what she'd learned? How could she not? This changed everything.

"And then what?"

Bianca shook her head. She didn't want her sister to endure further pain. "Nothing."

Her sister studied her for a moment. "It was something all right." Gia lifted the still open journal and read the page. By the bottom line, her mouth gaped and her eyes were rounded. "Seriously?"

Bianca shrugged her shoulders. She wasn't sure what to say. At least she wasn't the only one who didn't know about this affair.

Knock. Knock.

Enzo opened the door. "What's going on with you two? Everyone is waiting downstairs for us?"

Gia motioned for him to come in. "Close the door."

He did as she asked. When he stopped in front of them, he asked, "Why are you reading Mamma's journal? You need to put it back. It's none of your business."

When he went to reach for the journal, Gia was too fast for him. She leaned back on the bed, out of his reach.

Bianca spoke up. "It was only going to be one page. Just enough to feel like Mamma wasn't totally gone. And then—"

"Then we discovered something. Something big."

Enzo shook his head. "Whatever it is. It's none of our business."

"Did you know Mamma had an affair?" Gia blurted out.

"What? No. That can't be right. She wouldn't do something like that." He shook his head as though to chase away the troubling thought. He stepped back from them, distancing himself from the world-shattering news.

Gia scooted back on the big bed, crossed her legs and focused on the journal. She started to read their mother's troubling words. Bianca's gaze stayed on her brother, watching him as the wave of emotions washed over him. It was obvious that he hadn't known about this affair. And the journal didn't say when it'd taken place.

Gia turned the page.

He said that he still loved me and forgave me for what happened, but when we fight, when the distance looms between us, I wonder if he remembers that bad time in our marriage when we separated.

I was so sure that he was never coming back. That we would end up divorced. Days turned to weeks and then to months. I was weak and let a handsome man sweet-talk me into his bed. I've never regretted anything so much in my life. And then the worst happened...

"Stop," Enzo said. "This is wrong."

"I can't stop," Gia said. "This affects us all."

Enzo shook his head. "I don't want to know." Then his gaze narrowed and his voice shook with anger. "Isn't it enough that we lost both of them? Do we have to do this today?"

He might not need to know but Bianca couldn't live with the not knowing. What could be worse than her mother cheating on her father? Bianca needed answers as much as she needed oxygen.

As her sister argued with their brother, Bianca grabbed the journal from her. Her siblings' voices faded into the background as she took in her mother's words.

And then the worst happened. I became pregnant. Aldo said he'd forgiven me and would accept the baby as his own...

Wait. What? One of the three siblings wasn't a true Bartolini? Bianca's gaze hungrily sought out the next words, anxious to know that the family she'd known all her life was truly hers—that she wasn't an outsider.

...but now I wonder if he meant it or if he just accepted the baby because our families were pressuring both of us to get back together.
Am I overthinking his words? Maybe he just spoke in the heat of the moment. Tonight, when he comes in from the vineyard, we'll talk. It's the only way to fix things.

Who? Who isn't a Bartolini? Frustration, anger and sorrow churned in her stomach, making her nauseated. The journal was jerked out of her grasp before she could turn the page.

Enzo held the journal. Anger sparked in his eyes. "Stop! We're not doing this. We have a will to read. We have our parents to mourn. The past must stay in the past."

"What are you going to do with the journal?" Gia asked.

"I'm taking it downstairs and burning it in the fireplace—"

"No." Bianca jumped off the bed. "You can't do that."

"Why not?"

"Because one of us isn't a Bartolini. And that's the only key to the past."

CHAPTER ONE

Six weeks later, Bartolini Villa

HE NEEDED THIS EXCURSION.

He wished it could last longer—much longer.

Crown Prince Leopold stood in the lush garden of an Italian villa. He was surrounded by a group of lavishly dressed people. They all wanted a word with him. Why did he think coming to Tuscany would be any different than attending a social occasion in his homeland?

But in that moment, everyone's attention gravitated from him to a woman who'd joined their group. Her bold makeup and flamboyant hot pink outfit matched her personality. He was grateful the woman enjoyed being the center of attention. All he wanted to be was just another person in the crowd. What was it about people always wanting what they didn't have?

Just as his sister, the Princess of Patazonia, wanted a wedding that reflected her personality instead of a traditional royal wedding. But the queen insisted that tradition must rule above all else. Just as his father had said to him, right before he died:

Traditions are the bedrock of this kingdom.

Leo gave himself a mental shake. Now wasn't the time to get caught in the past—in the regrets—in the what-ifs.

Right now, he had his hands full with his feuding mother and sister. The battles between the two headstrong women was a daily occurrence. So when he was invited to this wedding of a childhood friend, he'd ordered up the family jet. Since he was of no help back at the palace, he figured he might as well wish his friend the very best.

Leo moved away from the flamboyant woman. He could take her high pitched, nasally voice only in small doses. Truth be told, there was another woman that had caught his attention. Her hair was dark and her skin glowed a warm tan. He noticed that she spoke when addressed but for the most part she was quiet. And when she did speak, her voice was soft.

He caught himself staring at her more than once. Maybe it was because she didn't make a point of walking up to him and introducing herself like so many of the other people. In fact, she acted as though she didn't even know he was royalty. Could that be possible?

Regardless, his interest in the beautiful woman increased. It'd been a while since he'd enjoyed a woman's company. With his pending engagement and marriage—a necessity in order to ascend to the throne—he wasn't in a position to start anything. But for the moment, he was still a free man.

He noticed how the other men stared at this woman—even the men that were in committed relationships discreetly turned their heads when she walked by. He couldn't blame them. She was stunning. He had to know more about her.

Noticing that she didn't have anything to drink, he snagged two flutes of champagne. He weaved his way through the crowd, dodging attempts at conversation, on his mission to meet the mystery woman. She was difficult to catch up with as she didn't stop to talk to any person for more than a second or two.

At last, he came up behind her. "Excuse me. I believe this is yours."

The woman turned to him. He held the glass out to her. Her brown eyes were filled with confusion. "But I didn't have any champagne."

"I noticed. That's why I retrieved this for you."

She accepted the glass, but he noticed she didn't drink any of it. "Are you enjoying the wedding?"

"I am. The setting is well done. And the gelato treats are unique."

"That was the bride's idea to help keep guests cool."

"You know her—the bride that is?"

"I do now."

"Ah, so you're a friend of the groom."

"I am now." She smiled.

He was confused. Was this beautiful woman some sort of wedding crasher? Was that why she was quiet? He quickly dismissed the idea. There was nothing about her that said she was anything but cultured.

"I'm confused," he said. "Are you a guest of the bride or the groom?"

"Neither. I'm their wedding planner, Bianca Bartolini."

He hadn't expected that response. He must be slipping. He was usually very good at reading people. It probably had something to do with the turmoil back at the palace. By the time he turned in at day's end, he usually had a headache that kept him up until late into the night.

He needed to do something to bring peace back to the palace. If he couldn't do that for his family, how would he ever keep peace over the nation?

He turned his attention back to his beautiful acquaintance. "It's a pleasure to meet you. I'm Pr...erm... Leo."

"It's an honor to meet you."

"You've done a lovely job with the wedding. The groom seems quite pleased."

"Thankfully."

He hesitated. "You say that like there was a chance he wouldn't be happy."

"I only had six weeks to plan this wedding. Six weeks. Do you know how short that is in wedding time?"

Before he could reply, Bianca was called away by the

waitstaff. With a curtsy and an apology, she was gone and he found himself disappointed to see her go.

A prince.

A real live, sexy-as-sin, bona fide prince.

And he'd been talking to her. Her heart fluttered. It was all Bianca could do not to spill the drink he'd so kindly gotten for her. But she didn't dare drink it. She had to maintain all her senses throughout the ceremony and reception. Everything had to go perfectly. Her future was riding on it.

Still, no one, including the bride and groom, had told her that the prince, whose face graced every gossip magazine, would be in attendance. Someone should have told her. She would have gone to great pains to make sure he had everything he needed.

Instead she'd stood there trying to keep her knees from shaking. And she had absolutely no idea what she'd said to him. She'd been so nervous. She'd probably made a complete fool of herself. And that curtsy. Did people still curtsy to royalty? She wasn't up on her royal etiquette.

Her rambling thoughts and precious memories of meeting the dashing prince would have to wait until later. Right now, she had a job to do.

She approached the bride, who was waiting to walk down the aisle. "Camilla, is everything all right? What do you need?"

Camilla looked flustered. "I forgot my gift for the groom." She paced around the study. "I don't know how I could forget the watch. It took forever to pick out the right one. And I had it engraved."

"Don't worry. Everything is going to be all right."

The bride's eyes shimmered with unshed tears. "No. It's not. This is an omen. Our marriage is doomed."

Bianca reached out, taking the bride's ice-cold hands in her own. "I just need you to breathe. Can you do that?"

"But—"

"No but's. Just breathe. Inhale. Deeply." Bianca demonstrated, hoping the bride would follow her example.

Camilla nodded. Her chest visibly expanded.

"And now breathe out." When the bride did as instructed, Bianca said, "Again."

Once the bride was looking a bit calmer, Bianca said, "You keep taking those deep breaths, and I'll be right back. This is all going to work out. I promise."

Bianca let go of the bride's hands and rushed out of the study, closing the door behind her. The ceremony was already a few minutes late. She walked calmly outside to the string octet and asked them to keep playing, entertaining the guests.

As she headed inside, her brother caught up with her. "What's wrong? Does the bride have cold feet?"

"No." Bianca said it firmly. "I just have to take care of one thing."

She dashed past her brother and headed up the stairs to the second floor. Her high heels didn't slow her down as she headed for the bridal suite. Bianca was certain everything would be all right. This was far from her first wedding—but it was her first wedding all on her own.

Using a master key that each of the Bartolini siblings had, she let herself into the bride's room. The bed was unmade, pillows were tossed about and there were heaps of clothes strewn everywhere. She'd known three-year-old's who kept their rooms tidier. She'd send one of the staff up here to tidy things up before the couple turned in for the night.

It took Bianca longer than she'd have liked to locate the bride's luggage. She searched through the carry-on first, knowing the bride wouldn't want the expensive watch to be far from her during her flight. It was on the third try that she found what she'd come for.

With the watch in hand, she raced out of the room and down the steps. She rushed into the study where Camilla once more looked like she was just about to have a meltdown.

"Here it is." Bianca placed the watch in the bride's hand.

"You found it. But how? Where?"

"None of it matters. All that matters is that your groom is waiting for you. He's starting to wonder if you're going to walk down the aisle."

"Oh, no! Please go reassure him that I want to marry him more than anything in the world."

Bianca didn't want to ask, but she felt obligated. "Are you sure you want to get married? It's okay if you've changed your mind. I know you were worried about omens—"

Camilla brushed aside Bianca's words. "I was just panicking. Everything is right now." She glanced down at the box containing the watch. "Thanks to you."

Bianca pressed a hand to her chest. "Me?"

"Yes. You've done everything to keep this wedding on track even though it was short notice, and I know I haven't been the easiest bride. I just want to thank you."

"You're welcome. And now I just want to get you down the aisle."

The bride smiled and nodded. "Let's do this." When Bianca turned for the door, the bride followed her. "Oh, here." She held out the watch. "Could you put this in our room for later?"

"Certainly." Bianca smiled and took the box. "You're a beautiful bride."

And with that Bianca headed out the door. She set the watch in a safe spot inside a buffet until she could get to it after the ceremony. And then she rushed out the back where all the wedding guests were looking a bit anxious.

A number of people turned her way as though wondering what she was doing and why the wedding had yet to start.

The groom paced in front of the minister and the groom's younger brother. He stopped when he spotted Bianca.

He rushed up to her. "What's going on? Where's Camilla?"

"Don't worry. She'd misplaced something. But it's been located and now the bride is ready. Shall I have the orchestra play the wedding march?"

"Yes, please. I was so worried she'd changed her mind."

Bianca reached out and squeezed his forearm. "She loves you with all of her heart."

"Thanks."

As Bianca turned away, her gaze caught that of the prince's. He didn't make any pretense to act as though he wasn't watching her. His stare was direct and observant. It made her heart skip a beat.

But she couldn't stop now and talk to him—as much as she wanted. She moved to the orchestra and the wedding music started. Bianca moved toward the French doors that were now open. This was where the bride was to make her grand entrance. The bride's father was standing outside waiting to escort his daughter down the aisle.

When Bianca saw the bride make her entrance, she backed away. She was no longer needed. All her work was done. Now she could take a seat at the back and watch the nuptials. It didn't matter how many weddings she attended, they never became any less romantic.

And it helped that the prince was in her line of sight. She was drawn to him. His bronze skin, dark hair and mysterious eyes were so attractive. A soft sigh passed her lips. If only she could get to know him. But that would never happen.

CHAPTER TWO

WEDDINGS WERE NOT his favorite events.

But Prince Leo had to admit, if only to himself, that the element of *will-they-or-won't-they?* made this particular wedding interesting. He had been leaning toward *they won't.* And by the worried look that had been on the groom's face, he had been leaning the same way.

And then the calm and unflappable wedding planner had made her entrance. She'd spoken softly to the groom and immediately put him at ease. Leo couldn't help but watch her as she took control of the situation. Her demeanor was casual. If she'd been worried about this event reaching its happy conclusion, she hadn't let on.

When he had to get married, he'd want someone like her to organize it. She seemed to roll with the punches as though she'd been through it a million times and knew that all would work out in the end. His sister probably wished she had a wedding planner like Miss Bartolini too.

Right now, the woman organizing the wedding was the same one who had planned his parents' wedding. His sister had tried bringing in her own wedding planner from the nation's capital, but the woman had caved when opposed by the queen and her crony. So his sister's most important day was about to be his mother's vision of how things should be without the bride's input. Leo had tried to help, but he'd been at a disadvantage, not knowing anything about weddings.

He'd known most of his life that when he married, it would be an arranged marriage—a logical, beneficial union. The fact that his parents had planned to have him betrothed as a teenager still soured his stomach. It'd been the last thing he fought about with his father before he'd died suddenly.

It'd taken Leo years to accept that he would marry and have children with a woman he did not love. And so he'd told himself that when he married, it wasn't going to be a big deal to him. It would be done out of duty and obligation—one more thing to tick off the royal duty list.

Love was intended for other people, like his sister. Giselle had found the love of her life and Leo couldn't be happier for her. And that was why her wedding was so important to him. One of them deserved to be truly happy.

"Looks like you have the weight of the world on your shoulders."

Leo turned to find the groom at his side. He smiled, happy for his childhood friend. "Not the entire world, just the weight of Patazonia."

Benito arched a brow. "Problems at home? I hadn't heard anything."

"Oh. You will. Pretty soon my mother and sister are going to have a nuclear meltdown over the upcoming wedding."

Benito laughed. "I can see that happening. Those are two really strong-minded women. You have my sympathies. I'm lucky. Even though our wedding was spontaneous, we had the perfect wedding planner. She took on the big things, including Camilla's parents, and let us enjoy our short engagement. Maybe you should hire her."

Leo was about to dismiss the idea when he realized this might actually work. "You were that impressed by this woman?"

Benito nodded. "Bianca is amazing. She interned with one of the greatest wedding planners in Venice. And now she has returned to her childhood home to start up her own wedding business."

His friend wasn't one to say things he didn't mean. So

for him to speak so highly of this Bianca, it meant a lot. If he were to consider hiring her for his sister's wedding, she would report to him. He would at last have some control over this event that was spiraling out of control—and causing a rift between the bride and groom. Best of all, Miss Bartolini wouldn't be a subject of the queen. Therefore, she wouldn't be under her thumb.

The more he thought about hiring his sister a wedding planner, the more he warmed to the idea. And the fact that Bianca was beautiful as well as composed was just a bonus.

"Have you met her?" Benito asked.

Before Leo could respond, Benito was off seeking out the woman who just might be the answer to his problems. The woman who might bring peace back to the nation. And quiet the gossip floating through the media of unrest in the royal household.

And with that in mind, he didn't try to stop his friend. He was looking forward to doing business with the wedding planner. If this all worked out, he could get back to his search for a bride. And soon he would become king.

A contest.

Not just any contest but one that pitted sibling against sibling.

Bianca still couldn't believe her parents' will had spelled out a competition between her and her siblings to decide who would end up inheriting the vast Bartolini estate. It included the villa, the vineyard, the stables with its award-winning stallions and mares as well as hundreds of fertile acres. It was a paradise of luxury and tranquility.

The siblings who didn't win the contest would lose their childhood home in exchange for an equivalent amount of investments and cash. The money didn't interest Bianca. It was cold and impersonal.

All three of the Bartolini siblings had been raised to appreciate the beauty of this land. And within the walls of this vast villa were all of their childhood memories. And for Bianca, it was crucial to succeed and win this contest.

For it was here in the lush, rolling hills of Tuscany that she intended to establish a destination wedding-planning service. And she was off to a mighty fine start.

Bianca glanced around at the mingling guests. And there was her brother, all dressed up in his finest suit and tie. He definitely didn't look like he spent his days out in the fields tending to the grape vines. In actuality, he cleaned up really well.

After the reading of their parents' will, tensions between the normally civil siblings was running high. It took a bit but the siblings all agreed that they would go with their strengths. Gia would run the boutique hotel, aka their family's sprawling villa. Enzo would oversee the vineyard with its world-renowned Chianti wine. And Bianca had agreed to coordinate weddings at the villa—talk about a romantic backdrop.

An outside accounting firm would be hired to tally their net incomes. Everything was to be aboveboard. And the family's attorney would oversee the contest. Nothing would be left to question. Everything would be certified and final. It seemed so cold—so final.

Enzo smiled at the beautiful young woman next to him. It was then that Bianca realized it was the first time she'd seen Enzo smile since the journal with their parents' devastating secret had been discovered. It had rocked the very foundation of this family—leaving their relationships vulnerable and strained.

Her gaze moved across the garden area, searching for her sister. Gia hadn't wanted to attend the wedding even though she managed the hotel. Bianca had pushed until she'd agreed. Bianca wanted the Bartolini estate well represented to the influential guest list. She was hoping for new clients—for all of them.

All her life she'd felt as though she didn't fit in. She was different than her siblings. While her brother and sister had enjoyed horses and grapes, she enjoyed the finer things in life. Her father used to get aggravated with her reluctance to get dirty.

And when she was pushed out of the nest, just like her siblings, so they could go off and seek their own path in life, she'd ended up in the UK where she'd worked her way through school. Once her education was completed, she moved to Venice. It was there that she followed her passion with a career in wedding planning. And when she landed a prestigious position as assistant to a world-renowned wedding planner, she thought her wishes had come true.

At first, that had been the case. Things went amazingly well. It was later, when Bianca was ready to put what she'd learned into practice that she realized she was terrible at following directions exactly as they'd been told to her.

She had a penchant for embellishing and taking the bride's ideas into consideration instead of convincing the bride that the wedding planner's methods were the best. Her mentor couldn't deny that Bianca had a flair for wedding planning, even if it wasn't quite the way she'd been instructed.

But now as the bride and groom were surrounded by their guests enjoying the afterglow of the ceremony, Bianca was able to take her first easy breath. Striking out on her own had been the right decision. Things were looking up—

"Bianca, there you are." Benito rushed up to her. "I've been looking everywhere for you."

Immediately she assumed her wedding planner persona. She stood a little taller and straightened her shoulders, prepared to deal with the latest developments. "What's wrong? Whatever it is, we'll deal with it."

Benito shook his head and smiled. "Nothing is wrong. In fact, something is right. Come with me."

He motioned for her to follow and then began walking away without any further explanation. She fell in step behind him, wondering what the normally quiet groom had on his mind.

When he stopped, she stepped up next to him. Her gaze met that of the man standing across from them, Prince Leopold. His eyes were a warm golden-brown that made her empty stomach suddenly feel as though a swarm of butterflies had invaded it.

She didn't know how long she stood there, caught up in his gaze. But when Benito cleared his throat, breaking the connection, heat swirled in her chest, rushing up her neck and setting her cheeks ablaze.

"Bianca Bartolini, I'd like to introduce you to His Royal Highness, Crown Prince Leopold of Patazonia."

Once again, Bianca curtsied. She willed her face to cool down, but it only succeeded in making her warmer. Goodness. What was he going to think of her? First, she was openly staring at him. And now her face must look like a roasted beet—all red and steamy. Not good. Not good at all.

"You've put on a splendid wedding," the prince said. "I've quite enjoyed it."

"Th...thank you, Your Highness."

"The prince is searching for a wedding planner," Benito said. "And I was telling him what a great job you did with our wedding."

"You did?" Then catching herself, she said, "I mean, thank you." She'd wondered after the wristwatch delay if Benito would still be happy with her services. "I'm sorry for the slight delay."

"Don't worry about it. Camilla told me what happened. Thank you for helping her and calming her down."

Bianca's eyes widened. "She told you all of that?"

"She did. I told her that she just wanted to keep me guessing for as long as she could."

Bianca wasn't used to brides standing up for her. Usually she took the blame, even for something that she had no control over. And when something stunning happened, the bride would take the credit. But every once in a while there were brides that were considerate and kind. Camilla was both of those.

"Anyway, Prince Leopold might be in need of your services. I'll let you two talk." And with that Benito made his way toward his bride.

Bianca's gaze moved to the prince. Her mouth suddenly went dry and she wasn't sure what to say.

What does one say to royalty? Hi? How are you? Beautiful day?

A nervous giggle welled up within her. She stifled it. What was wrong with her? She wasn't the nervous type. She'd worked with the very rich and the very famous. In the end, they were all just people. As her mother used to say, they put their pants on one leg at a time, just like everyone else.

But this man standing before her was most definitely not just another person. When he stared at her, like he was doing now, her pulse raced. Her insides shivered with a nervous energy. Her whole body reacted in the most unnerving ways.

She attempted to compartmentalize all these new and exciting sensations.

Focus on business.

If he had a job for her, it must be something big, something important. And it might be what she needed to launch a successful wedding business.

Coming to her senses, Bianca said, "If I may be of service to you, Your Highness, please let me know."

"There's going to be a wedding. And I think you might be just the right person to help plan it."

He wants me to plan his wedding? Me...planning a prince's wedding?

The honor of such a position was quite apparent to her. To plan such a wedding would mean she would have her choice of weddings going forward. She wouldn't have to search for prestigious clients, they would seek her out.

It would be sad that such a handsome and intriguing man would soon be off the market—not that she was in any position to be courted by anyone— most especially not a prince. With her heredity in question, it was best to keep to herself. But it didn't hurt to daydream.

"Um...thank you, Your Highness. I'm honored to be considered for such a role. Please let me know what I can do to help you."

He didn't say anything for a moment. "Do you have references?"

She nodded. "I can forward them to you."

"I will need to know more about you before I hire you for this very important position."

"Understood."

His expression gave nothing away. "How old are you?"

"Twenty-nine." What did that have to do with anything? But she didn't know the ways of the royals so she kept her questions to herself.

His dark brows drew together as he studied her. "Do you have much experience?"

"I've been working in the wedding industry since I was eighteen."

A brief flicker of skepticism showed in his eyes but in a blink, it was gone. "That's mighty young."

She nodded. "I started interning with a wedding planner when I was at university. My parents didn't believe in coddling their children. When my siblings and I became adults, we were expected to find our own way."

"But this estate is your family's, is it not?"

"It is. But our parents wanted us to rely on ourselves and not our birthright. Even now…" She stopped herself. The wound of her parents' deaths was still too new—too raw—to discuss, not even to gain the wedding of a lifetime.

"Interesting." He held out his hand. "May I have your phone."

She pulled it from the hidden pocket in the folds of her blue satin skirt. When she handed it over, their fingers touched. A tingly sensation raced up her arm and settled in her chest, setting her heart aflutter.

He took her phone and ran his finger over the touch screen. "I have given you my contact information. I trust that you will not share it with anyone."

"You have my word."

He nodded and then returned the phone to her. "Very good. Forward me your references as soon as possible."

She took her phone and moved her fingers over the same touch screen where his long, lean fingers had just been. And in no time, she had completed her task.

His phone chimed and he withdrew it from his pocket. She subdued a smile when his eyes widened as he read his phone. "You have forwarded me the information already?"

She nodded. "I like to be prepared. I keep relevant information on a cloud account."

"Thank you. I will be in touch." And then he turned and walked away.

She wanted to rush after him and ask when he would be in touch. This week? This month? This year? How was she supposed to plan anything when there was a real possibility of working for the Prince of Patazonia?

Or was it nothing more than a fantasy? Would a prince who could hire the best of the best want to hire a no-name like herself? Sure, she'd worked on the biggest and best weddings, but it hadn't been her name associated with those weddings, it had been her boss's. Bianca was still working to make her name known in the wedding world. So thinking a prince would hire her, well, it was nothing more than a fairy tale.

CHAPTER THREE

HE LIKED HER.

He liked her style. He liked her lack of pushiness. He liked her confidence.

And most of all, he liked the thought of her bringing peace to his home.

As the wedding reception wound down, Leo decided to make his move. His assistant had run a preliminary background check on Miss Bianca Bartolini and as for the references, each and every person had nothing but glowing compliments for Bianca and her capabilities.

He'd been observing Bianca. She was not a loud woman, not by any stretch. When the buffet table had run out of pastries, she'd quietly reminded the young woman to refill the tray. No matter what came up, she was on top of it. And had he not been keenly observing her, he wouldn't have noticed that she was constantly working to make the event seamless.

And now he was armed with the information he needed to put his plan into action. He approached Bianca, who currently had her back to him. It gave him a moment to notice the gentle curls of her dark hair with its half up and half down hairdo. The curls settled on the exposed nape of her neck before falling partway down her back. Her narrow waist was accentuated by the sash of her dress.

He followed the dress down over the curve of her hips to where the hemline stopped just a couple inches above her knees. He shouldn't be checking her out, especially not when he was about to hire her. Still, his gaze did its own thing, continuing to the end, where he found she wore a pair of silver stiletto heels.

She was a knockout. So much different from the very prim, very proper wedding planner that his mother preferred to work with. But if he was about to become king, then it was time everyone in the kingdom, including his mother, learned that traditions have their time and place but the future of their nation relied upon their ability to stay current and evolve with the times in order to remain relevant. And Miss Bartolini was going to be his first statement to his mother and the staff.

Next, he'd have to announce his choice for a bride. And he didn't have much time to make this monumental decision. By the end of the year, he would be married. The happily part was doubtful.

The ridiculous requirement in the country's charter about him being married in order to become ruler—talk about your archaic notions. Try as he might to get around that sticking point, it was law. One of his ancestors had written it into the country's charter and now he must abide by it, if he were to step up and be the king that people needed. It was something he intended to change once he was king.

Though he'd dragged his feet about taking on the position, he'd grown a lot in recent years. He'd gotten involved in politics and government, finding that he had a real head for these things. And then he'd gone out in disguise amongst his people and seen how the decisions made by government affected everyday citizens. And he wanted to be a part of that—he wanted to help the people of Patazonia.

But first, he had to see to his sister's happiness.

As though Bianca sensed his presence behind her, she turned. "Your Highness." She dipped her chin. "Is there something I can do for you?"

Just then the orchestra started to play a new song. It'd been a while since he'd danced and from what he'd observed, Bianca hadn't let up on her duties long enough to enjoy the evening. It was wrong for her to miss out on such a marvelous evening.

With the lanterns sending a warm cast over the patio area, he asked, "Would you care to dance?"

Her expressive eyes widened before she resumed her neutral expression. "Thank you. But I shouldn't be seen dancing. I have work to do."

He was surprised by her refusal. He couldn't recall the last time he'd been rebuffed. This just made him all the more determined to get her out on the dance floor.

"You've worked so hard to make this the perfect evening for my friend and his bride. You should take a moment to enjoy the fruits of your labor."

She smiled but didn't say anything.

"Why are you smiling?"

Immediately the smile slipped from her lips. "It's just the way you say some things. It's different."

"Ah, I see. I was taught by older scholars who believed formal speech is befitting a king. Or a king in the making."

"And what do you believe?"

"I believe a good king can speak any way he wants. It's what's in his heart that matters most. And now that I've indulged your curiosity, it's time you indulge mine as well." He held his arm out to her. "Shall we?"

She glanced around as though checking to see if she was needed. And when there was no one around clamoring for her attention, she placed her hand in the crook of his arm. "Lead the way."

That's exactly what he did. Once among the other couples, he clasped her one hand with his own and wrapped his other arm around her waist. Leaving a modest distance between them, they began dancing.

"It was so nice of you to attend the wedding," Bianca said. "Benito must be a really good friend."

"He's a very old friend. I'm happy he found his soul mate."

Her finely plucked brows lifted, but again she didn't say anything.

He couldn't help but be curious about her reaction. "Are you surprised that I'm happy for the couple?"

She shook her head. "I'm just surprised you believe in soul mates."

Perhaps he should watch his wording with her going forward. He didn't like explaining himself, especially about such a sensitive subject. "I do believe in love and soul mates. I just don't believe everyone has one." He noticed the frown on her face. "Has your heart been broken?"

The thought of it didn't sit well with him. He didn't know how a man lucky enough to win her heart could turn around and break it. If it was him—

He halted his thoughts. He didn't even know where that thought had come from. He wasn't looking for love. He was looking for a princess. They were two mutually exclusive things.

"No, it wasn't my heart. Not directly."

Talk about your cryptic answers. But before he could delve further into the subject, the music ended and a round of applause filled the air.

"If you'll excuse me," Bianca said, "I have things to attend to."

His phone chimed. He didn't have to look at it to know his car was out front, waiting to escort him to his hotel room in Florence. But he had one more thing to do.

"Bianca, I would like to offer you the job."

Her lush lips gaped. It took her a second to regain her composure. "Really? I mean, that was so fast. Are you sure?"

He smiled at her shocked reaction. "Would you like that I change my mind?"

She shook her head as she smiled. "No, I wouldn't."

"I have some business in Florence. Will you be ready to go in two days' time?"

"Two days? Boy, you don't give a girl much warning, do you?"

He hadn't considered that she might have another wedding. "I could definitely make this worth your time?"

Her eyes were like windows to the wheels turning in her mind. If her request for her services was within reason, he would grant it. And then the wedding planner would be all his for the next seven weeks.

"Where are you going? You can't just leave now."

Bianca stopped packing and turned to her sister who was standing in the doorway. She didn't know why Gia cared if she left. All they'd been doing was fighting. And that broke Bianca's heart. She was starting to worry that they'd never be a real family again.

"I have to go. It's for the best," Bianca said, calmly and emotionless. Tensions were so high that she didn't know what would set off one of her siblings.

"So that's it," her brother chimed in. "What about the estate?"

Bianca looked at Gia, then at Enzo. "I'm leaving because all of this fighting isn't good for us. It's tearing apart."

Gia crossed her arms and glared at her sister. "You're bailing on us. And leaving me to fight it out with Enzo."

"That's the reason I'm leaving. I don't want to fight anymore. It's exhausting. And it hurts too much." Bianca placed her makeup bag in her suitcase and then crossed it off her packing list. At this point, she had three suitcases. And, according to her lists, everything she would need was packed. It might look like a lot, but she would be working for a prince and she had no idea what she'd need to wear.

"I agree," Gia said.

Bianca closed her full suitcase and then turned to her sister. "You agree with what? That we shouldn't argue anymore? Or that I should leave?"

Gia sighed. "Really? You honestly think I want you to go?"

Bianca shrugged. "I don't know. So much has been said. And…and what if I'm not a real Bartolini. What happens then?"

Gia pressed her hands to her hips. "What if I'm not a Bartolini?"

Bianca didn't know what words to say to her sister. She couldn't think of any words that would make this situation any better for any of them. They just had to wait it out.

"We'll know soon." Enzo started to pace.

Her brother was referring to the DNA tests they'd submitted last week. But they'd been warned it would be a while until they heard back. Until then, they would have to find a way to deal with the unknown.

"Not soon enough," Bianca muttered.

Gia stepped up next to her sister. "Don't give up on being a part of this family."

"I won't. You either."

"I won't." And then they hugged. When they pulled back, Gia asked, "Do you want help getting these suitcases downstairs?"

"Sure—"

"Hey." Enzo stopped in front of the window. "There's a car here." His gaze moved to the luggage. "I guess it's for you."

She was having the most trouble with him. Everything she said struck him the wrong way. She hoped the distance would help their relationship.

"Enzo, don't just stand there," Gia said. "Grab a suitcase." She gestured to the largest piece.

He hesitated. Then with a sigh, he did as instructed. On

the way downstairs, he said, "I don't think you're doing the right thing."

"You never do." Bianca moved to the front door, stopped and turned to face her siblings.

"I can't believe you're giving up on the estate," Gia said.

"She won't have any worries," Enzo said quickly. "She's working for a prince. She'll be paid a fortune."

Gia's lips formed an O. "I didn't think of that. This DNA stuff has me so distracted."

The thing they didn't know was that she was being paid very little. She'd negotiated for something more important—a national marketing campaign for her destination wedding service.

A heated discussion of the ramifications of Bianca's actions on the contest ensued. Should the money she earned for the royal wedding be counted toward her total? Bianca settled the argument by voluntarily excluding the profit from the royal wedding.

But that wasn't enough to bring peace to the family. The heated debate segued to the subject of whether the sibling without Bartolini blood should inherit. Bianca's stomach turned. She was certain they were talking about her.

It all fit. The way she wasn't like her siblings and taking part in the heritage laid out for them by their parents. She'd always felt like a square peg in a round hole—never measuring up in her parents' eyes and always a mystery to her siblings.

Not able to stand the pain in their eyes, she said, "I can't do this! This fighting, it's not us. We never used to fight."

Her brother and sister looked as though they'd been about to say something, but then lowered their gazes and nodded in agreement. It was then that she felt she had to say something—something important.

"I've got to go," Bianca said, "but before I do, I want you both to know that no matter how this contest turns out or what the DNA says, we're family. We're all the family we have left. And…" Her voice faltered. She wasn't used to talking about her feelings to her siblings. "I love you both."

"Aww…" Gia's eyes misted.

And the next thing she knew Gia pulled both her and a reluctant Enzo into a group hug. The closeness didn't last all that long, but it was enough to assure them that they could face these challenges and get through them together.

When they pulled apart, Bianca regretted having to leave, but she'd already given her word and signed a contract. "I can't miss my flight. But I'll be back soon."

"Aren't you flying on a private jet?" Enzo asked.

"The prince's jet?" Gia's eyes were wide with amazement.

A smiled pulled at Bianca's lips as she nodded. And then she was out the door, promising to keep Gia informed about the upcoming royal wedding.

CHAPTER FOUR

He'd agreed.

Inwardly, she squealed with delight.

She'd asked for the moon and she'd been given not only it but the stars too.

Bianca sat in the leather seat of the prince's jet as they neared Patazonia. She couldn't believe she was about to become the prince's wedding planner. He'd still not told her the details of his upcoming nuptials. Since she'd boarded the plane, he'd been busy either on the phone or working with his assistant on what she surmised was a very big export deal.

It gave her time to update her day planner as well as make phone calls. Even if she was out of town, it didn't mean she couldn't book weddings at the Tuscany estate. The truth of the matter was she didn't have any other weddings booked, just a handful of people making inquiries.

The reason she'd landed Camilla and Benito's posh wedding had been a fluke. The original wedding planner was pregnant and when complications ensued, she was ordered on bedrest for the remainder of her pregnancy. And taking an immediate liking to Bianca when their paths had crossed in Venice, she'd recommended her services.

Bianca was anxious to get to work on the royal wedding, but the prince kept putting her off. She'd already made an extensive list of questions for him.

As she stared out the window at a passing white puffy cloud, she recalled their dance at the wedding. There had been some sort of connection between them. She'd felt it in his touch and the way his gaze had lingered on her longer than necessary.

Was it wrong that she wanted the prince to notice her as a woman as well as a wedding planner? After all, she was here to plan his wedding—his wedding. Her shoulders sank. Here she was worrying over a man who was taken. What was wrong with her?

Those moments on the dance floor, they must have all been in her imagination. After all, he was so invested in his wedding that he'd taken it upon himself to go out and find a wedding planner instead of leaving all the details up to the bride.

Just then the pilot came over the intercom to let everyone know they would soon be on the ground of Patazonia. It was a small kingdom just off the French border.

In the time since the prince had proposed the job to her, Bianca had been online researching customs and weddings within this foreign land. The problem was there wasn't much detailed information about Patazonian matrimonial traditions.

"See anything you like?"

She turned to find prince Leo now in the seat next to hers. "I was thinking the land looks so lush. I'm hoping to have a chance to explore the area just a little." And then realizing how that sounded, she rushed to say, "But not before I have all of the wedding preparations in place. Don't worry. The wedding will be my top priority."

"I have no doubt or I would not have hired you. This wedding must go off without a hitch. I am counting on you."

"And the bride, she'll be meeting with us when we land?" She pulled out her notebook. "I have a whole list of questions for her."

The hint of a smile played at his lips. "I doubt she'll meet us at the airport, but she'll be at the palace."

"Good. Good." Nervous energy flooded Bianca's system. She felt like an athlete preparing for their biggest event. She was ready to spring out of the gate and get as much done as fast as she could—all the while paying attention to the details. Because like it or not, as her mentor used to say, the devil is in the details.

"You seem anxious to get started."

"I am."

"I didn't anticipate you would want to start today after traveling."

"There's no time to waste. The wedding will be here in no time." And she'd never done a royal wedding. It would be daunting compared to the garden wedding where she'd met the prince.

Her stomach churned with nerves. What if she had taken on too big of a task? She should have hired an assistant. Maybe she could hire one in Patazonia. In fact, that might work out better. This person would have a full working knowledge of the local traditions.

"Bianca, is everything all right?" The prince's deep, smooth voice drew her from her thoughts.

"Yes. Why do you ask?"

"You looked worried."

She bestowed upon him her brightest smile. "Not worried at all."

And if he believed that she had a Christmas elf to introduce him to. But she was a professional. She could do this. She kept telling herself that as the plane touched down on the tarmac.

Had he made a mistake?

He didn't care what Bianca said. She was worried.

As a dark sedan moved them from the airport to the palace, Leo couldn't tell what it was about this trip that bothered her. And he had yet to tell her about the tension between his mother and sister. Perhaps he should have, but he hadn't wanted to scare her off. He'd already had all the qualified wedding planners in Patazonia turn him down when they realized the queen already had her own planner.

He needed someone on his sister's side. And Bianca was that person. He was pretty adept at reading people. She may be apprehensive now, but he'd seen her in action. He knew when she was in planner mode that nothing ruffled her.

Maybe he should warn her about the exact details of this wedding. He didn't want her totally blindsided—

"I will need an assistant," Bianca said.

"Don't you already have one?"

Her gaze didn't quite meet his. "I thought by hiring one here, they would be able to help with the local customs."

He had to admit it did make sense. "I'll have my assistant provide you with a list for you to choose from."

"Thank you." She glanced down at her list. "And I assume I'll have an office. I mean I could work out of my room, but that would be crowded and awkward—"

"Yes, I'll see that you have a set of private offices."

Bianca rattled off a couple of other items on her list and he was able to appease her. Nothing she'd asked for had been outrageous or over-the-top and by the time she'd checked off everything on her list, they'd pulled up to the palace. His explanation of how things would work would have to wait.

When he'd spoken to Giselle last, he'd told her he had a big surprise for her. He knew how much his sister loved surprises. Even though she was now in her twenties, she was still the first one up on Christmas morning, eager to find out what was in the garishly wrapped packages under the tree.

When the car pulled to a stop, the doors were opened by the staff. Leo stepped out of the car into the late afternoon sun. It didn't matter how many times he traveled, returning home always felt amazing. This place was in his blood—it was a part of him. He couldn't imagine wanting to live anywhere else.

He rounded the back of the car and stopped next to Bianca as she craned her neck, staring up at the palace. "What do you think?"

She continued to take in the enormity of the very old structure with its detailed stonework and its soaring turrets. He stared up at the palace, trying to see it as she did. The gray stone with the ivy climbing up it against the blue sky with the sun's rays peeking out was portrait worthy. Along the border were flowering shrubs. The fuchsia pink blooms added softness to the hard stone. The grounds were perfectly manicured in distinct designs. This place looked the same as it had when his father was alive. Leo couldn't decide if the lack of change was good or bad.

The enormous wooden doors to the palace swung open. The rest of the staff, in black-and-white formal attire, rushed out to greet them.

Leo stopped just outside the doorway next to one of the maids. "Bianca, this is Zola. She will see to anything you need during your visit."

The young woman briefly curtsied.

"Thank you."

Just then his sister came rushing to the doorway. Her long golden-brown hair fell over her shoulders. Her face lit up at the sight of him. He didn't know whether to be flattered that he was missed or concerned that yet again, something was amiss with the wedding.

"You're home." Giselle hugged him, as was her nature.

When they pulled apart, Leo said, "I wasn't gone that long."

"Long enough." His sister frowned. "You should hear what they want to do for the wedding now—"

"Not now, Giselle." Leo's voice was low but firm. "We have a guest."

It was only then that Giselle's blue gaze met Bianca's. The friendly smile returned to his sister's face. She moved to stand in front of Bianca. "Welcome. Leo didn't say he was bringing home company. He can be forgetful that way."

Forgetful? He took exception to that comment. He had a lot on his mind at the moment. And he didn't want his mother to know about Bianca until he'd had a chance to speak with her.

"It's so nice to meet you." Bianca curtsied. "I can't believe I'm here. This place, it's amazing."

Giselle's smile broadened as she moved next to Leo. "She's marvelous. Where did you find her?"

"At a wedding."

Giselle's brows rose. "Really? And you went there voluntarily?"

Leo shrugged off the question. "I've hired Miss Bartolini to plan the wedding."

"And I'm quite honored," Bianca said, punctuating her words with a smile. "But we don't have much time so if you two could sit down with me and tell me what you have in mind for your big day, we can get started."

"We?" Giselle's fingers moved between her and Leo. Her eyes glittered with amusement. "You think *we* are getting married?"

When Bianca turned a questioning gaze in his direction, Leo cleared his throat. "I suppose I was rather light on the details. My apologies. You will not be planning my wedding. You are here to plan my sister, Giselle's, wedding."

Bianca's gaze moved back and forth between the two siblings. "I... I'm sorry."

"It's okay," Giselle said. "It's like my brother to leave out the most important bits of information." Then she turned to Leo. "I can't believe you hired a wedding planner. Mother is going to have a fit."

"If you'll let me, I can be a big help to you with planning your big day," Bianca uttered. "I have a lot of experience with big weddings, famous weddings and difficult weddings."

That bit of spunk was why he'd hired her. He just hoped Bianca didn't back down when it came to dealing with his mother. Only time would tell.

Giselle's wary gaze turned to Bianca. "How well do you cope with difficult people?"

"Giselle," Leo said, "let's not scare her off before she's even started."

His sister shrugged. "Fair enough. Bianca, once you're settled, we can go over the plans that have been made so far."

Bianca smiled. "I'll be ready."

"I'll show you to your room," Leo said.

"That's okay. I've got this." Giselle moved to Bianca's side. "It'll give us a chance to get acquainted while you go speak to Mother."

Leo had been looking forward to spending more time with Bianca, but arguing with his sister would only arouse his sister's suspicions about his intentions with Bianca. And that was the very last thing he needed at this point.

He nodded. "I'll see you both at dinner."

His gaze briefly connected with Bianca's. It was long enough for his heart to pick up its pace. They'd been together for hours on the trip here and yet they'd barely had a chance to say more than a few words to each other. He deeply regretted it. And now he had to walk away. Why did dinner have to be so far off?

Disappointment shrouded her in its murky grayness. She really had been hoping to talk to him—to get to know him better. There was an air of mystery that surrounded him.

Prince Leopold was different. And it wasn't just that he was royalty, though that was definitely enough to set him apart from anyone else she'd ever known. But there was this invisible yet impenetrable wall that he kept himself cloaked in at all times, much like a body of armor.

As she watched him walk away, she noticed his broad shoulders were pulled back in a straight line. He held his head high as he took long, sure steps. She couldn't help but wonder about the man behind the facade. He might have all the physical things one could want, plus some, but what had happened to him to keep him segregated from the rest of the world?

Once he was out of sight, it gave her a chance to look around. She wasn't sure what she expected to find inside. It wasn't like she'd ever been in a palace before, but this place, it was enormous. The foyer was larger than the flat she'd had in Venice.

From the gleaming marble floors to the sparkling crystal chandelier, she realized this place was ripped out of the pages of a fairy tale. In that very moment, the enormity of the task before her became crystal clear. Not even the biggest, most star-studded wedding could compare to this affair. Her stomach knotted with nervous tension. This wedding would come with challenges, which she couldn't even comprehend at this point.

But she couldn't let Leo or Giselle see her insecurities. She stilled her rambling thoughts. She focused her gaze on her newest client.

"This way." Giselle's sweet voice drew Bianca from her wandering thoughts.

Bianca glanced around for her luggage but didn't see it.

"Don't worry. Your bags are already in your room. Come on." She headed for the grand staircase in the middle of the great foyer.

As they climbed the staircase with a royal red runner up the center, the princess said, "You must be very good at your job for my brother to hire you."

"I am." The admission might sound like bragging. It wasn't. It was the truth.

Bianca might be a train wreck in other areas of her life, but when it came to planning weddings and looking after the details, she was in her zone. Lists were her friends. Her digital calendar ran her life, from a reminder to get up in the morning to the reminder to wind down for the night.

At the top of the steps, the princess paused and turned to her. "I don't know if you know this, but my brother does not make spur of the moment decisions often." The princess's expression was quite serious. Her gaze searched Bianca as though hunting for answers to unspoken questions. "When he does, it has to be for a very special reason."

She didn't want Giselle to think ill of her. "I can assure you that I did nothing to sway your brother's decision. I didn't even know of your wedding until he brought it to my attention."

For a long tenuous moment, Giselle didn't react. Then as though mulling over Bianca's response, she smiled. "I'm glad he hired you because this wedding needs help." She turned and began walking once more. "And if my brother believes in your skills, then so will I."

"Thank you. I won't let you down."

Giselle led her down a wide carpeted hallway with so much expensive artwork that it felt as though they were visiting a museum. They stopped before an open door and Giselle turned to her.

"Here we are. Your things should already be in your room."

Bianca glanced in the sunny room. It was no less stunning than the other parts of the palace. "Would you like to come in? We could start going over details for the wedding."

Giselle shook her head. "I have to meet with William, my fiancé. But we can speak after dinner." She turned to walk away but then turned back. "Did my brother tell you about dinner?"

"No." She had to wonder what was special about dinner.

"It's sharply at seven. Don't be late. It will be in the formal dining room and dress appropriately. There will be guests."

She was hoping for something more casual, more conducive to work. But when in the palace, do as they do. "I'll see you then."

"One more thing. Did my brother mention our mother?"

"The queen? No." Bianca had a feeling he'd left a lot out and she couldn't wait to speak with him.

"You should know that my mother has very definite ideas of how the wedding should go."

Bianca relaxed a bit. "Most mothers do."

"But my mother is different. She's used to getting her way. But this is my wedding—my day. I want some say in it."

"I'm sure compromises can be made. I'll do my best to incorporate both of your ideas, if that's what you'd like."

"It is. As long as it's more my ideas and less hers."

Bianca smiled. "I understand. I will keep that in mind."

Just then a phone buzzed, and it wasn't Bianca's.

"That's William." Giselle's face lit up. "I must go. I'll see you later," she called over her shoulder as she rushed away.

Bianca smiled at the young woman's excitement over seeing her fiancé. A deep, abiding love was something special to witness. And that meant Bianca didn't have time to rest before dinner. She stepped into her spacious room and the first thing to draw her attention was a crystal chandelier. It caught the sun's rays shining in through the French doors and sent a cascade of colors across the walls. She'd never stayed in a place so fancy that chandeliers were placed in bedrooms.

But this was far from a bedroom. The beige-and-cream

room had a spacious bed with a quilted velvet headboard and footboard, but it also had a full-size couch, two chairs and a fireplace. Her gaze moved slowly around the room. There was just so much to take in, from the intricacies on the ceiling and wall, all the way down to the oriental rug.

Next to the French doors was a small table and chairs. She had a feeling she would be spending countless hours sitting there strategizing particulars for the wedding. She knew that the prince had assured her of having an office, but her working hours never fit into a normal business day. Ideas would strike at all hours of the day and night. And with the high importance of this wedding, she knew her mind would be on business 24/7.

And then there was the prince. A soft sigh escaped her lips as she pictured him. She definitely wanted to impress him—for more than one reason.

CHAPTER FIVE

"I WON'T STAND for this!"

The queen's harsh words echoed in Leo's mind. He knew she wasn't going to take well to his interference in the royal wedding plans, but it was time his mother realized her time as regent—of steamrolling over everyone—was almost at an end. By the end of the year he would be king.

As his mother glared at him, he couldn't help but wonder if part of her hostility was due to the part he played in his father's death. Ever since that horrific day, his relationship with his mother had been strained.

Or it could be that she resented having to step in as regent. Though if that were the case, why had she given him so much freedom up until now? If it weren't for public pressure, would she have pushed him to marry—to step into his birthright?

He had a lot of questions, but he couldn't bring himself to dredge up the past—the most painful period of his life. Because even though he and his father disagreed on certain things, Leo had looked up to his father like some kids idolized sports figures and actors. His father had been his role model.

"Mother, I know you love Giselle, but if you keep interfering with her wedding, you're going to drive a permanent wedge between the two of you."

The queen's eyes flared with anger. "And you think bringing in some stranger that knows nothing of our customs is the solution?"

"I do." He made sure to keep his voice calm. "Bianca is quite capable—"

"Bianca?" His mother crossed her arms as she continued to frown at him. "You're on a first name basis with this woman?"

There was no point in denying it. "Yes, we are on a first name basis. It is not uncommon to call people by their first names."

"And this woman, is she beautiful?"

His jaw tightened in frustration, but he immediately released the tension. He didn't want his very astute mother to get a whiff of his discomfort. She would take it and turn it on him.

"She's a wedding planner. I did not notice her looks." He was lying, but his mother didn't need to know everything.

The queen arched a penciled brow. "I do not believe you."

"This isn't about me or for that matter Bianca. This is about stopping the fighting between you and Giselle. Her wedding is supposed to be a happy time for her—"

"Her wedding is a duty—an obligation—just as yours will be. It's about forging an alliance with another country. It's about the future of Patazonia."

Leave it to his mother to remove the emotions and go straight for business. Many outsiders thought being part of the royal family was all about sitting back and letting everyone wait on them. But there were things that an outsider didn't know or stop to consider.

As a prince, he was raised to consider how his choices would affect the future of Patazonia. Everything he did was scrutinized by the press—most of the time their headlines were erroneous. But it didn't diminish his need to make careful decisions.

Just like now when there was a growing divide between the royal family and its citizens. The woman he married needed to bridge the gap between the palace and the commoners. It was imperative.

His mother had picked up right where the king had left

off with the old-school philosophies. She preferred to remain on her side of the palace wall and rule while the citizens were to remain disconnected on the other side.

When he became king, things were going to change. He wanted to be a king of the people, not a distant, cold ruler. He could do better. This whole dynasty could step up their game by being more interactive and breaking down some of the traditions that had kept them locked in their ivy tower.

He met his mother's angry gaze. "Does the future of this country include fighting?"

His mother gasped. "We were not fighting. We do not fight."

"Then what would you call the slamming of doors and the yelling that has disrupted the entire household?"

His mother's gaze lowered. "Your sister might have gotten a bit emotional over some points with the wedding."

"Some?"

"She wants to throw away everything traditional. But she's a princess. A princess must adhere to certain protocols."

"And was that how it was for you?"

"I don't know what you mean?" His mother glanced away.

This was his opportunity to ask her a question he'd wondered about for a long time. "Did you love my father? Or was it all about obligation?"

The queen, who always prided herself on maintaining her composure, looked at him slack-jawed. Was what he'd asked really that out of line? He supposed. Still, he needed to know the truth.

"This isn't about me or your father." The queen's voice was strained. Her face had noticeably paled.

"It might not have been but it is now—"

"No. It's not." Her firm tone let him know that he'd most definitely crossed a line. "Mrs. Schmidt knows what's best for your sister's wedding. After all, she's been planning royal weddings for nearly fifty years. She helped plan your father's and mine."

"And therein lies the problem, Mother. Giselle is young and times have changed. She doesn't want the same things that a bride of fifty years ago would want." When his mother went to argue, he held up a hand stopping her. "And, as the soon-to-be king, I believe the bride should have a say in her wedding."

"But she'll ruin everything."

"I highly doubt it. I believe a compromise can be reached, marrying some of the old traditions with some of the current trends. And before you resist, remember your future relationship with your daughter is at stake."

His mother huffed. "You're exaggerating."

"Am I?" He'd soothed his sister's tears. He'd listened to her vent about moving away from Patazonia—away from his mother—and moving to her groom's country. Leo knew it wasn't all talk. There was some serious consideration going on.

His mother didn't speak for a moment. At last he'd gotten through to her. "You really believe she's that upset over this?"

"I do. And you need to be careful how you handle things going forward."

"And you just want me to trust this stranger—this outsider?"

"I do. I think if you give Bianca a chance, you'll like her. She's a people person and well organized. Giselle has already met her and they've hit it off." Now that he was finally getting through to his mother, he didn't want to walk away without an understanding. "So will you give this a chance? Let Bianca try to bring peace to this family?"

His mother stirred her tea and then removed the silver spoon, setting it on the fine bone chine saucer. Even standing halfway across the room, he could see the wheels of her mind turning. This wasn't going to be the easy agreement that he'd been hoping for.

Oh, well. So be it. He'd been negotiating with his mother since his father had died. He told himself it was just training for his future as king.

The queen took a sip of tea. Returning the cup to the saucer, she turned her full attention to him. "I'll give your wedding planner a chance, if you'll do something in return."

And there she went with her negotiations, just as he'd predicted. At this point, he was willing to do most anything for some peace in his own home. And most of all, he wanted his younger sister to have the wedding of her dreams with the man she loved.

But he'd been down this road before. To have a party with his friends after graduation, it had cost him. He'd had to wear a suit and tie all summer as he'd visited country after country throughout Europe as part of a goodwill campaign. He couldn't even imagine what this wedding would cost him.

He stifled the resigned sigh. "What do you want?"

A slight smile lifted the queen's lips ever so briefly. "I want you to announce your engagement the day after your sister's wedding."

The day after? As in just a matter of a couple months? Seven weeks, give or take a day?

Leo swallowed hard. He struggled to maintain his composure. His gaze never wavered from his mother's. He didn't want her to detect any weakness. He knew his engagement must be announced soon if he were to be king by the New Year, but this felt so sudden—so final.

The queen held up a finger. "There's one more caveat."

Acid swirled in the pit of his stomach. "I'm listening."

"If you don't choose an appropriate wife by your sister's reception, I'll choose one for you."

He schooled his features as he'd practiced since he was a child. Because a future king could not be emotional. His tutors had drilled that into him since he was just out of diapers.

He intended to tell his mother that horses would fly before he'd allow her to pick his wife, but instead he uttered, "It's a deal."

That little smile on his mother's face bloomed into a full-fledged grin. She got to her feet and approached him. "This is for the best. You'll see."

He highly doubted it. "And you will play nice with the wedding planner?"

It was his mother's turn to sigh. "I will do my best—"

"Mother?"

Her lips pressed into a firm line. "I will hear her out."

"No." He shook his head. "I will receive regular updates and I'll hear everything. I will also have the final decision on the details of the wedding."

"What?" His mother looked horrified. "But you know nothing about weddings."

"I guess it's my caveat. Now, do we have an agreement?"

"You drive a hard bargain." His mother gave him an appraising look. "You're so much like your father. He would be proud of you."

"No one can ever replace him, but I try to do what I think he'd want of me."

"Like the wedding." The queen glanced away. "He would not approve of the bickering. Therefore, I will agree to your plan. However, you must keep in mind that this will be a state wedding with dignitaries in attendance."

"Yes, Mother. But it's also a personal, deeply touching moment for Giselle."

"Agreed. Since we're speaking of your father, you should know that he would not approve of you putting off your destiny for so long."

"I know." The weight of her words had been pressing on him for some time. It's why he was willing to go along with his mother's bargain. At least Giselle would end up happy. "I will take the throne by the New Year."

His mother turned back to the table. "I have a list of appropriate women for you to consider for your queen."

He'd already been introduced to some women his mother deemed "appropriate." His mother's ideal woman was quiet, meek and dare he say it—boring. He needed a strong woman who spoke her own mind and had a sense of humor so he wouldn't bore of her too quickly.

Sadly, he'd squandered his time to find a wife on his own terms. Now he was left to choose from his mother's preapproved candidates. And his mother knew she had the upper hand. If he had any doubts, the Cheshire smile on her face said it all.

He needed a bit of time to accept what was about to happen—he was going to marry a woman of his mother's choosing. "I must go check on our guest and make sure she has settled in."

His mother turned back to him. "But I'll see you at dinner?"

"I would not miss the kickoff to your birthday celebrations." This was a milestone for his mother. She would turn sixty and a lengthy celebration would ensue over the next few weeks. "We'll both be there."

"Very well."

And with their agreement in place, he departed. His mother wasn't quite herself. Sure, she was one to cling to traditions, but behind closed doors she normally relaxed a bit. That was not the case lately. This wedding had everyone on edge. He was really hoping Bianca would help bring his family back together again.

Speaking of Bianca, he should check on her before dinner, just to make sure she'd settled in without any problems.

At least that's what he told himself. Because the truth was that the flight home hadn't gone the way he'd planned. One problem after another kept creeping up and stealing away his time.

But no more. He took the steps two at a time, anxious to see Bianca once more. He wanted to show her around the palace and help her get her bearings as she launched into the wedding preparations.

He stopped outside her door and knocked. "Bianca? It's Leo."

Nothing.

He should probably just walk away and leave well enough alone, but he couldn't resist trying once more.

This time he knocked harder. Louder. "Bianca?"

With a resigned sigh, he turned toward his own private set of rooms. He'd taken no more than three steps when he heard her door swing open.

"Were you looking for me?"

He turned. "I was."

"Sorry. I was out on the balcony, enjoying what's left of this beautiful day."

He retraced his steps. "Your room, is it to your liking?"

"Yes, it is. I think it's the most beautiful room I've ever stayed in."

"That's good." That's good? Was that the best he could do?

But the thing was that every time he was within Bianca's gravitational pull, it messed with his thinking. His thoughts got tangled and his words seemed to lack substance.

It wasn't like him to be caught up in a beautiful woman. Yes, he'd admired many attractive women and he'd definitely enjoyed their time. But none of them had ever driven him to go out of his way to know more about them.

"I was just working on some preliminary plans for the wedding," Bianca said, interrupting his thoughts. "Well, it's more like a list of questions." Her glittering brown eyes lifted until their gazes met. "Perhaps you'd care to help me."

"Yes." What was he saying? He knew next to nothing about weddings. And that was being generous.

But if this gave him more of an opportunity to spend time with Bianca, then he was all for it. He stepped into the room, closing the door behind him. It was then that he inhaled the gentlest scent of wildflowers. It wasn't the first time he'd come across the unique scent.

As he followed Bianca to the balcony, he realized it was her. She was the one who smelled like sweet blossoms. He didn't think he'd ever come across a field of wildflowers without thinking of her.

When she came to a sudden stop, he nearly ran into her. As it was, his hands reached out for her tiny waist, his fingers wrapping around her so as not to bump her into the table.

She turned in his hands. "Sorry." Their gazes met once more. This time he was holding her and he didn't want to let go.

The breath hitched in his throat. His gaze dipped to her berry-red lips. They looked so full, so succulent. What would she do if he were to draw her to him and pluck a deep, long kiss?

He could have his choice of women. There was even a stack of biographies from available, eager women waiting for him on his desk. So why was he drawn to this quiet wedding planner?

Though Bianca was beautiful with her long loose curls, a golden complexion and dark lashes that framed her eyes, which were the mirrors to her soul, she was not from Patazonia. She was not royal. She was not even the daughter of an influential businessman. In his mother's eyes, Bianca was a nobody.

But to him, she was intriguing. She was tempting. And the more time he spent with her, the more captivated he became.

As though Bianca could read his thoughts, she moved out of his grasp. "I... I meant to offer you some coffee. I just brewed a pot."

He raked his fingers through his hair. A cup of coffee would be good. It would give his hands something to do besides finding their way back to her. Because if he were to pull her close again, he couldn't guarantee that things wouldn't move from a business relationship to something much more intimate.

"That sounds good." He took a seat at the small table on the balcony.

A minute later, Bianca returned with a full cup. "I forgot to ask what you take in your coffee."

"Black is fine." Right now, he wasn't sure he would actually notice what he was drinking. As Bianca took a seat next to him, his full attention returned to her. "How may I help with the wedding?"

She opened her laptop and moved her cursor to the top of a form. "Do you know approximately how many guests to expect?"

While the sun began its slow descent toward the horizon, he answered as many of her questions as he could. He surprised himself by how many details he'd picked up on by listening to his sister and mother argue.

He knew things about his sister's dress. Whether the ceremony would be ultraformal. And he knew where the reception was being held. Even the number of courses to be served for dinner.

"I'd like to do something for my sister on her wedding day," he said. "She's making a lot of concessions to please my mother and go along with tradition, but I think she needs a chance to let down her hair and live it up on her big day. Do you have any ideas?"

Bianca stopped typing and thought for a moment. "Since the wedding is early in the day, you could do an after-party."

"An after-party." He mulled this over. "Does this mean we could have a select list of guests?"

"Certainly. You could exclude some of the guests from the ceremony and include some others that were not fortunate enough to receive a ceremony invite. The after-party can be as formal or informal as you'd like."

This appealed to him. He knew his sister and her fiancé had a lot of friends—friends that had to be overlooked for invitations to the ceremony in order to invite heads of state and dignitaries from all over Europe and beyond. This would be a way for his sister to have everyone she cared about around her on her big day.

"I like it," he said. "But for the moment, let's just keep this between us. I'll have a list of guests for you by the end of the week."

"That's good because we don't have much time to plan something like this." She hesitated.

"What's bothering you?"

Her gaze lifted to meet his. "With it being so close to the wedding, a lot of people might have other obligations already?"

"Let me worry about it. You pick out an appropriate invite and I'll put together the list."

"What about the venue?"

"That's the easiest part. We will have it at the Hampstead estate next to the lake. It's about fifteen kilometers from here. Far enough that it won't bother my mother with the loud music."

Bianca's eyes widened. "You were serious about letting your hair down."

"Definitely. I just wish I'd have thought of it."

"Why? I don't mind sharing ideas with you. After all, it's my job."

He shook his head. "It's not that. If I'd have had this idea a lot sooner, I could have booked some headline bands. As it is, they are probably all booked."

They continued to talk about bands. He named the ones he'd heard his sister mention. Then he inquired about Bianca's favorite band and in turn, he told her his. For a moment, it wasn't work. It was like they were two friends getting to know each other.

"Thank you." Bianca finished her list of potential bands. "I'll do the best I can to get someone your sister will approve of."

"And my mother doesn't need to know about any of this for now. Speaking of which, it is time to dress for dinner." He got to his feet. And then he realized he needed to make something else perfectly clear. "You will be reporting to me on this wedding. I know my mother likes to think she's in control, but I would like to have dinner with you each evening to go over everything—to make sure we're on track."

Bianca nodded. "Understood. And we can discuss my promotional campaign."

He couldn't help but smile. "I won't forget. I already have my people working on some preliminary mockups. I'll have them for you to approve shortly."

Her face lit up with excitement. "Thank you."

"I'll stop back and walk you to dinner." And with that he left.

CHAPTER SIX

IT WASN'T A QUESTION.

It wasn't an invite.

It was a declaration. Prince Leopold would be escorting her to dinner.

As Bianca stared into the mirror, she became distracted. Try as she might, she couldn't forget the turmoil back in Tuscany. Her attention focused on her face. She searched for signs that she was a Bartolini. Her nose—was it too small? She turned this way and that way.

Her eyes—were they too close together? Were they the same size and shape as her father's? She struggled to conjure up the exact details of her father's face. The more she struggled to recall, the more frustrated she became.

As she continued to stare at her reflection, she remembered people commenting on how much she resembled her mother. Was that a clue? Did she look like her mother because her father wasn't truly her father?

And if she wasn't a Bartolini, who was she?

The questions tumbled through her mind. They weighed on her, putting everything she thought she knew about herself into question.

Tears of frustration pricked the backs of her eyes. She blinked repeatedly. How long were those DNA tests going to take? The wait was agonizing.

But right now, she had an important dinner with the royal family. She put on diamond stud earrings followed by diamond dangle earrings. She may be a poor pauper compared to the wealth of this royal family, but back in her own world, the Bartolini's had made a name for themselves.

She gazed down at the navy-and-silver dress she'd selected for this evening. It was formfitting and hugged her curves. As she stared in the mirror, she sucked in her breath, pulling in her stomach. Maybe this wasn't the right dress to wear for meeting the queen for the first time. But when she checked the time, it was a quarter to seven. Too late to change now. She expected Leo to arrive any minute.

Bianca slipped on the silver rhinestone–studded stilettos. Still, she was stuck on the fact that a prince—a sexy, gorgeous prince—would be her escort for dinner. Who cared if he was a bit presumptuous? She knew how to put him in his place if he got obnoxious. Though she just couldn't imagine Leo being an overbearing jerk.

As she finished with the delicate strap on her shoe, her attention focused on her nails. She'd had them done for the wedding at the vineyard. She lifted her hands to her face and inspected them. Other than a slight tremor, they looked good. The French manicure was holding up nicely. The last thing she wanted was to greet the queen looking anything other than her best.

The nervous tremor that had started in her hands moved to her stomach. She was meeting a queen. Who did that? People with a much higher social status than her. She didn't even know what to say to the woman. Her mouth grew dry. Her brain drew a blank.

Don't think about it. Think about something else.

She wanted someone to share this moment with. Her thoughts turned to her sister. She knew Gia would be in awe over this just as she was. And she had promised to let her siblings know when she'd arrived safely.

She reached for her phone. As she went to pull up her sisters' number, she paused. The last time she'd seen them, there had been a big argument. She didn't want to go there again. Perhaps a text message would be best.

Arrived safely.

Immediately a response pinged on her phone.

Exciting! What's it like?

Amazing!

And the prince?

Bianca thought for a moment. Scads of adjectives raced to the front of her mind.

Amazing!

#jealous Tell me more.

> *Knock. Knock.*
> "Coming," Bianca called out.

Can't now. My prince...

Bianca groaned. *Erase. Erase.*

Can't now. The prince has arrived for dinner.

#exciting Don't forget. Details. Lots of details.

LOL. Talk soon.

Bianca smiled as she set aside her phone. Things were starting to seem normal between her and her sister. Perhaps she'd had the right idea about putting a little distance between them. Because during this whole thing of losing her parents and the mess with the will, she could really use her friend—her sister.

Knock. Knock.

"Bianca, are you ready?"

"Yes. I'll be right there." She glanced in the mirror. She adjusted a stray hair and then smoothed the makeup under her left eye. It was as good as it was going to get.

She moved to the door and swung it open. She didn't know it was possible for Leo to look any better than she'd seen him so far. But she'd been wrong.

His short dark hair was still damp from his shower. The sides were clipped close to his head while the curls on top were short but just long enough for them to do their own things. And what they did made Bianca want to reach out and run her fingers through the damp curls.

Her gaze met his smiling eyes. Her heart raced. His face was clean-shaven. She paused to inhale, imagining the slightest hint of a spicy aftershave. Mmm… She longed to take a step forward and lean into him for a real whiff.

"You look beautiful." His voice drew her from her meandering thoughts.

"Th-thank you." She needed to calm herself.

Otherwise she was likely to make a fool of herself in front of the queen. If she did that, she'd end up fired before she even began her job. And she didn't want to think of the negative consequences to her business.

"Are you ready to go?"

She glanced back at the room just to make sure she hadn't forgotten anything. She leveled her shoulders and turned back to him. "I'm ready."

He arched a brow. "Are you sure?"

"Positive."

In true princely fashion, he held his arm out to her. "Then let's go."

She stepped out, pulled the door shut behind her and then placed her hand in the crook of his arm. The heat of his body radiated into her skin, warming her cell by cell, bone by bone. Did he have any idea what he did to her heart rate?

She hoped not. As it was, she had to concentrate on walking. She didn't want to trip over her own two feet. How embarrassing would that be?

She swallowed hard, trying to put on a calm exterior. "What's your mother like?"

"Hmm... How long do you have?"

"Oh, boy."

A soft deep laugh rumbled in his chest. "Relax. I'll be there with you."

That was of little comfort considering she didn't rely on others to fight her battles. It was one of the lessons her father had instilled in her and her siblings. To make it in this world you have to be strong with a kind heart.

"How do I address her?"

"Don't address her unless she speaks to you first. And then you may refer to her as Your Majesty."

"Oh, my. That formal, huh?" This definitely wasn't like any other time where she'd gone to meet a boyfriend's mother. Far from it.

Leo nodded. "My mother is a stickler for titles, duty and tradition."

"What do you call her?"

"Mother, in private."

"And in public?"

"Your Majesty."

It took a second for Bianca to realize that her mouth was agape. She couldn't even begin to imagine what it was like to grow up the way he had.

Sooner than she was prepared for, they arrived just outside the dining room. Leo turned to her. "Are you ready?"

Bianca nodded.

With her stomach twisted in a nervous knot, she entered. She found Giselle standing by a tall handsome man who must be her fiancé, by the way she was looking at him.

Next to them stood another couple. They were older.

The man looked quite distinguished and though he didn't smile that often, his wife beamed as she made small talk with Giselle.

And then Bianca's attention moved to an older woman with silver hair. It was cut short into a neat bob. That she presumed was the queen. Her stomach shivered with anxiety. Surely that queen couldn't be as intimidating as she was imagining. Could she?

Leo came to a stop near the group and waited for a pause in the conversation. "Mother," he waited until she turned her attention to them, "I'd like to introduce Bianca Bartolini of Tuscany, Italy." And then he turned to Bianca. "Bianca, I'd like to introduce the Queen of Patazonia."

Bianca's mouth went dry but her brain worked just enough for her to remember to curtsy to the queen. She hoped that was right. When she straightened, the queen was staring at her with a hawk-like stare. Bianca's breath stilled in her lungs.

She felt so out of place—so out of her realm. But she couldn't falter. She had to stay strong for Leo, for Giselle, for herself. Without this account, the future of her wedding business looked uncertain. She needed her business as her touchstone. Without it she'd be adrift.

Leo had warned her not to speak until spoken too. And yet she felt compelled to say something—anything to break this awkward silence.

"It's so nice to meet you, ma'am. I'm honored to be here. Your palace, it's quite extraordinary."

A penciled brow rose. "Perhaps if my son isn't too busy, he can give you a tour of the gardens before you leave. They were my husband's passion."

"Thank you but…" Just then Leo gave a slight shake of his head. Bianca adjusted what she was about to say. "I will definitely make a point of visiting the gardens."

"Very well. Shall we eat?" The queen started for the head of the table.

The queen acted as though she were there just for the evening. Did the woman not know that she was the wedding planner? Had Leo failed to tell her?

Bianca glanced over at Leo who was making conversation with a gentleman who had such a sour expression that it looked as though he'd just sucked on a lemon. She had no idea who the man was but he obviously didn't have a very optimistic view of life.

Thankfully she'd been seated near Giselle. She really liked the young woman. She was warm and vivacious, unlike her mother. Bianca also noticed that the bride-to-be mentioned the wedding only once in passing. She found that odd. Most of the brides she'd worked with were quite excited for the big day and would talk about the preparations almost nonstop. Perhaps the rift between mother and daughter was the reason for the quietness on the subject.

The queen made a point of talking to each person at the table except Bianca. It was as though she were invisible. It wasn't an ideal way to begin a working relationship, but at least she hadn't been banished. That had to count for something. Right?

When the queen mentioned the gardens once more to her guests, Bianca seized the opportunity. "I'm very anxious to see the gardens. It would be a beautiful backdrop for the wedding. In fact, I just hosted a garden wedding at my family's estate. It's where I met L…erm…the prince."

"Is that so?" The queen turned to her son.

"Yes. I attended Benito's wedding."

"I see. Now I understand why you feel like an expert on the subject."

The seconds ticked away as mother and son stared at each other. A war of wills quietly ensued. Bianca felt bad for Leo. He was only trying to help his sister have a happy wedding. This wasn't his fight but he was taking it on for his sister's sake. Bianca's respect for him escalated.

"I hope to be able to make this wedding a very memorable and happy occasion for everyone," Bianca said, trying to diffuse the situation.

The queen turned to her. "This is not your typical wedding. Giselle is a princess and certain obligations go along with that title—even if she doesn't like it."

She's the mother of the bride. Just the mother of the bride.

Bianca lowered her hand to her lap where no one could see its slight tremble. And then she pasted on a bright smile. "I'm eager to learn of your traditions."

The queen arched a disbelieving brow. "Are you? Because I already have a wedding planner that knows everything about planning a royal wedding."

"And I'm looking forward to working with her. I think we'll be able to make room for your traditions and for Giselle's wishes." Bianca could now understand why Leo had brought in reinforcements. The queen was very determined to have her way, no matter how unhappy it made her daughter.

And that was it. The conversation ended as the queen turned to the female guest to her right.

CHAPTER SEVEN

HER CONCENTRATION WAS AMISS.

It might have something to do with a very handsome prince staring across the table at her.

Every time Bianca's gaze met his, he would glance away. Was it possible the prince was interested in her? Or was it a case of wishful thinking?

She didn't know how she did it, but she made it through the seven-course dinner without spilling her water, dribbling her wine or dropping her fork, even though her hands insisted on trembling. Giselle included her in a friendly conversation, but Leo for the most part was quiet. He paid attention to the conversations around him, but he didn't participate unless someone directly addressed him.

When dinner was concluded, the queen, the prince and Giselle's fiancé spoke with their guests about a matter of government while Giselle pulled Bianca aside. They walked to the terrace, which overlooked the gardens that were highlighted by a vast array of soft lights. They were huge and looked exactly like a maze. Her inner child was anxious to go explore.

"I think you impressed my mother," Giselle said. "But she would never let on. She isn't used to someone standing up to her."

Bianca worried that she'd said too much. "I hope I didn't offend her. That was not my intention."

"My mother does not respect many people. And certainly not the ones she can easily walk over. That's why my brother is the perfect person to be king. He stands up to our mother and calls her out on things when she goes too far."

"And what about you?" It would be helpful to get more

information about the dynamic between the bride and her mother.

Giselle shrugged. "Before the wedding, my mother and I never had much of a reason to clash because I was never interested in the inner workings of the country. There were always enough people handling affairs of state, allowing me to concentrate on my own life. But this wedding, it went from being my marriage to William to being world-wide publicity for our country. There are news networks bidding for strategic camera placements within the cathedral." There was a tone of disbelief and disgust in her voice. "Can you imagine?"

Actually, she could. She once did a wedding for two American movie stars. The paparazzi was everywhere. And the first photo of the newlywed couple sold for millions. But that wouldn't do anything to soothe this bride's nerves.

"I'll handle the press. That's not for you to worry about."

Giselle studied her for a moment as though trying to figure out if she should trust her. "You've dealt with big weddings before?"

"Yes. I've worked for some very famous people. Some of them had huge weddings and others preferred privacy. Every wedding is different. Just as every bride is different."

"My brother must really like you." Giselle smiled like she knew a secret.

Bianca glanced around, afraid someone might overhear them. Luckily there wasn't anyone too close to them. "I think he likes the way I do my job."

Giselle's smile broadened. "He's never brought home a woman before."

Heat engulfed Bianca's face. "It's only work."

"Uh-huh." But the look in Giselle's eyes said that she didn't believe her.

"We're working on your wedding and—" She caught

herself, not sure if Leo would mind if she shared their arrangement.

"And what?" Giselle drew out the words with a definite note of interest. "Do tell."

"It's no big deal." That was a lie. It was a huge deal to her. "In exchange for me planning your wedding, he has agreed to sponsor an advertising campaign to draw people to my family's vineyard in Italy for my wedding planning business."

Giselle didn't even attempt to hide her gaping mouth. It took her a couple of seconds to speak. "My brother is doing all of that?"

"Yes. For you. To give you the wedding of your dreams."

"My brother isn't the kind to go out of his way for just anyone. Trust me. He likes you."

"It's not for me. It's for you."

"Uh-huh." Her eyes said that she didn't believe her.

Bianca's stomach fluttered as though it'd been invaded by a swarm of butterflies. Giselle had to be wrong. Leo wasn't interested in her—

"There you are." Leo's voice came from behind them.

Both Bianca and Giselle turned. When Bianca's gaze met his, her heart beat wildly. And this was all Giselle's fault for putting these wildly inappropriate thoughts into her mind.

Giselle glanced around. "Where's William?"

"He's waiting inside for you. Everyone has called it an evening."

Giselle turned to Bianca. "I'm glad you're here. I like you. And I think together, we'll plan a great wedding. Can we meet first thing tomorrow to go over details?"

Bianca nodded. "That would be perfect."

"I'll see you then." Giselle headed back inside. She paused next to her brother. "You have good taste. Just don't go and scare her off."

Leo arched a brow at his sister but didn't say a word. Giselle giggled as she headed inside, leaving them alone in the moonlight.

He approached her. "You did well at dinner. My mother is not an easy woman."

"But I don't think she likes me."

"I'll let you in on a secret—I don't think she likes many people. But give her time. She won't be able to resist liking you."

His words warmed a spot in Bianca's chest. That warmth radiated up her neck and once again set her cheeks ablaze. She wasn't one that normally blushed but there was something about being here—talking with Leo—being so close to him.

"I think you're trying to put me at ease, but I know dealing with your mother over this wedding is not going to be easy. She has her thoughts and they aren't easily going to be swayed, but I intend to do my best. I can at least run interference for your sister. Your mother can yell at me—"

"My mother rarely raises her voice. It's more along the lines of looks that could kill as well as a warning tone in her voice that makes people quiver."

"Quiver, huh? Are you trying to get rid of me?"

"Not a chance. Instead, I came out here to see if you'd like to stroll through the gardens with me." He once again held his arm out to her. "Shall we?"

She loved his gentlemanly ways. The guys she'd dated didn't do things like offer their arm, get her chair for her or open her car door. But Leo, he was definitely different.

She placed her hand in the crook of his arm and walked with him as they moved to the sweeping stone steps that led to the gardens. As they moved along the cobblestone walkway, she inhaled a sweet floral scent. It was delightful.

"This is beautiful. How big is it?"

"Every year, they expand it. I don't know exactly how

big it is. I just know that when I was little, it was fun to play in. But the head gardener wasn't so happy when we veered off the path and trampled the plants."

The thought of Leo as a young boy made her smile. "I bet he wasn't that upset with you."

"Oh, I think he was, but there wasn't much he could do since I was a prince. And so we kept playing out here and getting in more trouble."

"I can't blame you. When I was young, my brother and sister would play with me among the grapevines at the vineyard. But it was nowhere near as fun as this winding garden path. There are so many hiding places."

"There's a lot more to Patazonia than the royal gardens. I hope to show you around while you're here." He stopped and turned to her. "You haven't changed your mind about the wedding, have you?"

She shook her head. With him gazing into her eyes, her heart had leaped into her throat. Was that desire reflected in his eyes? The prince desired her? Her heart tumbled in her chest.

She didn't know how long they stood there staring into each other's eyes. It was like Leo had a gravitational force around him and she was being drawn in. Though she knew letting anything happen between them would be a mistake—compounding all of the other uncertainties in her life—she remained rooted to the spot in front of him.

Her heart raced as she found herself getting lost in his dark gaze. Her fingers tingled with the urge to reach out to him—

Someone cleared their throat. Loudly. Annoyingly.

And in that second, the connection dissipated. Bianca blinked and glanced away. Heat returned to her face. She was grateful she didn't have to speak because she didn't trust her tongue to work correctly.

Leo cleared his throat. "Yes, Michael. What is it?"

"You are needed, sir. The call from Canada."

Leo sighed. "I'll be right there." Once the man moved on, Leo turned his full attention to her. "I'm sorry. I've been expecting this call all day."

"I understand. You have important business to attend to."

Reality had come crashing in on them. And none too soon. He was a royal prince. She was a wedding planner with an uncertain heritage. They did not belong together.

"About this…" As his voice trailed off, he looked at her with confusion reflected in his eyes.

He wasn't the only one to be confused. Her heart had betrayed her mind in wanting what it could not have. And now that her feet were once again planted firmly on the ground, she couldn't forget that she was here to do a job. That needed to be her focus. Not getting swept up in some fairy tale.

"It's okay," she said. "You have important work to do."

"You're not upset about ending the evening so soon?"

She shook her head. "Not at all. I understand that business must come first."

As he escorted her back to the palace, he didn't offer her his arm. And she made sure to keep a reasonable distance between them. Because as much as nothing had happened between them, something most definitely had almost happened.

For a brief moment awareness had passed between them. It had been something genuine. Something not quite tangible but utterly unique. But for both their sakes, it was best neither of them examined it too closely.

CHAPTER EIGHT

HE'D ALMOST KISSED the wedding planner.

And the only thing he regretted was that they'd been interrupted.

A hectic week had flown by since that very memorable moment and Bianca filled every nook and crevice of Leo's thoughts. He sighed. He was playing with fire. He was supposed to be choosing a wife in order to announce his engagement after his sister's wedding, not indulging in a fleeting desire. But, oh, what a desire.

"What are you smiling about?"

Immediately Leo cleared his facial expression. His sister stood in front of his desk studying him. How long had she been there? He'd been so caught up in his thoughts that he hadn't heard her enter his office.

He leaned back in his chair. "Good morning, Giselle."

"From the look on your face you must have had a good night too."

He frowned at her, warning her off the subject. But his sister wasn't good with warnings. She dared to tread where most people would veer away.

"If you must know, I worked late into the night. And it was a very successful meeting."

Giselle crossed her arms. "If that's what you need to tell yourself, then go ahead. But I think it was something far more personal that had you smiling."

He cleared his throat. "Did you need something?"

"You didn't show up at breakfast—"

"I was working."

"And Bianca wondered where you might be."

He leaned forward and straightened the papers on the

desk. "I thought you would be working with her this morning and going over all of the relevant details for the wedding."

"We are. I'm just waiting for her to grab her things and then we're off." He could feel her gaze on him the whole time she spoke. "I just stopped by to see if you would want to accompany us."

His gaze moved to the stack of bios of potential wives for him to choose from. He'd been dragging his feet long enough. The time had come. It wasn't just his mother who was pushing for him to move into the role of king. It was the cabinet too. And, truth be told, he'd been allowed his freedom to be young and a bit adventurous. Now, it was time for him to assume his responsibilities. Even if marrying for duty wasn't something he relished.

He stared blindly down at the papers on his desk. "Thanks. But I have a lot of work to catch up on."

He'd used the excuse of urgent business to cancel his daily meetings with Bianca. Though he really did have pressing matters, he needed the time and distance to regain a certain level of detachment where the alluring wedding planner was concerned.

"You're sure? You and Bianca seem to enjoy each other's company."

His sister was right, but he wasn't going to encourage her. "I'll catch up on the wedding plans this evening."

Now that Bianca had had a chance to settle in, it was time she filled him in on the progress with the wedding. If there were problems, he wanted them addressed straight away. Nothing would ruin this event for his sister.

Giselle turned to leave but then turned back to him. "How did you get Mother to go along with this plan?"

His gaze met hers. "It's not for you to worry about. I told you I would work this out so that you could enjoy your wedding and I've done just that."

Giselle rushed around the desk, wrapped her arms around him and pressed a feathery kiss to his cheek. "You really are a great brother. And someday I'll pay you back for all you've done for me."

"I didn't do it for payback."

Giselle pulled away. "I know. You did it because you love me." She moved to the other side of the desk. "I'm your favorite sister."

"You're my only sister. Now go before I disown you." He sent her a teasing smile.

She smiled back at him. "I'll tell Bianca you're sorry you were detained, but you're eager to see her this evening—"

"Giselle—"

She scurried out of the office, giggling the whole time.

He shook his head. His sister had a good heart, but she could be relentless at times. He just hoped when he did pick a wife that she would be friends with his sister. It'd be nice to finally have some family harmony.

At last, he'd run out of excuses to resume his search for a wife. As the queen had reminded him that morning in the hallway, only six weeks remained until Giselle's wedding followed by his official engagement announcement. And there was no way he would allow his mother to choose his wife. He inwardly shuddered at the thought.

He reached for the first bio on the rather large stack. As he started to read the page, he found himself comparing the woman to Bianca. He stopped, trying to clear Bianca's beautiful image from his thoughts. He started to read again. This candidate's photo had short hair unlike Bianca's long hair—he stopped again. This was going to take a long, long time.

Was he avoiding her?

Had that moment of attraction unsettled him?

Those were the questions that snuck into Bianca's

thoughts as their dinner meetings had been cancelled night after night. She'd scarcely seen him since that moment in the gardens.

She tried to tell herself that he was a prince and therefore very busy. And that had worked the first day. But she couldn't lie to herself any longer. Leo was avoiding her. It hurt.

And for that reason, Bianca had kept herself busy from first thing in the morning until she'd passed out from utter exhaustion late at night. Planning a national event was not for the faint of heart.

This morning, Giselle was giving her a tour of the cathedral. Its soaring arched roof was jaw-dropping. The stained-glass windows were stunning works of art. And the suspended lanterns were absolutely charming. This church would provide the most stunning backdrop for the wedding. Bianca made a list of items she'd like to address later, after she'd given them some thought.

At lunch in the nearby village, Bianca tried her best to catch everything Giselle said. However, the princess was the opposite of her brother. Where he was reserved and spoke only when he had something substantial to say, Giselle rambled on about this, that and another thing.

The princess was like a sunny ball of energy. And Bianca could easily imagine them being lifelong friends. Not that it was possible. When the wedding was completed, her time in Patazonia would also be completed.

But would Leo avoid her until then?

"What's the matter?" Giselle asked as the chauffeured car whisked them back to the palace earlier than expected.

"Um...nothing." Bianca lied. There was no way she was discussing Leo with his sister. If Giselle didn't approve of the match, she would fire Bianca on the spot. And if she did like them together, she would just make the whole situation even more awkward.

"That frown on your face says you have something on your mind," Giselle said. "You can talk to me."

"I was just thinking about the wedding." She needed a diversion. "You've told me what you want for the wedding and now I have to speak to your mother and her planner to find out what they expect."

"Do you have to?" Giselle's voice carried with it a slight whine.

"My goal is to give you the best day of your life. A day you can look back on and smile. If you're fighting with your mother throughout the whole ordeal, you aren't going to enjoy your big day and you definitely won't want to remember it."

"You're right." Giselle looked down at her skirt and picked a piece of lint from it. "You know, William and I have even talked about eloping. But please don't tell my brother and certainly not my mother. She would explode and then lock me in the tower until the wedding."

"My lips are sealed. But is that what you really want to do?"

Giselle shrugged her slim shoulders. "It's better than fighting about everything, even down to the table linens."

"Then it's a good thing I'm here. You don't have to fight anymore. I'll be your go-between."

"Thank you. I feel so much better with you here." The car pulled to a stop at a side entrance to the palace. "Now, let's get you back to your office."

"That would be nice. I have so much to do."

"And I believe someone will be waiting for you."

Bianca's heart raced with anticipation. She couldn't wait. Her steps were quick through the maze of hallways until Giselle stopped outside the door. "I won't keep you any longer."

"Thank you for everything. I won't let you down."

"I know you won't. I can see why my brother hired you on the spot."

Bianca sent her a reassuring smile. "I'll send you the questionnaire I use for the details of the ceremony. If you could get that back to me right away, it would be helpful."

"I will." Giselle took a few steps down the hallway before pausing and turning back. "You know this is the first time I've been truly excited about the wedding. I just know with you here it's going to be extra special."

Once Giselle was gone, Bianca opened the office door fully expecting to find Leo waiting for her. Instead, standing behind an oversized dark wood desk was a beautiful young woman.

"Hi." The young woman straightened. "You must be Bianca." She moved from behind the desk. "I'm Sylvie. I'm your assistant for the wedding."

The young woman appeared to be about her age and she had the friendliest smile. "It's nice to meet you, Sylvie. Have you ever arranged a wedding before?"

She nodded her head. "I work for a wedding planner in town. The prince—" just the mention of him had the young woman blushing "—hired me to help you."

"I hope he didn't take you away from anything important."

Sylvie vehemently shook her head. And then with a perfectly serious expression, she said, "Nothing could be nearly as important as the royal wedding. I just can't believe I was chosen over all of the other more experienced people."

Bianca couldn't help but smile at Sylvie's sense of awe. "I'll tell you a secret. I was surprised too when the prince hired me."

"You were?"

Bianca nodded. "I've done a lot of big weddings but nothing this big and not on my own."

"You aren't alone. You've got me."

"And together, you and I will give Giselle and her fiancé the wedding of the century."

"Let's do it."

They sat down and went over what Bianca had sorted out so far. They made lists because nothing got done in Bianca's world without detailed lists. Sometimes she even made lists of lists. But her curiosity of when she'd see Leo again was a constant distraction.

CHAPTER NINE

BEING A PRINCE did have its drawbacks.

From marrying out of duty to his lack of anonymity.

Leo might have grown up in the spotlight but that didn't mean he'd grown accustomed to always standing out in a crowd. Instead, he found ways of creating his own privacy. One such way was moving into his own private apartment right here in the palace.

He made his bed every morning. He picked up around the apartment. He liked a neat space. He cooked for himself regularly during the week. He had to admit that cleaning wasn't his thing and so he did let the staff go through the apartment once a week vacuuming, dusting and tidying everything.

But when it came to cooking, he found, to his mother's horror, that he enjoyed it. He had taken many lessons from the palace chef over the years. Not that he was an expert now, but he could make a number of reasonably easy dishes. Tonight's menu included a tossed salad followed by fettuccine Alfredo.

He set the small table on the balcony. It was simple but cozy. He assured himself that it was nothing more than he would do for a friend. Then again, maybe not just any friend—

Knock. Knock.

He gave the table one last glance and then headed for the door. When he swung it open and found Bianca standing there, he told himself that his racing heart was due to rushing around to get ready for the evening. It had absolutely nothing to do with how beautiful Bianca looked that evening.

She was wearing a black dress that dipped at the neckline, giving a hint of her cleavage. The straps over her shoulders left her arms bare. A belt showed off her delicate waist. The skirt stopped a couple inches above her knees. And on her feet were black sandals.

She was a knockout. He swallowed hard, hoping his voice didn't fail him. "You look amazing."

Suddenly his dark-wash jeans and white oxford shirt seemed quite underwhelming. "I should have told you tonight would be casual. My apologies." He moved to the side. "Come in."

She stepped inside and looked around. "Is this your place?"

"It is."

As she stepped to the center of the living room, she said, "It's like a home within a home."

"It's my private space. It's where I can unwind and be myself."

"It's very nice. And much more modern than the other parts of the palace."

"How is your office? Is it to your liking?"

"Yes, thank you. I like it a lot."

Things between them took on a nervous tension. He wondered if she was remembering their moment in the gardens. If they hadn't been interrupted, things definitely would have escalated. Not wanting to make this evening more awkward, he pushed aside the thoughts.

He cleared his throat. "I apologize for being detained the last couple of days. Something urgent came up and it took all of my time."

"No need to apologize. As a prince, your time must be constantly in high demand. And I was busy getting caught up on wedding details."

He nodded in understanding. He was grateful she'd let him off the hook so easily. Though he was busy catching up on matters of state, as well as busy searching for a wife, he'd needed the time to gather his senses where Bianca was concerned. She was the wedding planner—nothing more.

"And thank you for hiring Sylvie." Bianca's voice interrupted his thoughts. "I think we're going to work well together." Then Bianca frowned. "Will she be joining us this evening? Should I have waited for her?"

"No. This dinner meeting is just for us. I think you have some information to share with me and I have some to share with you."

"It sounds like this is going to be a very productive meal."

"I hope so."

He poured her a glass of white wine. He'd had two cases of each type of wine shipped from the Barto Vineyard. He wondered if she'd notice.

This had to be a dream.

A cozy dinner for two. Just her and a prince. A gorgeous, handsome, dashing prince. Definitely a dream.

And there was music playing in the background. There was the distinct moan of a saxophone floating ever so softly through the dimly lit room. If she were to close her eyes, it'd be so easy to imagine this was a date. A smile lifted her lips.

But this wasn't a date. Far from it. Bianca's eyes opened. This was a business dinner. She couldn't let herself forget it. Just like she'd forgotten what they'd been talking about.

Her gaze met his expectant one. She glanced down, remembering the glass of wine in her hand. Oh, yes, she was supposed to sample the wine.

First, she swirled the wine, inhaling its fruity fragrance. And then she sipped it. Immediately a moan escaped her lips.

Her gaze moved to meet his. "How did you know?"

"Know what?"

"That this is my favorite wine."

"I didn't. But I recalled you drinking it after the wedding at the villa."

"You're a very observant man."

"I try. I hope you're equally as impressed with the dinner."

"It certainly smells good." She reached for her tablet. "Before we eat—"

"No work before dinner. It'll ruin your appetite."

"But we have so much to go over and not much time until the wedding."

"There will be time tonight. I promise. But first, we eat."

He led her to a private balcony. The view of the lush manicured lawn stretched out before her. This place, it was amazing. It was like something written in a storybook. And yet it was real. She wondered what it must have been like to grow up in a place like this.

"This is beautiful. I just love what I've seen of Patazonia."

Leo stepped up next to her. "I get so busy that I rarely stop to appreciate the view."

Was he saying that he didn't regularly have romantic dinners here? The thought of him sharing this kind of moment with another woman soured her mood. She gave herself a mental shake. Where had that thought come from? It wasn't like she had a claim on him.

When she went to turn, she realized just how close he was standing. Her heart pounded in her chest. When she inhaled, she breathed in the light scent of his spicy aftershave mingled with his manly scent. It was quite an intoxicating combination.

He didn't move. He stood there right in front of her. All she had to do in that moment was to lift up on her tiptoes. Her gaze dipped to his mouth—his very kissable mouth. And then she could press her lips to his.

The temptation was more than she could take. After all,

he was the one to set up this very intimate dinner. Surely, he expected more to happen than business. Right?

With him staring into her eyes, she lifted up on her tip-toes. The common sense in her head was drowned out by the pounding of her heart. His hands reached out to her, wrapping around her waist, drawing her closer.

She leaned forward—

Beep. Beep. Beep.

As though the spell had been lifted, Bianca pulled back.

Beep. Beep. Beep.

Leo inhaled an unsteady breath. "Sorry. It's the kitchen timer."

He turned and headed inside. Bianca paused on the balcony, trying to slow the pounding of her heart. What in the world had gotten into her?

Well, he was amazingly handsome. He was available—sort of. He was, after all, a prince. And she didn't have a drop of royal blood—at least not that she knew of. And then the memory of her mother's journal entry came rushing back to her.

The uncertainty cast over her and her siblings brought her feet back to the ground. What was she going to do if she wasn't a blood Bartolini? Would her siblings look at her differently?

She pushed the troubling thoughts to the back of her mind. There was nothing she could do about her siblings and the fallout from their parents' deaths now. The only thing she could control was giving Giselle the very best wedding and growing her business as a result.

This meal was going to be a challenge. How was she supposed to sit there as the last rays of the sun disappeared and the stars twinkled overhead and stare across the table at the most handsome man and keep her thoughts focused on work?

She walked to the galley kitchen. "Can I help?"

"Would you mind grabbing that basket of bread?"

She turned to the counter and found the bread. "Anything else?"

He shook his head. In his hands were two plates of pasta. "I already put the salad on the table."

She didn't miss how amazing this dinner smelled. Her stomach rumbled its approval. "Did you make all of this?"

He set the food on the table. "Not the bread. I cheated and stole it from the palace kitchen. No one can beat their fresh bread."

He pulled out a chair for her and she sat down. She was tempted to ask if he went to all this trouble for every business meeting but didn't want to ruin this moment. She knew later, when she was alone in her room, that she would replay this evening in vivid detail.

Dinner was quiet without the constant interruption of his phone—or hers for that matter. She knew why hers was quiet—she'd totally muted it. It was a habit she'd gotten into before important meetings. There was nothing worse than a creative and productive meeting halted for a phone call that could wait until another time. In the time it took to answer the call, ideas may have been lost, enthusiasm for a more daring, more bold idea may have waned. And the thing Bianca disliked the most was letting a good idea slip away.

But right now, her ideas had strayed from flower arrangements and quartets to something far more daring—far bolder. As the prince ran the fine linen napkin over his lips one last time, she couldn't help but stare. She wondered what would have happened if they hadn't been interrupted out on the balcony.

In this very intimate setting with no guards, no family—absolutely no one to interrupt them—would they have even made it to dinner? Or would they be enjoying something far more delicious—

"What is it?" The prince's deep voice rumbled across the table, drawing her from her thoughts.

Did he know what she'd been thinking? No. Impossible. It was best to move things along to the business of the wedding. It would focus her thoughts. And once they wrapped things up, she'd be on her way before her thoughts had another chance to stray again.

She swallowed hard. "Thank you for dinner. It was delicious."

He shook his head. "You don't have to say that."

Was he serious? He doubted his skills in the kitchen? Was it possible a prince could have normal insecurities like everybody else in the world? "You're a talented cook."

Was it possible he was blushing? He moved so quickly to clear the dishes from the table that she wasn't able to get a good look at his face. Perhaps it was a figment of her imagination.

Then realizing she was just sitting there with the prince waiting on her, she jumped to her feet. "Let me help."

"I've got it."

"It's the least I can do after that amazing dinner." She followed him to the kitchen with the near-empty breadbasket.

He placed the plates in the sink and then he turned, almost bumping into her. "I can take that." He placed the basket on the counter. "Would you like some more wine?"

She shook her head. "No. I mean, I would but I still have work to do."

"Oh, yes. The wedding. Let's go to the living room and you can tell me your thoughts."

Her gaze strayed to the sink. "I should help you wash the dishes."

"There's no need because as much as I like to pretend that this apartment is my space to maintain, there's a staff that periodically puts everything to rights."

"Must be nice."

He smiled and set her heart pounding. "There are some advantages to being the crown prince."

"Talk about a charmed life," she teased.

The smile slipped from his face. "There's a lot more to it than most people know. There are expectations and demands. Sometimes your life is not your own."

"Sorry. I didn't mean anything by the comment."

He shook his head. "It's okay. How about we work on the wedding plans?"

Together they moved to the couch. Leo cleared off the coffee table and Bianca spread out her stuff. She wasn't exactly sure how this was to work. The truth was this evening was feeling more like a date than a business meeting.

A nervous giggle bubbled up in the back of her throat. She choked it down. She had to keep her composure, even if she was a jittery ball of nerves on the inside. What was it about this man that had her losing her calm, collected demeanor?

CHAPTER TEN

TWO LIT CANDLES.

Two wine glasses.

And this wasn't a date?

Bianca turned a questioning gaze to Leo, finding him sitting closer than she'd anticipated. When his dark, probing gaze met hers, her mouth grew dry. Did he have any idea how his close proximity made her heart pound? What exactly did he have in mind for this evening? Was she going to be dessert?

"Did you have a question for me?" Leo asked.

Act professional. Don't let him see how he gets to me.

She swallowed, hoping her voice didn't betray her. "Um, yes, I'm not sure how this is going to work. Are you planning to have input into the wedding? Or are you just looking for an overview?"

"An overview."

Thank goodness. There were already enough people fighting to have their way with the wedding. "Would you like an overview of everything? Or is there a specific area you're interested in? Such as the disagreements between the queen and the princess?"

His eyes widened with her last question. "I would be most interested in the differing opinions."

Bianca nodded. "Will you make the final decision in those cases?"

A thoughtful look came over his face. "Am I to take it that you would prefer if I were to take on a more active role?"

Bianca resisted the urge to shrug her shoulders. Though the prince had taken on a friendly persona with her, she realized their relationship was still grounded in business. And as a professional, she tried to maintain certain standards that left out shrugging.

She swallowed. "I believe if you were to take on such a role it would help alleviate some of the tension flowing between mother and daughter."

He nodded. "Then I will do it. Anything to bring some peace back to the palace."

"Great." She picked up her tablet. Her finger moved over the screen, searching for the photos she'd taken earlier. "The first disagreement is about the setting for the ceremony."

The prince sighed.

Bianca paused and turned to him. "Have you changed your mind about being the deciding voice?"

"No. Continue."

"Your sister is interested in having a small, intimate ceremony. The queen says she has a long list of relatives and dignitaries that must be allowed to attend without insulting anyone. I can see both points of view."

Frown lines bracketed his eyes. "I really want my sister to have the wedding of her dreams, but I know there are a lot of influential people that will expect an invitation."

"Would you mind if I made a suggestion?"

"Please do."

"What if we were to have the ceremony in the cathedral as your mother wants, but in order to create a cozy intimate ceremony, we can dim the stained-glass windows with curtains and we could use candles to illuminate the aisle and the front of the church. The focus then would be on the happy couple and the wedding party."

Prince Leo paused as though considering all sides of the scenario. And then he looked at her. "I like it. Do it."

"Your mother might not like it—"

"Leave her to me. Make the arrangements. Now, what else is there?"

They went over the guest list, trying to trim it back to the size to fit in the cathedral. The princess and the queen couldn't agree on who should be cut on the list so the formal invitations could be sent out. Surprisingly, Leo was able to glance down over the list and cut the necessary names.

"And how about my sister's dress?"

Bianca struggled to hide a smile. "She has that under control. No one is to see the dress. It is under lock and key in her suite of rooms. Only her and the dressmaker have access to it."

"My mother must be having a fit."

"I couldn't say. But your sister appears quite pleased with her selection. She said it's a real head turner."

"Oh, no. I'm afraid to imagine."

"Your mother said she won't stand for anything inappropriate so she's having her bridal gown resized for the princess."

Leo didn't bother hiding the fact that he rolled his eyes. "Those two are so stubborn. Should I be worried about my sister's selection?"

"I can't honestly say. I haven't seen the dress. But your sister seems reasonable to me."

"That's what I was hoping you'd say."

Now was the time for her to inquire about her compensation for planning the wedding, but how did one ask a prince if he'd followed through with what he'd promised her?

Hey, did you get a chance to call anyone? Um...do you want me to give you ideas—?

"It's my turn." Leo got up and moved to the desk in the next room, which looked to be his study. He returned with a laptop. "As soon as we came to an agreement, I had my people start on preliminary campaigns for your wedding business."

"Wow. You are very efficient." The words were already out of her mouth by the time she realized she wasn't talking to just anyone. Heat rushed to her cheeks. Leo was a prince, the crown prince. Soon he would be ruling a nation. Of course, he would be on top of things.

"I have five different approaches for you to consider." He acted as though she hadn't just stuck her shimmery heels in her mouth. It made her like him even more.

They went over the different themes. First, flowers everywhere. Second, location shots of her family's estate. Third, following an actual wedding. Fourth, a modern approach with romantic words for art. And last, her as the spokesperson and model.

The proposal was quite involved, more so than she'd ever imagined. "These are all so impressive. Would you mind if I took the night to consider them all?"

"Not at all. Take as long as you need."

"It won't take me long. It's just that the busy day is catching up with me."

"Of course. And I have some phone calls to return before I can call it a night."

She gathered her things. His fingers brushed over hers as he attempted to help her. His touch was like a jolt of static electricity. The sensation raced up her arm and settled in her chest where her heart beat wildly. She'd never experienced anything like it before.

She didn't remember moving to the door, but suddenly she was standing there. When she paused and turned back, Leo was standing right there next to her—closer than two business acquaintances and yet too far away for the perfect ending to an intimate dinner.

He didn't say anything.

She stood perfectly still.

And then his gaze lowered to her mouth. Was he going to kiss her? Her heart tumbled in her chest. This moment was surreal. She, Bianca Bartolini, standing in a palace with a dashingly handsome prince standing before her. Not only had he prepared her dinner but now he might actually kiss her.

If this was a dream, she didn't want to wake up. She was quite content to live the rest of her days in this delicious fantasy.

With her eyes, she willed him to her—like casting a spell over him. She knew it was ridiculous. Of course, it couldn't work—

But then he was there. His lips pressing to hers. Her heart suspended its pounding in utter shock. Could this be happening? Was Prince Leo really kissing her?

But as his lips moved over hers, as his hands wrapped around her waist, as her body was instinctively drawn to his, as her feet felt as though they were floating, she knew that this moment was real. This moment—this kiss—it was something that she would remember for the rest of her life.

His kiss was gentle at first but as she opened herself up to him, he wanted more and so did she. As the blood warmed in her veins, her responses to him became bolder. A deep moan of ecstasy filled the air. Was that her? Or was it him? In that moment, it didn't matter. Each was getting lost in this exquisitely sweet moment—

Knock. Knock.

They jumped apart.

Leo looked at her with desire still smoldering in his eyes. He ran a hand over his disheveled hair. Had she done that? Things had certainly moved beyond a simple goodnight kiss.

Her fingers traced over her still-tingling lips. All the while, she couldn't bear to take her eyes off him.

He cleared his throat. "I need to get this."

She nodded in understanding and then stepped back out of the way of the door. Luckily for her, the door would shield her because she had no doubt that one look at her and whoever was on the other side of the door would know what she'd been up to—getting lost in the steamy kisses of the prince.

Leo swung the door open. "Oscar, I thought I'd left strict instructions that I wasn't to be disturbed this evening."

Bianca wondered how far he'd anticipated that good-night kiss going. Had it been a sudden flare of passion? Or had it been something he'd been planning, anticipating even?

The last thought doused the remaining embers of passion as well as the hope that once the door closed, they would pick up where they'd left off.

"Sir," Oscar said with a baritone voice, "my apologies. It's the princess—"

"Is something wrong with Giselle?"

"No, sir. It's just she's been searching for Miss Bartolini. When she didn't find her in her room, she started searching for her. And when she couldn't find her anywhere, she worried that she'd wandered off sightseeing and perhaps had gotten lost."

Bianca took a couple steps back. She couldn't help but smile at the older man's obvious discomfort of delivering this news to the crown prince. And the frown that covered Leo's face was cute.

"She's not lost," Leo ground out. "She's here. We were just finishing our meeting."

"Very good, sir. I will let the princess know."

"And Oscar?"

"Yes, sir. No more interruptions."

Leo closed the door with a firm thud. Then he turned to her. "I'm sorry about that. Leave it to my sister to jump to farfetched conclusions."

"I should go." Thankfully it was Giselle searching for her, but it could have been the queen. Bianca didn't have to wonder what the queen would think of her lip-locking with the prince. The queen would have her on the first flight out of Patazonia.

"You don't have to." His eyes pleaded with her. "Not yet."

It was so tempting to stay—to find out where that kiss would lead them. But then again, she didn't have to stay to learn the answer to that question. She already knew if she were to stay that they were going to cross over a line they couldn't come back from. And that wasn't something she was ready to do. Not even for a strikingly handsome prince.

And now she had to leave before the little bit of common sense failed her. Because when she stared into his mesmerizing eyes, like she was doing right now, it was so easy to lose herself.

She glanced away. She had to stay focused on her job. It was important. Kissing the prince was not on any of her lists. The lists would get her what she wanted—her successful business, her security. She had to focus on her lists and not on how his enchanting kisses could cast the most delightful spell over her.

"I should be going," she said, glancing down at her hands.

"Are you sure I can't tempt you to stay a little longer? I still have some more of your favorite wine and I have some moonlight I can show you out on the veranda."

Did he have to make this so hard? It was as though she had a devil on one shoulder, telling her to live in the moment, and an angel on the other, telling her to march out that door. To say she was torn between her desires and her common sense was an understatement.

"As tempting as the offer is, if I don't go to the princess and find out what she needs, I'm pretty certain Oscar will be back. And I feel bad for him—being caught in between you and your sister."

"My sister can't possibly need anything important at this hour. Whatever it is can wait until morning."

"With the wedding so close, it might be urgent."

He rubbed the back of his neck. "Very well. We will meet again tomorrow evening."

Bianca nodded. "As per our agreement."

He opened the door for her. She moved past him, leaving a wide berth between them.

"Good night," she said.

"Till tomorrow."

His words sent a wave of excitement fluttering through her chest. Was that some sort of promise of more delicious kisses to come?

She kept moving down the hallway, not trusting herself to slow down and have one last backward glance. Because she'd been listening for the door to close behind her and it hadn't. Leo was standing there, watching her walk away.

It wasn't until she turned the corner that she stopped for a moment to gather herself. Had that really happened? She touched a finger to her well-kissed lips. Oh, yes, it had.

The moment though sweet and spicy must be a thing of the past. It was a memory she would hold dear. But now that she could once again think straight, she knew the knock had been her saving grace. Because to have a fling with the prince was to risk her entire future, which had enough uncertainty already. It was best that it ended here.

CHAPTER ELEVEN

HE'D BARELY SLEPT.

And he had no appetite.

In the two weeks since that earth-shifting kiss, Leo had taken every precaution not to be alone with Bianca. What was wrong with him? He'd never had a woman get under his skin the way Bianca had done. When he was around her, he longed to pull her into his embrace.

And that's exactly why they didn't dine alone again. They'd had their business dinners in the village a few nights, another night he'd invited Giselle and William to accompany them. Yet another night they'd had a working dinner with Sylvie. He'd even considered dining with his mother just so they wouldn't be alone, but he wasn't quite that desperate—yet.

Now, he sat alone in his office with two stacks of paper in front of him. They were the bios of candidates for his future wife. He'd been through the pages countless times. With his sister's wedding now only four weeks away, he had to get serious about his search. With a large portion of bios cast into the not-a-chance pile, it was time to meet the remaining women face-to-face.

A frown pulled at his lips. Why had he agreed to this? Oh, yes, so his mother would go along with his plan to let Bianca coordinate his sister's wedding. And now he had to hold up his end of the agreement.

The task left a sour feeling in the pit of his stomach. No wonder he'd skipped breakfast. Who could eat when they had to pick a marriage partner from a stack of biographies of strangers? Well, that wasn't entirely true. Some of the women he'd met on formal occasions. However, he hadn't dated any of them. He knew if he were ever to indicate a liking for someone his mother deemed appropriate, he would be formally engaged by the end of the day.

Maybe that would have been better than sitting here playing Russian roulette with his future. But there was something he'd rather be doing. He'd rather see how the wedding plans were progressing. Judging by the glance he'd had at dinner of Bianca's to-do list, she was hard at work.

He'd never met a person who ran their life by lists. He wouldn't be surprised if Bianca had lists for her lists. He had a lot of things to do as the next King of Patazonia, but even he left room for the unexpected—for a chance to enjoy life. He wondered if Bianca ever let herself enjoy spontaneous moments.

"Sir, your lunch date is here," Oscar said, standing in the open doorway of his office.

He checked the time. She was a half hour early. Normally he appreciated a visitor being prompt, even a few minutes early, but thirty minutes early. That was too much.

"Please tell Miss Ferrara that I'll be with her shortly. I have a few things I must finish up."

"Very well, sir." Oscar nodded and then backed into the hallway and walked away.

He liked Oscar. The older man was very good about keeping his thoughts to himself, unless Leo pushed for an answer. Other than that, the man did what was asked of him without causing any problems. The queen could take a few lessons from him.

"What are you doing in here?" came a familiar voice from the hallway.

He glanced up as his mother strode into his office. She didn't smile, but then again, she rarely smiled so that wasn't unusual. But by the etched lines across her forehead, she did have something on her mind.

"Mother, this is where I work."

"But you have a guest."

He arched a brow. "How would you know?"

She sighed. "Leopold, I thought you'd realized I know everything that goes on within these palace walls. Just like I know you've been spending far too much time with that... that person."

"I believe you mean with the wedding planner. And her name is—"

"I know what her name is. My question is what are you doing having intimate dinners with her?"

Leo refused to let his mother see that her question had poked him the wrong way. He met her gaze straight on. "They aren't intimate." Not anymore. "They are working dinners. Every evening, she dines with me and gives me a status report on the plans for the wedding."

His mother crossed her arms. "You expect me to believe you're really that interested in your sister's wedding? It's just an excuse to spend more time with that woman."

"Bianca is her name. And I'd appreciate you using her name instead of calling her that woman—"

"See, I was right. She's here because you're interested in her."

"She's here because you won't let Giselle have a hand in planning her own wedding and I don't have the patience nor the time to babysit the two of you."

His mother huffed. "Well, your dinner tonight will have to be cancelled."

"And why would that be?"

"Because I've invited the Duke of Lamar and his daughter to dinner. You will be there and you will spend some time with her."

"So this isn't a state dinner, it's a matchmaking ploy."

"Call it what you will, but you can't put off this marriage much longer. The press is already running negative stories about the royal family and your sister's wedding isn't enough to sway the growing discontent with the citizens.

They believe you have no interest in governing this nation. And frankly, I'm starting to think they might be right."

Leo stood. "If you believe that then you don't know me at all."

His mother arched a penciled brow. "Then I will see you at dinner."

He didn't want to go. He wanted to dine with Bianca. He'd been looking forward to that dinner—to, um, hearing about the latest wedding plans.

"I'll be there."

Without a word, his mother turned toward the door. "Don't keep your visitor waiting."

And with that his mother was gone.

His jaw tightened. He hated when his mother started throwing her weight around. He knew he'd started it by hiring Bianca without discussing it with the queen. But he knew she would have vetoed the idea. So he figured it was better to hire Bianca and hope for understanding than to mention it first and then go against his mother's wishes.

When he'd hired Bianca, he'd never imagined she'd be such good company. He wondered what she was doing now. He grabbed his phone to text her.

Are you busy?

He waited. No response.

Can't make dinner. Sorry. Something came up.

With a sigh, he placed his phone in his pocket. He'd put off meeting with—he glanced at his calendar—Jasmine Ferrara long enough. This was going to be more of a business interview than a date because he didn't have any interest in romance.

His thoughts returned to Bianca. He hoped cancelling

dinner wouldn't cause any problems. From what he could see so far, Bianca was quite capable of making sensible decisions concerning the wedding. She didn't need him looking over her shoulder, but he wasn't willing to let go of their connection. He needed to be on top of things should his mother decide to cause trouble.

Or at least that's what he told himself was the reason for insisting on dining with Bianca each evening. It had absolutely nothing to do with that unforgettable kiss. After all, he was supposed to be interviewing for a wife. He didn't have the right to kiss Bianca—even if it had been the best kiss ever.

How could the day be over already?

Where had the time gone?

Bianca made her way back to her office within the palace walls. She had so many notes. It was going to take her hours to sort through everything. But she was supremely pleased with how much she'd accomplished.

The ceremony, as well as the extensive security, had been planned down to the finest detail. And though it'd been a heated meeting with the queen and her wedding planner, they'd finally struck an agreement where the queen would get to keep her extensive guest list while the princess got to have a sense of intimacy with lots of candles and curtains that would be lowered over the stained-glass windows just as the ceremony was about to begin.

Bianca smiled as she entered the office.

"There you are." Sylvie glanced up. "I've been trying to reach you."

Bianca pulled out her suspiciously quiet phone. The battery was dead. No wonder she hadn't gotten any responses to her inquiries from that morning.

Nor had she heard from Leo. Not that there was any particular reason she should hear from him, but that hadn't kept her from hoping. Just the thought of him had heat rushing to her face.

"What has you blushing?" Sylvie asked.

Bianca swallowed hard. No one could know about the stolen kiss. Not even Sylvie, who was quickly becoming a good friend. The kiss had been a mistake. A moment of passion.

"I'm just warm," she said, hoping Sylvie would believe her and let the subject drop. "I was doing a lot of rushing around. For some reason, I imagined a palace would always be cold and drafty but that isn't the case here. Perhaps I should have packed more summer clothes."

"There are some great shops in the village. I could write down their names."

She didn't have time for shopping. It wasn't on her list of things to do. And she had something to do every minute of every day. The wedding was so close and there were still so many details to take care of, including the after-party.

Still, Bianca didn't want to be rude. "Sure. If you could jot those down for me that would be great."

Sylvie smiled. "I'll do that."

Bianca glanced at the time on the wall. "It's getting late. I'm surprised to find you still here."

"I didn't want to go home before you got back. You know, in case you had something that needed done ASAP."

Bianca glanced down at the stack of work she'd placed on her desk. "I do have a lot that needs done, but not tonight."

"Are you sure? I don't have any plans."

"I'm sure," Bianca said. "I need a chance to sort through my notes. I'll have a list for you in the morning."

"Okay. As long as you're sure."

"I am." The truth was she was so accustomed to working on her own that it was taking her some time to get used to having an assistant. "Go get some rest and I'll see you in the morning."

Sylvie grabbed her things and headed for the door. She paused and turned back. "I hope you have a nice dinner with the prince."

There was a look in her eyes like she knew what had gone down between Bianca and Leo. Was it possible rumors had started?

"I don't know what you've heard?"

"Heard?" A look of confusion came over Sylvie's face. "I haven't heard anything. Oh, gosh. I'm sorry. I didn't mean to imply anything. I just—I meant that I hoped everything goes well."

"Oh. Yes. Me too." She felt so ridiculous for thinking her secret had gotten out. She was going to have to be calmer going forward. "I think the prince will be impressed with what I was able to negotiate between the princess and her mother."

"I know that I am. I'm really enjoying working with you. I will see you in the morning. Good night."

"Good night."

Sylvie closed the door behind her. Bianca moved to sit down at her desk. She'd put an extra charger cord in her desk. She'd been meaning to replace her battery as it didn't last nearly as long as it once had. But one thing after another kept her from going into the village to buy one. She supposed she could order it online and have it delivered to the palace. Yes, that sounded like the best idea.

She plugged in her phone but it was so dead that it didn't immediately turn on. She set it aside to do its thing. But she didn't want to be late for dinner. Leo did have a thing for punctuality.

They hadn't discussed what time dinner would be tonight. If it was to be at the same time as usual she had to get moving. She didn't even have time to stop at her room and change clothes.

Bianca checked her makeup with her compact. She powdered her nose before reapplying her shimmery lip gloss. One final glance in the mirror and she decided it would have to do. It wasn't like she was going on a date. Right?

She stood up and checked her phone. It still had that blasted flashing red checkmark on the screen that let her know it was charging, but it wasn't ready to be used, just yet. And so she left it behind.

Thankfully she was good with directions because the palace was full of small staircases tucked discreetly in walls at the most unexpected places. When she reached the knight wearing the palace's coat of arms, she turned and headed up the carpeted steps. They were modest and absolutely nothing like the grand staircase in the front of the palace. If you didn't know about the steps, you might very well miss them.

At the top of the steps, she turned to the left. The prince's apartment was at the end of the hallway. It was very private. In fact, as she glanced around, she realized it was the only doorway. And considering Bianca hadn't passed anyone on her way here, she assumed not many people were welcome in this part of the palace. The fact that she'd been invited into this part of the prince's world made her feel special. A smile pulled at her lips.

She paused outside the apartment door. It was the first time she'd allowed herself to imagine how this evening might go. She envisioned another candlelight dinner with the prince flirting with her. Would it be proper to flirt back? Oh, who cared about proper? This was a fantasy.

Part of her said that she needed to stay focused on business, but the womanly part of her said that she was crazy to pass up a moment in Leo's arms. After all, what were the chances that another handsome prince would cross her path?

She halted her thoughts. She couldn't believe she was having this debate. It wasn't like the kiss would happen again. It was a fluke. A one-time thing.

With the internal conflict resolved, she leveled her shoulders and lifted her chin. It was time to do business. She inhaled a deep breath, hoping to slow her heartbeat. She raised her hand and knocked.

No response.

Perhaps she hadn't knocked loud enough. She tried again. Still nothing.

She turned and retraced her steps. At the bottom of the steps, she came across Oscar.

"Good evening, ma'am."

"Hi. Would you happen to know where the prince might be?"

"I just passed him heading into the gardens. But he—"

"Thank you. I'm late." She rushed off.

The gardens were down another floor. But when she got to the window, she saw Leo was already outside. Had he planned on having dinner in the gardens? The thought of such a beautiful romantic setting set her heart aflutter.

She started moving again, anxious to catch up with him. But when she reached the main floor and made her way out to the patio area, Leo was nowhere in sight. She set off down one of the paths but the shrubs and trees acted as walls, making the gardens more like a maze.

And then she spotted Leo just up ahead. She was about to call out to him when she noticed he wasn't alone. Bianca moved forward just enough to catch sight of a young woman smiling up at him. From that distance, Bianca couldn't make out what he was saying but whatever it was had his female companion thoroughly enthralled.

But then again, with his deep, rich voice he could be reading the information on the back of a medicine bottle and make it sound engaging. An uneasy feeling settled in the pit of her stomach.

Bianca took a step back. She didn't want them to see her lurking. Her foot landed on a fallen twig. The sound of cracking wood was much louder than she would have expected. Knowing it would draw attention, she jumped behind a bush. Her white heels sunk in the freshly watered dirt.

Tears stung the backs of her eyes. She told herself it was her being upset over ruining her cloth pumps and not the fact that Leo had gone from kissing her like she was the only woman in the world to romancing some other woman in the gardens instead of having dinner with her.

The murmur of voices faded away. They must have moved on. It was then that Bianca glanced around the bush, praying no one was around to witness her most embarrassing moment. To her relief, she was alone.

She stepped back upon the stone walkway. In the waning sunlight, she glanced down at her shoes. They were ruined—along with her daydream that the prince thought she was special. She was just another woman in his long list of admirers.

Avoiding the palace staff, she made her way back to her office where she retrieved her phone and a stack of work. She headed to her bedroom, skipping dinner altogether. She had no appetite.

Once in her room with the door closed, she looked at her phone. Now, it was charged and there were a couple of text messages. The first was from Sylvie. The second was from Leo, cancelling their dinner plans. And that was it. No explanation. No nothing.

She wanted to be angry with him, but she knew that wasn't logical. It wasn't like they were seeing each other. The kiss had been a mistake. They had a business relationship. Nothing more.

She would do well to remember that.

She needed to focus on her work. It was the only thing she could count on—the only thing in her life that she felt as though she had any control over.

CHAPTER TWELVE

SHE WAS TIRED of the games.

The prince could not kiss her one evening and then share moonlight walks with someone else another night. It didn't work that way. It didn't matter that he was a prince or that her heart raced every time they were in the same room. She had her standards.

And that's why for the next ten days, she'd reduced their meetings to daily status emails. It was much more efficient. And so much safer for her heart.

However, when she glanced up from her desk to find Leo standing in the doorway of her office, she was caught off guard.

She swallowed hard. "Your Highness, I wasn't expecting you. Can I do something for you?"

"Your Highness?" He frowned at her. "We're back to using titles?"

She gave a slight shrug before saving the current document on her laptop. She had a feeling the prince's visit would take a bit of time.

"Today is the final day of the queen's *la fête*."

"La fête?"

"Yes. Technically it's my mother's sixtieth birthday but she refuses to celebrate her birthday. She says she's too old to have birthdays. So they call her celebration the queen's *la fête*."

"Oh, I see. I'll make sure to keep out of the way. Besides I have plenty of work to do—"

"No, you don't understand. You are invited."

Bianca pressed a hand to her chest. "Me. But I'm a nobody."

"You are my guest."

Her heart stuttered. Was he asking her to be his date? Wait. No. He must mean his guest as in a general invitation because he'd moved on to that woman in the gardens. Bianca's mood dampened a bit.

She shook her head. "I couldn't intrude. It should be a private family event."

"It's not private nor a family-only event. This will be a big state dinner with fireworks afterward."

"Fireworks?" Now that was her kind of party.

He smiled and nodded. "And there is a place at the table with your name on it."

"But what's the dress code?"

"Formal."

"As in black tie?"

He nodded. "If that is a problem—"

"I've got a formal gown, but I had planned to wear it to your sister's wedding."

"Then I will see that you get a new gown for the wedding."

"No, you can't. That would be too much."

"You are doing me the favor. It is the least I can do."

"How so?"

"Because these events are usually stuffy and can veer into matters of state. I would like to avoid that this evening. And with you there, it will make the evening more festive. Perhaps the politics can be avoided for one evening. Your attendance would be in honor of the queen."

When he put it that way, how could she say no?

"Okay. I'll go."

"Good. I can stop by your room on the way to the cocktail hour."

That would be too much like a date and she needed to make sure the boundaries were clear. She couldn't let herself get swept up in the evening. She was hired help. Nothing more.

"It's okay. I'll make my way."

His eyes reflected disappointment, but in a blink it was gone. "Very well. Cocktails are at six in the library."

"I'll see you there." Bianca turned back to her laptop. She had so much work to do.

But she couldn't stop thinking about the fact that the prince had given her a personal invitation to a very important dinner. The thought of spending the evening with Leo made her heart race.

She told herself not to get too excited about it because they would be surrounded by heads of state and dignitaries. And then there was the queen. Bianca didn't care how much she told herself otherwise, that woman made her nervous.

This was it.

This was as good as it got.

Bianca gave her coral gown with its ivory and silver embellishments one last glance in the mirror. Her stomach shivered with nerves. She had no idea if she was overdressed or underdressed. Perhaps she should have consulted Giselle. She most likely wouldn't have minded giving her some fashion tips. But it was too late for that now.

She ran a hand over her pulled-up hair. It was then that she noticed the slight tremor in her hands. How could she have gone to some of the biggest weddings in the world with Hollywood stars and politicians but this birthday party made her quake.

Bianca sucked in a deep breath. She had to get a grip. She checked the time on the delicate diamond-studded watch that her parents had given her on her sixteenth birthday. It was stunning and something she wore only on the most special of occasions. But when she wore it, no matter where she was in the world, it made her feel like her family was a little closer. And now with her parents both gone, that connection was more important to her than ever before.

Sometimes she felt like a leaf just tumbling in the wind. There was no true place where she fit in. Her brother knew it. Her sister wouldn't say it, but she couldn't deny it.

But if Bianca were to make her wedding business a success, she would have a sense of security. She couldn't control the outcome of the DNA tests, but she could control the success of this wedding—so long as she stayed on top of every detail.

Buzz. Buzz. Buzz.

Her cell phone vibrated against the white marble vanity. Knowing it could be about any number of things regarding the quickly approaching wedding, she rushed to grab it. When the caller ID showed her sister's name, worry consumed Bianca for an entirely different reason.

"Gia, are the test results in?"

"Well, hello to you too." Gia expelled an exasperated breath.

"Sorry. It's just all this waiting. It's getting to me." If anyone would understand, it was her sister.

"You don't have to worry."

"What's that supposed to mean?"

"It's obvious you're a Bartolini. You look just like Nonna when she was your age."

"You really think so?" Bianca once more glanced in the mirror. She didn't see it.

"I do. I'm the one who should be worried."

"No, you shouldn't. You were Papa's favorite. And you can't deny it."

There was a moment of silence before Gia said, "That leaves Enzo."

They both hurriedly agreed that it couldn't be him. Could it? Secretly Bianca wondered if it was him as he and their father used to butt heads—a lot.

She stifled a sigh. The guessing game was getting old. And it was getting them no closer to the answers they so desperately needed.

They talked for a few more minutes, catching up on each other's lives. Then Bianca had to go. She couldn't be late for the queen's celebration. She promised to speak to Gia soon.

Bianca headed out the door. Truth be told, she wasn't sure where she was going, but she'd been too proud to admit that to Leo. But she figured if she could make it to the main entrance that she could just fall in line with the other guests as they made their way to the library.

And that's exactly what she did. Security was everywhere in dark suits and wearing earpieces. Since she was a guest within the palace, she was able to pass through the checkpoint without any problems.

She wondered if security was always this heavy. And then she realized that it would be this intense for the wedding. She would have to make allowances for that in her plans. She reached for her phone to make a note and then realized she'd left it back in her room. She tucked the information in the back of her mind.

She followed two couples to the library. As she glanced around, she was relieved to find her dress would fit in. At last, she took a full breath.

She could do this.

The funny thing was that everyone thought she didn't get nervous or filled with anxiety before a big event she'd planned. That wasn't true, but she didn't tell them. The trick was to put on a confident smile and never let them see her perspire. And that's what she intended to do this evening.

As she stepped into the massive room, she immediately searched for Leo. He was tall, so she hoped he would stand out in this crowd, but she didn't see him. And before she had a chance to make the rounds, Giselle rushed up to her.

"There you are." Giselle slipped her arm in Bianca's. "I've been telling everyone how you are putting a fresh spin on the wedding."

Was that what she was doing? Who was she to argue with a client? Correction: a princess.

"Bianca, I'd like to introduce you to the Duchess of Lamar."

Not sure how to properly greet a duchess, she said, "It's a pleasure to meet you."

The wedding conversation took off from there. The duchess said that she would be recommending Bianca's services to her nieces. That made Bianca smile.

When they entered the grand dining hall, it was stunning. The table was unlike any she'd ever seen as it must have seated at least a hundred people. Wow! She couldn't even wrap her mind around the size of the long narrow room with purple trim and portraits of the royal family through the generations.

She was seated in the middle of the table. Nowhere close to the queen at the head of the table, which was fine with Bianca. And nowhere close to the prince at the foot of the table, which she found deeply disappointed her.

But she was delighted that throughout the eight-course meal, she was entertained by the Earl of Saskan. By the looks of him, he was only a few years her senior. He was a delightful man, who could easily carry on an entertaining conversation. And he wasn't too bad looking, but he had nothing on the prince.

"It's nice that they invited you to dinner," the earl said. "They have such a tight knit group of people for these events that it's rare for an outsider to be included. Not that you're an outsider, but you know, not one of the group—"

With each word he spoke, her insecurities came rushing to the surface. She was an outsider in this grand, historic palace. Nothing would change that. She even felt out of place in her own family, she thought sadly.

"It's okay." She placed her hand on his forearm to get his attention. When his rambling stopped, she said, "I understand. I'm a guest at the palace, I believe they felt it would be rude not to invite me."

She felt someone staring at her. Could it be the prince? And then realizing that it was probably inappropriate to be touching the earl, she quickly withdrew her hand. When she lifted her gaze, the prince turned his head to the person on his right. Why should he care who she spoke to?

The earl looked at her with relief written all over his flushed face. "Sometimes, well, a lot of times I say the wrong thing. I didn't mean anything by it."

"No offense taken." But it was definitely time to change the subject. "And how are you connected to the royal family?"

She didn't know it was such a loaded question but it kept the earl talking of his lineage through most of the meal. All she had to do was interject an acknowledgment in the appropriate pauses as he regaled her with a detailed history lesson.

Surprisingly, the dinner didn't last as long as she'd imagined with that many courses. The queen didn't chat abundantly and when she finished the course, she signaled for the dishes to be cleared. In fact, during the salad course, the earl had talked so much that he'd squeezed in only one bite before the dishes were whisked away.

When the meal was over, they were escorted to the grand ball room. And grand it was with its gold trim and enormous landscape murals on the walls. A crystal chandelier was the focal point of the room. Bianca had never seen a chandelier of that magnitude. It took in the light, making the thousands of crystals shimmer and then cast a rainbow of colors throughout the room.

As the music started, Giselle sought her out. "Are you having a good time?"

"I am. Thank you. But I had no idea there would be dancing."

"My mother, though she hasn't danced since my father passed on, does enjoy the music. You should dance."

Bianca shook her head. "I don't think so."

Giselle frowned. "Why not?"

"I really should go back to my room. I have so much work to do—"

"Not tonight. There will be no work. I insist you enjoy yourself." Just then the earl passed by them and Giselle stopped him. "Donatello, my guest doesn't have an escort, would you mind dancing with her?"

The earl's face lit up. He turned to Bianca. "May I have this dance?"

"I… I don't think it's a good idea." She was a wedding planner, not any part of the royal society. It was more than enough that she'd sat at the dining table, but now to kick up her heels—it didn't seem right.

"Go ahead," Giselle encouraged.

The earl turned to Bianca. "If you don't know how to dance, I can show you. Trust me, it's not that hard."

Heat rushed to Bianca's face. How was she supposed to turn him down now? He was such a nice man, but he didn't make her heart race or fill her with giddiness like… like Leo.

In that moment, she realized she had a crush on the prince. Maybe it shouldn't come as such a shock. Probably most of the single women and maybe even some of the married ladies in the room had a crush on him. What wasn't to like?

But she couldn't just stand around here waiting for Leo to ask her to dance. That wasn't going to happen. And the best way to forget about how Leo made her feel was to get on with her life. Just one dance and then she would quietly slip away to her room.

"I'd love to dance." Bianca slipped her hand in the crook of Donatello's arm.

As he led her to the full dance floor, her gaze strayed across Leo's. This time she didn't have to wonder if he was looking at her. He was staring right at her. There was a frown pulling at his kissable lips. And his normally warm brown eyes were dark and stormy.

As the earl took her into his arms, she had to turn away from Leo. What was he frowning about? Leo might have invited her to the dinner, but it wasn't like he was her date. In fact, he hadn't spoken so much as a single word to her all evening. He didn't earn the right to be upset with her. She hadn't done anything wrong.

The earl hadn't been exaggerating about his skill on the dance floor. She knew how to dance, but her moves weren't as smooth as his. As they moved around the floor, she searched for Leo, but she wasn't able to locate him.

Maybe he'd been upset about something else. Yes, that must be it. Someone must have said something he didn't like. Perhaps it was the queen that had him out of sorts. Because there was no way he cared who she danced with.

When the music stopped, Bianca said, "Thank you so much for the dance. I enjoyed it." It was the truth. "And you are quite a talented dancer."

"Thank you. We could go again, if you want."

"Thanks. But I think I'll sit this one out."

"Perhaps later."

She nodded. "Maybe."

And that was it. The earl moved on. Without anyone around that she knew, Bianca was left to her own devices. She made her way to the edge of the crowd. It was time to make a quick exit, but she was on the opposite side of the room from the door.

She stayed near the wall as she made her way around the crowded room. She neared the corner where there were floor-to-ceiling purple drapes with gold trim that framed the wall of windows overlooking the gardens. She paused for just a moment to admire the view.

When she turned to continued walking, someone reached out. A hand pushed against her mouth, muffling her scream. Another arm wrapped around her waist and she was yanked back into the curtains. It all happened so suddenly that she didn't have time to fight back.

CHAPTER THIRTEEN

THE DOOR SLIPPED CLOSED.

Darkness surrounded her.

Bianca's heart raced. She was alone in the pitch black with her kidnapper. Her palms grew moist. Her mouth was dry. She had to do something. Fast.

Having gained her wits, she used all her might and kicked the person behind her. There was the muttering of a male voice. Immediately he released her. She spun around, but she couldn't so much as see her hand in front of her face.

"What'd you go and do that for?"

She immediately recognized that voice. It was Leo. Leo? What was he doing grabbing her out of the ballroom into—whatever this room was?

"Leo? Is that you?"

"Who else did you think it'd be?" He sounded a bit exasperated.

"I don't know. Some kidnapper. Or worse."

"You are safe. It's just me."

Her gaze moved around the room. Even though her eyesight had adjusted to the darkness, she couldn't make out anything, including him. "Leo, what are you doing? Why did you kidnap me from the ballroom?"

"I didn't kidnap you."

"Really? Because it sure seemed like it to me." She turned around. Her hands stretched out in the darkness, searching for the door. "How do I get out of here?"

"Come with me."

"No. Now turn on the lights."

It took a couple of seconds but then a bare lightbulb lit

up. She glanced around, finding that they were in some sort of passageway. And she couldn't make out a door.

"Where's the door?"

He pointed to a spot on the wall. It looked like the rest of the wall. And there was no door handle. She moved to it and tried to push it open but it wouldn't budge.

"Bianca, stop." The agitation had drained from his voice. "Let me explain."

Having no success with opening the door, she whirled around to him. "Is there another way out of here?"

"Yes."

"Then let's go."

"Aren't you even going to let me explain?"

She was mad at him. She didn't think anything he had to say at the moment was going to change that fact. "No. Let's go."

He let out a frustrated sigh. "Follow me."

He led her through a tunnel. In places the tunnel narrowed and they had to pass through it sideways. In other places there were wooden stairs.

"What is all of this?" she asked.

"So you're speaking to me again?"

She huffed. If he thought that he was off the hook, he was wrong. She didn't bother answering him. He could come to his own conclusion.

Not pushing his luck, the prince said, "These are secret passages that weave their way through the palace."

"I've heard of palaces having secret passageways but I thought they were just works of fiction."

"Now you know differently."

"But how do you know where you're going? There are so many different ways to go." She stayed close to him so as not to get left behind.

"I learned these tunnels when I was a kid."

"How did you keep from getting lost?"

"I did get lost, but my father found me. He taught me how to navigate the tunnels so I never got lost again. Once you figure it out, it's no harder than walking through the halls of the palace."

"Uh-huh." She didn't believe him.

If she was in here alone, not only would she be scared, but she was certain she'd never find her way out. She'd become a ghost that haunted the palace.

And then a thought came to her. "Is this place haunted?"

"Haunted?"

"Uh-huh. You know, ghosts that got trapped in these passageways."

Leo stopped and turned to her. In the cramped space they ended up being much closer than she was prepared for. His gaze met hers, making her heart pound. That's all it took—a look—for her body to respond to him.

She was so tempted to lift up on her tiptoes and press her lips to his. She wondered how he would react. Would he pull her closer? Would he wrap his arms around her, crushing her soft curves to his very muscular chest?

But that wasn't part of her plan. She was supposed to ignore these unwanted feelings. After all, he had practically kidnapped her from the party. Still, it'd be so easy to just live in the moment—this very intimate and most unique set of circumstances.

As though Leo could sense her conflicted emotions, he leaned forward as though to tip the scales in his favor. The breath hitched in her throat. He was going to kiss her.

But she couldn't let him off the hook that easy. Her hands moved, pressing against his very firm chest. Surprise flashed in his eyes.

"Don't even think about it." As the stern warning passed over her lips, her heart sank in her chest.

"Are you saying the thought hadn't crossed your mind?"

She wasn't playing this game with him because she knew

that she would end up losing. "I'm saying that you aren't getting off the hook that easily. Shouldn't you be here with your girlfriend?"

His brows drew together. "What girlfriend? I have no girlfriend."

She desperately wanted to believe him, but she knew what she saw. "The woman you were walking with in the gardens the night you cancelled our dinner plans."

His eyes momentarily widened. "You saw us?"

"I did."

"And that's why you've been so distant?"

"I've been busy." She answered a little too quickly—a little too vehemently.

He nodded in understanding, though they both knew it was much more than work that kept Bianca away from him.

"The woman you saw me with is an old friend of the family. I'm not now nor was I ever interested in her for anything other than friendship. We went for a walk while her father and the queen talked business. That is all."

"Really?" She wanted to take back the question, but it was too late.

"Really."

He said all the right words, but this thing between them—it was like playing with fire. It'd be so easy to get caught up in the flames—and get burned.

And then realizing that she was still touching him—still absorbing his body heat through his white dress shirt—she yanked her hands back to her sides. But it was too late. His energy had been absorbed into her body and it coursed through her faster than the speed of light. It warmed her chest and melted her core into a puddle of need.

No. This isn't going to happen. He isn't going to take what he wants.

She thought of stepping back, allowing more space between them, but she didn't want him to read weakness in her movement. And so she stood there, rooted to the spot. Her determined gaze continued to hold his. She would not let him detect any weakness in her.

But she was starting to wonder how long she could keep this up. Because every fiber of her being craved him.

He stood there for a moment as though questioning her decision. But her determination was stronger than the way his dark eyes could make her knees turn to gelatin. Wasn't it?

Before she could answer that question, he turned and continued through the passageway. She followed him as they ascended a set of narrow steps with no handrail. Bianca pressed her hands to the cold stone walls to balance herself. They kept going up and up. Then there was a switchback and they ascended another flight of steps.

"Where are we going?"

"We're almost there."

That didn't really answer her question. But she would be grateful to get out of this secret passageway. She felt totally disoriented and utterly reliant on Leo—the man of mystery. She wondered what other secrets he had and if any of them were nearly as interesting as these passageways.

At last they reached a doorway, if it could be called that. It was more like a movable part of the wall. A faint bit of light lit the way.

As they stepped out of the wall, Bianca asked, "Where are we?"

There wasn't a voice to be heard. So they were a long way from the ballroom. And there weren't any other sounds. They were alone. All alone.

Stay focused.

But he's so cute. And what happens here would be our secret.

But he hasn't apologized. He can't just do what he wants without consequences.

Leo turned to her on what appeared to be some sort of landing. There was a set of stairs to his left and a single step that led to a wooden door on his right. The window let in the moonlight.

"We are in the east tower," he said.

Her heart pitter-pattered in her chest.

Why had he brought her here?

Now that he had her alone, he wasn't sure this was such a good idea. But it was too late to back out now.

"I wanted you to have the best vantage point. Come on." Leo took Bianca's hand and led her up the step and out the door.

"Vantage point for what?" She glanced around.

In the moonlight, the general layout was visible. Leo let go of her hand and lit some torches. A warm glow filled the space and highlighted the large daybed with a twin mattress and a dozen plush pillows.

"What is this place?" Bianca asked.

"It's my private spot. It's where I come when I have a lot on my mind. Sometimes I sleep out here."

He gazed into her eyes.

His heart pounded against his ribs. All he wanted to do was pull her into his arms and crush his lips against hers. He wanted to forget his duty—his obligations. In Bianca's arms, he was certain he would find the release he was seeking.

But when she gazed up at him like he hung the stars—like she was doing now—guilt assailed him.

He needed to be honest with her. She needed to know the real him. Because he wasn't the perfect prince that his mother portrayed to the world.

His thoughts drifted back to the week he'd spent on this very terrace, refusing to go back inside the palace. It had been the darkest point in his life—

"Leo, what's the matter?" Bianca's voice drew him from his troubled thoughts.

He shook his head. "Nothing."

"It's something. The pain is written all over your face. I'm a pretty good listener—that is if you want to talk about it."

He hadn't talked about it with anyone. Not even his mother. And she had been there—she'd gone through the nightmare, not exactly with him. They'd each gone through it in their own individual ways.

Leo turned and gazed into Bianca's eyes. "I don't want to ruin this night for you."

"You won't. I'd like to think we're friends and that we can confide in each other." She stared into his eyes as though she could see clear through to his soul. "Does it have something to do with your father?"

How did she do that? How did she know what he was thinking? Did she have some sort of special power? Or were his thoughts that transparent?

"How did you know?"

She shrugged. "It was just a guess. But you never talk about him. How come?"

Leo took her hand and led her over to the daybed. They perched on the edge of it. He was trying to find a place to start. He supposed the best place to start was the beginning.

"I'd looked up to my father all of my life. When I grew up, I wanted to be just like him. The problem was that I had no idea what that would entail."

"I can't even begin to imagine. And I thought I had it hard fitting into my family."

He shook his head. "Don't feel sorry for me. I'm not the good guy you think I am."

"Sure you are. Look at what you're doing for your sister. And how you took time out of your busy schedule to attend your friend's wedding. And then there's what you're doing for me—"

"Stop." He held up a hand as though blocking her compliments. "You don't understand. None of that can undo the past."

He recalled how his mother made him promise to never speak of his father's death. She wanted to sweep all the unsavory details under the rug, where no one would notice them. His mother wanted the picture-perfect family and the unblemished prince to ascend to the throne. She wanted to live a lie because none of those things existed in real life.

But he'd already lashed out at his father and it had cost his father his life. Leo couldn't lose his only remaining parent and so he did as the queen wanted. However, it came with a price. Every time he had to gloss over the details or leave out a fact, especially when talking to his own sister, it'd killed a little piece of him.

He'd been living with the secret for so long that it felt as though it was going to smother him unless he let it out. And Bianca was so easy to talk to. It was though he could tell her anything and she would understand. But would she look at him the same way once he told her his secret?

He drew in an unsteady breath. Peeling back the scabs hurt just like the nightmare had happened yesterday. But this wasn't about his comfort. It was about proving to Bianca that he wasn't worthy of her.

He stared straight ahead into the black sky. "I was sixteen. And I wanted to go on holiday with one of my friends to the lake. But my father told me I had responsibilities to attend to. I was a kid. I hated being in the spotlight. I hated being escorted by bodyguards everywhere. I hated being different."

"It must have been difficult. I think every kid just wants to fit in. I know I did."

Her words of comfort gave him the encouragement he

needed to continue. "When I told him I was going with my friends and nothing he said could stop me, my father grew angry and started yelling at me. He told me it was time I grew up. He had plans for me to attend a royal wedding in another country. He said I would meet an appropriate young woman."

Leo could still recall his outrage when he realized his father had already chosen the young woman he was to marry. He wasn't even an adult yet and his whole life had been planned without even consulting him.

"I told him I didn't want to date anyone. My father said this wasn't going to be a date. This young woman would be my future wife." The exact words of that horrific fight were a little lost on him. "My father suddenly grew quiet. I thought it meant he was giving in to my demands. Being a kid, I told him I quit being a prince. That my sister could be queen. By then he was perspiring and his face was a pasty color." Leo could still see his father's sickly image in his mind. "He strode up to me. I never saw him so angry. Ever." Leo's voice faltered. "He told me I couldn't quit. I was a prince by blood. It was an honor—a privilege. And…"

Bianca reached out and squeeze his hand. There was so much to that innocent touch. There was kindness, compassion. Both of which he didn't deserve.

He swallowed hard, hoping his voice wouldn't fail him. He had to get out this secret that he'd been keeping so deep within him. It was as though it was choking him. And the only way he could take a full breath was to get it all out in the open.

"I should have known that something was seriously wrong with him. He'd been sweating profusely and he'd looked awful, but I was only worried about myself and being with my friends. I wasn't giving up. I kept yelling at my father. I… I can't believe those angry, hurtful words were the last ones I said to him." Tears stung his eyes as emotion choked off his next words.

Bianca shifted closer to him as though letting him know that she was there to lean on. Then ever so softly, she said, "He knew you loved him."

"Did he? Because when he stopped yelling midsentence the look in his eyes was full of rage. And...and then he collapsed." He ran the back of his hand over his eyes. "I don't know how long I stood there like a complete and utter fool."

"You were in shock."

"But it was my father—the king. If I'd acted faster, maybe things would have been different."

"I don't think a few seconds would have changed things. It was out of your hands."

"You might be the only one who thinks that. Because when I finally came to my senses and started screaming for help, my mother entered the room. When she rushed over to my father, she asked me what had happened. I told her we'd been fighting and he'd collapsed. She looked at me as though it was all my fault. Then she made me promise not to mention a word of what had happened to anyone, including my sister."

"That's a huge secret for a kid to keep. Is that why there's a distance between you and your mother?"

He shrugged. "Everything was different after that. She had to become the regent and it was a position she didn't want, but she said that duty must be upheld. So I guess she holds that against me too."

Bianca placed a finger on the side of his jaw, encouraging him to meet her gaze. "And you've been blaming yourself all of this time?"

"It was my fault. If I hadn't been so insistent on having my way, things would have been different."

"Or they might have happened the same way. I don't think anything you said or did would have changed your father having a heart attack. And did you ever think your mother was trying to protect you? Maybe she struggled stepping into such an important role and by taking a firm line, it was her way of proving to everyone, including herself, that she was up to the challenge."

He paused, giving Bianca's words some serious thought. "I never thought of it that way. My mother always seemed so calm, so in control."

"Maybe you only saw what she wanted you to see."

His gaze searched Bianca's. "You really don't think I had any part in my father's death?"

"I don't. And I think if he was here, he'd tell you the same thing."

Those are the words that he'd longed to hear. He just hadn't known it. And having shared his deepest-held secret with Bianca, they now had a bond he knew would never be broken.

Her heart raced.

She'd never felt as close to anyone as she did in that moment—

A great big boom shook the ground.

Bianca instinctively reached out for Leo. Her fingers wrapped around his muscular bicep.

"Relax," he said. "Everything is okay."

Was it? Okay, that is. Because she was beginning to wonder if those passageways had taken them back in time and they were suddenly a couple hundred years in the past. The boom could be that of a canon aimed at the palace. When she was with Leo, it was easy to believe that anything was possible.

But then again, maybe she'd had one too many sips of champagne. As another softer boom filled the air, she braced herself for the palace to shake, but instead she saw the sky fill with light—colorful shades of pink and blue.

Fireworks. She breathed more easily. And then quickly withdrew her hand from Leo's arm. She moved to the stone wall at the edge of the tower. There wasn't a soul near them. They were so high up that it felt as though they were in the sky with millions of stars sparkling around them.

And then she felt Leo's presence just behind her. She waited for him to reach out and touch her. Her traitorous heart picked up its pace in anticipation.

When she turned her face to him, he said, "I'm sorry. I handled this night all wrong."

He looked at her like she should say something here, but if he was waiting for her to disagree with him, he'd be waiting a long time.

As the silence stretched between them, Leo cleared his throat. "It's just when I saw Donatello flirting with you and you enjoying it...it bothered me."

When his gaze lifted to meet hers, she searched his brown depths. Not finding the answer she was looking for, she asked, "Why did it bother you who I was talking to?"

He stepped closer to her, so close that they were practically touching. All the while the booms of the fireworks sounded in the background and the sky lit up with a rainbow of colors.

And then he reached out to her, caressing her cheek ever so gently. "Because every time you smiled, I wanted you to be smiling at me. And when you let out that contagious bubbly laugh of yours, I wanted it to be because I made you happy. And when you danced, I wanted it to be my arms wrapped around you, holding you close."

She lifted her chin ever so slightly. And then in a breathy voice, she asked, "You did?"

He gave a slight nod of his head. "I did. Do you know how hard I've been fighting my attraction to you?"

"I have some idea. I've been doing the same thing."

Desire reflected in his eyes. "I've wanted to do this since

the first moment I spotted you this evening." He lowered his head and caught her lips with his own.

The breath stilled in her lungs. There were a million reasons why this shouldn't be happening. And in that moment, those reasons dissipated into the starry night.

With the cascade of white-and-blue fireworks overhead, Leo's mouth pressed to hers. Her heart leaped into her throat. This was really happening. Leo was kissing her again.

In that moment, it didn't matter that he was a prince. To her, he was just Leo—the man who made her heart race with just a look. There was so much more to him than a fancy title. And she was anxious to continue peeling back the layers that made Leo such an exceptional man.

As his lips moved over hers, she let herself get wrapped up in the moment. The boom and crackle of the fireworks faded into the background. Right now, Leo was shooting off fireworks in her mind...and her heart.

Her arms, almost of their own volition, moved up his chest, over his broad shoulders and wrapped around his neck, drawing him closer. She wanted more. She needed more.

And yet, he took an agonizingly long time savoring her lips—refusing to rush the moment like she was apt to do.

She couldn't tell if it was the boom of the fireworks or the pounding of her heart that filled her ears. Not that it mattered. The only thing she cared about at the moment was that this kiss never ended. Because she knew deep in her heart that this moment was very precious. They were making a memory that she would cherish for the rest of her life.

When Leo pulled back all Bianca wanted to do was to draw him near once more—to feel his warm lips pressed to hers. She struggled to calm her rushed breaths.

"Bianca, if you want me to stop," his voice was raspy as he drew in one quick breath after the other, "tell me now."

Was he serious? "Don't stop."

"You're sure? Because I don't just want you for this moment—I want you to stay the night with me beneath the stars."

She glanced around. "Won't someone find us here?"

A deep laugh bubbled up from deep in his chest. "Trust me, they know better. When I'm up here, I want to be alone."

"And how many other women have you brought here?" She didn't know why she'd asked, but she knew the answer was important to her. The breath hitched in her throat as she waited.

"You, *ma chère*, are the first."

Knowing this was as special to him as it was to her warmed a spot in her chest. She took him by the hand and led him to the daybed. She sank down on the soft cushion as Leo joined her.

When she turned her head to him, he claimed her eager lips once more. Oh, yes, this was most definitely what she needed. He was what she needed…as much as her lungs needed oxygen.

That evening, she let go of all her worries about the DNA tests, the plans for the royal wedding and the future of her business. Lying there wrapped in Leo's very strong, capable arms, all she could think about was him, her, them.

All the problems could wait. Right now, there was a driving need to see where their star-studded night would take them.

CHAPTER FOURTEEN

LAST NIGHT HAD been amazing, spontaneous and unforgettable.

But in the light of day, she knew it had been a mistake.

Bianca groaned in frustration. Her heart said one thing while her mind said the opposite. All her insecurities floated to the surface.

She paced back and forth on the balcony of her room. What had she been thinking to let down her guard and make love to the prince? For a moment, the memory of the night before came rushing to her mind. Leo had been so gentle with her, so loving and thoughtful.

But it hadn't been all sweet and tender. There had been some heady passion that left her utterly breathless and begging for more. It was a night that she would never forget. But it couldn't happen again—no matter how much she wanted to relive it.

It had been a mistake.

She'd put everything she held dear in jeopardy for a man that was out of her reach. She wasn't royal. She didn't have an aristocrat cell in her body. And worst of all, she had the DNA test weighing over her. When it came back and proved she wasn't a Bartolini, who would she be?

She certainly wasn't going to ask Leo to go through this nightmare with her. It wasn't fair to him. This was her burden to carry on her own.

Bianca stopped pacing. She knew what needed to be done. The sooner, the better.

She headed out the door. She knew where to find Leo—in his royal office. On her way, she practiced what she'd say to him.

The clean-cut, always proper assistant stopped typing on his desktop and turned to her when she arrived. "May I help you?"

"I need to speak with the prince."

In total sincerity, Michael asked, "Do you have an appointment?"

In her rush, she hadn't thought of that. She didn't usually have to see Leo during business hours. "No, I don't. But this won't take long."

"I'm sorry. The prince has asked not to be disturbed."

She wondered what that was all about. Did it have something to do with what had happened between them last night? Or did he normally ask for privacy while he worked?

She wanted to ask but it was none of her business. Instead she said, "Thank you."

Just as she was about to turn away, Michael said, "I could give him a message."

She shook her head. This was something that needed to be said in person. "I'll speak with him later."

She moved to the doorway and started down the hallway when she heard her name called out. She paused and turned to find Leo standing there.

He rushed to catch up with her. "Did you need to speak to me?"

"I did."

"What did you need?" His voice and expression were neutral so she wasn't able to figure out what he was thinking.

She glanced around as people passed through the spacious hallway. Offices lined both sides of the hallway. There was absolutely no privacy. "Not here."

"Then come to my office."

In his office, it'd be easier to stick to the matter at hand. She wouldn't let herself get distracted with how good his lips felt pressed to hers—

She halted her meandering thoughts. This was what she feared would happen when they were together. She needed to make this meeting short and straight to the point.

"Let's go." Her stomach shivered with nerves, but that didn't stop her from leveling her shoulders and following him.

Once they were in his office with the door closed, she turned to him, finding that he was standing closer than she'd been expecting. She swallowed hard. "It's about last night—"

"I wanted to speak with you about that too."

"You did?" Her gaze met his.

He nodded. "Yes. But you go first."

This was it. All those practiced words fled her. And now she was left scrambling for a way to phrase this that would leave them in as good a place as possible.

Drawing upon the calm exterior she used for her wedding planner position, she lifted her chin just a bit. "Last night...it was a mistake."

"It was..."

Was that a question? Or was he in agreement? She wasn't able to discern his intent. Her heart raced, pumping her body with nervous energy.

"I shouldn't have let things get out of control," she said.

"You think we are better off sticking to our working relationship?"

"You do understand, don't you?"

He didn't say anything for a moment as though absorbing what she said. "So you would like to pretend like last night never happened?"

"Yes. Exactly."

There was some emotion reflected in his eyes, but before she could define it, he blinked and his feelings were locked behind a wall of indifference.

"We will forget it ever happened."

She held out her hand to him. "Then we have an agreement that our relationship will be nothing but business?"

His thumb stroked the back of her hand, sending tremors of yearning flooding her system. He looked at her with desire in those warm brown eyes.

"Be careful what you ask for," he said. "You might end up regretting it."

She was already regretting many things—none of which were spending those precious hours wrapped in his arms or tasting his addictive kisses. She was in trouble. Big trouble.

The week was getting away from him.

And nothing was going right.

First, the fact that his fling with Bianca was over before it'd really begun bothered him.

Second, his mother was on his case every chance she had, pushing him for the name of his chosen bride. There was little more than a week until his sister said "I do" and his engagement would be announced to the kingdom. His fate would be sealed.

And Leo was not ready. In the beginning, it'd appeared to be an easy enough task. Find a friendly woman whose goals aligned with his. They'd marry, he'd become king and the rest would hopefully fall into place. But somewhere along the way, the gravity of this decision had set in.

Maybe it was seeing how happy his sister was with William. Or maybe it was how happy he was in Bianca's company. Or perhaps it was that magical night beneath the fireworks. Whatever it was, he couldn't settle for mere tolerance of his wife. There had to be more...

His mind filled with the image of Bianca smiling and laughing. How it filled him with such warmth. He recalled their many meals together and though they'd started off discussing his sister's wedding, they'd eventually end up on a far more personal note. Those were the sort of experiences he wanted to share with his wife. Was that asking too much?

But if he didn't make a decision and soon, his mother would take the matter into her own hands. His hands clenched. This was an utterly impossible situation.

And he'd only compounded the matter by acting upon his growing feelings. How was he supposed to choose a wife when all he could think about was Bianca?

Leo frowned as it was now early Friday morning and he hadn't seen or spoken to Bianca since their business lunch yesterday. She'd kept her word about their relationship being all business. He didn't like it. He didn't like it at all. And that's why he'd planned something special for them this morning.

Knowing Bianca was an early riser, he went to find her. It took a bit but he finally tracked her down in the library with his mother. It definitely wasn't the ideal place to meet up with her, but he was determined to see her. His surprise couldn't wait.

The doors were open and he slowed as he heard his mother's voice.

"And why are we supposed to take your advice when you dress like—like that."

Without missing a beat, Bianca spoke up. "Pardon me, ma'am. But this isn't about my personal tastes. We're talking about the princess and what she would like for her wedding. And I must say your daughter has exceptional tastes. She must take after you."

"I, uh, thank you." There was a slight pause as though Bianca's compliment had knocked his mother off her game. But the queen was quick and she soon had the conversation back on track. "However, the princess will wear my wedding dress."

He recognized the stern tone of his mother's voice. She was in no mood to bend or be persuaded from her decision.

Leo stepped into the room. "There you are." His gaze settled upon Bianca just as her mouth was opening to argue with his mother. "We have a meeting."

"We do?"

"Yes."

"But—"

"Leopold, don't forget you are to have lunch with Elizabeth." The queen arched a penciled brow.

"I haven't forgotten. Plans have changed." He was tired of his mother's constant interference. Today, he was going to do what he wanted to do, not what he was expected to do. "Are you ready to go, Bianca?"

Bianca's confused gaze moved between mother and son. Her mouth opened but nothing came out. That was a first.

A smile pulled at Leo's lips. "We don't want to be late." He turned his attention to his mother. "Please excuse us."

His mother looked exasperated. She waved them off.

Once out in the hallway, Bianca stepped in front of him. She glared at him. "Why did you interrupt my meeting with your mother?"

"I was doing you a favor."

"A favor?" Her voice rose with agitation.

He took her hand in his. They moved swiftly down the hallway. It wasn't until they were out of earshot of his mother that he stopped. Bianca yanked her hand free as she shot him another angry glare.

"I'd appreciate if you would let me do my job," she said. "And we don't have any plans."

"That's where you would be wrong."

"No. I'm not." She reached for her phone and ran her finger over the screen. Then she turned the phone to him. "See, I don't have you on my calendar."

"Then your calendar must be wrong."

"My calendar is never wrong. It's what keeps my life, my business, on track."

He wasn't going to argue the point. He had more important matters in mind. "My car is waiting for us. This way."

"And if I refuse?"

"You'll regret it. I promise you're going to love this." He could tell by the widening of her eyes that she was hooked.

Did he have to interrupt her meeting with the queen?

She'd just started to make some headway.

Bianca admitted that she might have pushed the queen hard, but someone had to stand up to her. Otherwise the queen was about to roll right over her daughter. It was Bianca's job to make sure that didn't happen.

When she went to speak to Leo, she realized he was already walking away. She rushed to catch up with him. His long legs took lengthy strides and she had to take two steps for every one of his.

"Do you mind telling me where we're going?"

"Out." He stopped and opened the door for her.

She stepped out into the cool morning air. The sun was shining in the cyan blue sky. There wasn't a cloud in sight. It was going to be a beautiful day.

When Bianca lowered her gaze, she noticed a sleek black sports car sitting in the middle of the drive. It wasn't a new model. This car was a classic but in mint condition. The top was down, revealing its black leather bucket seats. It looked perfect for cruising around and taking in the sights. Not that she had time for sightseeing.

As though Leo had read her thoughts, he moved to the car and opened the passenger side door for her. Just then her phone vibrated in her hand. Her breath hitched as she wondered if it was a message about the DNA results. She glanced at the phone, willing the results to be in—so she'd at last know if she was a true Bartolini...or not.

However, the text message on her phone was from Sylvie. The replacement linens were to be delivered that afternoon. Though it was good news so far as the wedding, she was still left wondering about the DNA results and how they would change her life.

"Bianca? Hey Bianca?"

She glanced up to find Leo waving at her. She pressed her lips into a firm line as she sent off a quick text to her assistant, thanking her for following up on the order.

"Sorry. I have a lot going on right now."

"Exactly why you need a little break."

"You aren't going to let this go, are you?"

"Not until you come with me."

She climbed into the car. The leather seats were so soft it felt as though they'd been wrapped around her. After Leo climbed in the driver's seat, he fired up the powerful engine. It purred, but Bianca sensed the purr was deceptive. A little pressure on the accelerator and they roared off, down the driveway.

As he adjusted the rearview mirror, she asked. "Are you allowed to do this?" When he glanced at her with a questioning arc of his brow, she added, "You know, go off on your own. After all, you're the crown prince."

A smile lit up his face. Oh, my, was he handsome. Her heart swooned. The traitorous thing.

"It took a lot of negotiating but I've been allowed a certain bit of freedom."

"I bet the queen wasn't happy about that."

He laughed. The sound was warm and rich. "It's not the queen that I had to convince. It was Sir George."

"Who is Sir George?"

"He's the head of my security detail. In fact, he's the head of the royal protection for the palace and the family. But he personally oversees my protection and I've been a challenge to him over the years."

"And he agreed that you could go out driving by yourself?"

"Hardly. Behind us is a dark SUV filled with heavily armed guards. If anyone were to stop this vehicle, they would have an ex-military team to deal with. I can assure you, we are quite safe."

The low-set car clung to the road as they whipped around the mountainous curves. Bianca's hand tightened around the door handle. It'd been a long time since she had been in a sports car. She remembered not long after her brother started to drive that he would be given the task of driving her to visit with friends. He drove so fast, as though he were a race car driver, only he'd had a lot less experience at the time than Leo had now.

Still, Enzo had been a good sport. Without him, she wouldn't have been able to see her friends since they lived so far apart. And her parents were always busy. Her father with the winery and her mother with the horses and the gardening. None of which interested Bianca all that much.

But Enzo made sure she didn't get forgotten in the rush of everyday life. She smiled at the memory. Maybe the distance between them now was something that could be overcome. Maybe they could be close once more. She didn't realize until that moment that it was something she wanted, something she wanted as much as—no, more than—she wanted to win the contest.

"What are you thinking about?" Leo's voice interrupted her thoughts.

"My family. Actually, my brother."

"And that made you smile?"

"Yes, it did. Riding in this sports car reminded me of him when I was a kid and how he would drive me around so I could see my friends. I'd forgotten about it—about how we'd crank up the music and I would sing at the top of my lungs. He'd laugh and we, well, we just had fun."

"And you two don't have fun any longer?"

She glanced down at her hands. "We haven't in a lot

of years. We drifted apart when I was a teen. I was more worried about my hair and my clothes than hanging out with my family."

"Isn't that normal for a teenage girl?"

She shrugged. "Maybe. But once the distance was there, we were never able to overcome it."

"By the smile on your face when you thought of your brother, I don't think it'll be hard to repair your relationship."

"It might be harder than you're imagining." And then the story of finding her mother's diary and the fact that one of the three siblings was not a Bartolini by blood all came spilling out.

She didn't know why she'd confessed to Leo. She'd been intending to keep the secret until the DNA results proved what she already surmised—she wasn't a Bartolini. But it felt good to get it out—even if the results were not what she wanted for herself or either of her siblings.

Leo took his gaze off the road for a moment to glance at her. Sympathy reflected in his dark eyes before he focused back on the road. "You shouldn't assume you are not a Bartolini. It could be any one of you. Or maybe you misunderstood—"

"There was no misunderstanding." Bianca wrung her hands. "It makes sense that it's me." Her voice crackled with emotion. "I never lived up to my parents' expectations. I always marched to a different drummer. I wasn't like my brother or sister."

He reached out and took her hand in his. "It doesn't mean you aren't a Bartolini."

"If only that were the truth," she muttered under her breath.

Leo gave her hand one last reassuring squeeze. And then the car pulled to a stop.

She glanced around. "Where are we?"

"This is the best view of the palace and the surrounding area. I like to come up here just to get away from all the pressures. Though I don't get time to do that very often these days."

"I can see why you'd want to come up here. The view is stunning." She stared out at the land as the sun's early morning rays highlighted it. She reached for her phone and snapped a photo through the open window.

When she went to open her car door, he said, "Wait. I have an even better view for you."

"Better than this? Impossible."

"Trust me." He started driving again.

They moved further along the tree-lined road. The car climbed a gradual rise and at the top, a rainbow of color came into sight. It hovered there in all its big, bright brilliance. As the car moved closer, more color was revealed, and soon Bianca realized what she was looking at—a hot air balloon.

"Oh, look." She lightly clapped her hands together in excitement. "I just love hot air balloons. Do you think they'll fly it while we're here?"

Leo pulled the car to a stop. "We can ask."

"Do you know these people?"

He offered only a smile in response. What did that mean? Was he going to use his status as prince to get what he wanted?

As soon as the thought crossed her mind, she felt guilty. In all the time she'd known Leo, he'd never once abused his position as the crown prince. He was better than that.

Leo was a good man. No. He was a great man with a generous, caring heart. When it came time for him to take over the throne, the country of Patazonia would be very lucky.

Her door swung up, startling her from her thoughts. She glanced up to find Leo standing there.

"Are you coming?"

"Of course." She alighted from the car and walked beside Leo.

She thought they would be moving toward the edge of the mountainside for a view of the area, but Leo was headed for the hot air balloon. Suddenly she started to worry that he was doing this for her.

"Leo, we shouldn't interrupt them. They look busy."

"It'll be okay. I'm sure they won't mind letting us take an up-close look."

He took her hand in his. A rush of tingles started in her fingertips and worked their way up her arm. They settled in her chest and had her heart racing.

In that moment, her awareness of their bodies touching—of the smoothness of his palm brushing over hers—was all she could think about. Did he mean something by the touch? Did he need the connection of their laced fingers? Did he crave it like she did?

She felt like a girl once more with the biggest crush on the most popular guy in school. Only Leo was so much more than that—he was an intriguing puzzle of contradictions. And she wanted nothing more than to figure him out.

Leo released her hand to go and speak to the three-man crew filling the balloon. Two men, one on each side, held up the opening of the balloon, while the third man worked the controls. A blast of flames would shoot forth filling the balloon with hot air. It was marvelous to watch as the colorful material rippled and expanded. Up and up it went.

And then Leo was once more by her side, taking her hand in his. "Come on."

She walked with him. "Leo, are we allowed to get this close?"

"We are."

And the next thing she knew, she was being helped inside the basket. Her heart raced. This was the experience of a lifetime. She was never going to forget this—or the very special man sharing this experience with her.

CHAPTER FIFTEEN

THIS WAS DEFINITELY one of his better ideas.

Leo stood at the edge of the basket as Bianca filmed the lush landscape with her phone. The truth was that he hadn't noticed the passing scenery as he was entranced with the beautiful woman next to him.

Was it wrong that he was supposed to be looking for an appropriate wife and yet all he wanted to do was kiss Bianca? There was something about her—something that drew him to her. She filled his thoughts when he was supposed to be working, when he was supposed to be getting to know some young woman—he was always comparing them, and when he was alone at night, his thoughts were all about her.

He shoved aside his problems. Right now, all that mattered was making Bianca happy.

His gaze moved to her. The big smile on her face was brighter than the morning sun. And there was a gravitational pull to her that drew him close.

"Are you enjoying yourself?" he asked.

She lowered her phone. "I can't believe you did this." Her eyes glittered with happiness. "It's amazing. I love it. Thank you."

Oblivious to the pilot firing the flame to keep them aloft, Leo leaned toward Bianca and pressed his lips to hers. It was a quick kiss, but it had a big effect on the pounding of his heart.

If only they didn't have an audience, he would pull her into his arms and kiss her deeply and thoroughly. Her sweet, sweet kisses were addictive.

She pulled back and gazed up at him with her big round eyes. "What was that for?"

He shrugged, not sure what she was thinking. "Just seemed like the right thing to do in the moment."

A hint of smile pulled at her berry-red lips as she turned her head to the magnificent view. He gazed at the distant horizon, but all he could see in his mind's eye was Bianca.

All too soon the balloon lowered toward a large field not far from the palace grounds. The first touch-down was gentle. It was the second touch-down that jolted the basket and had Bianca reaching out to him to help steady her. He held on to the basket with one hand and placed an arm around her waist with the other arm. She melted into his side, her curves aligning with him as though they'd been made for each other. Her arm wrapped around him too as her other hand white-knuckled the edge of the basket.

When the basket came to a final rest, the relief was written all over Bianca's face. The chase vehicle hadn't caught up to them. Leo helped Bianca from the basket.

In the distance, they heard a vehicle approaching.

"That must be our ride," Leo said.

"You think of everything."

"I try." He sent her a smile, hoping she'd send one back. And she did.

There was no way he wanted this morning to end. And then a thought came to him. As soon as they got back to the palace, they could share a leisurely brunch. He liked that idea. Anything that kept Bianca close by appealed to him.

When he turned back, he noticed the vehicle rushing toward them wasn't a palace vehicle. And there were more vehicles behind it. When someone leaned out the passenger window and started yelling, Leo knew they were in trouble. Without his security team, they were in serious danger.

"Come with me." Leo took her hand in his and headed for the wooded area.

"Leo, what are you doing?"

"That's the paparazzi." At least that's who he hoped it was and not some anti-government group. "We have to go."

For several moments they ran, moving through the thick underbrush. He knew where he was going. He just hoped the paparazzi didn't know these woods.

"Leo?" Bianca called out in a breathy voice. "Leo, please stop."

He came to a complete halt and turned to her. "Are you okay?"

"I… I just need to catch my breath." She huffed and puffed. "I didn't know we were going for a morning run."

"I'm sorry." He felt terrible that their wonderful excursion was ruined. "I never meant for this to happen. Sometimes I forget that I'm a target for headlines."

"Do you think they got a photo of us?"

"I'm not sure. If they did, it was from a distance. Don't worry about it."

"And do you think they're following us?"

He didn't want to think that was true. But he knew that the paparazzi would go to great lengths to get a good photo or a juicy story.

"It's not far from here. Can you keep going?"

She nodded. "But could we slow down a little? The ground is uneven and there are roots sticking up."

He glanced around as he strained to hear any sign that they'd been followed. "I think we're good."

"Maybe you should call someone. Your security will be worried."

He pulled out his phone, but there was no reception out here in the middle of nowhere. "I can't call now, but I will as soon as we get back."

"Then we better get moving before the queen sends out every guard on the palace grounds."

They set off once more at a much more reasonable pace. He told himself he kept ahold of Bianca's hand to help her along the way.

Twenty or so minutes had passed when Leo came to a stop. He released Bianca's hand. She didn't say anything. He could tell she was tired and definitely not happy. The entire day had been ruined. And it was his fault for not doing a better job of planning ahead.

He knew there was an entrance around here somewhere. The problem was that it hadn't been used in so many years there was a significant amount of overgrowth.

He pulled on the vines and at last he found the bars over the entrance. "Here it is."

Bianca moved to his side. "What is it?"

"An entrance to the palace."

Bianca started to laugh. "You can't be serious. It looks like a drainage pipe."

"That's what it's supposed to look like."

"But I'm confused. Why would you want the entrance to the palace to look like a neglected drainage pipe?"

"Because it's a secret entrance."

He hunched down as he worked to release the lever that held the iron grate in place. There had been so many years of disuse and rain that it was rusty. Leo made a mental note to have someone come out here discreetly and make sure it was in better working order.

It took several minutes and all his might, but finally the latch gave way. And then he pulled the grate open.

He stepped inside and then turned back for Bianca. "Come on."

She shook her head. "I… I don't think so."

"Trust me. This a lot shorter than climbing the hillside to the palace."

"But there might be snakes or worse in there." She visibly shuddered.

"What's worse than a snake?"

Softly she uttered, "A spider."

He wanted to tease her, but he saw the genuine fear in her eyes. Instead he pressed a hand to his heart. "I swear upon my life that I will protect you from any snake or spider."

"You think I'm silly."

He shook his head. "Everyone is afraid of something."

"That's not true." Her gaze searched his. "You aren't afraid of anything."

Oh, there was something he feared. But it wasn't some eight-legged creature or the fangs of a reptile, no, what he feared went much deeper.

He feared having his heart broken again. He feared speaking too loudly—too harshly. The image of his father clutching his chest came to mind. If only he'd done what was asked of him—if he hadn't made waves—then maybe his father would still be here with them. Not wanting to delve further into the subject, Leo didn't correct her.

Using the flashlight app on his phone, he guided them through the tunnel until they came to a steel door with a keypad. He punched in the security code. The heavy door swung open with ease.

He stood aside and waved Bianca into the secure tunnel. He followed her, pausing to press the button for the door to swing shut behind them.

"We are safe now. No one can get in here." He took the lead, using his memory to lead them to the lower level of the palace—the old portion that no one bothered with anymore.

They walked in silence. After a series of turns and a few flights of steps, they'd reached the end. Leo released the catch on the secret movable wall panel. It took some effort, but he finally got it open.

He'd just stepped out into the hallway when he heard: "Leopold. There you are." He didn't have to turn to know it was the queen. And she was none too happy with him.

He inhaled a deep breath and then turned. "Mother."

It wasn't just the queen facing him. There were a half-dozen royal guards behind her. This was bad. Very bad.

The queen turned to the guards and dismissed them. Once they were gone, she turned back to him. Anger lit up her eyes like little bolts of lightning.

"What is the meaning of this?"

"How did you even know about this passageway?"

She arched a penciled brow. "Leopold, there isn't much around this palace that I don't know about. I've known about the secret passageways since your father took me through them when we were first married. Did you really think I didn't know about your adventures when you were a kid? I'd have thought you would have grown out of such things."

"I didn't have a choice today. The chase team was delayed and instead the paparazzi tracked us down. Do you really think it was a good idea to hang out and let them come up with whatever scandalous drivel sells their papers?"

"I suppose not. But did you stop to think about this before putting yourself in such a precarious position?" She didn't wait for him to answer. "Taking off on a hot air balloon ride of all things when there is work waiting for you. Not to mention—"

Bianca stepped out of the shadows of the secret passageway and stood next to him. The queen's gaze settled on Bianca as her frown grew deeper.

Leo cleared his throat. "I wanted to give Bianca a view of the land. And what better way than from above."

The queen crossed her arms, as though preparing for war.

Leo rushed on. "It was a beautiful morning. But I'm sure Bianca has to get back to work."

Bianca was spurred into motion. "I do. There's a gown fitting shortly. I should go and make sure everything is on track."

When Bianca went to move, the queen spoke up. "Not so fast. I would appreciate it if going forward you would curtail yourself to your work. That is what my son is paying you a fortune for, is it not?"

Leo considered telling his mother that technically he wasn't paying Bianca much, but then he decided that information might work against them. His mother might use it as an excuse to send Bianca packing.

"I assure you, ma'am, that everything for the wedding is on track," Bianca said before Leo could figure out the best way to placate his mother. "I have a checklist to keep us on a timely schedule."

"I hope that list doesn't include any fashions like that." The queen gestured to Bianca's white skinny capris and colorful top.

It wasn't the first time his mother pointed out that Bianca's fashion sense didn't align with hers. The truth was Leo enjoyed Bianca's colorful outfits. This palace certainly could stand to be brightened.

"I like Bianca's sense of style," Leo said, taking the heat off Bianca. "I'm hoping she'll add color to the wedding."

"Leopold—"

"Mother, not everything should be a shade of gray. Sometimes there needs to be bright oranges, pinks and purples. In fact, purple would suit you."

The queen remained quiet for a moment, not used to Leo getting in her face and disagreeing with her. The quietness didn't last for long. "Then maybe she should pay more attention to her color choices instead of taking up your time. You have other matters of great importance—"

"Bianca," he said, cutting off his mother because he

knew where this conversation was headed, "would you mind leaving my mother and me alone so we can talk?"

"No problem." Bianca nodded to the queen and then quietly escaped.

Lucky her. Leo wished he could follow her.

He turned his attention back to his mother. "I know you're frustrated with me but that's no reason to take it out on Bianca. She's doing a really good job with the wedding and Giselle is happy. Isn't that the important part?"

"You're falling for her."

"Bianca?" He shook his head. "No. I'm not."

It was just a passing attraction, nothing serious. When this wedding was over, she'd return to Italy. And he would get on with his royal duties. First, he would get married. And then he would ascend to the throne. It was all planned.

His mother's gaze searched his. "Do you really believe that?"

"Bianca is nice. And I enjoy her company, but that's all it is."

His mother sighed. "Then you are a fool. And I didn't raise a fool."

Without another word, she turned and walked away, leaving him alone with her words. Was she right? Did his feelings for Bianca go deeper than he allowed himself to believe?

CHAPTER SIXTEEN

LAST NIGHT HAD been the most boring date of his life.

And his lunch date wasn't faring much better.

Neither woman would do as his princess.

Leo set aside his now-empty coffee cup. When he glanced up, he found his luncheon companion staring at him. Immediately she smiled at him, like that was going to change things.

There was no spark between them. There wasn't even a fizzle. There was nothing. No chemistry. No anything.

Bridgette was the daughter of an earl of a small country in the Mediterranean. And though many had gone on about her beauty, all Leo could think was that she didn't hold a candle to Bianca's glittering eyes and her sparkling smile.

And then there was the fact that conversation between him and Bianca flowed easily. He didn't have to work to keep the conversation going like he did tonight. How was he supposed to marry someone when they had nothing to talk about?

Bridgette lit up with a smile. "This has been the most enjoyable evening."

She surely couldn't mean it. After all, they hadn't found one subject to talk about that they had in common.

"It was a nice meal. And I enjoyed your company." Was it wrong that in his mind he pretended he was speaking to Bianca?

"I've heard so much about your lovely gardens."

He followed her over to the glass doors that led out to the expansive patio on the edge of the famed gardens. All the while, he was thinking of how to get out of this. Because he knew as sure as he was standing there that they didn't have a chance for a future. There was no point in getting Bridgette's hopes up.

"Leo, there you are." Giselle rushed into the room. "I've been looking everywhere for you."

"Well, you've found me."

She glanced over at Bridgette. "There's a problem with the wedding."

"What sort of problem?"

Giselle shook her head. "I can't tell you. You have to come see."

"Now?" He knew his sister could get excited about things, but something felt off here.

"Yes, now. Right now—"

"We'd be happy to help," Bridgette interjected as though they were already a couple.

"Um, no. Sorry," Giselle said. "This is delicate and only my brother can handle it."

It was then that Leo glanced toward the interior doorway to find the butler waiting in the wings. His sister had planned this. And for once, he was grateful for his sister's schemes.

"Then let's go," he said. Before walking off, he turned to Bridgette. "It was lovely meeting you. Thank you so much for making the journey here. Oscar will see you out."

He turned and walked with his sister toward the door. They were just steps away from the hallway—

"Wait. That's it?" Bridgette called out from behind him. "I got all dressed up for this? We didn't even kiss. How are we supposed to get married if you won't even kiss me?"

Giselle grabbed his arm. "Don't you dare stop. If you saddle me with her as my sister-in-law, I will never speak to you again."

Leo smothered a hearty chuckle as they set off down the hallway, but he couldn't resist smiling. "So is there truly an emergency? Or did you simply feel sorry for me?"

Giselle shrugged once more. "There's only so much anguish I can watch my brother endure."

"You were watching us?"

"No. I mean I saw you through the doorway and then I inquired about your guest. When I found out it was Bridgette, I knew you were in trouble."

"You know her?"

Giselle shrugged. "We've met up before at various events. I know all I want to about her and trust me, she's not right for you."

"Maybe I should have you sort through my stack of possible brides."

Giselle stopped walking and frowned at him. "You're making a mistake."

"I'm not any happier about this than you are. But you know I have to marry in order to take the throne. They need to know there's a good possibility of an heir. I am doing what is expected of me. I've put it off as long as I can."

"You need to marry someone you love. Someone you trust. Someone who makes you smile."

He rubbed the back of his neck and glanced away. "That's a luxury I can't afford."

"It's a necessity you would be wise not to overlook."

"Since when did you become an expert on marriage? You haven't even said 'I do' yet." He regretted the words as soon as they slipped past his lips.

Pain reflected in his sister's eyes but in a blink, it was gone. "I have to go."

"Giselle, I'm sorry—"

"Forget it." She turned to walk away.

"What about the wedding?" he asked. "You know, the problem?"

"There isn't one."

And with that his sister marched off in the opposite direction. He knew she was upset with him and he would have to work on making it up to her.

His phone rang. He immediately answered it, hoping it was the news he'd been awaiting. And it was. By the time he disconnected the call, he had the perfect excuse to go see Bianca.

He set off with quick strides. With each step, his anticipation grew. He had a surprise for her. Something she was going to love.

"Come with me."

Bianca glanced over her shoulder to find Leo standing in the doorway of the palace's grand ballroom. Her fingers tightened around the stylus and her tablet. She was working on the setup for the reception—the best way to use the space available considering the large number of guests. They'd barely started.

"Hi." She couldn't help but smile. Every time he was around, a bubbly feeling sprang up inside her. "I can't leave now. We're working on some last-minute modifications to the layout of the reception."

He walked up to her and glanced at the tentative setup on her tablet. "Looks good. Let's go."

He grabbed her hand and started walking. Bianca dug in her heels, refusing to move. When he noticed her resistance, he stopped and turned back to her.

"What's wrong?" he asked.

"I told you I'm working."

"I know and I'm sorry, but this just can't wait." His eyes pleaded with her to follow him.

"Wait? What are you talking about?"

"Just come with me."

And then a worrisome thought came to mind. Was there some part of this royal wedding that she'd overlooked?

Her heart clenched with dread. There were so many

moving parts to this wedding that it was tough staying on top of anything. But in the end, if she could handle this wedding, she could handle any wedding. The trick was getting the princess down the aisle and then onto the dance floor. It was only then that Bianca would be able to take her first easy breath.

"Tell me," she said. "What's wrong?"

"Nothing is wrong." A smile pulled at the corner of his lips. "In fact, something is very right."

"But I need to finish here—"

"Sylvie," Leo called out.

Immediately, Sylvie dropped what she was doing and rushed over to them. She stopped in front of Leo with rounded eyes and a timid smile. She noticeably swallowed before gazing up at him as though he were some sort of god. "Yes, Your Royal Highness?"

Leo took the tablet from Bianca and handed it over to her assistant. "Could you continue to work on setting up the room?"

"I… I…uh…um…yes." Her eyes rounded like saucers. "Definitely. I'd be honored to, Your Highness."

"Thank you." Then he took Bianca by the hand and led her from the room.

"Leo, what are you doing?"

"We have to go. We don't have a lot of time."

"But I need to tell her what I have in mind for the changes."

At last, he stopped and turned to her. "Do you have it written down?"

"Yes—"

"Of course, you do." He turned and keeping his hand clasped around hers, he headed for the door. "I bet you have your entire life planned out in one big list."

She frowned at the back of his head. "Don't make fun of the lists. They keep everything organized and on time."

His pace didn't slow down. In fact, it might have sped up. "But where is the room for spontaneity and fun?"

She didn't respond at first. She'd been so busy proving herself to her parents and her siblings that even though she didn't have the same interests as them that she could still be a success.

When Leo stopped and turned a questioning look at her, she said, "Maybe I'm not the typical young person. So what if I don't live for Friday nights out on the town with my friends, hitting all of the hot spots. And maybe I didn't vacation in Monaco or sail the Mediterranean, but I've worked hard. I've accomplished a lot. If I hadn't, you wouldn't have hired me. Right?" When he didn't immediately respond, she asked again, "Right?"

He sighed. "Right."

"So then don't diss my lists. You might live your life without the need for organization—but being the crown prince, I can't see that lasting—but I need the lists. They make me feel like I have a handle on things. They make it possible for me not to stress out about everything."

Leo looked at her like he was seeing a whole new side of her. "You really enjoy those lists?"

"I know it might be strange for a lot of people, but yes, I like my lists. I need my lists. If I follow my lists, they'll get me where I need to go."

"Hmm… Perhaps you should start a list of fun things."

Now that was something she hadn't considered before. A list of restaurants she'd like to try out. A list of locations she'd like to visit. She already had a list of movies and television shows that she'd like to watch but as yet hadn't gotten around to them.

"So I'm forgiven?" Leo's voice drew her from her thoughts.

"Um…what?"

"You know, for dragging you away from your work?"

"I still don't even know why you drew my away."

"Can I show you?"

"Well, considering Sylvie looked excited to do anything that you asked, I wouldn't want to ruin it for her." And secretly she was curious to know what was so important to him. "Let's go."

Hand in hand, he led her out to a waiting car. The driver opened the door for them. Before Bianca climbed in, she looked back at Leo. "You aren't driving today?"

"I thought this would be easier."

"Easier? Easier for what?"

"You'll soon see." A big smile lifted the corners of his mouth and lit up his eyes.

Whatever he was up to had him very excited. In fact, she'd never seen him this excited. She wouldn't admit it, but his mood was contagious. After keeping her in suspense, he didn't deserve to see her smile. Two could play this game.

As the unmarked sedan moved out through the service entrance of the palace, no paparazzi noticed their exit. It was rather freeing after seeing how the press camped at the front gates and clambered over the official flagged cars as they emerged from the palace grounds.

Bianca wondered what it was like to live under a microscope. She glanced over at the prince. He didn't seem to let it get to him. But growing up in the spotlight must give him a different perspective versus someone like her who had lived a rather anonymous life.

A part of her felt sorry for him. Because not only were his greatest achievements on display for the whole world to see, but his failures and heartaches were all out there for people to criticize and dissect.

Maybe being a prince wasn't all it was hyped up to be, but as she leaned back against the buttery soft black leather seat and stared out the window at the passing greenery that was quickly giving way to more buildings, more cars, more people, there were definitely some pluses to this life as well.

Bianca questioned him a couple more times about their destination, but he wouldn't crack. And when the car pulled to a final stop and the driver got out to open their doors, she was confused. Leo donned a dark cap and sunglasses. He looked very mysterious.

She stepped out onto the asphalt, raised a hand to her forehead to block the bright sunlight and gazed around at big nondescript buildings.

She turned a questioning gaze to Leo. "You brought me to the warehouse district?"

He laughed. "Not exactly. Come with me and I'll show you the magic that lurks inside."

Magic and this place didn't seem to go together, but she had to admit he had her full attention now. "Leo, what are we doing here?" And then a worrisome thought came to her. "You don't want to move the princess's after-party here, do you?"

The deep rumble of laughter filled the air. "Bianca, do you trust me?"

"No. I mean... I guess—" She halted her rambling. Why did this man get to her and make her a blubbering mess?

When her gaze met his, she found that no harm had been done. He was still smiling.

They headed toward the side of the building. There was a nondescript door with a red light next to it. As they approached, the light went out.

Leo opened the door and stood aside for her to enter. It was darker inside and it took a moment for Bianca's vision to adjust. She let Leo take the lead. He quickly made his way to a group of people and bright lights.

"What is this?" she whispered while glancing up at the spotlights suspended from the ceiling. Then the cameras came into view. "A television station?"

"Close. It's a sound stage. And they are filming your advertisement for your business."

"What?" She slapped a hand over her mouth when her voice was a little too loud and heads turned in their direction.

Leo's smile lit up his eyes. "I told you I would take care of you. And soon this will be on the internet and network television."

"Quiet on the set," a man called out.

No one seemed to notice that beneath the dark baseball cap was the prince. She stood next to him and watched as a bride entered the scene carrying the biggest, most splendid bouquet of pink and white ranunculus and peonies. They were hands down Bianca's favorite flowers.

Leo guided her over to one of the monitors. It was there that they could see the background. In the distance were the green rolling hills of home. In the foreground was her courtyard. But how?

Her gaze moved to Leo. He sent her a knowing smile. That man was good, very good.

They stood quietly while lines were spoken, scenes and retakes were filmed. Bianca wasn't sure how much time passed as she was totally mesmerized by everything that was going on around her.

Leo had taken her marketing preferences and taken them a step further. As the reality of the situation sank in, it was getting harder and harder for her to stifle her excitement. She wanted to speak. She wanted to celebrate the moment.

This wasn't just any commercial. This was a chance to make her dream a reality. This was going to make her a household name in the wedding world. And it was all thanks to Leo.

She didn't know how to thank him, but she would figure out something special. She just had to think about it for a bit.

During a break, someone nudged the director and then pointed over his shoulder at them. Oops! They'd been spotted.

The director rushed toward them. The man made a big flourish of bowing to the prince. Leo stiffened ever so slightly. If she hadn't been standing so close to him, she never would have noticed. So, all of the pomp and circumstance didn't come so naturally to him. Interesting.

"Your Royal Highness, I didn't know you'd be stopping by today. I hope I haven't kept you waiting."

"Not at all." Leo smiled as though to put the man at ease. "We've enjoyed watching the filming."

"Thank you, sir. Is there anything I can do for you?"

"I would like you to meet Miss Bianca Bartolini. She is the woman behind BB Wedding Dreams."

Again, the man bowed. He took her hand and gave a feathery kiss to the back of it. "It's an honor. I hope when we are finished, you'll enjoy the image."

"I've already enjoyed what I've seen. When I see the film merged with the background, it's like I'm home once more."

"Your home, it's gorgeous. People are going to be clamoring to marry at your lovely villa."

"I hope you're right."

They talked for a few more minutes and then they left, leaving the crew alone to finish their work. Bianca couldn't quit smiling.

As soon as they stepped outside, she turned to Leo. "That was amazing. Thank you. It's more than I ever imagined."

His brows rose. "What were you expecting?"

She shrugged. "I don't know. But certainly nothing that elaborate. And you even filmed my villa."

"I thought it should show people exactly what they'd be missing by not getting married there."

Excitement and anticipation bubbled up in her and she acted without thinking by throwing her arms around Leo for a hug. It was when she leaned into him—when she breathed in his clean, masculine scent—that she realized she'd overstepped. His body remained stiff, as though she'd caught him off guard.

She quickly pulled back. "Sorry. I just lost my mind for a moment there."

"I take it you approve?"

She eagerly nodded her head. "I do."

And now the pressure was on her to do something extra special for him. She just had no idea what that might be. But she would think of something.

CHAPTER SEVENTEEN

Buzz. Buzz.

She didn't have time for phone calls.

Still, Bianca couldn't just ignore the call—not until she knew who was on the other end. She removed the phone from her purse. Her heart stilled in her chest when she saw the name of her family's attorney flash on the caller id.

There was no way this was anything but bad news. She'd been dreading this day for the longest time. And now it was here.

Maybe she should just ignore it. She could let it ring over to her voicemail. After all, today was the royal wedding. Giselle and Leo were counting on her to make this day go smoothly for everyone.

She had to bring her very best game today. She couldn't be upset. But she also couldn't be distracted wondering what the attorney wanted.

With great trepidation, she answered the call. "Hello. This is Bianca Bartolini."

As she said her name, she wondered how much longer she would have a right to it. When all was said and done, would everything about her life be a lie—even her name?

"Ms. Bartolini, this is Lando Caruso," the family's attorney said. "I've spoken with your brother and sister. They've informed me you're out of the country."

"That's correct. I'm working on a wedding."

"I see." His voice didn't give any hints as to what he was thinking. "The reason for my call is that the testing facility says they'll have the DNA result in a couple of days."

"Oh." Her heart was heavy and sank all the way down to her silver heels. Not wanting to have any witnesses to her utter meltdown, she said, "Can you give me the results over the phone?"

"No. The agreement with your siblings was that the results would be revealed when you were all in the same room."

"Right." She recalled making that agreement. It seemed like a lifetime ago.

"How soon will you be returning home? As you can understand, your siblings are quite anxious for the results."

She understood very well. "The wedding is today. I'll be able to fly home tomorrow or the next day."

"Very well. I will arrange to be at the villa on Tuesday. Will that give you enough time?"

"Y-yes." Her stomach shivered with nerves.

They ended the call and then Bianca stood there as though in a trance. This could very well be the end of her life as she knew it. With the results at hand, the stark reality of her future was daunting.

Knock. Knock.

Her future and the uncertainty of that future would have to wait for another time. She had a wedding to oversee. And absolutely nothing was going to go wrong today. She owed both Giselle and Leo her undivided attention.

There was another knock.

"Coming!" She glanced in the mirror to make sure she hadn't forgotten anything. She could do this. Because whether or not she was a Bartolini, she was a wedding planner. No one could take that away from her.

The bride was stunning.

The groom, eh, not too bad.

And the entire wedding had gone off without a hitch.

Leo knew who to thank for making his sister's big day so perfect—Bianca. She'd once again worked her magic. She'd smoothed out the rough edges, covered over the imperfections and highlighted the beauty of the day. The only thing that bothered him was that she'd been so busy he hadn't had a moment to so much as thank her.

But there was another part of this day that he dreaded. It meant the deadline for choosing a wife was at hand. It was like a ticking time bomb. And when it went off, life as he knew it would be over. How was he supposed to spend the rest of his days with someone he didn't love?

Because after spending time with Bianca, he'd realized how he longed to share his life with someone he cared about. Waking up in the morning, eager to see that person. Finding out something exciting and anxiously seeking out that person to share the news.

And then there were Giselle and William. They were so in love. They practically glowed when they were in the vicinity of each other. That's what he wanted for his life. Not a cold, heartless business deal—

"Come dance with me."

Leo turned to find the radiant bride next to him. "I'm not much of a dancer."

"We both know that's not true." She grasped his arm. "Come on."

With this being the formal reception, the music was more sedate. It made dancing and talking much easier, which didn't thrill Leo. His sister was good at reading his moods and he didn't want to get into what was on his mind at the moment. This was her wedding. A time for celebration. Not a time to dissect his life.

"You look beautiful," he said.

"Why thank you. You look pretty dashing yourself. Except for that frown on your face."

"What frown?" He didn't know he was frowning. He forced a smile to his lips. "Better?"

"You don't have to put on a show for me."

His muscles stiffened. "I don't know what you're talking about."

"Yes, you do. Mother gave you a deadline to find a wife and the time is up."

He stopped dancing and looked at his sister. "How do you know?"

She smiled and shrugged. "Mother isn't the only one with spies."

He shook his head. "You weren't supposed to know. This is your big day and it isn't your problem."

They started to dance again. "But I want to help."

"No one can help. At this point, I'm considering putting the names in a hat and pulling out one."

Giselle arched a brow. "You're joking, aren't you?"

Part of him was, the other part was seriously considering the option. "How do you choose a spouse that you don't care about?"

"Do you really need me to answer the question?" When he nodded, she said, "You don't."

"But I have to. I need a wife in order to become king. And I need to step into the role by the New Year. The nation is becoming restless." His gaze searched hers. "Who do you think I should marry?"

"I think the answer is right in front of you. All you have to do is open your eyes."

For a few minutes, they didn't speak. He knew his sister was referring to Bianca. He'd thought of her too. But she didn't fit into the mold of a princess. She was different from all the other prospective brides.

Still, he could see his future with Bianca. He could imagine waking up next to her each morning. He could see having a family with her—a happy family.

But he knew his mother would not approve. Not by a long shot.

"Stop fighting it," Giselle said, drawing him from his

thoughts. "You've fallen hard for her. Anyone can see it. Even Mother."

"Bianca is so easy to get along with. Everyone loves her—except Mother."

"Forget Mother for a second." Giselle stopped dancing and stared at him. "Do you love Bianca? Really love her?"

"I do." There was no hesitation. It was a fact that he hadn't been willing to acknowledge until now.

"Then stop standing here. Go get her."

That was easier said than done. He had no idea where she was and the reception was ending. But he would find her. He would tell her how he felt. And then he had to hope she felt the same way.

CHAPTER EIGHTEEN

THIS WAS IT.

The end.

Sadness assailed Bianca. It was the strangest reaction she'd ever had to the end of a wedding. Not just any wedding but a royal wedding that had received international attention. Her phone was ringing off the hook with people eager to have her plan their big days.

She should be thrilled. She should be out on the dance floor of the after-party celebrating, but instead she'd been busy ironing out small wrinkles in the background, from missing appetizers to a shortage of serving staff.

But now with the party in full swing and the prince's favorite band playing, she spotted him smiling and chatting with his sister and a group of guests. That was all the thanks she needed—

"Miss Bartolini, I'd like to have a word." The queen signaled for her to follow.

Once in the hallway, Bianca bowed her head. "Good evening, Your Majesty."

"It was a lovely day. And that in large part was due to you."

Bianca could hardly believe what she was hearing. The queen had just complimented her. After all the rows they'd had and how the queen was certain Bianca was going to make a disaster of everything.

"Thank you." Bianca didn't know what else to say.

"Perhaps my son should consider hiring you for his wedding." Apparently, Bianca failed to keep the surprise from showing on her face as the queen continued. "So, he didn't tell you that he will be announcing his engagement tomorrow. And his wedding will be later this year."

Bianca struggled to speak. "That's exciting news."

Inside she felt anything but excited. She felt sad. She felt as though she were losing the most special person from her life—not that he was ever hers to start with. Just the thought of Leo with another woman filled her with jealousy. She quickly reined in her rising emotions.

"Very exciting. Everything is working out." The queen beamed with happiness. "I've had my assistant forward you a bonus for your success tonight. And I know you must be anxious to get home to your villa so I've had my jet put on standby. It's yours tonight or tomorrow."

"Thank you. I really appreciate it."

"I won't keep you. Since this party isn't really my style, I'm going to call it a night and let the young people live it up. Goodbye, Miss Bartolini."

"Good night, ma'am." Bianca bowed her head once more.

She watched as the queen made her way to the door. There was nothing left for Bianca to do. Sylvie was seeing to any lingering details.

The thought of flying home tonight was tempting. It would be nice to get back to the villa while she was still a Bartolini—

"Bianca! There you are." Leo stepped out of the party, closing the door behind him. "I've been looking everywhere for you."

"Sorry. There were a lot of things to do today." Like saying goodbye to him. But she wasn't ready to do it. Not yet.

"You did a positively fabulous job. Not even my mother could find anything to complain about."

"I know. She gave me both a compliment and a bonus. Can you believe it?"

Leo's brown eyes widened. "You really impressed her.

I am not surprised. Everyone is calling it the perfect wedding. And it's all thanks to you."

She couldn't put on this "nice" show any longer. She had to know if it was true. Was Leo getting married? "And I heard about your engagement." Her voice wobbled. "Congratulations."

Confusion clouded his eyes. "How did you hear—wait, my mother, right?"

She nodded. "She's very excited."

"I didn't want you to find out this way."

"What way? The fact that I thought what we shared meant something and all of this time you were planning to marry someone else—"

"Bianca, stop." He reached out, gently grasping her upper arms. "It isn't like that."

She yanked free. Her gaze narrowed in on him. "How is it?"

"It's you."

"What's me?"

He rubbed the back of his neck. "This isn't how I meant for any of this to happen."

"You aren't making any sense. What about me?"

His gaze met hers. "It's you I want to marry."

She pressed a hand to her chest, feeling as though the air had been sucked from her lungs. "Marry me?"

Leo nodded.

She shook her head. This couldn't be happening. Leo wanted to marry her but she was a wedding planner, not a fitting wife for the crown prince. She was a nobody, a commoner. The prince must marry someone of noble birth.

"No." She took a step back. "You don't mean this. It would be a mistake."

"Bianca, I love you."

She took another step away from him. Her heart was

cracking and her vision blurred with unshed tears. "No, you don't."

He stepped up to her. His unwavering gaze met hers. "I don't know where all of this doubt is coming from, but if you're worried about my mother, don't be. I'll deal with her."

"It's not your mother."

"Good. Then what is it?"

"Will you still feel the same way about me if the DNA results reveal that I'm not a Bartolini? What happens if I don't know who my father is? For all I know, I could be the daughter of a criminal." Her voice wobbled. She blinked repeatedly, struggling to keep her emotions at bay. "I can't marry you with that hanging over our heads."

Silence filled the air between them.

The silence was more painful than acknowledging that everything she thought she knew about herself might be wrong. Because Leo's continued silence meant he agreed with her.

Unable to take the silence any longer, Bianca said, "My job is complete. Sylvie is inside and will oversee the cleanup. I need to go."

The door to the party opened. The blast of music echoed through the hallway. Giselle beamed at them and then yelled over the music. "Come on guys. Let's party." She moved over and latched her arm with Leo's. "I requested your favorite song."

Giselle motioned for Bianca to join them before disappearing inside. Bianca moved toward the door but remained in the hallway. She couldn't go back inside. She closed the door.

This was difficult enough. She just needed to get it over with. She needed to take the queen up on her offer and return to Tuscany as soon as possible.

Because if she loved Leo—and she did love him with all

her heart—she would be on that plane tonight. Leo needed to live the life he was destined for—the throne that he always wanted. He deserved to have a wife by his side that the people looked up to and respected.

And it wasn't her. She probably wasn't even a Bartolini. If she were to marry Leo and the press got ahold of the story it would ruin Leo. She would do anything to protect him, including sacrificing her heart.

The acknowledgment hurt Bianca more than she knew possible. She didn't fit in with her family. She didn't fit in Patazonia. Where did she belong?

CHAPTER NINETEEN

HE'D MESSED UP.

Big time.

Leo had taken time to think about what Bianca had said to him instead of following his heart. In his defense, he never expected her to turn down his marriage proposal. But that was becoming a thing with Bianca—not reacting the way he expected.

By the time he'd gotten his head screwed on straight, Bianca had left the party. He'd quietly slipped away, eager to find her. He had to convince her that they belonged together. Maybe theirs wouldn't be a fairy-tale marriage, but truth be told, he didn't believe in fairy tales.

He wanted a relationship that was real—a relationship that was strong, reliable and enduring. He could have all of that with Bianca. He firmly believed it. In fact, he couldn't imagine his life without her in it.

He demanded the keys to the SUV that his security detail had used to escort him to the reception. He was in no mood to be coddled by his team. He needed some space to himself. He tramped the accelerator. When he found the inside of the vehicle too constricting, he put down the windows and let the cool night air rush over his face as he raced back to the palace.

This can be fixed. It isn't too late.

He kept repeating the mantra the whole way home. It was as if he said it enough, it would be so.

The SUV's tires screeched to a halt in front of the palace. He raced inside. He could feel curious stares from the staff, wondering what had him in such a rush, but he didn't have the patience or the inclination to explain.

He took the stairs two at a time. He racewalked down the hallway. He rapped his knuckles on Bianca's door.

"Bianca?" He waited. No response. "Bianca, we need to talk."

The door opened but it wasn't Bianca on the other side. It was one of the staff.

"Where is Bianca?" he asked, not caring how anxious he might appear. He didn't have time to worry about appearances.

The young woman looked confused. "Miss Bartolini isn't here."

"Do you know where she is?"

"She left."

"Left?" That couldn't be. "As in left the palace? To go back to the party?"

The young woman looked flustered. "I don't know where she went. I was instructed to help her pack and then I started to straighten up. Was that a mistake?"

The mistake was all his. The weight of his error mounted with every passing moment.

Noticing the maid's worried look, he said, "You've done nothing wrong. Continue what you were doing."

He turned and strode away. She'd left already? The after-party hadn't even wound down.

He wasn't giving up yet. He could catch her at the airport. He'd do whatever it took.

Leo retraced his steps down the staircase, but at the bottom stood the queen. "Leopold, what is the meaning of this? You're racing up the driveway, screeching tires and running through the palace as though it's some sort of gymnasium."

He descended the stairs. "It's Bianca. I have to find her."

The queen's brows rose. "Is there a problem with the party?"

"No. It's fine." He raked his fingers through his hair. "There's something I have to discuss with her."

"Well, if that's all, you'll have to phone her because she's already in the air. I gave her my personal jet to return home."

"You did what?" He couldn't believe what he was hearing.

The queen frowned at him. "Come with me."

He followed her to her office, where most of the kingdom's decisions were made. It was where his ancestors including his grandfather, father and eventually he would rule from. This seemed like a fitting place to have this life-altering conversation.

"I've chosen a wife," he stated boldly. "If she'll have me."

His mother's frown lifted into a smile. "Very good. And I take it you'd like Bianca to plan the wedding. I will admit that she did a pretty good job with your sister's wedding, but you have to realize with you being in line for the crown, traditions must be strictly adhered to—"

"Mother, stop!"

She blinked as though surprised by his interruption. "Leopold, I'm not going to be as agreeable this time. Bianca cannot be your wedding planner."

"You're right. She's going to be my bride."

His mother's penciled brows rose high on her forehead. "Leopold, if you're trying to be funny—"

"I'm being perfectly serious. I want to marry Bianca. I want her to be my princess—"

"Stop! No." The queen vehemently shook her head. "It's not going to happen. I gave you a whole selection of very fine women to choose from. Just because you couldn't find your version of the ideal woman—"

"But I did. Bianca is everything I've ever wanted and more."

His mother shook her head again. "Leopold, you're missing the fact that she doesn't have noble blood. She isn't from a politically influential family. She brings nothing to the nation. She's…she's a wedding planner."

"She's the woman I love. And she loves me in spite of my faults—"

"Faults?" The queen's eyes narrowed. "This woman has convinced you that you are full of faults?"

"No, Mother," his voice filled with pent-up emotion. "You did that the day Father died." His mother's mouth opened but he didn't give her a chance to speak as he kept going. "When he died, you looked at me like it was all my fault. And you've been blaming me ever since."

"That's not true."

"It is true. Whether you admit it or not."

The composed look on her face crumbled. In its place were deep worry lines that aged his mother. She sat down on the window seat as though her legs would no longer hold her up. "I had no idea that's how you felt."

"How could I not when you sent me out of the room after father died as though you couldn't bear to look at me. And you made me promise not to tell anyone what had happened. Do you know what keeping that secret cost me? I couldn't even talk to Giselle."

For so long, he'd kept this torment of emotions locked up inside of him. But after confiding in Bianca, he realized the secret was destroying not only him but also his relationship with his family. He'd been distancing himself— avoiding conflicts. And it was no way to live life. It was no way to rule a country.

"But you told Bianca?" His mother's troubled gaze searched his.

"I did. I trust her. And I don't regret it."

"And she convinced you that I blamed you for your father's death?"

"On the contrary, she defended you." His mother's eyes widened. Maybe at last his mother would see that there was so much more to Bianca. "She suggested you might have been trying to protect me."

"I was." The queen's voice was soft as though all of the fight had gone out of her. "Our enemies will use anything to hurt us, even twisting innocent facts into something sinister."

He could barely allow himself to believe what he was hearing. "You never blamed me?"

She shook her head. "Your father had health issues."

"I never knew."

"Only four people knew of them. Two of them were your father and myself. A king must not look vulnerable."

Leo had a feeling his mother's last comment was aimed at his relationship with a commoner. "Bianca will not make me vulnerable. With her by my side, we can do great things together. I love her."

"But does she feel the same way?" The queen stood. "Maybe she doesn't love you and that's why she left so quickly."

"She left because I made a mistake. Now I need to make things up to her."

"You really love her, don't you?" When he nodded, his mother said, "There's a commercial flight tomorrow."

It was his turn to arch a brow. "You aren't going to try and stop me?"

"Maybe I should. But when it all comes down to it, I want my children to be happy. And Bianca makes you happier than I've ever seen you. So go get her. Make her your princess."

"Thank you." He hugged his mother, something they rarely did, but he had a feeling that was about to change. When he pulled back, he said, "You try to put on a crusty exterior but on the inside you're just a marshmallow."

She sent him a playful frown. "Go. Before I change my

mind." His mother turned and walked away. She called over her shoulder, "And have someone move that vehicle."

Now he had to wait through the night to get to his princess.

It was going to be the longest night of his life.

CHAPTER TWENTY

"YOU'RE BACK."

It was almost lunchtime when Bianca dragged herself to the main house. She glanced over at Gia as she entered the kitchen. Bianca smoothed a hand over her mussed-up ponytail. She'd forgotten that her sister had turned the place into a boutique hotel and that there might be guests lurking about. She peered past her sister, relieved to find her alone.

"I got in late last night."

Gia had already turned in by then, but Enzo had still been awake. He knew Bianca was upset but he hadn't pried. He just let her know he was there if she wanted to talk.

She turned her back to her sister to avoid questions about the shadows under her bloodshot eyes.

"I loved the photos you sent," Gia said. "Do you have some of the wedding?"

"Um… I do. But not on me." The last thing she wanted to discuss was the royal wedding. "I was so tired last night that I forgot to plug my phone in and now it's dead, kind of like me. Do you have some coffee you can spare?"

Gia made them both a cup and then joined Bianca at the kitchen island. "You don't look so good, considering you just planned the wedding of a lifetime."

And had my heart torn out and shredded.

"How am I supposed to look?"

Gia shrugged. "Like you're on top of the world. The phone has been ringing like crazy with people trying to reach you to plan their wedding."

"Sorry about that."

"Sorry?" Gia studied her. "Now I know something is

wrong. Bianca, what is it? Tell me what has you looking like you just lost your best friend."

Bianca needed someone to talk to and so she started at the beginning. She left out some of the steamy bits, some things weren't for sharing. And then the proposal—

"And you turned him down?" Gia's voice rose.

"Shh…" Bianca glanced at the doorway to assure herself that they were still alone. "I don't want anyone to know."

"I wouldn't want anyone to know you lost your mind either. I mean, it's obvious by the look on your face when you mention Leo that you love him. And he's a prince. What else do you need?"

"You don't understand. What happens when the DNA test says I'm not a Bartolini?"

"You're still you and he loves you."

Bianca shook her head. "He loves the idea of me. But when I pointed out about the DNA tests and that I could be anyone's daughter, including a criminal's, he went silent." It was only when her sister's face paled that Bianca realized she'd said too much. "Gia, I didn't mean that. I… I was just being thoughtless."

"It's okay." The look on her face said it was anything but okay. "It's the truth. We don't know anything about the biological father."

Not sure what to say, Bianca opted to distract her sister with her story about Leo. "Anyway, Leo didn't say a word and then he walked away. That was all the answer I needed."

Gia grabbed a tray of pastries and placed them in front of Bianca. "I think you're going to need these." When Bianca arched a questioning brow, Gia added, "You know, comfort food."

Bianca's gaze moved to the tray. "I'm going to need a lot more sweets than this. Do you have any chocolate?"

Before Gia could answer, sounds of a commotion came

from the front of the villa. What was that all about? Some rowdy guests?

"I'll be right back." Gia rushed out of the room.

Bianca browsed the cabinets for some chocolate. The voices in the front room grew louder and she could hear Gia's raised voice. Alarmed, Bianca pushed the cabinet door shut and rushed after her sister.

Bianca came to a halt when she spotted Leo.

Her heart leaped into her throat.

What was he doing here? Not that she should care. Whatever they'd shared was over.

"Go away."

Leo braced himself for a prickly reception. He just hadn't expected the hostility to come from Bianca's sister. It didn't surprise him. He'd handled things poorly with Bianca. He just needed a chance to make it up to her.

Luckily for him, the private jet had returned earlier than expected and he didn't have time to wait until noon for the commercial flight. It was refueled and ready to go early that morning. Still, it had taken him longer to get to the Bartolini estate than he'd planned because he had to make an important detour. It was a crucial part of his plan to win Bianca back. He hoped it would prove to her once and for all how much he cared about her…if only he could get past her brother and sister.

"I'm not leaving until I speak to Bianca," Leo said as Enzo continued to stand in front of him with his fists pressed into his sides.

"She doesn't want to see you," Enzo said while Gia agreed with him. "I don't care if you are a prince, you can't hurt my sister."

"You don't understand—"

"I understand that my sister was crying and that's all I need to know."

The fact he'd caused Bianca such pain weighed heavy on him. He had to make it up to her, if she'd let him. "I can fix this."

Gia stepped between the two men. She leveled her shoulders and tilted her chin upward. "If you've come to tell my sister that she's not good enough to be a royal, you can leave now."

That's what she thought? It couldn't be further from the truth. But he didn't want to explain himself to Bianca's siblings. The person he needed to explain things to was Bianca—

"Leo, you shouldn't be here." Bianca stepped into the room.

"Don't worry about him," Enzo said. "He was just leaving."

"No. I wasn't." Leo frowned at the man. And then he turned his attention to Bianca. "I need to speak with you. Alone."

"We have nothing left to discuss."

"Listen, I messed up and I'm sorry." He pulled a huge bouquet of red roses from behind his back. "These are for you."

Bianca's eyes paused on the flowers before meeting his gaze once more. He couldn't read her thoughts. It was as though she'd put up a protective wall and now he had to find a way to breach it.

"Please go, Leo. It's over. It was a mistake." She turned and walked away.

He desperately wanted to follow her—to tell her that nothing was over between them. They were just getting started, but her two protective siblings weren't about to let him get past them.

He placed the flowers on a stand by the door. "I'll be back."

He wasn't giving up. He loved Bianca. And she loved him too. She was afraid of the results of the DNA test and he had to prove to her that they didn't matter to him.

CHAPTER TWENTY-ONE

THE FLOWERS STARTED showing up the next day.

"I don't know where to put them all," Gia said. "It's starting to look like a florist shop in here." Gia looked at Bianca with sympathy in her eyes. "I know he screwed up, big time, but would it hurt to hear him out?"

Before Bianca could answer there was a knock at the door. She didn't have to wonder. She knew who was there—the florist. Again.

Bianca moved toward the door. "Don't worry. I'll have them take the flowers away."

She swung open the door, but the words lodged in her throat. There stood Leo.

"You can't be here," she said. "A guest might see you and it'll end up on social media."

"That's a risk I'm willing to take."

"Why are you making this so difficult?" Every time she saw him, the feeling of loss washed over her. How was she ever going to forget him—her very own Prince Charming?

"Just hear me out. That's all I'm asking. And then if you still want me to go, I will." He could see the indecision reflected in Bianca's eyes. "Please."

"Okay. We can go outside—"

"I have a car." When her eyes widened in surprise, he added, "It's getting late. I thought we could talk over dinner."

"I don't know."

"Go with him," Gia said. "Give him a chance. We don't have room for more flowers."

Maybe it was the best way to set things straight with

him. Bianca glanced down at her skinny jeans and purple top. "I should change."

"You look perfect," Leo said. "You're always beautiful."

Meanwhile, her sister stood to the side, urging them out the door.

Bianca said, "A quick dinner and then you'll leave?" When he nodded, she added, "And no more flowers?"

"I promise."

She grabbed her purse and shoes. Then they were out the door. She noticed him messaging someone as they headed toward the car. Then he slipped the phone in his pocket and opened the car door for her.

Why was he making this so difficult?

Bianca's heart ached.

There was nothing that could change things between them. Leo was royalty. She was not. And the DNA tests were delayed so it'd be another few days until they received the results.

Still, her body longed to fall into his strong arms— to rest her cheek against his muscular chest—to hear the steady pounding of his heart. It might have been a little more than twenty-four hours since she saw him last but she'd missed him dearly. How was she going to exist without seeing him again, except for on the front of a glossy magazine?

"We should talk now," she said as the car headed toward Florence.

"Not yet."

"Leo, nothing you say is going to change our circumstances."

"Just wait. We're almost there. And I'd like to be able to look at you when we talk instead of concentrating on the road."

The red sports car he'd rented slowed as they made their way into the city.

"There it is." Leo pulled into a parking spot.

Before she could get out, he'd rushed around the car and opened the door for her. As they started up the sidewalk, she noticed a group of photographers. They started snapping pictures as flashes repeatedly lit up the sky.

Bianca stopped walking. "Leo, we can't go in there."

"Sure we can."

"But the paparazzi—"

"It'll be okay."

"But how did they know you would be here?" She stared at him. Something was up, but what? "I didn't even know you'd be here."

"I told them," he said matter-of-factly.

"You did?" Her words got lost in the frenzy of questions volleyed at them from the reporters.

Leo took her hand and led her through the crowd. At last they were inside the restaurant. They were immediately seated—next to the window.

"Excuse me," Bianca said to the maître d'. "Can we have another table? Away from the window?"

"It's okay," Leo said. "I requested this table."

"You did?" She didn't understand. What was going on?

Leo took her hands in his as they stood next to the table. On the other side of the window flashes went off. But in that moment, as Leo stared into her eyes, he was all she could see. His voice was all she could hear.

"Bianca, I'm sorry about what happened back at the after-party. I didn't react the way I should have. When you started throwing out all those excuses of why we shouldn't be together, I got nervous. But now I want the entire world to know how I feel about you."

"Th-those weren't excuses. They are the truth. I'm not a part of your world. I don't even know what world I belong in. The DNA results—"

"I know where you belong. With me."

Tears stung the backs of her eyes. He was saying all the right things. "But what happens when the DNA results say I'm not a Bartolini? Those reporters out there will have a field day. It could threaten your position as king."

"It doesn't matter. Don't you know how much I love you?"

Her heart pounded in her chest. "But what about when you become king—?"

"I would step down from the throne if that's what it took for us to be together."

"You would?"

He nodded. "I would."

"But the queen—she'll never approve."

"I told her I love you and it took some convincing but she's coming around. I'm sure you can win her over."

How was it that he was overcoming all her objections? Her gaze searched his. "What are you trying to tell me?"

"Bianca, I love you and it doesn't matter about your heritage. I know you have the biggest, most caring heart." He removed a small black velvet box from his pocket and opened it. The camera flashes were now almost continuous. He held the biggest teardrop diamond ring out to her.

A tear of joy splashed onto her cheek. "Leo, what have you done?"

He dropped down on one knee. "Bianca Bartolini, I fell for you the day I saw you at the wedding at the villa. Since then I've come to love your company, your sense of humor and your warm smiles that light up my darkest days. No test is going to change my feelings for you. I love you with all my heart. And I just have one question for you: will you be my queen?"

Her heart pounded with love for this man. It was then that she realized exactly where she belonged—next to the man she loved.

"Yes. Yes, I will. I love you."

He pulled the ring from the box and slipped it on her trembling hand. And then he stood. He peered deeply into her eyes. "You're the most amazing woman. And the people of Patazonia are going to love you as much as I do."

And then he lowered his head and pressed his lips to hers as flashes lit up the entire room. Fairy tales really do come true.

* * * * *

A PROMISE TO KEEP

ALLISON LEIGH

For my family.

Chapter One

The house—a generous term if there ever was one—sat on the side of the mountain. The wood had gone gray with weathering and the windows were miserly in number as well as size—probably to keep out the cold. Even on the warmest of summer days, there would be the wind that never, ever seemed to let up.

Summer hadn't hit this part of Wyoming yet. During this time of year—well, March to May, pretty much—it could be warm one day and a blizzard the next. Squarely in the middle of April—the month after which she was named—it was colder than a witch's tongue and a foot of snow still clung in the shadows.

Which meant the wind was sharper and more stinging than ever, and from the moment April Reed left the warmth of her car's heated interior, it furiously whipped her hair straight into her eyes as she squinted up at the mountain.

Up at the odd-angled, wood-sided house.

It had to be constructed of sterner stuff than it appeared, or it would have blown off Rambling Mountain long, long ago. Either that or it was a testament to the sheer stubbornness of the house's occupant.

Her grandfather, Squire Clay, had always said that nobody was more stubborn than Otis Lambert. Not even Squire, himself.

Which was saying something.

She pulled the collar of her leather coat against her throat and reached inside the car for her briefcase. When she straightened, the wind slammed the car door shut for her. She yanked the edge of her jacket free where it had caught and squinted into the wind as she moved past a dusty blue pickup and stepped around the wooden barricade blocking the road leading up to the weather-beaten house. Even without the barricade, she wouldn't have been able to drive the last half mile up to the house. Not with the rockslide. The boulders weren't enough to block passage entirely, but they were definitely enough to block a vehicle.

She chewed the inside of her cheek as she weaved

her way around a four-wheeler parked on the other side of the blockage and glanced back down the road. Developing the road would be costly. When she was finished meeting with Lambert, she'd take some photos of the damage and email them to her boss. Gage Stanton wasn't likely to let a few boulders stand in his way, but he'd still want a general sense of what they'd be facing. Ultimately, her boss had in mind a sumptuous resort catering to outdoor enthusiasts, because Rambling Mountain could offer it all. Rock climbing. Hunting. Fishing. Whatever. The only road on the mountain was this one. It would need to be passable even if Gage chose another location on the mountain for the resort.

The wind whistled and she pulled her collar close again, turning to head up the road. It was steep. Treacherously narrow. She instinctively moved away from the side that overlooked the sheer drop-off. Hundreds of feet below glistened a pristine lake fed by natural underground springs. A lake that would provide endless recreational opportunities. If a person could reach it.

It might seem strange for one person to own an entire mountain, but one did.

Otis Lambert.

Technically, water was the property of the state, but Lambert and his ancestors had always exercised their water rights when it came to the lake. It wasn't that they'd unreasonably withheld the natural stream water that flowed from it. Down the mountain, that water helped irrigate the region, including the town of Weaver and a whole lot of ranch land. But the only accessible point to the lake from a recreational standpoint lay entirely within Otis Lambert's property. Thousands and thousands of acres of it.

And one week ago, Otis had contacted her boss, Gage Stanton. Founder of Stanton Development. A Colorado-based company known for everything from award-winning, master-planned communities to hospitals to amusement parks.

The very fact that Otis had requested a meeting with a developer would seem to imply that he was softening when it came to sharing his mountain.

"Won't happen, girl."

Her grandfather's words from just that morning swam in her mind. They'd been sitting at the round oak table in the middle of the kitchen at the big house. The stack of golden waffles that her grandmother, Gloria, had set on the table had been quickly decimated by Squire and her uncle Matthew. He was Squire's son and had run the Double-C for as long as April could remember.

And all four of them—Squire and Gloria, Matthew and his wife, Jaimie—lived together in the sprawling old house everyone referred to as the "big house." As one of the largest cattle operations in the state of Wyoming as well as several states beyond, the Double-C commanded considerable influence and wealth. Considering that, the big house was actually somewhat modest in size. And even though Squire was supposedly retired as the head of the ranch, he could still ride and rope as well as any one of his progeny and he'd never stopped looking for an opportunity to add to their holdings.

"Won't happen, girl," he'd said, his icy blue eyes squinting at her as he sipped his steaming coffee from a china cup. "I've spent more 'n half my life trying to negotiate a deal with Lambert to connect those two sections o' land we own down on the southwest corner. Old hermit isn't even willin' to discuss leasing a couple hunnert acres that he'd never miss. The man's sitting on millions but he lives like a pauper 'cause that's the way he likes it. Waste of time goin' up the mountain to see him. Be better off tryin' to sell ice to a glacier."

"Stop trying to discourage her," Gloria had chided as she gave April a quick wink. "Not everyone is as stubborn as you. Maybe Otis'll have a soft spot for a red-haired girl."

Squire had grunted at that, a faint smile on his lips. "Well, I guess that worked for me back when you were a nurse poking me with needles 'n' naggin' me about drinking my coffee."

"Keeping you alive," Matthew had reminded his father as he pushed away from the table and dropped a kiss on Jaimie's head. "Everyone's heard

that Lambert's sick. Really sick. You're just aggra-
vated that your granddaughter's beating you to the
punch getting a meeting with him."

Squire had made a face, but his eyes, which
could look cold as winter, had been warm and kind
as he'd eyed her. "Do your best, girl. But be pre-
pared for disappointment. Lambert's never shared
an inch of land. Sick or not, can't see him chang-
ing now."

Loose gravel slid under April's boot and she
barely caught herself from landing on her knee.
Cussing under her breath, she stopped still and
hauled in a deep breath. If she'd known she'd be
having this hike ahead of her, she would have worn
more suitable boots.

She looked back down again toward her red car,
then up toward the house. She'd only gone halfway.
Even though she was accustomed to living with
elevation—Denver wasn't called the Mile High City
for nothing—the air was even thinner up here and
the ramshackle house wasn't situated anywhere near
the summit.

She knew why Gage had sent her to take the appointment with Lambert. She may have grown up
mostly in Arizona, but she'd still spent plenty of
time in Wyoming. Visiting her grandparents for
holidays, spending summers there. Her boss had
sent her, ostensibly, because she had an edge, being
"sort of" a local girl.

She knew it was more than that, though. If Lambert's health were really as bad as it was rumored, there'd be a lot of interested parties where his land was concerned. And first in line would be her grandfather, Squire Clay. The only thing more important than that land was his family. If April could successfully negotiate a deal with Lambert now, it was guaranteed that Squire wouldn't try to get in the way.

There was good reason Gage was so successful.

She swiped her hair away again, took another deep breath and set off once more.

She hadn't gone twenty yards before a figure appeared from behind the house. He was too far away to make out his features, but his stride wasn't slowed at all as he kicked through a mound of snow, aiming her way.

It wasn't the sight of the man that was alarming, particularly. She'd never met Otis Lambert. Never seen him before, even. But this man's head was bare and she doubted Otis—who, like Squire, was somewhere in his nineties—had a full head of dark hair.

Which meant he was the ranch hand. Jed Dalloway.

Otis had taken him on several years back, according to Squire. And he was almost as reclusive as Otis.

No, the man didn't alarm her. But the fierce dog at the man's side, curling back its lips to expose wickedly sharp teeth, was another matter.

She was used to dogs. Liked them. The only reason she didn't have one herself was that she lived in a loft apartment in downtown Denver and spent more hours at the office than she did at home. She couldn't give a dog the attention it deserved.

But this shaggy gray growling beast looked more wolf than dog.

A wolf had once come down from the mountains at the Double-C, picking off cattle along the way until Matthew and his brothers had gone out with a rifle to take care of it. She'd been sixteen at the time and full of outrage toward them.

Now she felt more like the poor cow must have felt, finding itself in a wolf's stare.

She lifted her chin, swiping the hair away from her eyes yet again. "Does he bite?" She'd raised her voice, but the wind nearly tore it away.

The man was coming toward her, the dog keeping pace. "What'd you say?"

The closer man and dog drew, the faster her heart beat. He was a good thirty feet away when he stopped. The denim shirt he wore open over a white T-shirt strained at his wide shoulders and yanked in the wind. The dog leaned against the side of his muddy jeans, teeth still bared. The growl was no longer imagined, but perfectly, nerve-rackingly audible.

It took every speck of willpower she had not to take a step back. "I asked if he bites."

"When he needs to."

She swiped at her hair again. Dragged her focus from the fearsome canine to the man. His eyes were narrowed. Unwelcoming.

But she had a reason to be there and wasn't going to be cowed just because a man gave her a narrow-eyed look. "That's not exactly a comforting answer."

"Wasn't intending it to be." But he lowered a raw-knuckled hand and touched the dog's head. The animal promptly sank down on its haunches. The growl ceased, though the teeth remained visible. "You're trespassing. Signs are posted on the road. The *private* road. You ignored them."

She tightened her grip on the leather strap of her briefcase. She'd never been a ninny and she wasn't starting now. She stepped toward him. "I'm not trespassing. I was invited. I'm April Reed with Stanton Development. I have an appointment with Mr. Lambert."

His eyes narrowed even more. If it weren't for the frown lines creasing his forehead and drawing down his lips, he might have been a nice-looking man in a rustic sort of way. "Otis isn't available."

She stopped. "Are you *his* guard dog like this one—" she waved her fingers toward the dog "—seems to be yours?"

His frown seemed to lighten a little, which didn't explain why her heart pounded even more nervously.

Nevertheless, he stayed hostile. "You've wasted a trip." He turned on his heel and the dog followed suit.

She gaped as he started walking back toward the house. She set off after him. "Wait! Hold on!"

She read impatience in the way his wide shoulders moved. The way he stopped, yet took a moment before turning toward her. When he did, his frown was firmly in place. She was close enough now to see his eyes were dark, though she couldn't tell what color of dark.

"You're Jed, right? Jed Dalloway?"

He didn't answer. Just kept looking at her with those dark, soulless eyes as she continued walking toward him, finally drawing even with him. With the chunky high heels of her leather boots, she stood close to six feet tall. He was still taller.

"I assure you, Mr. Dalloway, that your boss *is* expecting me." Projecting assurance had never felt quite as challenging as it did just then. She forced a small smile as she stepped past him, angling toward the weathered deck lining the front side of the house, as yet still several hundred feet away.

The deck was cantilevered over the cliff side. And looked to her pretty much like a death trap.

"Guess you're the reason he left, then."

She looked back at him. "He's not here?"

Jed gave a brief shrug.

She eyed him suspiciously. Tried to ferret some

hint of anything from his expression. "I understood that Mr. Lambert rarely leaves the mountain."

"Didn't say he wasn't on the mountain, Miss Reed."

Her gaze flicked away from him to their surroundings. The jagged rocks sloped gently here and there with stretches of somewhat level ground—much of it still covered in snow. In addition to the house, there was a small shed with a window, and an even smaller shed without one. A horse with a heavy coat was standing in the shelter of it. The cattle that were supposedly being run on the ranch were nowhere in sight. Not unusual. Reportedly, there were less than a hundred head. On thousands and thousands of acres. "You're saying he just, what?" She waved her hand. "Went out for a stroll?"

"I'm saying he's not available." He gestured toward the deck. "You want to check it out for yourself, be my guest. Meanwhile, I have things to do." He angled away from her, heading toward the back of the property from where he'd appeared in the first place. The dog lingered behind, his lip curled up again to deliver his last thoughts before finally trotting off.

She waited until both beasts had disappeared from sight, and deliberately relaxed her jaw. "Pleasant," she muttered under her breath, and closed the distance to the deck. She chewed the inside of her lip, looking underneath it, and then straightened again.

She hoped it was sounder than it looked as she gingerly went up the creaking steps. She stepped her way around the missing boards, then stopped in front of the door, knocking several times. Loudly.

There was no answer.

She exhaled and walked to the far end of the deck, where it wasn't projecting off the edge of the cliff. She looked off to the side of the house. There was no sign of man—young or old. No sign of the dog.

She tried knocking on the front door again, to no avail.

She still wasn't inclined to believe that Lambert had forgotten the appointment.

She returned to the steps and sat down on the top one, feeling relatively secure since there was at least solid earth beneath the wood, in case her rear end went through it. She dragged her briefcase onto her lap and delved inside. She pulled out her cell phone and checked it for a signal, not surprised there was none. There were still many places around Weaver where cell signals didn't yet reach. At times, like now, it was entirely frustrating. At others, when a person wanted to get entirely away from the outside world, it was an absolute delight. Remained to be seen what Gage would do about that fact.

She shook her hair out of her eyes as she slid

the phone back in its pocket and took out a business card and a pen instead.

"What's she doing out there now?"

Jed frowned, looking out one of the square, high-set windows. "Still sitting on the step." She'd been there a solid thirty minutes now. As if she were waiting for Otis to drive up the broken road. He glanced at his boss. "Next time you think twice about keeping a meeting you arranged, cancel it yourself."

Otis sucked at his teeth as he rocked in his wood-slatted rocker. For anyone else, the rocker would sit on a front porch. For Otis, it sat in front of the woodstove. No cushion for comfort. The ancient knitted blanket on his knees was a recent addition. Along with the hacking cough that was never going to go away. "I didn't expect a girl."

Jed looked out the window once more. From his angle, he could see the back of her copper-colored head and a bit of shoulder outlined in sleek black leather. If she sat there five more minutes, he was going back out there, no matter how pissed off Otis got.

"Man. Woman." Which April Reed definitely was. "Does it make any difference, Otis? We both know you're not gonna sell. Particularly to a developer." God knew they'd had enough arguments about it, especially in the last few years.

The only sound that came from Otis's direction was the rhythmic creak of wood runners on the wood floor.

Jed grimaced. "Stubborn old man."

The creaking didn't hesitate. "Keeps me alive, boy."

For how much longer?

Jed didn't ask the question. He didn't want to hear the answer. Ornery or not, Otis was the last thing left in the world that Jed cared about and he was dying. Dying because he wouldn't seek the medical care that he'd probably needed since before Jed had met him five years ago.

But he didn't have to test Otis's temper, because the redhead was moving finally. Standing.

She walked back to the door and he expected to hear a knock, but none came. Instead, after a moment she headed back to the steps, avoiding the rotten boards that Jed needed to repair once the weather finally improved. Then he caught a glimpse of her again, walking toward the road.

Tall. Slender. Dressed in a trim jacket and sexy-as-hell boots.

She looked like she belonged on a magazine cover. Or in an office cracking out orders to her minions.

Instead, she was being snubbed by a cantankerous old man.

As he watched, she slung her briefcase strap

across her chest like a messenger bag and pulled something from it.

A cell phone, he realized, watching her hold it out in front of her. She was obviously taking pictures. Maybe recording video. Her arm panned around until she was aiming it toward the cabin. He didn't worry about her seeing him from his vantage point inside.

Eventually, she panned the other direction and started making her way down the road again. When she was out of sight entirely, he went to the front door and pulled it open.

The business card she'd tucked in the doorjamb slid free and landed on the floor near his boot.

He picked it up and read the embossed black printing. It told him little more than what she'd told him outside. April Reed. Stanton Development. Denver, Colorado.

On the reverse, she'd written a telephone number and a brief note.

"She's going to be back," he told Otis. He wasn't sure if he was glad about that or not.

"How do you know?"

He flicked the business card onto Otis's lap. "She told you so."

Otis harrumphed. He looked at the note. "You can deal with her."

"She's not my problem."

"She is if I say she is." Otis smiled slyly. "That

bother you for some reason? Been a while since you've gotten off the mountain to see a woman."

"It's been a while since I've gotten off the mountain because I've been stuck up here all winter with *you*."

"All the more reason." He waved the note. "You know how to make a business deal. Or have you forgotten?"

Jed ignored the dig. "You're not going to make a deal with anyone and we both know it. I run the Rad for you, Otis. But that doesn't make me your lackey." He headed out of the room.

"Where you going?" Otis's querulous voice followed him.

"To take care of the stuff you *do* pay me for."

Chapter Two

"Well? How'd it go?"

April made a face at her friend Piper Madison and began shrugging out of her jacket as she slipped onto the barstool next to her. "It didn't."

They were at Colbys Bar & Grill, which was doing brisk business for a Thursday afternoon.

Piper looked sympathetic. "Sorry. I know you hate disappointing that sexy boss of yours."

April rolled her eyes. "That's what I get for introducing you when you came to visit."

Piper chuckled. "You're probably the only female on the planet who wouldn't be attracted to Gage Stanton. Tall, dark, rich?"

"How about demanding, a perfectionist and arrogant?"

"Sounds like someone I used to know." The pretty blonde owner of Colbys stopped in front of them on the other side of the bar. "Let me guess." Jane's smile was wry. "Talking about your boss? How is it working for Gage?"

April figured her smile was equally wry. She knew that Jane and Gage had been briefly married ages ago, before Jane had moved to Weaver. Long before she'd married April's cousin Casey Clay. "Never dull, that's for sure."

Jane chuckled. "So, what can I get you?"

"Just some coffee to start." Deciding she was too chilly, she pulled her jacket back on. "What's the special for lunch today?"

"Chicken enchiladas."

"They're good, too. Had them last week," Piper offered. She already had a salad in front of her that she'd partially consumed.

"Enchiladas it is," April told Jane. "How's life with my cousin and those babies?" Casey and Jane had recently adopted twins.

Jane winked as she keyed in the order. "Never dull, that's for sure." She turned up a mug in front of April and filled it with coffee. She wiped the gleaming wood bar top with her towel. "Piper, you need a refill?"

"Not yet." Piper waited until Jane had moved

down the bar again before she spoke. "I completely forget that Jane was ever married to Gage. Criminy. Where's the fairness in life? I can't get a date, and she has had not one hottie hubby, but two."

"You most certainly *can* get a date," April chided.

"Sure, if I lived somewhere other than Weaver," Piper complained. "Here, I'll forever be just the preacher's kid who teaches sixth grade."

"Then move to Denver," April said immediately. "You can split the ridiculous rent on my apartment with me."

"Much as I love that fancy loft of yours, you know I can't."

"I know you won't," April countered without heat. "So stop complaining. If I've said it once, I've said it a hundred times. If there is someone you want to date, ask *him*. You don't have to wait around waiting to be asked."

"Too bad all women don't have your confidence. You've always had guys falling at your feet, too. Maybe it's the fact that you're tall, svelte and red-headed while I am a short, round and forgettable brownette."

April couldn't help but laugh. "You exaggerate more than anyone I've ever known." She was tall, but keeping from looking like a living scarecrow was as much a problem for her as Piper's lifelong battle against the fifteen extra pounds she didn't want.

Her friend's eyes were twinkling. "It's not an

exaggeration when it comes to Mr. Perfect Financial Planner."

April sighed faintly and stirred milk into her coffee. "Kenneth was fun, but—"

"He made the ultimate mistake. He got serious and you didn't."

"Unlike you, I'm not interested in settling down yet." She started to lift her coffee, but set it down again. "Who proposes to a woman they've only been dating a few months? We never even slept together." Exasperation suddenly churned inside her because she knew she'd hurt Kenneth, no matter how unintentionally. "I mean, really. Who would take a proposal like that seriously?"

Unfazed by April's waving hands, Piper pushed her salad to the side and scooped up a blob of guacamole with a tortilla chip. "All the people who've fallen in love at first sight? Maybe Kenneth's just the old-fashioned type." She popped the chip in her mouth and crunched on it.

"No man I've ever met is that old-fashioned." April exhaled. Piper might lament her romantic vacuum, but on a daily basis, she successfully corralled a roomful of hormonal preadolescents. What was one agitated redhead? Piper's equanimity was soothing.

"Well, I forever live in hope that there are a few old-fashioned guys still out there," Piper said wryly. She took another scoop of guacamole, this time eschewing the chip and going straight at it with the tip of her fork. "But back to your meeting. What do you mean, *it didn't?*"

"I mean I never even had a chance to see Otis Lambert." Jed Dalloway's face swam inside April's head. She shivered and not even wrapping her hands around the hot coffee mug helped. "Did you know the road up to his place is blocked off? Probably a half mile back from the house. There was obviously a rockslide at some point. Huge boulders on the road. The wood barricades look like they've been there awhile."

"Since there's never been any reason for me *to* drive up there, no, I didn't know. So when he set the meeting, he didn't mention it."

"Nope." She stretched out one leg. "Had to walk the rest of the way in these."

"You've routinely worn four-inch heels since you earned your first paycheck. You expect sympathy?"

April grinned. "Obviously not from you."

"So, you hoofed it in high heels and then what?"

"And then nothing. He wasn't there. At least that's what I was told."

"By whom?"

"Jed Dalloway." She eyed her friend. Except when they'd spent four years as college roommates, Piper had lived her entire life in Weaver. "Have you met him?"

"Not that I recall. I've heard his name, of course,

but unless he has kids in school, not much reason I would have."

"He didn't exactly strike me as the family type."

Piper chuckled. "Why? Wasn't he wearing his sign?"

"Ha ha." She looked down at her coffee, seeing instead Jed's dark eyes. "Otis Lambert doesn't need to post No Trespass signs. All he has to do is post Jed Dalloway on the road."

"Off-putting, I take it."

"His attitude is." She shook her head, as if to rid him from her thoughts. "I left my card. Said I'd be back." She was briefly interrupted when a server delivered her meal. She thanked the teenager, and began unfolding her napkin. "Why did you say of course you've heard his name?"

"Jed Dalloway's name?" Piper shrugged. "You know this town. Everyone hears about everyone, sooner or later. You want that black olive?" She was reaching even before April shook her head and Piper popped it in her mouth. "Ooh, hot." She chewed quickly, gingerly. "Heard he's from Chicago or thereabouts. Some scandal involved. So they say."

"*They* being the grapes on Weaver's prolific vine?"

"You know it." Piper dashed her fingertips with her napkin. Her smile was mischievous. "Not that *I* listen to gossip."

April's lips twitched. "Of course not." She cut into her steaming enchiladas. "So what *is* the good gossip around town?"

"As usual, half of it involves members of your family. You think I'm going to say?"

April laughed. "Now I know you're exaggerating."

Piper chuckled. "Maybe a little." She glanced at her watch. "I have fifteen minutes before I need to be back at school for a teachers meeting. Pick a category." She held up her hand. "Money problems? Marital discord?" She ticked them off on her fingers. "Politics? Sex scandals?"

"Oh for Pete's sake. Sex scandals?"

"Just because we're small town, doesn't mean we're not keeping up with the Joneses. There's a rumor that Vivian Templeton is paying for more than architectural designs when it comes to the new town library she's trying to get built."

April rolled her eyes. Vivian Templeton was the sister-in-law of Squire Clay's deceased first wife. Even though she'd never met the woman herself, she knew Vivian had to be well in her eighties. Maybe more. April wasn't related to her, but her mom's stepbrothers were. Which meant the wealthy eccentric was family of a sort. "I have a hard time imagining it, but Vivian's first husband made his fortune in steel. Supposedly she can afford whatever she wants to spend her money on, so if she's not hurting anyone, who cares? I mean other than

Squire." Her grandfather held a grudge against Vivian over a supposed insult to his first wife.

Piper shrugged. "Beck's firm is handling the design."

That *was* news. "People think Beck would cha-cha with an elderly rich lady when he has my cousin at home? Talk about ridiculous."

"He's not the only architect at his firm."

"Yeah, there's Nick," she said dismissively. "Can't see that one, either." Nick was Beck's son from his first marriage. "He's two years younger than me."

Piper spread her hands. "I'm just the messenger. So, what's your plan with Mr. Lambert?"

"I'll go back tomorrow. And the next day. And the next if I have to."

"That would be Sunday. Easter Sunday."

April made a face. "Okay, maybe not Easter Sunday."

"How long're you planning to be in town?"

"Depends on how things go. I'm meeting with Archer Templeton next Tuesday." The attorney practiced in Colorado and Wyoming and, among other things, represented Stanton Development in both states. "He's doing research on possible claims that might arise against the Rambling Rad."

Piper rolled her eyes. "Another hottie. Man, you do get all the luck."

April made a face. "Archer's cut from the same cloth as my boss. Not my type. At all."

"Do you even know what your type is?"

Once again, Jed's face flitted through her mind. Strong legs braced and short dark hair whipping in the wind.

Fortunately, Piper was pulling out her wallet and didn't seem to think anything about April's lack of an answer. "Just stay long enough that we can get together again before you leave."

"I will. And put your money away. I told you I'd get lunch."

"Just because you earn three times as much as I do and have a trust fund the size of Alaska doesn't mean I can't buy my own lunch."

"That's true." April plucked the wallet out of her friend's hands and zipped it shut again. "But I've got per diem expense money to use up one way or another and staying at the big house means either buying you a bunch of lunches or going shopping. I'll never use up the funds otherwise."

Piper grinned. "Life is really rough working for that sexy developer of yours." She put away her wallet and slid off the barstool. She gave April a quick hug and gathered up her belongings before sending a wave toward Jane as she pulled on her coat and left.

When her friend was gone, April turned back to her sufficiently cooled enchiladas. When she finished eating, she pushed the plate aside and pulled out her phone, studying the photographs she'd taken up on the mountain. She discarded a few, forwarded the rest to her boss and continued reviewing the emails she'd received.

She'd only gotten through two when her phone vibrated. She swiped the screen and held it to her ear. "That was fast."

"Landslide." Gage's tone was typically brief and to the point. "Happen often?"

"I have no idea," she admitted. "I'll find out, though." She could see Jane from the corner of her eye, pulling drinks at the other end of the bar and wondered, not for the first time, if Gage's ex-wife was one more reason why he hadn't come to Weaver himself. Jane was now a happily married woman with a family. Gage—for all of his eligible bachelor reputation—had always struck April as distinctly lonely.

"Let me know." On that, he ended the call in his typically abrupt way and she went back to answering her emails. Two cups of coffee later, she'd finished. She paid the bill and headed out.

The clouds had blown away. The sky was a bright blue, the air brittle and cold even through her leather jacket. She debated driving back up the mountain to see if Lambert had suddenly become "available," but decided against it. In the note she'd left, she said she'd return the next day. Whether or not Otis Lambert stood by his words, she would stand by hers. Ambushing a man who was ill just wasn't her style.

She drove to the far side of town, where Shop-World was located and where she knew the cell signal was the strongest of anywhere in town. She found an available parking spot in a sunny corner and pulled out her laptop. Even though she knew the contents of the Rambling project file backward and forward, she read through it again while she called the State Geological Survey. The woman on the phone told her that Lambert had made no report of the landslide. Strictly speaking, he didn't have to. The only thing that appeared to have been impacted had been the road. His private road.

Nevertheless, she retrieved all the history she could of geological events that had occurred in the area and sent the information in a summarized email to her boss.

By the time she finished, she was colder than ever from sitting in her idle car and the bright lights of Shop-World were beckoning. She put away her computer and grabbed her wallet and headed toward the busy supersized store. She went first to the clothing department and found an inexpensive, insulated coat. She added a knit scarf with a matching beanie and gloves to her armload, and then swung by the grocery department to grab some chocolate, because—well, there never needed to be a specific reason for chocolate.

Her phone buzzed and she juggled her armload as she pulled it from the pocket of her jacket. Another message from her boss. While Gage was unfailingly brief verbally, the same couldn't be said when it came to his texts and email messages.

Reading through his latest, she headed toward the registers at the front of the store only to bump right into a pyramid of paper towels. She cursed under her breath, dropping the coat and scarf and trying to keep the entire display from toppling. She managed, but several rolls escaped her, and she chased after them, snatching them up.

"…*and* that's why I keep telling you to watch where you're going," she heard a woman say as a noisy cart rumbled past her.

"And that's why we should keep our noses out of our phones," April mumbled after her, meeting the little boy's eyes as he trotted after his mama. He smiled at her and she couldn't help smile back as she stuffed one roll after another back onto the now-lopsided pyramid.

"You missed one."

She looked up, first at the extended roll of towels. Then the long, square-tipped fingers grasping it. The masculine wrist beyond. Her stomach was sinking even before she got to his face.

She grabbed her items and straightened from her

graceless crouch, taking the roll from him to set on the pile. Brown, she realized. His eyes were a deep dark, chocolate brown. "Mr. Dalloway."

And there was definitely a bite of amusement in those eyes, even though it didn't translate to any other part of his face. Maybe he wasn't handsome in a conventional sense. But he was definitely arresting.

"Miss Reed." He turned on his boot heel and started to walk away.

She renewed her grip on her items and followed. "I left my card for your boss," she said to his back. She was purchasing a cheap coat. He only wore the same clothes he'd worn earlier that day as if he were impervious to the cold weather. "I told him I'd be returning tomorrow."

His shoulders moved impatiently and he stopped to look at her. Lines radiated from the corners of his eyes, and she could tell he spent a lot of time squinting in the sun. She had a dozen relatives who possessed those exact same kind of lines.

But what put the lines around his tightly held lips?

"Another day's not going to matter," he was saying. "He's not going to see you tomorrow. Or any other day. He's not selling. And definitely not to a developer."

He wasn't saying anything that her grandfather hadn't already said. She wanted to believe Jed as little as she wanted to believe Squire. "Then why'd he ask to meet with Stanton Development?"

"Why does Otis do any of the things he does?" He spread his hands and she noticed then the small brown prescription bottle he held. "Not even sure Otis himself knows."

"You, ah, you run the ranch for him, don't you? The Rambling Rad. Are you afraid of losing your job?"

His lips twisted. "He's not going to sell, Miss Reed. My involvement with the ranch, such as it is, is as immaterial to him as it is to you."

"It's not immaterial! I assure you, the company I work for isn't about putting people *out* of work. It's about creating *more* opportunities!"

His expression didn't change. She couldn't tell if he believed her or not. "My advice would be to go back to Colorado. Focus your efforts on greener pastures." He turned to go again.

"I'm sorry that he's ill, Mr. Dalloway."

He didn't look back. "So am I, Miss Reed."

She chewed the inside of her cheek, watching him step around a Shop-World employee stocking a shelf with Easter candy. He was aiming for the pharmacy.

If she were really a bloodthirsty developer, she'd race for her car to get up the mountain for a chance to get to Otis before Jed could.

Instead, she joined the lines at the registers, paid for her items and drove back out to the big house.

By the time she let herself in through the back door, it was nearly dark outside and the smell of home cooking was heady.

Everyone was already seated around the kitchen table and she dumped off her briefcase and purchases in the mudroom before washing her hands and joining them. "Sorry I'm late." She slipped into the empty chair next to her grandmother.

"Don't be silly." Gloria handed her a steaming platter piled high with roasted vegetables and beef. "We just sat down anyway."

April took the platter and scooped a helping onto her plate. Despite the lunch at Colbys, her stomach was already growling. "Smells wonderful." She passed it on to Matthew, who was at the head of the table. "At the rate I'm eating, I won't fit in my clothes by the time I go back to Denver."

Squire snorted. He was at the other end of the table. "Too thin as it is. Could stand some meat on your bones. Just like your mama."

Gloria tsked. "Leave her alone."

April didn't bother hiding her smile as her grandfather harrumphed. Squire Clay might have the sternest face imaginable, but he was a complete softie where his grandchildren and great-grandchildren were concerned. Whether they were grown like April, or still young, he was guaranteed to be their biggest partner in crime. Which was pretty sweet, considering the stories April had grown up with about what a hard-ass he'd been as a father.

"I thought I'd go see Aunt Belle soon," she told Gloria. "If you want to come?" Belle and April's mother, Nikki, were twins. "I'll see if Lucy can join us, too." Lucy was Belle's stepdaughter.

"It's a plan." Gloria smiled.

Eventually, talk turned to ranch business, and April let it wash over her as she worked her way through her food.

"How'd things go up on the mountain?"

The question was inevitable, of course. She gave her grandfather a grimace. "Like you expected."

"Sorry to be right, girl."

"No you're not," Matthew scoffed, giving April a wink. "You love being right."

"When I'm dealing with sons who don't know their heads from a hole in the ground," Squire shot back without heat.

"Regardless, I'm not giving up," April assured them.

"Damn straight," Squire said, nodding approvingly. "This family never gives up."

"True," Gloria said brightly, giving her husband a deliberate look. "Which is why I've sent in our RSVP for the fund-raiser." She extended a basket of golden rolls toward him. "*Two* will be attending."

His brows pulled down. He ignored the basket. "I told you we were *not* going to that thing."

The hand holding the basket didn't move an inch. "And I told you that we were."

His lips thinned.

There had always been plenty of standoffs between her grandparents so April knew better than to worry as the tension between them thickened. "What's the fund-raiser for?"

"New library," Jaimie said. "Vivian's latest project. She's hosting a big do at her home. Has invited half the state, from what I hear."

Understanding hit. Squire detested anything related to Vivian Templeton. And he considered the lavish home that she'd built to be an eyesore. "Building a new library is a good thing, though."

"And long past due," Gloria said in agreement. "The one we have occupies that small two-story down by the town square and it's nowhere near large enough anymore to serve the entire town. Enlarging the present location isn't feasible, so that means finding a way to build a new one." She was still giving her husband a stern eye and the basket of rolls was still extended. "Regardless of who is spearheading the effort."

He grimaced. "Doesn't mean I am going to go out to her house and pretend we're all friends." He snatched away the basket, grabbed a roll and pointed it at Matthew. "That woman shunned your mama," he reminded before slapping the roll down on his plate.

"Before we were born," Matthew said mildly.

"S'pose that means *you're* going, too?" Squire looked even more annoyed.

"Squire, Vivian has made some significant contributions in the few years since she moved here," Jaimie tried in a pacifying tone. "The new hospital wing, the—"

"People like her can always throw money at a cause," he cut her off. "Thinking it covers up what they're really like."

"Vivian isn't trying to cover up anything," Gloria said wearily. "She's been perfectly honest about regretting the things she's said and done in the past. She's apologized. You're the one who won't accept it. And if you won't go with your own wife to the fund-raiser, I'll find someone who will." She pushed away from the table and stomped out of the room.

Squire cursed under his breath and stomped out of the room, too. A second later, they heard the back door slam as he left the house.

Standoffs between her grandparents were normal. Walking away in opposite directions was not.

Alarm gurgling inside her, April looked from her aunt's face to her uncle's. "Should we go after them?"

"Not if you want to keep your head attached to your body," Matthew advised.

Jaimie got up and began clearing the dishes. "They'll be fine," she soothed. "Squire must feel like he's on the losing end of the battle where everyone's acceptance of Vivian is concerned. You know him. That just isn't going to sit well."

April handed Jaimie the roll basket. "Was what she did really so bad?"

"You know what Squire is like when it comes to family," Matthew said. "When her husband found out that my mom was his illegitimate half sister, Vivian lost it. Those were the days when anyone illegitimate was treated like a pariah, but her husband was all set to bring my mother into the family fold anyway. He died in a car accident before he had a chance to actually do that. Evidently there were rumors it was suicide."

"Which Vivian categorically denies." Jaimie slid her hand over Matthew's shoulder. "And your mother died when she had Tristan around that same time. One of those weird tragic coincidences."

"I can still remember Squire coming home from the hospital with Tris wrapped in a blanket. Alone." Matthew shook his head and brushed an absent kiss over Jaimie's knuckles. "Who knows what kind of relationship they might have had if they'd lived."

"Even though their marriage was far from perfect, Vivian says her husband loved their sons too much to leave them deliberately," Jaimie told April.

"In any case, Squire's never likely to forgive Vivian for treating my mother the way she did." Matthew rose with his plate in hand.

Jaimie spoke gently. "I think Vivian's contributions around Weaver—the money she's investing—is a way of atoning for that. She's going to do what she's going to do regardless of what anyone—particularly Squire—thinks about it. Since he was elected to the town council, he hasn't been able to avoid her as much as he'd like to."

"He seems to be going to great lengths to avoid her," said April.

"Don't worry about him and your grandma," Matthew advised. "The old man doesn't have a lot of things these days to be obstreperous about, so when he has a chance, he really goes at it. He'll come around if only to appease Gloria."

"He can save his appeasing," Gloria said, sailing into the kitchen in time to overhear. "That coot of mine can just stay home. April will be my date for the fund-raiser, won't you, dear?"

"When is it?"

"Week from Saturday."

She chewed the inside of her cheek. "I'd be happy to, but I'm not sure I'll be here that long. Depends how things go with Mr. Lambert."

"Well, I want you to succeed, of course," Gloria said, "but anything that keeps you here with us a little bit longer is just fine with me. Next time you go up the mountain to see Otis, take a covered dish.

Have never known two men living on their own to turn down a pretty girl bearing home-cooked food."

April groaned. "Grandma, that is so old-fashioned."

"Maybe so." Gloria nodded sagely. "But I'll bet you it works."

Chapter Three

The next afternoon, April—wearing her new coat and scarf and gloves—went up the mountain again. She was not resorting to her grandmother's suggestion of taking a covered dish. She wasn't meeting Lambert for a church potluck dinner, for heaven's sake.

But once again, she went back down the mountain after an hour, having failed to get past the front door of that miserable little shack. Like the first time, she spent the rest of the day with her computer and her phone, gathering more research and reporting it all back to Gage.

That evening, when she got together with some of her cousins at Colbys, she had to recount the effort to meet Lambert yet again. "The only bright spot, if I can call it that," she said over the hot cider she was drinking, "was that Jed Dalloway wasn't around this time to witness my failure."

"It's not a failure," Lucy assured. She was sitting across the tables they'd shoved together to accommodate the number of cousins who kept showing up. "Unless you're giving up already."

"Squire would kick me out from under his roof if I were." April pulled a crispy French fry from the enormous mound in the center of the tables and dredged it in ketchup. "Not to mention my boss would probably give me the boot, too." She wasn't really worried about that, but neither did she want to return to Colorado with nothing to show for it. Not on the very first assignment she'd been charged with heading. She wouldn't exactly blame Gage if he didn't repeat the mistake any time soon.

"I'm sure that wouldn't happen." That came from Sarah, who was Matthew and Jaimie's daughter and taught at the same school as Piper. She kept casting an eye toward the pool tables where her nineteen-year-old daughter, Megan, was playing with friends. "You know the worst part about kids turning nineteen?" She jabbed her French fry in the air. "You lose your ability to ground them when they keep doing dumb things."

April looked over toward the group in question. Despite the cold weather, Megan wore a pair of denim shorts, cowboy boots and a skintight T-shirt. She was blonde and impossibly lovely in the way that only nineteen-year-old girls could be. "What kind of dumb things?"

"The usual. Staying out too late. Hanging with the wrong crowd."

"How does the sheriff's daughter manage to hang out with the wrong crowd?"

"Probably because she *is* the sheriff's daughter." The suggestion came from their cousin Courtney as she slipped into a free chair. "Trust one who knows."

"Don't worry so much about Megan," Lucy soothed. "All of us around that age tested the boundaries. We've all come out on the other side more or less intact. And her brother has a good head on his shoulders. Megan always listens to him."

April felt the whoosh of cold air when the door started to open and she glanced over, half expecting to see another one of her cousins arriving.

But the man who entered was no relative of hers.

And for whatever reason, Jed Dalloway's focus seemed to land right on her face when he let the door swing closed behind him.

She felt a rush of heat in her face and quickly looked away, which only made her feel stupid. For all of Vivian Templeton's fancy fund-raisers for new libraries and such, Weaver was still a small town. Running into familiar faces in public establishments was commonplace.

A bright peal of laughter rose above the general noise of voices and jukebox music, and April glanced toward the pool tables to see Megan leaning against a young man, laughing merrily. He slid his hand down Megan's backside. April grimaced and looked away, glad that Sarah hadn't seen.

In truth, at twenty-eight, April was as close to Megan's age as she was to Sarah's. She felt for both mother and daughter.

"So what's everyone wearing to the library fundraiser?" The question came from Courtney. "I don't think my closetful of scrubs will quite cut it at a Vivian Templeton production."

The topic made April think about her grandparents. Squire and Gloria still hadn't been speaking that morning at breakfast. "It's not a formal affair, is it?" She couldn't imagine how such a thing would be particularly successful in Weaver, where a lot of folks' idea of dressing up meant washing the mud off their boots and pressing a crease into the legs of their blue jeans.

"Cocktail attire," Courtney answered, "according to the invitation."

"In other words, wear a couple sequins with the jeans," Jane suggested dryly. "I know Vivian pretty well by now. She might seem like an eccentric snob at times, but she's a lot less uptight about that sort

of thing than appears. And she knows people will
kick in money for her library project if only for
the chance to see inside her mansion." She looked
around her and muttered something under her
breath as she pushed to her feet and began clearing the empties from a nearby table to carry back
to the bar.

Jed had taken one of the few empty barstools and
despite her best efforts, April's attention kept sliding to him. He was facing away from her, which
didn't help any. It only meant some kernel of her
mind decided it was okay to study him, free from
discovery.

A ridiculous notion, of course. The man could
look up at any moment and see what was going on
behind him courtesy of the long mirror hanging on
the wall behind the bar.

Nevertheless, she continued to study him.

The wide shoulders, bowed a little. A result of
the arms he'd propped on the gleaming wooden bar
top? Or the weight of working for a man like Otis?

She looked down at her hands, more than a little
oblivious to the conversations flowing around her.

She wasn't aware of any plan to stand until she
found herself on her feet. But there she was, skirt-
ing tables and making her way to the bar.

She angled between Jed and the person occupying the barstool next to him. "Buy you a drink?" It
came out more breathless than she intended.

He didn't look up at her, but looked up to face the mirror instead, catching her gaze in the reflection there. "I don't drink."

She couldn't help the way her eyebrows rose a little. He had a squat glass sitting in front of him, half-filled with amber liquid, and when she lifted it and sniffed, she knew it was scotch. "Okay." She set the glass precisely where it had been. "Buy you a coffee, instead?"

He finally shifted, looking at her straight on with those dark, chocolate eyes.

For no reason whatsoever, her mouth suddenly felt dry.

"You won't get to Otis through me."

"Sometimes the offer of a coffee is just a coffee, Jed."

"What happened to Mr. Dalloway?"

She glanced around the bar. "I don't know." The woman on the barstool beside him shifted, forcing April to shift, as well. Her shoulder brushed accidentally against Jed's before she managed to scoot back a few inches. "It's Friday night. The mister and miss stuff can come back out on Monday morning."

His lips actually stretched into a semblance of a smile. Just enough to make something unfamiliar inside her flitter around.

He turned slightly, and his thigh brushed against her leg. Only *he* didn't scoot back.

"The gesture's appreciated," he finally said.

"Miss Reed." He twisted on the barstool again. No longer touching.

That flittering fizzled and sank.

She managed a smile but could see by her own reflection in the mirror that it looked just as tight as it felt.

She looked down at his seemingly untouched glass of whisky. "Enjoy your—" she turned her palm upward "—whatever, then. Jed."

She skirted the crowd that had been thickening and returned to her seat only to find that three more relatives had joined their group.

She pushed cheerfulness into her voice. "Definitely turning out to be ladies' night," she said as she sat back down after exchanging quick hugs with them all.

"Hey." Nick, Lucy's stepson, tossed a balled-up napkin toward her. "What about me? I pee standing up."

April grinned, managing to push off the worst of her Jed-lag. "Charming as always, Nick."

He flashed a dimple and tilted his bottle of beer in her direction.

She leaned toward him. Of all of her cousins, he was the closest to her in age. "Rumor has it you're romancing Weaver's newest billionaire widow."

He looked only vaguely chagrined. "Vivian Templeton is too much for any sane man to take on. Young or old."

She laughed. "Congratulations, though. I hear you're working on the big library project."

He nodded. "I had to promise Dad the moon for him to give it to me. After working with her for the past few months, I'd steal the moon just to give the project back to him."

"She's that hard to work with?"

"Let's just say she's…different." He held up his palms. "She wants the Taj Mahal. Has me work up something." His right hand dipped and his left rose like a scale. "Then practicality strikes. Has me changing it all again. Back and forth. Up and down. Every time we meet. Extravagance one day. Then the next it's 'Dear Arthur' and she backtracks all over hell and back again."

"Ah, *Dear Arthur*." Jane had returned with another tray of drinks.

April lifted her brows. "Who is Arthur?"

"Vivian's last husband and according to her, the great love of her life. Unlike all the rest of her husbands, he was a regular guy. Didn't have money, and evidently being with him taught Vivian the error of her ways. Since he died, she's been trying to right all the wrongs of her life. I think she's afraid if she doesn't she won't be joining him."

April frowned. "Morbid."

"Not from Vivian's perspective. Until Arthur, she had all the money in the world, but little happiness. She's outlived all four of her husbands. The oldest of her sons died when he was a young man. She's been estranged from her other two since they were old enough to get away, and she's spent the last several years trying to restore a relationship with them. Not having much success, I'm afraid. All of her grandchildren get on with her, but her own sons still don't want anything to do with her."

So Squire wasn't the only one who wasn't in a forgiving mood when it came to Vivian. "She sounds…interesting."

Jane chuckled. "I think she's pretty entertaining, actually. She's trying to be a better person. Personally, I think that's something to admire."

"You don't have to work with her," Nick said with feeling.

"Hey." Megan had left the pool tables momentarily. "What time is Easter dinner over at Uncle Jefferson's?"

"Two o'clock." The answer was more a chorus of responses. The whole family was going to be there.

Megan huffed. "Why couldn't they just do it right after church? It's gonna take up the whole day."

"It's Easter," Sarah reminded evenly. "It's a time for family." Her gaze traveled past her daughter. "Your new friends can wait."

The young woman rolled her eyes and turned on her heel, sashaying back to the pool tables.

Sarah sighed noisily.

"April, I imagine Kenneth will be happy when

you get back to Denver." That was from Lucy in an obvious attempt to change the focus.

"Don't think so," she answered absently. Jed had moved away from the bar and was making his way around the tables. And that flittering inside her re-appeared. "He was getting too serious for me. We broke up a few weeks ago." Her eyes caught on Jed's face but he did nothing more than glance her way as he passed right by, going out the exit.

"Know him?"

April looked from the door swinging closed to Jane. "Sorry?"

"Do you know Jed?"

"Do you?"

"He comes in now and then. More often this time of year. You know how the winter gets to people."

April waited, sure there was more. "And?"

Jane shrugged. "And nothing. He lives up on the Rambling. Know he isn't a drinker. Orders a dou-ble. Doesn't drink a drop. That's about it. He's not very talkative."

"I heard he's from Chicago," someone offered.

"Thought it was Atlanta," someone else said.

"It doesn't matter to me where he comes from," April said. She looked beyond Nick's shoulder to-ward the exit. "As long as he doesn't get in my way."

"What does my beloved ex plan to do with the mountain if he succeeds?"

April lifted her hands. "You know Gage. Make use of as much of the mountain as he can."

"Well, at least we can trust him to be responsible with it," Jane said.

"If he gets it," April cautioned. "Right now, it's not exactly looking likely. I've tried twice to meet with Mr. Lambert and haven't managed it yet. Parked myself right on his front porch for an hour this afternoon but he never answered the door."

"He's a stubborn one all right," Courtney said.

Surprised, April looked down the table. "You've met him?"

Courtney nodded. "Once." But she didn't say anything more. April could only assume it had something to do with the old man's health. Her cousin was a nurse at the hospital, after all.

"So what happened with Kenneth?"

April looked at Nick. It was absurdly difficult pulling her thoughts away from Jed and Otis. "Kenneth? Right. Yeah. He proposed. We broke up." She suddenly pushed out of her chair. "I'll be back."

She grabbed her jacket and hurried out the door. It was already dark outside but the old-fashioned lampposts lining Main gave enough light to see along the street. She didn't see Jed, though. Not when she walked to the end of the building. Then back again.

Disappointed, she sank down on the iron bench outside of the grill and slowly pulled on her jacket.

She exhaled deeply and stretched out her legs, crossing her boots at the ankle. From inside the bar behind her, she could hear the faint pulse of country music. From the dusty pickup truck driving slowly down the street, she could hear the louder pulse of classic rock. She looked in the opposite direction and could see the mountainous peak of the Rambling, a dark shadow against the sky.

"What are you really doing up there, Otis? Is it just a mistake? Or some game you're playing?"

"It's no game."

She jerked, sitting upright. "Jed. Where'd you come from?"

He jerked his thumb and she looked across the street.

"The park?"

"Is that surprising for some reason?"

She pressed her lips together. Shook her head while she curled her fingers around the cold metal seat beneath her. "It's a nice park. The town square," she finally said. "I had my first kiss under the gazebo in the park when I was thirteen."

His only response was to tuck the tips of his fingers in the front pockets of his jeans.

She let out a breath, feeling idiotic. "I don't know why I said that."

"Is it true?"

"Yes."

"Who was the kisser?"

"Just a boy."

"Kenneth?"

She gaped. "Your hearing must be very good."

His lips compressed and he looked across the street toward the park and the gazebo that was a shadowy monolith in its own smaller way. "First girl I kissed was named Tanya."

The name itself wasn't what shocked her. The fact that he'd offered the information at all was.

She moistened her lips. "Um…his name was Scotty. Scott. He was a friend from summer camp."

"And Kenneth?"

She narrowed her eyes, studying his face. His eyebrows were dark and level. The equally dark eyes were impossible to read. He had a small white scar near the corner of his unsmiling mouth. And as usual, he seemed impervious to the cold air, wearing merely a long-sleeved T-shirt with his jeans while everyone else wore jackets and thick sweaters.

"That's actually none of your business," she finally said. "Are you impervious to the cold? It's freezing out here."

"It'll get colder. Storm is coming."

"That's not an answer."

He shrugged.

She exhaled, struggling against impatience. "Is the reason your boss hasn't met with me because he's too sick? Frail?"

"That's actually none of *your* business."

"A deal with Stanton might help him."

Jed just looked at her and she felt that weird fluttering start up again. "You know," she added hurriedly. "We're talking significant money. That goes a long way for treatments. Or medicine. Whatever he needs."

"You think he doesn't know that?"

She swallowed and rubbed her palms down the front of her jeans as she rose. Remaining seated while he stood was just too much of a disadvantage. "I don't know what he knows, do I? Having not had an opportunity to actually speak with him." She crossed her arms and eyed him suspiciously. "Are you preventing him from having visitors?"

He gave a snort that sounded genuinely amused. "You seem to be under the delusion that I can control anything where Otis is concerned. The man does what he wants, Miss Reed."

She spread her arms. "Oh, come on. It's still Friday evening. Can't we dispense with that? I mean, you know my romantic history now," she said lightly. "I know yours."

His dark eyes seemed to go even darker. "No." He pulled his fingers from his pockets. "You don't." He started to walk away but stopped after a few feet. "Come tomorrow around three." His voice was low. Gruff. "I'll see what I can do."

She nodded, because she was too surprised to actually get out a word.

Then, he was gone, disappearing around the corner of Colbys.

She ought to feel some sense of success. But all she felt was bewildered.

"Hey, April." Nick stuck his head out of the door. "You all right?"

She nodded. "Needed some fresh air."

He looked concerned. "You rushed out after I mentioned Kenneth." He made a face. "And all that. I didn't mean to upset you."

"I'm not upset."

He was obviously unconvinced. "You're sure?"

She tucked her arm through his. "Honestly."

"Then come back in. I'm feeling outnumbered by females."

"You know, I *am* a female, too."

"Eh." Nick made a face. "I s'pose."

"Like I said. Charming as ever, Nick."

"That's me. Nick Charming."

She laughed and headed back into the warm, bustling bar, determined to leave thoughts of Jed Not-Charming out in the cold where he belonged.

Chapter Four

"She won't come," Otis said. "Rain's on the way. Only fools would drive up in the rain."

Jed stirred up sparks in the woodstove and tossed in another log. He shut the door and adjusted the air intake to make sure the flame took. Just because he always ran hot, didn't mean Otis did, and the woodstove was the only source of heat in the cabin.

"Sick o' winter," he muttered, straightening from his crouch.

Otis laughed, though it was at least 70 percent cough. "You picked a bad place to live then," he wheezed. "In a place where winter can use up three of the four seasons."

"Didn't pick Wyoming." He shoved his fingers

through his hair and rolled up his sleeves as he moved to the window. "Picked me, if you remember." More accurately, Otis had picked him.

Literally off the floor of a bar in Texas. Out of the bottle and the drugs. Away from anything and everything that Jed had used to forget the past. To forget everything and everyone he'd lost.

If it weren't for Otis, Jed would probably be dead. Or still wishing he were.

He still kept the past at bay. Now he just did it working a small herd of cattle on the side of a mountain, where one misstep could be the difference between life and death.

The thick clouds hanging around the mountain obscured the view of the town far below. Visibility driving up there would be particularly bad.

He'd told her to come at three because that was usually the time that Otis was awake between naps. When he'd have enough energy and appetite to swallow down some stew or, if it was a really good day, some eggs or even a few bites of steak.

It was only two o'clock now. He hoped to hell the redhead had the good sense not to come up the mountain. Not in this weather.

He looked over at Otis. He doubted the man had ever been built like a bear. More like a wily fox. In the five years since Jed had been with him, the fox had withered. Weakened.

The wily, though?

Jed wasn't putting any bets on that trait diminishing at all.

"What did you do with that business card she left the other day?"

"Tossed it."

Jed gave him a look.

Otis rubbed his hand over the sparse white whiskers sprouting unevenly over his bony jaw. "Don't recall."

He raised his eyebrow.

The old man sighed noisily. He lifted one of the library books that Jed kept him supplied with and pulled the card from inside the pages.

Jed took it and went into the kitchen. There was one phone on the mountain and it was straight out of another era. Heavy black plastic with a rotary dial and a long curly cord.

He dialed the number that April had written on the back of the business card, but the line went straight to voice mail. Common occurrence when it came to calling cell phones. Even more so when there was a storm brewing.

He didn't figure the message would ever be received, but he left one anyway. "Stay off the road in the rain."

He turned down the heat under the venison stew he'd picked up the night before from Bubba Bumble down in Weaver. The guy was a short order cook at Ruby's Diner, but he kept Jed supplied with home-cooked meals for Otis. Jed could manage scrambled eggs and standard meat and potatoes, but not anything much fancier. The few times he'd tried over the years had not been successes. It was a lot easier to go to a source who knew what he was doing.

Jed had hoped the stew—something Otis used to want routinely—would be a temptation now for Otis's dwindling appetite.

He left the card sitting on the counter next to the phone and went back into the other room. Otis was slumped in his chair, book open on his lap, but his eyes were closed. Snoring slightly.

He was sleeping more and more.

Jed moved the book to the table by the chair and Otis didn't stir. The fire was burning well so he adjusted the intake, then snapped his fingers at the dog.

Samson uncurled and shook himself, then followed Jed out of the room and back into the kitchen. Aside from the kitchen and living area, there was a single bathroom and a single bedroom and the entirety of the whole place could have fit into the master bedroom that Jed once shared with Tanya.

He knew why she kept sneaking into his thoughts.

It was like that every spring. After eight years, the memories ought to have dulled. After eight years, he'd given up thinking that they would.

Samson followed him out the back door and his ears perked up. The shepherd mix took off running, but Jed didn't worry about him. The dog had been with Otis longer than Jed had.

He crossed to the shack that had been his home ever since Otis had come into his life. Otis told him it had originally been a potting shed for his mother. Apparently the concession on his father's part hadn't been enough to tempt her to stay on the mountain, where life was just too damn hard.

Until Jed came along, the structure had mostly been used to shelter calves when necessary.

Jed had shared the space with more than one orphaned calf in the years he'd been there. But he'd made a few changes.

He had a bed on one side of the room. An efficiency kitchen on the other, where the potting bench had once stood. The bathroom was in one closet, his clothes in the other. His only indulgence where modern technology was concerned was the radio that ran under any circumstances. If the electricity went, if the batteries went, if the sunshine went, it would run by hand crank.

Besides the radio, the appliances—stove, tiny fridge, water heater—all ran on propane. The woodstove was similar to the one that Otis had, and could heat the tiny space for a whole day on a single piece of wood. He had one lamp, a stack of his own dog-eared library books and a padded bed for Samson when the dog chose to sleep in the shack rather than the cabin.

Ten, fifteen years ago, if anyone had suggested there'd come a time when Jed Dalloway would be content with such a simple, meager existence, they'd have been laughed out of Chicago. And Jed would have been laughing hardest.

Even though the wind was sharp, he left the door open to clear the air inside the shack while he stuck his metal coffeepot on a lit burner. The coffee inside was just starting to gurgle when he smelled the rain beginning to fall.

He moved to stand in the doorway. The shack was situated somewhat higher than the cabin, which meant that Jed's view off the mountain wasn't entirely blocked. Not that he could see anything anyway with the clouds lying over every surface like a wet blanket.

He inhaled deeply. Unlike Otis, his lungs worked fine.

The thought was depressing and he turned back to the stove. The days of coffeehouses and designer grinds were long over. Now his coffee came from a can he opened with a can opener and he'd reheat the boiled stuff until it was gone and then he'd start again.

He turned off the flame and filled a thick white mug with the near-black brew. He'd even mastered the knack of pouring without ending up with a layer of grounds in the bottom of his mug.

He was heading toward the threadbare recliner next to the lamp when he heard Samson bark.

Sighing, he swallowed a swig of burning, bitter coffee before setting the mug aside and heading out into the rain to investigate.

The dog barked if a cow got too far afield or if a hungry predator got too far infield. Other than those reasons, the dog kept to threatening growls and a general tendency of ignoring everyone's plans but his own.

A more perfect match for Otis didn't exist.

The rain was more spit than shower as Jed followed the barking, but still, by the time he found the dog, he was pretty wet.

No less wet than the redhead, who was standing with her back to one of the fallen boulders where the dog had her pinned.

"Samson," Jed called sharply, and the dog fell back, landing on his haunches. He walked past him toward April. "You're either crazy or desperate," he said flatly. "Why on earth did you drive up that road with a storm coming?"

Her chin came up. "I live in Colorado," she said crisply. "We have storms there, too."

"Yeah, well, this is the side of a freakin' mountain and it's pretty damn easy to go off the edge." His words were drowned out by the sharp crack of thunder. He gestured sharply. "Come on." There was no way she could drive back down the treacherous road now.

She started forward, carrying her briefcase under

one arm and some sort of padded carrier in the other, giving the dog a wide berth.

He sighed impatiently and relieved her of both. "Samson won't hurt you. Watch your step. Rocks are constantly rolling and they're slick to boot. Don't want to turn an ankle." Or worse.

He led the way to the cabin. He had no desire to have her in his shack. She was already memorable enough.

They went in through the back into the kitchen. "Sit down," he told her, dumping her stuff on the small table. "I'll get you some towels."

She swiped her hand over her hair, slicking it back from her face. Her eyes, blue to start with, were deep and clear like sapphire. "Thank you."

Otis was still sleeping. Jed didn't disturb him when he retrieved the towels from the dryer wedged into the bathroom and went back into the kitchen. April'd pulled off her coat to reveal a white shirt that was soaked through.

"Looks like you wasted your money on that coat." He dumped the towels on the counter, keeping the smallest one for himself. They were old. Thin. But they'd do the job. He dashed it over his head and face.

"To be fair, its main selling point besides inexpensiveness was warmth." She plucked at her blouse, which at least meant he couldn't so clearly see the lacy outline of her bra beneath, and leaned to one side to rub her hair between the folds of a towel. "Not water resistance." She sounded breathless. "This is just not how I pictured this afternoon going."

"You didn't picture the rainstorm?"

She straightened and draped the towel around her shoulders like a cape. Her hair was messy. Tousled. And her sapphire eyes were snapping. "What a sense of humor you have." Her slender fingers flicked over the water-spotted leather briefcase. "I suppose Mr. Lambert still isn't available, either."

Jed held his finger to his lips. "Listen."

Her eyebrows pulled together, creating a line in her otherwise perfectly smooth face. He wasn't entirely sure the red hair didn't come out of a bottle, because she didn't have a single freckle on her strikingly beautiful face. "Listen to what?"

"Shh."

She pressed her lips together. A faint dimple appeared in her slightly pointed chin.

Then she obviously heard it.

Otis's snoring.

Her frown cleared. Her lips relaxed.

"I'm not waking him up," he said in a low voice.

She looked insulted. "Did I ask you to?" She lifted the corners of the towel around her shoulders again and rubbed at her hair. "The opinion you have of me must be really spectacular," she murmured.

It was just as well she couldn't know what his thoughts were where she was concerned. His emotions had died along with Tanya and the babies, but that didn't mean everything else about him had died.

"Here." She stopped messing with her hair to mess with the padded carrier. "Courtesy of my grandmother." She slid out a foil-covered rectangular glass pan. "Strawberry-rhubarb cobbler. She seems to think a couple of men on their own would be in need."

That was an appetite he *could* appease.

"Thanks." He controlled the urge to get out a fork right then and there. "Otis will enjoy it."

"And you?"

He smiled slightly. "Maybe."

She rolled her eyes a little and moved the pan from the table to sit it on top of the cold stove. "It's still a little warm." She whipped off the foil and gave him a look. "In case that's of interest."

"Subtle." He opened a drawer and got a fork. Remembering that he wasn't entirely a caveman, he got out small plates, as well. "You?"

"Oh God no. I hate rhubarb."

"Sacrilege."

She smiled and quietly slid out one of the table chairs to sit.

He scooped up a healthy portion of the dessert. She was right. It was still warm.

He pounded down half of it standing right there beside the stove before he could speak. "My compliments to your grandmother." He set the plate and fork on the table and sat down across from her.

She was plucking at her wet blouse again.

He ground his molars together for a second, and then exhaled. He got up and went back to the bathroom. He pulled open the dryer and shuffled his hand inside until he found a suitable shirt and a pair of sweatpants.

He took them back to her. "Here." He dropped them in her lap. "Bathroom's through there." He jabbed his thumb. "Try not to wake up Otis while you're at it."

Her lips parted. He could read the thoughts forming on her face.

"You're not leaving anytime soon," he said. "It's not safe. Not until the clouds lift at least. Considering the sound of the rain—" He didn't bother finishing because the rain was an audible drumroll on the roof.

She still debated it. Silently. But then she stood, the clothes bundled at her waist. "Through there?" She nodded toward the doorway.

There was no danger of her getting lost. "Yup."

She sucked in her pale pink lower lip, then left the kitchen. She was walking gingerly, obviously being careful to be quiet.

He let out a long breath, rubbing his hand down his face when she was gone.

* * *

The faded black T-shirt hung halfway down her thighs and she had to roll up the long sleeves. The ugly green sweatpants were too long too, even after she folded over the waistband twice. But they were clean and warm. And far preferable to her wet jeans and cotton shirt.

The washer and dryer were right there, jammed against the wall next to the sink and the door to the dryer was ajar. She peeked inside. Heart pounding as if she were sneaking around doing something she shouldn't, she pulled out the mound of clothes inside the dryer and pushed her wet things inside. A quick twist of the dial and the dryer began softly tumbling. Then, because of that guilty feeling, she started to shake out the items she'd removed, thinking that she ought to at least fold them.

The theory worked well enough through three long-sleeved shirts and two short-sleeved. Obviously Jed's. All soft and faded from who knew how many washings. When she reached a pair of gray boxer briefs, however, theories burst in a puff and she dropped the underwear like a hot potato. Feeling flushed, she left the stack of folded shirts on top of whatever remained and, boots in hand, padded quickly back to the kitchen.

She couldn't avoid seeing the emaciated, white-haired man slumped in a rocking chair near the woodstove as she went. But he was facing away from her and she was glad.

. There just seemed something wrong about being there while he slept, unaware that she was even under his roof. It felt unfair. To him.

In the kitchen once more, she pulled the swinging door shut, then sat down across from Jed. His plate was empty.

"I don't feel right being here," she told him quietly. "Not like this."

He lifted a brow. "Because?"

She exhaled. "Because, because I don't know! Like I'm taking advantage of the situation or something. This isn't a fair negotiation."

"You need more than one party at the table for a negotiation."

"Exactly."

A muscle in his jaw flexed. It made the scar near his mouth shine more whitely. "Look." His brown eyes snared hers. "When he is awake, he's not going to negotiate. Trust me on this, April. I've tried to get him to sell for the last two years. Ever since it was obvious he wasn't going to get better."

She moistened her lips. "I know it's none of my business, but—"

"Cancer," he said succinctly. "Invasive and unstoppable."

"I'm sorry," she whispered.

He looked away. "Yeah."

His expression was so carefully blank, it was heartbreaking.

She closed her hand over his arm and felt heat center in her palm and zing right up her veins. The last thing she wanted to be was attracted to him, but pretending she wasn't was getting harder by the minute. "Jed. I know this isn't easy. Does he… Do you know if he has a will?"

"He doesn't talk about it." He was silent, and for a moment, she thought he wasn't going to say more. "Knowing him, I doubt it," he finally added.

She realized he was looking at her hand on him as he spoke, and she quickly pulled back, curling her fingers into her palm. She wondered if she should warn him that there might be a relative of Otis's. Someone who'd inherit the property if Otis really hadn't made other plans. Wondered, too, if Jed already knew.

Which just made her feel even more like some sort of circling vulture.

She rose restlessly and hitched up the sweatpants when they wanted to slip down her hips. She moved to look through the small window situated over the sink. The rain was still coming down in sheets, but she could see the two sheds she'd noticed the first day she'd come up the mountain. She didn't see the horse.

She turned and leaned back against the sink. It was an old-fashioned thing. Porcelain-covered cast iron, with drain boards attached on both sides. The kind that people nowadays paid thousands for to achieve that whole "farmhouse" look.

The stove was somewhat more modern, but still looked like it was out of the fifties. There were no true cabinets. Just open shelves on the wall and below the wooden counter. A threadbare stretch of beige fabric hung in front of the ones below, but it was pushed aside, as if it were a nuisance, but not a big enough one to just take it down altogether.

She looked up from the messy collection of old bowls and foodstuffs. "How old is this cabin?"

"You'd have to ask Otis."

Old enough to be of historical value? If so, that might be one way of protecting at least the cabin, regardless of who ended up with it after Otis was gone.

She heard a chest-rattling cough from the other room and winced.

Without a word, Jed got up and pushed through the door. It swung a few times, then stilled. Despite the age of everything, those hinges were oiled and silent as could be.

It was still pouring rain, but she pushed open the back door anyway and stepped just outside. A paltry effort to allow the ailing man as much privacy as she could.

She was still standing there when Jed returned and pulled open the door behind her.

"What the hell are you doing?"

She moved past him to the table and swiped the mist of rain from her face with the towel. She opened her briefcase and pulled out the preliminary proposal that Gage had drawn up before sending her to Wyoming and set the glossy covered presentation on the table.

"Feel free to read that yourself," she invited. "Nothing in there is set in stone, obviously." She spread her hands. "Maybe most of the ranch proper could be excluded." Gage had never said such a thing, but he wasn't entirely unreasonable. "This cabin, for instance. Otis and his, ah, his assignee could remain here for as long as they wanted. Keep back enough land to run the cattle and still benefit from the sale of the rest. Whatever was in Otis's mind when he reached out to my boss? He simply needs to tell us what that is, and I believe Gage would do what he can to make it work."

Jed's face was still painfully expressionless. "Anything for the deal."

She had no answer to that. "You might like thinking otherwise, but something *is* going to happen with this land. Sooner or later. There are too many natural resources here for it to be simply ignored. At least read the proposal. I'm, um, I'm going to go now."

"You can't drive on the road in these conditions."

"I won't drive," she assured. "I can wait out the

rain in my car." She gestured at the door. "The
clouds are beginning to lift. It won't be long. And I
really don't feel right staying here. When Mr. Lambert is up to meeting, I'll come back."

"You are crazy. It's cold. Wet."

She pulled on one boot then the other, hopping
around slightly as she did so. "I have a tank full of
gas and a good car heater. I'll survive." She picked
up her wet coat and replaced the towel around her
shoulders with it. She waved her hand toward the
dessert. "Save some for Mr. Lambert. Happy…
happy Easter."

Then, before she could let common sense over-
ride the instinct for escape, she grabbed her briefcase and hurried out into the rain once more.

She was drenched and shivering all over again
by the time she made it past the wooden barriers
and the boulders.

She started her car and cranked the heater and
huddled in her seat wearing Jed's T-shirt and sweats.
Within a matter of minutes, heat had filled the interior and the windows were clouded with steam.

She thumped her head against the headrest. "Stupid, stupid, stupid."

Even though she knew it was pointless, she
pulled her cell phone out of her briefcase and tested
the signal. It was entirely flat.

She opened her contacts, selected Gage and
quickly typed in a text. Her thumb barely hesitated

before she hit Send. The message would be delivered the moment there was enough signal.

She took a deep, cleansing breath and tossed the phone back into her briefcase.

And then she waited for the rain to end.

Chapter Five

"*No. Not only no, but hell no.*"

April turned the phone to show Archer the screen and the text message she'd received from her boss.

It was Tuesday. Three days since the rainstorm.

Gage had sent the response to her on Sunday. She'd received it right in the middle of Easter dinner at her aunt and uncle's horse farm.

He'd ignored every attempt she'd made to reach him in the time since. When April called the office, his secretary had told her that he'd gone on a short trip.

"You've known Gage a long time," she said to Archer. "You've got to convince him I'm right."

Archer gave her a tilted smile. His green eyes

were full of a sort of biting mirth. "I give the man legal advice, doll. That's it."

She huffed disgustedly. "Don't call me doll. It's disrespectful."

"I have the utmost respect for dolls," he assured, not in the least fazed. He nodded toward her phone. "Gage obviously wants you working on this. He denied your request to be taken off the deal. Clearly. You may not think you're the right man for the job, but he does." Finished with his summation, he picked up his icy glass of beer.

Even though one of Archer's offices was in nearby Braden, they were sitting at a corner booth in Ruby's Diner because he had a court appearance with a client in Weaver later.

Through the window beside them, all vestiges of the rainstorm were gone. Easter was past and it was as if spring had suddenly sprung. Nearly an entire month late, according to the calendar, but who was counting?

Temperatures had suddenly warmed enough to melt away the last bits of snow. Flowers were already poking up their cheerful, colorful heads. Grass was greening. Trees were budding.

The only flies in the ointment were her grandparents still barely speaking and April's inability to both quit the assignment she'd been given or succeed at it.

She rotated her own glass of soda between her

fingers. "I should have stuck to marketing," she said. "That's how I started working for Stanton in the first place, you know. I was doing PR for Huffington's expansion in Colorado Springs. Stanton was a partner on the project."

Archer laughed. "He hired you away from your dad?"

She nodded, almost smiling at the memory. Her dad hadn't been upset about her branching out beyond the family fold; he'd done the same himself. But he'd been somewhat put out having to explain to his wife that their daughter was moving away to Denver. "It doesn't matter how many other projects I've worked on. I'm obviously not cut out for bringing in deals like this."

"Not all deals involve situations like this," Archer reminded. "And I thought you were all about the 'never give up' tradition."

"It's easy to say," she muttered. "Not so easy to do."

"Yeah, well." He shifted and pulled a folder from the briefcase sitting on the bench beside him. "Maybe this'll help change your mind."

He flipped open the folder on the Formica tabletop and turned it so it was facing her. He tapped the report inside. "Louis Snead. Otis Lambert's only living relative. At least that we could find. He's a distant cousin. Lives in Texas. Forty-seven years old. No career to speak of. Last job was selling used cars in a buy-here, pay-here lot. Before that, he spent a couple years at a phone bank. Defaulted on a mortgage a good ten years ago. Been unemployed for several months and he's in debt up to his pornesque mustache."

"I take it you're trying to tell me he'd jump at the possibility of inheriting the Rambling."

"I guarantee he's not interested in taking over running the ranch. Judging by his past, he'll turn everything for a quick sale. Of course, that's only if Lambert dies without a will that instructs otherwise."

"And we don't know if he has one." She gathered up a hopeful tone. "You think Snead would deal with Stanton Development?"

"I think Snead will deal with whoever gets to him first with cash money," Archer said. "Look. I'm a fan of the way Gage operates. But as successful as he is, there are deeper pockets out there. And frankly, it's not going to be long before there are more developers than just you lining up at the scent." He spread his hands. "The minerals and the water? The State itself has a vested interest in Rambling Mountain. They'll be part of the equation if there's any way they can be. Maybe Snead would care about the way the land is handled. Without actually talking to the guy, it's all speculation."

He rested his arm on the table and leaned toward her. "Considering Lambert's situation, if you're really interested in protecting his interests, the best way to do that is to make sure Stanton Development is first in line."

"He doesn't want to meet with *me*! I've tried twice." She didn't count the last time, during the rainstorm. Jed may have suggested the time for the meeting, but he'd never expected her to drive up the mountain when the storm was descending. She felt certain that would have been Otis's assumption, as well.

If the old man hadn't been sleeping, she would probably have never made it inside the cabin, rainstorm or not.

"I don't know what to do to convince him to see me," she said, which just earned her a steady look from Archer.

She let out an impatient huff. "Fine. I know. I try again."

He gave her a wink. "There you go, doll."

She huffed again and rolled her eyes.

His smile merely widened.

The next morning, April drove up the mountain for the fourth time. The black T-shirt and sweatpants were folded on the passenger seat, freshly laundered. She also had a plastic container of leftover glazed ham from the family's Easter meal three days before.

The sky was as blue as a robin's egg and as she drove up the winding road it was hard not to get distracted by the spectacular view. She was becoming so familiar with the road that she knew when to slow for the hidden curves and when she could speed up through a straightaway. She knew where to avoid the potholes and where to watch for fresh slides of rock.

What she wasn't familiar with, however, was the sight of a man sitting directly on the edge of the drop-off about half a mile below the location of the barricade.

He was old. Wizened. And leaning so far forward that it looked as though he might simply roll off, right into the sky.

Feeling like her nerves were shooting straight out the top of her head, she swerved to a stop and shut off the engine. There was enough room for one car on the road, but not two, and simply walking beside the car toward the man was enough to make her feel slightly queasy. "Mr. Lambert?" The man couldn't possibly be anyone else. "Mr. Lambert, are you all right?"

His head turned and his eyes squinted at her from a pallid, lined face. "If I planned to do a header off the edge, I'd a' done it by now. I wanna be buried on my mountain. Not at the base of it down there."

His voice was stronger than his appearance suggested. But the assurance was also followed by a racking cough that had her breaking into a jog to close the last several feet.

She reached him, extending a hand but he just waved her off, yanking a blue folded bandanna out of his jacket to hold to his mouth. Beneath the jacket, she could see his thin shoulders jerk before the coughing finally subsided.

He might not intend to jump, but that terrible cough was enough to knock anyone off their feet, much less a weak old man from his precarious perch.

She pressed her hand against her thumping heart and gingerly knelt on the road near him. "Why don't I drive you back up closer to the house?" Better yet, drive him straight to the hospital, because he looked like he belonged in a hospital bed. She knew better than to make that suggestion, though.

"Walked down on my own steam," he said crankily. "I can walk back up on it, too."

She shifted until she was sitting on her rear, legs crossed like a school kid. She really didn't like being so close to the edge and the jagged rocks below. "Not sure I could do that from here," she admitted. "I'm April Reed."

"I know who you are." He peered at her with faded blue eyes. "Owe you my apology, too."

Everything she'd ever heard about the man hadn't led her to think he was an apologizing sort. "Not at—"

He cut her off with the wave of a gnarled hand. "You make a lot of these kind of deals?"

She wasn't going to lie. "This would be my first."

"I ain't selling," he said bluntly. "Was never my intention to waste your time, though. Entertainin' as it's been seeing ol' Jed twist a little."

"Twist?" It seemed a cold way to treat the man who was caring for him. And there was no doubt that Jed cared about Otis.

"Where you're concerned," he said.

She frowned, moistening her lips. "I can't imagine what you mean."

"Then you're not as smart as you look, girl. I've known Jed five years now. That man's got an eye for you."

Her stomach fluttered and she pressed her lips together. This was getting way, way off track. She steered it back. "Coming to Weaver is never a waste of time for me."

He pocketed the bandanna. "I know you got kin here. Ain't selling to your grandpa, either."

"Well, I guess if you had been going to sell anything to Squire, you could have done so by now."

His thin lips twisted in what she supposed was a smile.

A bird flew past, its long, tapered wings flapping elegantly. They both watched it circle and dip, then rise again and fly out of sight.

It felt almost holy, sitting there looking at the magnificence spread before them. Some would want to share it. Some, like him, obviously wanted to hold it close. She could actually understand both ways of thinking.

"It is really beautiful here, Mr. Lambert. I can understand why you've never wanted it changed in all these years. If that's something you're concerned about, Stanton Development could make sure it's preserved the way you want."

He squinted even more. "When I called that company o' yours, I expected your boss to come."

"Gage." She couldn't keep the surprise out of her voice. "I'm sorry he didn't realize that. I'm sure he would have never sent me if he had. If that's why you've changed your mind about—"

"Haven't changed my mind about nothin'."

She couldn't help feeling stymied. "Mr. Lambert, why *did* you contact Stanton Development, then? If not because you know about our policies of responsible development and—"

"I knew your boss's mama, once upon a time."

Her words dried as her mind caught up.

"Althea Stanton," he murmured. "Helluva woman. Was real sorry to hear she died a while back." His attention was still trained out beyond the mountainside. "Was curious about her son."

April studied his profile while her mind ticked busily. Gage's mother had died before April had started working for him, but he still had a framed photo of her in his Denver office. She knew he had a younger brother somewhere and that was it. "He's a good man, Mr. Lambert. Doing business with him—"

Otis gestured yet again. More impatiently. "I got plans of my own for the Rambling."

"Do they involve your cousin? Mr. Snead?"

Otis snorted, setting off another coughing fit. "Girl, do you think I'm stupid?" he asked when his shoulders stopped shaking.

"Then have you shared your plans with anyone?"

He gave a cackle of a laugh. "Got me a sweet little will."

Relief swept through her. Not because she believed the presence of a will helped Stanton's cause in any way. If anything, it most likely complicated it. But a will would make things simpler for everyone Otis left behind.

For Jed.

As if her thoughts had conjured the man, she spotted him and that scary dog heading on foot down the road toward them.

She quickly pushed to her feet and brushed off the seat of her pants. "I won't take up more of your time, Mr. Lambert." She extended her hand to him. "I hope things turn out well for you." It seemed like such a paltry thing to say in light of his health. "I know my grandfather would want me to tell you that if you should need anything—"

He let out that crack of a laugh again. "Your grandpa is just gonna wanna know if he's finally getting a chance at that pass of land he's wanted for fifty years."

Since he was probably right, she couldn't make herself deny it. "People like you and Squire are the heart of this land, Mr. Lambert. I can promise you. Like respects like."

He made a sound and finally took her hand. Giving it more of a shaking squeeze than an actual shake. "Be careful on the road," he said a little gruffly.

Her eyes suddenly burned. "I will. You, too."

Then he noticed Jed and the dog approaching and she went to her car to retrieve the clothes and the container of ham.

She met Jed halfway and his fingers brushed hers as she handed everything over to him. "Thank you." Her voice sounded thick and she quickly turned away, jogging back to her car before she made a total ass out of herself.

She got behind the wheel, started the engine and crept past them, because she had to go farther up the road before there was a space wide enough for her to turn around.

When she'd done so and passed the two men again, Otis was standing, obviously leaning against Jed as they slowly headed back up the mountain road.

Jed's head turned and he watched her as she passed.

She drove back down to Weaver with Otis's words circling in her mind.

That man's got an eye for you.

* * *

"So your boss wants you to stay here." Piper read the text message on April's phone before handing it back. "Explain to me again why that's a bad thing?"

April propped her elbow on the bar and threaded her fingers through her hair. "He still thinks I'm going to be able to bring in a deal on Rambling Mountain. It's not going to happen." And she still hadn't been able to get the annoying man to return her calls.

Now it was Friday night already and she was having appetizers with Piper at Colbys.

"Okay, so let's not talk about work anymore."

"Fine. Want to talk about my grandparents still not speaking? Let me tell you. Last Sunday's Easter dinner was a *real* delight."

Piper made a face. "Want to talk about my home-room class? Ben Scalise and Lucas Taggart glued all the school desks shut with construction adhesive this morning before the bell. Principal Pope was so mad he wanted to expel them both. They're suspended for a week, and Lord only knows what sort of punishment they'll get as a means of restitution."

"Ouch."

"And that was just the *start* of my day," Piper said. She drained her lemon-drop martini and gestured to the bartender. Jane wasn't pulling duty that night. Instead, there was a lanky young man April didn't know serving up the drinks. "How is it that

I studied theater in college and end up a teacher and you study marketing and end up a real estate developer?"

"I'm not a developer. Gage Stanton is." She toyed with her own glass, still half-full, and thought about the drink that Jed had ordered but not touched. "You and I would be better off at a yoga class tonight or something. Moods we're in? Liquor and happy hour appetizers are probably not the wisest course."

"I'm sure you're right, but that just sounds like way too much work." Piper waved at the bartender again. "Christian's new," she said from the side of her mouth. Then she spun around on her seat until her back was to the bar top. "What're you wearing to the fund-raiser tomorrow?"

"I dunno." She'd left her favorite black jeans in Otis Lambert's dryer up on the mountain. She could have worn them with a dressy blouse. She hadn't brought a lot of options for this trip. "I suppose I'll borrow something. You?"

"Oh, I bought a dress that I can't really afford."

April chuckled. "Good for you." She pushed away from the bar. "I'm hitting the ladies. Order another round if you ever get the bartender's attention. If we're going to drown our week's stresses, let's do it right. We don't even have to worry about driving home. Weaver might not have rideshare services yet, but I have a connection with the sheriff's department." She grinned. "Pretty sure we can get courtesy rides."

"Ooh, I love connections." Piper crossed her ankles and swung her legs back and forth.

April worked her way through the Friday night crowd to the restrooms. She had to wait in line to take her turn and when she headed back to her place at the bar, she stopped short at the familiar figure occupying her stool next to Piper.

Her stomach sank, making her regret the number of spicy wings she'd consumed.

She rejoined Piper, who was giving her an arch look, and managed to find a friendly expression from somewhere. "Kenneth," she greeted. "What an…interesting coincidence."

He hopped off the stool, looking as tall and urbane as he always did in a perfectly fitted sport coat over his studiously casual striped shirt and narrow trousers. He clasped her hands in his. "Sweetheart." Before she could evade it, he was pressing a kiss on her lips.

His kiss wasn't unpleasant. Nothing about Kenneth had ever been unpleasant, except his unexpected seriousness. But neither did a simple brush of his hand send heat whipping through her veins.

She wasn't inclined to make a scene, but she was glad when he finally lifted his head, saving her the trouble of digging her heel into his foot.

She pulled back as far as his hands allowed her. "What are you doing here, Kenneth?"

"You had to know I'd come after you, sweetheart."

She shook her head. "No. We broke up weeks ago."

He slid his hand along her cheek. "Absence makes the heart fonder and all that. Doesn't every girl want a man to chase after her?"

Piper was watching the exchange with interest. April gave her a sideways look and her friend just lifted her shoulders.

Big help *she* was.

April looked up at Kenneth's face. Classically handsome. Impossibly neat, well-trimmed beard. The man even smelled good. On paper, that should have made him a perfect match. "How did you even know I was here?"

"Your office, of course." He rubbed his hands up and down her arms.

Interesting that her office couldn't share Gage's whereabouts with her, yet they felt free to share hers with a former boyfriend.

"And *here* tonight?"

"Your grandma." He smiled easily, either far more obtuse than she'd ever known or he was being deliberately oblivious. "Why don't we go somewhere quieter?"

"To do what? Kenneth, I thought I was clear. I'm sorry you've come, but—" A glimpse in the mirror on the wall above the bar caught her attention and she broke off.

She turned to see the source of that reflection and her eyes collided with Jed's where he stood just a few feet away. In contrast to Kenneth's fashion sense, Jed wore ancient blue jeans and worn-down cowboy boots. His T-shirt was faded from washings rather than design. She knew, because she was pretty sure she'd folded the one he wore when she'd pulled it from Otis Lambert's dryer. His hair was short and tousled and the only scent he carried was soap and mountain air.

She knew that, too, because she hadn't been able to get it out of her head.

"But there's, well, you see, there's—"

"Someone else?" Kenneth's voice was incredulous.

She pulled away from him, latching onto the excuse and nodding quickly. "Yes."

Without stopping to consider the wisdom of her actions, she went to Jed and slipped her arm through his, stretching up to brush her lips against his hard cheek. Even prepared for it, the sensation that rippled through her was more quake than ripple. "You're late," she said loud enough for Kenneth.

Thankfully, Jed didn't jerk back from her, which he could well have done. But the slow hand that traveled up the small of her back was wholly unexpected. The rough knit of her turtleneck provided no protection at all from the sensation. And the way he lifted his eyebrow slightly, it was as if he knew it.

"Sorry," he murmured, and then his mouth grazed over hers.

Half a kiss.

Less than that.

It still felt like the earth shifted under her feet.

Maybe he knew that, too, because his arm came around her shoulders, holding her close. Close enough to feel the heat that radiated from him. The man was like a furnace and for a woman who was often chilly, it was a cherry on the sundae.

"Going to introduce me to your friends?" His voice was deep. Tone intimate.

She moistened her lips, tearing her gaze from his with difficulty before looking toward Piper.

Her friend's eyes were wide.

Her heart felt like it was ready to explode out of her chest. "Jed, this is Piper Madison. Friends forever. Past, present, future. And this is, ah—"

"The old boyfriend," Jed finished. "Kenneth, I assume." He stuck out his big, calloused, square hand. "No hard feelings, man."

Kenneth looked considerably more bewildered than Piper. Obviously reluctant, he finally shook Jed's hand. "You know about me. But I don't know about you."

Jed's lips lifted in a semblance of a smile that made the hairs on the back of April's neck stand up like they'd done the first time she'd seen Samson on her first trip up the mountain. "Kind of how it goes, Ken," he said casually.

He looked past them and garnered the elusive attention of the busy bartender with a single lift of his finger. "Another round for the ladies," he said. "What about you, Ken? You look like a scotch and soda kind of guy."

Kenneth pushed his hand in his pocket. He could have been posing for a catalog. "I'll have a merlot."

Jed's half smile stayed put, but April sensed he was laughing on the inside. As if he knew that Ken never drank anything harder than beer or wine.

"You heard the man, Christian."

"And for you?"

"I'm designated driver tonight. Coffee'll do."

"You bet. Soda and coffee are free for DDs," Christian said.

"Even better." Jed's fingers were cupped around April's shoulder and the way he slowly rubbed his thumb back and forth over the point of it was entirely distracting. "So, Ken. What brings you to this neck of the woods?"

Kenneth looked from April's face to that hand on her shoulder, then back to Jed's. "Guess I took a wrong turn somewhere along the way."

Her conscience nipped. "Kenneth—"

"Happens to the best of us," Jed assured, as if they were just two guys discussing a missed golf putt.

In record speed, Christian had set up their drinks and Jed had pushed the glass of wine into Kenneth's neatly manicured fingers. With his own wrapped around the thick white coffee mug, he lifted it in a toast. "To safer travels."

Kenneth's lips were thin. He was too polite to ignore the toast, though. "Safer travels," he said evenly.

Piper suddenly hopped off her barstool and grabbed Kenneth's arm. "Come on, handsome. You look in need of a good ol' two-step."

Once again, politeness ruled. With one last look toward April, he set aside his glass and followed her friend out onto the small, yet crowded dance floor.

In their absence, awkwardness was quick to descend and April hurriedly stepped away from beneath Jed's encircling arm. "Uh, thanks." She rubbed her hands down her jeans and slid her fingertips into her back pockets. That was safer than taking her drink and pouring more alcohol on her swimming senses. "You were quick on the uptake."

He set his coffee mug next to the other drinks and she had the suspicion that he intended to escape while the escaping was good.

Only instead of turning away, his eyes looked into hers.

"Dance?"

Chapter Six

Dance?

April stared up at Jed, feeling the world around them shrink away, leaving only him at the center of a pinpoint.

His lips twisted a little at her failure to offer a coherent response, and his hand closed around hers.

Without waiting for her agreement, he tugged her onto the dance floor and then swung her into his arms. "Don't pretend you don't know how to do this." His deep voice was low against her ear.

She could hardly breathe being pressed up so closely to him. For one, there was the incredible heat of him. For another, the man had rock-hard muscles. Like he'd been hewed from the granite rocks of Rambling Mountain.

And lastly, the man could dance.

He didn't just stand there, arms around her, shuffling his worn cowboy boots an inch here, an inch there. He could really dance.

And simply keeping up with him kept her mind occupied enough that she actually forgot to feel awkward.

She forgot most everything. Including keeping track of where Kenneth and Piper were and the fact that she was going to owe her best friend big-time for helping to ease that particular situation.

When the music slowed, so did Jed.

Instead of the whirls and twirls, she ended up pressed against him. Despite herself, her hand found the back of his neck. Her head the curve in his shoulder. She could feel the imprint of his spread fingers against her spine. "Who taught you to dance?" She sounded breathless even to her own ears.

"My wife."

Everything inside her froze. She accidently stepped on his toe and her head hit his chin when she jerked it up to look at him. "You're *married*?"

As if she hadn't turned to an inflexible board, he kept on moving, more than capably keeping her moving, also. "Not anymore."

She waited, but that was it.

No explanation.

No nothing.

Which just left her with a pounding heart and every point of contact between her body and his feeling warm and tingly.

And that's when she realized that handling Kenneth would have been a much easier road.

And one that would probably be a whole lot safer.

She flexed her fingers against Jed's. "Do you always come to Colbys on Friday nights?"

"No."

"So it's just my lucky day, then?"

"Evidently."

A few more bars of music passed while she cast around for something to say. Anything to say that would adequately pave an escape without making her feel like even more of a fool. "H-how is Otis?"

His brown eyes darkened even more. "Ever Otis. What were the two of you talking about the other day on the mountain?"

"He didn't tell you?"

His hand tightened against her spine, and the space between them shrunk a little more. "Would I be asking if he had?"

Breathing evenly was beginning to take an effort. "Afraid he made a deal with me behind your back?" Otis had said Jed had been with him for five years. Maybe Jed wanted the ranch.

He didn't look unduly concerned, though. "Did you?"

"Otis's interest in Stanton Development wasn't because of the mountain."

"I could have told you that." He turned her smoothly, avoiding another couple.

Kenneth and Piper, she realized, feeling even more bemused when Piper gave her a sly wink.

"Then you *do* know why he called?"

"I didn't say that."

"I've noticed that's a habit of yours. Not saying much."

The corner of his lip quirked. "I said enough to get you out of trouble with the boyfriend. Who, by the way, is now heading off to a corner with your forever friend."

"Ex-boyfriend. Remember? And if Piper likes him, then more power to her. She could do a lot worse than Kenneth."

"Your castoff? You trying to say you don't have a jealous streak?"

"He's not my castoff! I can't help it if he wanted mo—" She shook herself. "There's nothing to be jealous about. Not when it comes to Kenneth at least." She didn't want to think very hard about the way she'd felt when Jed had said those two words… *My wife.*

She also didn't care for the way he could so easily shift her right off course. She touched her fingertip boldly to that raised white line near his mouth. "How did you get the scar?"

"Knife. Is the red real?"

Her breath seemed to stop up somewhere in the middle of her chest. *Knife?* "If you ever saw my mother, you wouldn't need to ask." Nikki Reed's hair was as vibrantly red now as it had been when April was a child.

She was vaguely aware another song had started. Laughing women were clustering all around them, stomping boots, clapping hands, sliding forward, sliding back.

Line dancing.

But he didn't move.

Nor did she.

"Otis told me he has a will."

If she hadn't been watching him closely, she would have missed the flicker deep within his dark gaze. She didn't know if it was relief or something else.

"He tell you what's in it? Where he's stashed it?"

She shook her head and moistened her lips. "Do you have a plan for yourself? For...after?"

"Until someone makes me stop, I'll keep doing what Otis brought me here to do. Keeping the cattle alive and healthy to get 'em to sale."

"It's always possible that Otis could leave the ranch to you."

He shook his head. "No."

"Why not?"

"We don't agree on what he should've done with the land."

"What's that mean?"

He just shook his head. "The only thing Otis wants from me after he's gone is to bury him on his mountain. That's as far as my plans go."

She couldn't bear it. She slid her arms around his neck and pressed her cheek to his. "I'm sorry," she whispered. "He's lucky to have you."

"It's the other way around." He closed his hands around her forearms and gently pulled them down. Let her go. "The music's stopped."

Chilled, she pushed her fingertips in her back pockets and looked down, letting her hair fall forward over her cheeks as they walked away from the dance area.

The drinks were still waiting on the bar, though when she looked for Kenneth and Piper there was no sign of them. Another couple had commandeered their barstools. Music was quickly pounding again. Garth and his friends in low places rocking through the bar.

April took one sip of her drink, but set it back down and flagged down Christian.

He had to lean toward her over the bar top to hear her.

"If my friend Piper comes back, would you tell her I left?" She pulled a bill out of her pocket and slid it to him.

He nodded and slipped the bill into the glass behind the bar with a wad of others.

She tugged her jacket free where it was still hanging on the barstool, earning an annoyed "excuse me!" look from the woman who'd taken the seat. She made sure her phone and keys were still in the pocket and started for the door.

Jed followed. "Where are you going now?"

"Home." At least to the Double-C. She pushed through the door and went outside, but stopped at the sight of snowflakes floating in the light cast off by the lampposts.

"You've been drinking."

She gave him a look. She hadn't finished even half of her first drink. She had taken one sip of the second. "Want to give me a sobriety test?" Not waiting for an answer, she pulled the front of her jacket closer together and headed down the sidewalk toward the parking spot where she'd left her car.

His footsteps followed her.

She whirled on her heel. "Oh for heaven's sake. I'm sober as a judge!"

"Good for you."

"Then what are you doing? Following me?"

"Doing the same thing as you." He held up his hand. A key dangled from it. "Home."

She swiped a snowflake from her nose and started off again. Her cheeks felt hot. Redheads' curse.

And again, his footsteps sounded behind her.

There were cars and trucks and SUVs slanted into the parking spots all the way down the block. It was reasonable that one of them was his.

"How'd you meet Loverboy?"

She flipped up her collar and quickened her step. Half a block to go. She didn't look back at him, but raised her voice so he'd hear her. "How'd your chin get sliced by a knife?"

"One of those online romances? Www-dot-getadate?"

Despite herself, her lips twitched.

She schooled her expression and shot him a look over her shoulder. "You talking about me, or the source of your knifer?"

He lifted his hand. "Hey, watch—"

Her shoulder bounced hard and she stumbled, grabbing the lamppost she'd walked into. "Oh that's just perfect." She righted her course, determined not to rub the pain in her shoulder.

"You all right?"

She rolled her shoulder, grimacing a little. "Right as rain," she assured without looking back. She realized she was starting to walk faster, but there wasn't any way to slow down without looking obvious. Sort of like pretending she hadn't just plowed into a lamppost.

Meanwhile, his footsteps behind her were steady as ever.

She shoved her hands in her pockets. Clasped her car key in her fist. Quarter block now. Parked in front of the feed store, next to a pickup truck that was more about fancy wheels and special lights than it was about utility.

"Bar fight."

She stopped walking and turned to face him.

"In Texas. Five years ago." He stopped walking, too. Right beside the lamppost she'd run into. The light shining down on his head made his hair look vaguely reddish. "Same night I met Otis."

She absorbed that. Then frowned. "Wait. He wasn't the one who—"

His lips stretched. He didn't try to close the distance between them. "No."

She let out a breath. "Oh. That's good, then. Is that where you come from? Texas?" He didn't have any sort of drawl that would have given it away. In fact, when he did string more than two words together, his speech bore no hint toward any particular region at all. "Is working cattle in your blood?"

He actually smiled outright at that. "Everything I know about working cattle came from the School of Hard Ranching according to Otis Lambert."

That smile was so arresting she actually started to take a step toward him.

"He's the one who bailed me out," he added. "Stitched me up."

She froze again. "Bailed?"

"Bar fight," he said again. As if that were the only explanation a person needed. His hand flipped. "Your turn."

She swiped another snowflake from her cheek. Fair was fair, she reasoned. "It wasn't www-dot-getadate." She rocked back on her chunky heels. "My boss does business with Kenneth's firm. He's a financial analyst."

His lips twisted. "I recognized the type. All he's missing is the bespoke suit."

She chewed her lip. His smile was so much better than the grimace. It took years off his face. "It wasn't serious," she added abruptly.

"He followed you all the way from Denver."

"Not because I wanted him to. We never even—" She huffed. What was *wrong* with her? "It wasn't serious," she said again, and turned to head for her car once more. This time, she didn't even try to measure her pace.

She hit the fob in her palm to unlock it and yanked open the door when she reached it. A quick check in her mirror and she backed out of the parking spot and gunned it down Main as if the devil was at her bumper.

Flying past the sheriff's department reminded her to lighten up on the gas at least, but she didn't manage to draw an even breath until the lights of town were in her rearview mirror.

It wasn't long before those dwindling lights were replaced by bright headlights.

She angled the mirror a little so the reflection wasn't shining in her eyes. She didn't feel particularly compelled to speed up to accommodate the driver following her. She was already going faster than the speed limit and the snow flurries were getting heavier. It wouldn't be long before she hit the turnoff for the ranch.

Those bright beams stayed on her tail, though. Annoying. She didn't have a hope of making out what sort of vehicle it was. For all she knew, it was one of the officers from the sheriff's department. And even though she had connections, she didn't want to test them too hard by getting pulled over for speeding.

She let off the gas a little, edging the shoulder in case the driver wanted to pass. It'd be easy enough to do since there was no oncoming traffic at all.

But those lights stayed with her.

Her fingers tightened on the steering wheel. "Just go around me," she muttered.

But the vehicle didn't budge.

She sped up again.

Telling herself to relax didn't accomplish anything. Reminding herself that the highway was the main road between Weaver and everywhere else didn't help, either.

The sky was black. The road ahead illuminated

only by the sweep of headlights. Her wipers were on low, swiping over her windshield and the little buildup of snow. Then waiting. Waiting. Waiting while the highway was a high hum beneath her tires before swishing again.

And still, those lights remained in her rearview mirror. Never inching closer. Never backing off.

Her fingers were like vises around the steering wheel.

Every roadside slasher movie she'd ever watched in her teens had come back to haunt her and when she finally—thank heavens!—*finally* reached the turnoff for the Double-C, she barely slowed as she spun the wheel.

Her tires skidded as they hit the graded gravel and she fishtailed through the timber-framed entrance, narrowly avoiding sideswiping one of the yard-wide side pillars.

Nerves tight, she regained the wheel as she slowed, and finally rolled to a stop. Her chest ached from the way her heart pounded and she dropped her forehead to the steering wheel. "You're a crazy person, Reed." And if any one of her family members had witnessed the way she'd turned off the highway, they'd have skinned her.

She screamed outright when the door beside her yanked open.

"Who the *hell* taught you to drive?"

She stared at Jed, speechless.

For all of two seconds.

Then she threw off her safety belt and launched herself out of the vehicle at him. "That was *you*?"

She planted her hands on his chest and shoved.

"You scared the *life* out of me!" She went to shove him again but he caught her wrists in his, holding her at bay. She twisted her wrists, but he held her fast. "What is *wrong* with you?"

"What is wrong with *you*?" His voice was just as angry. "Driving that way? Do you have any sense at all?"

She finally managed to yank free and glared at him.

There was plenty of light. The headlights on his truck bathed them both in white, and the falling snow glittered like diamonds around them.

"You were tailgating!"

"The hell I was." His hands went to his hips as he glared back. "You knew that was me. You could have gone off the road. Hit something even worse than that gate!"

"I most certainly did not know it was you!" She wrapped her fingers in the front of his shirt, wanting to shake him and shove him all at the same time. "How was I supposed to know you would follow me?"

"There's one damn road," he said through his teeth. "Your turnoff just comes a damn sight sooner than mine!"

The fight abruptly drained away, leaving her feeling spent. Her shoulders sagged and she exhaled shakily. Her head fell forward, landing on the center of his chest. "God. You really scared me."

He swore softly. "I'm sorry." His arms came up. Surrounded her. "You really scared me."

Then she felt his fingers slide over her head. Slip down through her hair. And the pounding in her chest took on a whole new element.

She looked up at him. Despite the white glare of headlights, his eyes were canyons of dark. His face was pale, his square jaw flexing.

She dropped her gaze to that small scar.

No, that was an excuse. An easy excuse, because it was so close to his mouth. So close to those lips that rarely softened into a smile.

"Don't look at me like that, April."

She raised her gaze to his. "Like what?"

His fingers tightened in her hair and her mouth ran dry. She swallowed. Moistened her lips.

She wasn't sure if she moved first. Or if it was him.

But then his mouth was on hers and she felt engulfed by an inferno. Or maybe the burning was coming from inside her.

There was no way to know.

No reason to care.

Her hands slid up the granite chest, behind his neck, where his skin felt even hotter beneath her fingertips, slipping through his thick hair that was not hot, but instead felt cool and unexpectedly silky.

His arm around her tightened, his hand pressing her closer while his kiss deepened. Consuming. Exhilarating. Her head was whirling, sounds roaring.

It was only a kiss.

But she was melting.

She was flying.

And then she realized the sounds weren't just inside her head.

Someone was laying on a horn.

She jerked back, her gaze skittering over Jed's as they both turned to peer through the curtain of white light shining over them.

"Mind getting at least one of these vehicles out of the way?" The shout was male and obviously amused.

"Oh for cryin'—" She exhaled. "That's my uncle Matthew," she told Jed, pushing him away. "And I'm sorry to say, but we are probably *never* going to live this down."

Chapter Seven

"Soooo." Piper, looking particularly pretty in a fluttery pink dress, sidled next to April. She was waiting with the people clustered in line for the bar that was set up in front of the enormous windows inside Vivian Templeton's lavish home. "How's it going?"

"I don't buy that wide-eyed act for a second," April told her dryly. She inched forward as the line moved. "What have you heard?"

Piper grinned and bumped April's arm with her shoulder. "You and Jed left Colbys last night together."

At least it wasn't the fact that Matthew had caught her and Jed kissing like a couple of teenagers.

"I could say the same thing about you and Kenneth, I think." Not a soul was paying them any attention. All of the guests passing through Vivian's front door were too busy gawking at the gold furniture and the artwork on the walls to be interested in their conversation. "The two of you disappeared before Jed and I left."

"Aha!" Piper had arrived earlier than April and Gloria and she already held a crystal champagne flute in her hand. She tilted the delicate rim toward April. "You *did* leave together."

"No. We left at the same time." They moved forward again. April could see around the people in front of her to the table where dozens of flutes exactly like Piper's were lined up. "Big difference." She angled her head. "Where do you suppose Vivian managed to get that many crystal flutes?"

Lucy stuck her blond head between them. "You haven't seen her butler's pantry. She could open a catering company with all the party stuff she owns."

"Subtle way to cut the line," April murmured wryly.

Her cousin winked. "I try." They moved forward again. "Thank goodness I see some beer bottles there," she said. "Beck'll be relieved. If it weren't for Vivian's business, I'd have never gotten him through the door here." She lifted her arm, sending a thumbs-up, and April looked over to see Lucy's husband standing near one of the windows looking as though he'd rather be anywhere else. When she dropped her arm, she settled it over April's shoulders. "So what's this I hear about you and the mountain recluse getting caught making out?"

Piper's head whipped up. *"What?"*

April grimaced. "Who'd you hear that from?"

"Oh, just…around." Lucy's eyes were full of mirth. "So? Getting busy while you're in town, are you?"

"No," April denied. "Look. We're next." She shoved her cousin ahead of her. "Better grab the beer before it's all gone."

Lucy laughed softly, but did exactly that.

Then it was her turn and April took one of the champagne flutes, holding it up for one of the white-suited caterers to fill before moving out of the way.

Piper tucked her arm through April's, keeping her from getting too far away. "You trying to keep secrets from your bestie?"

"Of course not."

"Making out with Jed?"

She spotted her grandmother across the room, laughing as she talked with a group of people. "It was just a kiss." Major understatement. "Who's that man over there by my gram? The one holding the gray cowboy hat."

"That's Tom Hook. He's an attorney. Your grandmother looks great, by the way." Piper propped her hand on her hip. "Wish I could look that good right now."

"Oh, stop. You look amazing." But April's grandmother did look particularly attractive.

Gloria's hair wasn't as red as it once had been, but it still remained as much auburn as silver. She'd left it down for the fund-raiser and it swirled around the shoulders of her close-fitting ivory dress. Squire was in his nineties. Gloria, however, was more than twenty years younger and had a figure that was enviable at any age. Combine all that with intelligence and an engaging wit, and was it any wonder that she drew eyes?

Particularly Tom Hook's.

"What's his deal?"

"Who? Tom?" Piper spread her palms. "I don't know. He has a small ranch, I think. I know he's a lawyer, though. He's handled some stuff for my dad. And don't think I haven't noticed you avoiding the conversation."

"We're having a conversation." She tapped her glass lightly against Piper's. "I wonder what my grandfather would think if he could see her right now." She doubted he'd still be acting like such a stick in the mud. She suddenly handed her champagne to Piper. "Hold that."

She pulled her cell phone out of the small sequined purse she'd borrowed from Jaimie along with a black turtleneck and skirt, and aimed the camera toward her grandmother. She snapped off several shots before tucking it away again.

"You're going to show your grandfather the pictures? You think that's going to get them talking again?"

"I don't know. It could backfire just as easily. And it *was* one kiss." She took the flute back from Piper and lowered her voice. "One rock-the-world kiss." She shook her head, the memory still so fresh it made her warm just thinking about it. "Matthew interrupted us."

Piper winced. "Oh. Nice."

"It was a fluke."

"Getting interrupted?"

April couldn't help but laugh. "That, too." This time, she slipped her arm through Piper's. "I might be my grandmother's date, but she's obviously blowing me off. So let's go explore. And you can tell me just what you got up to with Kenneth."

"Not a thing," Piper assured her. "Only thing that boy wanted to talk about was you."

It was April's turn to wince. "I'm sorry." They walked down a wide corridor, peeking in doorways as they went.

They weren't the only lookie-loos. Attendees were everywhere they turned, and the crowd thickened when they reached a two-story atrium that opened to a fancy brick patio that led down to those spectacular grounds that had been visible from the living room.

"Holy cow." Piper was looking up at the filigreed

balustrade running around the perimeter of the second level landing where even more people were congregating. "I've heard rumors about this place, but until you see it in person…" She spun on her high heels, trying to take it all in. "He's gone back to Denver, by the way. Your brokenhearted hottie."

"I never wanted him to chase after me."

"I know. So when do you plan to see Jed again?"

April let out a laugh steeped with futility. "There's no plans for anything. And what good would it do, anyway? There's nothing for me to do here. Otis owns the land and he's not budging."

"Yeah, but he's—"

"—don't say it."

Piper looked solemn. "Not saying it doesn't mean it's not going to happen. If he's really that ill and not getting any sort of medical treatment? Even if he were as healthy as a horse, he's an old man. My dad was talking about him the other day. Said the church records show Otis is ninety-nine years old! He won't live forever."

"I'm sure Jed would rather lose Otis to old age than to cancer," April said. "Until we know what arrangements Otis has made in his will, there's no reason for me to try to persuade him to sell. I'd only be bugging a sick old man if I kept pursuing it."

"So you have to wait until he's gone?"

"I don't want to think about it. Makes me feel like a vulture."

"You think Otis might leave the ranch to Jed?"

"Jed says he won't." She chewed the inside of her check. "Gage finally got back to me this morning. He wants me to finish up a few things with Archer since we're both here in town. After that, I'll be heading back to Denver."

"I'm sorry things haven't worked out the way you'd hoped."

She spread her hands. "At least I had an opportunity to visit Weaver."

Piper's eyes suddenly danced. "And kiss the mountain man—oh. Look. There's Vivian." She gestured toward one of the staircases leading down from the second level, where a diminutive woman with stylish silver hair was descending. She wore a knee-length chiffon dress with a beaded bodice and the hand she closed over the banister winked with diamonds and gems.

April leaned toward Piper. "Remind me—we're in Weaver, right?"

"I know," Piper whispered back. "She wears Chanel suits when she goes into town. In a Rolls-Royce, mind you. And you're related to her."

"*I'm* not. It was Squire's first wife who was related to Vivian's first husband."

"Details, shmetails," Piper dismissed as they watched Vivian greeting people as she went. "Close enough. Come on." She pulled April toward the door leading outside. "If she gets any closer to us, she might ask for a donation. And thanks to this dress, I have a whopping twenty-five bucks in my savings account right now."

April covered her laughter as they went out onto the patio. The snow flurries from the night before had been too light to leave any lasting evidence. Particularly under the sunny afternoon skies. It was chilly, definitely. But not uncomfortably so thanks to her borrowed turtleneck.

There were fewer people outside, even though a bar was set up there as well as portable heaters and a long display of library books. In the middle were several large artist renderings of the proposed new library and they wandered over to look at them.

"Nick's doing himself proud," April murmured.

"Move over Frank Lloyd Wright?"

April chuckled. "That would be something all right."

While they'd perused the display, more catering staff had appeared, this time circulating with trays of hors d'oeuvres. Along with everyone else there, they ate their fill and crowded around when Vivian took center stage to discuss the library project.

Gloria, April noticed, never got too far away from Tom Hook. Even when she drew April forward to introduce her to their hostess, the lawyer was near.

April hadn't been sure quite what to expect upon meeting Vivian. Not when there had been so many stories about the wealthy widow. The woman was unfailingly gracious, though. She was clearly in her element when it came to asking for money for the project. But also, when April pulled out the check that Gage had instructed her to donate when they'd finally connected that morning, she seemed sincerely grateful.

Eventually, it was time to leave, and April drove them back to the big house. Matthew and Jaimie were still out. Squire was nowhere to be found. Gloria didn't say a word. She simply went off to change her clothes, leaving April sitting alone at the big round table in the kitchen.

When a chime sounded, it took her a minute to even recognize that it was the doorbell.

Nobody ever came to the front door of the big house. Everyone always came around to the mudroom entrance.

The chime sounded again and she hurried through the house, into the living room that was rarely used, and pulled open the heavy door.

Jed stood on the step. "Here." He handed her the plastic container from the ham and the glass dish from the cobbler. Folded on top of them were her black jeans and white blouse.

She felt hot inside as she took the items. All she could think was that it had been less than a day since his mouth had been on hers. "Thanks. You didn't have to bring them here. I'd have—"

"Otis died this morning."

Shock rocked through her.

Then she shoved the stuff on the table next to the door and put her arms around him. "I'm so sorry." Her voice was hoarse. "So sorry, Jed." She felt his hands on her back.

But it was too brief. Too little. As if he didn't want her sympathy.

He pushed her back altogether and his gaze went past her.

She looked over her shoulder to see her grandmother. "Gram…" She had to clear her throat. Her voice was thick. "This is Jed Dalloway. My grandmother, Gloria Clay."

"Otis enjoyed the cobbler, ma'am," Jed greeted. "Wanted me to tell you thank you."

"My pleasure," Gloria said with a friendly smile. Her eyes were a little searching. "Nothing like a covered dish from a pretty girl."

Jed's jaw canted. "Pretty much what Otis said."

April's eyes burned. She looked away to swipe her cheek.

"I've got things to take care of," he said abruptly, turning to go. His eyes skated over hers.

"Jed—"

But he was already heading down the wide steps of the porch, his long legs eating the distance to the dusty truck parked in the circular drive fronting the house.

"Honey." Gloria came up and rubbed her shoulder. "What is it?"

April turned into her grandmother's arms. "He's gone."

"Jed?"

Him, too. "Otis."

Like all things Otis Lambert had done in his life, he did the same in his death.

Everything his way.

He'd ordered his own cremation. Chosen his own plain, flat headstone. He'd even gotten the paperwork that allowed his ashes to be buried on his own land—a task he'd made Jed promise to handle himself.

Since the only reason Jed figured he was alive today was because of that long-ago Texas night when a complete stranger saw something worth saving in Jed's miserable soul, he figured he owed it to Otis to live up to his word.

Otis had marked his chosen spot a year ago. Despite the elements in the months since, the big red X he'd painted on the rocks was faded, but still there.

Which left Jed with nothing to do after his boss was gone, besides finish the work. He'd had to wait for the doctor to come up and certify the death and then wait some more for the mortuary to perform their part. They'd been doing their thing when Jed had driven down to the Double-C ranch.

Some things he just hadn't had the strength to witness.

By the time Jed received the wooden box of ashes, it was nearly nightfall. The ground was more rock than soil and it took more pickax than shovel to dig the hole once he'd managed to get past the boulders blocking the way. Samson lay on the ground nearby, his head on his paws. Not even chasing after a rabbit when it got curious enough to come close and see what was going on.

One box of ashes shouldn't be so hard to deal with. But it was still backbreaking work to get the hole deep enough for that box.

But at last the deed was done.

Jagged boulders moved. Earth briefly disturbed.

A plaque situated.

The words were simple. "Otis Lambert. Born here. Died here."

No dates were included. Otis never figured it was anyone's business, anyway. And who, in their right mind, would ever climb up onto the edge of earth where Otis had chosen to spend his eternity?

Only Jed, because he'd promised. Certainly nobody from town. Otis had flatly forbidden any other mourners.

In the moonlight, Jed carried the shovel and pickax back to the UTV he'd had to leave parked down the hill a hundred yards off. One last time he went back up to the ridge carrying the bedroll that was always stowed behind the seats of the UTV and the truck. You never knew when you'd get stuck out on the land for a night. It wouldn't be long before Jed would have the roll fastened to the back of his saddle, because during calving season it was sometimes just easier to bed down where the mamas were.

He flipped open the roll and sat down on it beside Otis.

He was no different than Samson.

"It's a good view, Otis."

The dog woofed softly and crawled forward to put his head on Jed's knee. He rubbed the dog's head. "I know, buddy."

There'd been hardly anyone to come to Tanya's funeral, either. Everyone had either been in jail by then or had put Jed at a distance. And Tanya's only family was already gone by then.

The day he had put his first and only love in the ground, it had been just him and a minister. A guy he'd never seen before. One who had never known Tanya. Just someone who'd answered the phone number provided by the funeral home.

In a way, this was better. Truer.

"Guess you knew that, too, you old man." Otis had never said who he'd been in Texas to bury five years ago. Jed had known better than to ask.

Samson scooted again, pushing his eighty pounds

of determination against Jed in his effort to take over some of the bedroll.

Jed was weary enough, he didn't care. He let the dog take his share while he looked up at the stars.

They looked close enough to touch.

He'd given up on heaven. But he still believed in hell.

Otis was the one who'd shown him the way out.

He'd brought Jed up to this very spot when he'd arrived that first day on the Rambling Rad.

"You think your life is so bad? You really want to end it? Stop playing around at it and do the job right." He'd gestured at the sheer drop-off. "You won't survive going over that. And there are plenty other spots down the road. Don't have to look hard. Otherwise, work starts early here. You can fix up that ol' potting shed however you want. I need someone with a strong back and tight lips. In return, you'll get room and board and a percentage of whatever profit the ranch makes for as long as you're working it." Then he'd let out that cackle of a laugh. "'Course a hunnert percent of nothing is still nothing."

"You can be glad I didn't walk off the edge," Jed muttered, resting his hand on the freshly turned earth beside him. "Nobody else'd be fool enough to bury you on the side of a mountain."

He'd sure thought about walking off the ledge, though.

But as the weeks, then the months and the years passed, he'd climbed up to this spot less and less.

The last time he'd been up here had been to help Otis paint that damn red X.

The dog had stretched out. Jed pushed with his own weight to gain enough space and stretched out, too.

He propped his hands behind his neck and stared down at the lights sparkling in the distance. Was April still down there somewhere?

Working out Stanton Development's next move?

Or had she already gone back to Denver where good ol' Kenneth would be waiting with open arms?

Jed couldn't really blame the guy.

He'd set his eyes on Tanya more than a decade before she'd even given him the time of day.

If she had never done so, she'd never have died.

And as far as Jed was concerned, that was the very definition of hell. Knowing that if it weren't for him, Tanya and the babies she'd carried would still be alive today.

Chapter Eight

The house—a generous term if there ever was one—was still sitting on the side of the mountain.

Wood still gone gray with weathering. Worn deck still lining the front side of the house.

April zipped up her leather jacket and reached inside the car for the padded carrier. She started to close the car door but the wind finished the job first, yanking it right out of her hand.

It hadn't even been two weeks since she'd made her first trip up the mountain to see Otis.

It felt like so, so much longer.

Now the only thing she could do coming up the mountain, was to pay her respects.

She made her way past the wooden barricade

and the boulders and aimed toward the front of the house.

She didn't see the rocking chair sitting on the deck at first. Not until she'd picked her way up the ragtag steps.

Jed was sitting in it. One bare foot propped on the splintering rail in front of him. He wore jeans and a striped shirt that he hadn't bothered to button and one of the shirttails flapped in the wind.

A bottle of scotch sat on the deck beside the chair.

"Do you have a drinking problem, Jed?" For a greeting, it wasn't what she'd intended.

Certainly not what she'd been rehearsing all the way up the winding mountain road.

He didn't look at her. "What do you want, April?"

She pressed her tongue against the back of her teeth, exhaling. She hurt inside. "I came to see how you are."

He spread his hands and she saw the short glass he was holding in one of them. "This is how I am."

She walked toward him. It was almost automatic now to step over the boards that looked as though they were ready to split right in two.

"My family sends their condolences."

He didn't respond. There was about an inch of alcohol in the bottom of the glass.

"When's the last time you ate?"

Again, no response. He lifted the glass, watching the whisky swirl. But he didn't drink. Just lowered the glass again, resting it against that hard, bare abdomen.

Her hair blew across her face and she pushed it back behind her ear, looking out from the deck. Weaver lay in the distance, a small town shaped a bit like a cross. Another range of mountains lined the far side, separating Weaver from its sister town of Braden. Yet up here on the mountain, they could have been the only two people in the world.

"It's very windy out here. Aren't you cold?"

"I don't get cold."

She looked at him. His eyes were bloodshot and his knuckles looked raw. "Everyone gets cold."

"Thank you for your condolences."

"Now go home? Is that going to be the end of that thought?"

"There's no reason to stay here." He gestured with the glass. "You said it. It's windy and cold."

"Then come inside." She lifted the insulated carrier. "I've brought you a meal."

"No point in trying to bribe me. I can't help you acquire the ranch."

"It's not a bribe." Because he didn't seem inclined to invite her inside, she just went to the door and let herself in.

The chair that Otis had sat in the day of the rainstorm was gone and she realized it must be the same one that Jed had taken out onto the deck. There wasn't much other furniture to speak of. The wood-stove was stone cold when she checked.

She went through the swinging door to the kitchen and set everything on the table, then went back in the living area. The wood was stacked against the wall near the woodstove. She opened the door and laid a new fire, silently blessing the fact that she'd learned how to do so when she was just a kid.

Flames were licking well from the kindling into the log when she closed the heavy door on it and went back into the kitchen. She propped the door open with a chair so it would get some of the heat from the fire. The most modern thing in the place seemed to be the phone, and it looked nearly antique. No coffeemaker. No microwave. She remembered that from the last time she'd been up there.

She searched behind the curtain hanging from the counter and found a tin of ground coffee. The metal coffeepot sitting cold on the stove was the same style that Squire always used when he'd taken his grandkids out camping and fishing.

She gave it a thorough wash, filled it with water from the tap and stuck it back on the stove, fiddling with the burner a bit before the gas flame lit.

There was a bowl of eggs in the ancient refrigerator. Freckled and colored and probably farm fresh versus the supermarket. She cracked one into a small bowl and stirred several scoops of coffee into it. When the water was boiling, she dumped in the slurry and stirred it until it foamed up. Then she poured in a bowlful of cold water settling the whole mess and turned off the flame.

When Jed finally came in, she was sitting at the table sipping at a cup.

It was too late for lunch. A little early for supper. But she'd set the table with a plate from his shelf. Folded one of the napkins from her carrier and placed it beneath the mismatched flatware that had been piled in the sink.

She didn't say anything while he studied the display. Just used two fingers to push his steaming cup of coffee across the table toward him.

His lips compressed. He dumped his glass into the sink, pouring out about an inch of whisky, she noted. Then he picked up the coffee cup. "Looks more like tea than coffee. I don't drink tea."

She smiled faintly, focusing hard on the coffee so she wouldn't get caught staring at that slice of bare chest showing between his unbuttoned shirt. "It's not tea," she assured. He surely knew it. The kitchen was redolent with the scent of coffee. "Give it a try anyway."

He took a sip. Narrowed his eyes at her. "All right," he finally said. "It'll do." He flicked his free hand, taking in the set table. "Is this part of the whole condolence package?"

She noticed again the scrapes on his knuckles.

They hadn't been there the day before when he'd come to the Double-C. "Ordinarily, I'd have just left the meal. But I didn't want you having to eat alone."

"I've been eating alone a long time."

"If you're saying that you and Otis didn't share meals, I don't believe you." She sipped her coffee, pretending a calmness that she didn't really feel. "Have you made any arrangements yet?"

"For what?"

He was being deliberately obtuse. But she wasn't going to rise to it. Not when she knew it was caused by grief. "Piper's father is a minister if you don't have someone in mind already to handle the service for you."

"It's taken care of."

She wasn't really surprised, she decided. "Otis left instructions, I suppose."

"You could say that."

"Will it be soon? I know Squire will want to—"

"He's already buried. I buried his ashes myself."

She stared, feeling a sinking sense of dismay. "When you say you did it yourself—" she glanced at his raw hands "—you're not saying you *did* it yourself. Are you?"

"I had the proper permit," he said flatly. "I told you he wanted to be buried on his mountain and I promised him I'd do it."

"Oh, Jed."

"Just leave it." He looked grim and he lifted the

coffee cup again, taking a drink. "What's different about this? It tastes—" He broke off, shaking his head.

"Smooth? No bitterness? It's egg coffee. Squire's favorite."

He shoved the cup onto the table as if he were appalled. "What the hell is egg coffee?"

"You stir an egg into the grounds. And some shell. It clarifies the coffee." She caught one of his hands in hers. Studied the knuckles that were scraped raw. When she turned his hand over, the ridge of callouses on his palm hadn't been enough to prevent a blister. "You used your bare hands?"

"I used a shovel and a pickaxe." He opened the back door and pointed to a spot beyond the two sheds. "He's up there on that ridge. Staring down at all of Weaver forevermore. Lording over things from his position on high."

She closed her eyes, swallowing dismay. When she opened them again he'd closed the door and was toying warily with the coffee cup. She knew that if he liked coffee as much as Squire, he couldn't help but like the old-timey recipe. She hadn't met a coffee drinker yet who didn't. "You could have had help, Jed."

"Somebody else dug the hole when my wife died. It wasn't any easier that way. At least this time, it wasn't strangers doing the job."

She curled her fingers in her lap. "When, uh, how long ago did she die?"

"Does it matter? Tanya's gone. Whether it happened yesterday or a decade ago."

Tanya. The name sank through her. "You married the first girl you kissed?"

"I kissed a few others between that first one with her and the last. She didn't make it easy catching her. She had—" He broke off and looked down at his mug.

"Had what?"

He didn't immediately answer. "High standards," he finally said abruptly.

April dragged her eyes away from his chest again and trained her attention on the food. "You, ah, you don't have to bring back any of these containers. If you're not up to eating now, I can package it all up and put it in the fridge for later."

In answer, he grabbed the chair she'd used to prop open the swinging door, flipped it around toward the dinky table and sat. "Why do people send food?"

She made a soft sound. "For support. Comfort. Surely that's not an unfamiliar concept for you."

His lips twisted. "You ought to be celebrating."

She sat back, stiffening. "Why?"

"He told you he had a will, but I haven't found it. Looked all day. Not in his room. Not tucked among the ranch books. It's nowhere."

"Why would he have lied to me about having a will?"

"Why bother calling Stanton Development? Otis likes…liked…yanking people's chains."

"He seemed genuine when he said his interest in Stanton was centered on my boss." She fiddled with the strap of the food carrier still sitting on the table. "I can't help but wonder if maybe Otis is Gage's father." The notion had been percolating ever since Otis admitted knowing Gage's mother.

"That'd be convenient, wouldn't it? Your boss would get the mountain without the heavy price tag. And don't pretend you didn't think about that already."

She folded her arms, wishing she hadn't said anything. "If you want me to go, just say so. You don't have to resort to insults to accomplish it."

He didn't apologize. Didn't say anything. He just drank the coffee. And when the cup was empty, he took a piece of the fried chicken she'd set out and bit into it. A minute later, he scooped potato salad onto his plate.

Satisfied that he was at least consuming something besides coffee and—presumably—scotch, she went to check the fire. The log was burning well and she adjusted the venting. She suspected the interior would warm up in short order. The cabin didn't sport a lot of square footage.

She went down the short hall to the bathroom and

opened the wooden cupboard above the washer and dryer. She was hoping to find a first aid kit. All she located amid the congestion of stuff—everything from rusty tools to a can of peanut brittle and a copious supply of kitchen matches—was a brown bottle of hydrogen peroxide that looked as old as she was. She took it down anyway and twisted open the lid to pour a small measure of the clear liquid into the cracked porcelain sink. The peroxide bubbled, which was good enough for her.

She capped it again, then poked through the rest of the cabinet, finally finding some bandage strips inside a silver metal box that looked like it had once held jewelry.

There wasn't anything remotely like a handy stack of clean washcloths. So she took the peroxide and bandages and went back to the kitchen.

He'd eaten two chicken legs. The potato salad was gone. She set the bottle and box on the counter and poured more coffee carefully into his cup. In general, the grounds tended to rest in a clumpy mess at the bottom of the pot, but she was also used to pouring through a little strainer. Which she doubted existed in this particular kitchen.

Then she sat back down across from him. "How are you doing? Really?"

He pushed aside the plate and leaned his elbow on the table, pinching the bridge of his nose. "I'm fine. This wasn't unexpected. It just—" He sighed and dropped his hand. "He sat down in his chair and took a nap. He didn't wake up. Just like that." He snapped his fingers. "Gone."

She closed her hand over his. "I wish—" She broke off, shaking her head. She moistened her lips. "I wish there were something I could do."

His fingers slowly curled around hers. "You're doing it."

Her throat tightened and her chest ached even more. It was either start crying right then and there or do something. She slid her hand from his and got up to grab the bottle of peroxide and the metal container of bandages. She pulled the rest of the cloth napkins from the carrier and then crouched in front of him. "Give me your hand."

His eyebrows pulled together. But he put his hand in hers. She cradled it with one of the napkins. "I don't think this will hurt." She dribbled peroxide over the scrapes and scratches and then dabbed them dry with another clean napkin. "When was the last time you got some sleep?"

He let out a rough sound. "You saying I look like I need it?"

She raised an eyebrow, giving him a look.

He made a face. "It's been a while," he admitted grudgingly.

She could well imagine. She rinsed the scrapes on his other hand with the peroxide, then fit the adhesive strips over the worst of them. "I wish I had some antiseptic cream," she fretted as she carefully smoothed the edges of the bandages with her fingertip. "I hope it helps. That it didn't hurt too much."

"It's killing me."

"I only meant to help." She curled her fingers lightly around his hand and looked up with dismay.

His gaze caught hers and her mouth dried.

He cupped her cheek. His hand felt warm. The bandage cool. The look in his eyes stole her breath.

And then he let out a muffled curse. "Sorry."

He stood abruptly, stepping around her and pushed out of the kitchen through the back door.

She hovered there, still kneeling on the ancient linoleum floor. Maybe she was crazy. Coming here at all.

She cleared away the bandage wrappers and covered the food and stacked the containers on the metal shelves in the old refrigerator. She checked the woodstove and closed down the air control to let the fire burn low and very slow.

Then she went out the kitchen door he'd left open.

She told herself she was going to leave. Jed clearly didn't want company. At least not hers.

But instead she looked up at the ridge where he'd buried Otis.

And her footsteps started that way.

The hill angled sharply upward, but there was a path of sorts worn into the long grass whipping around in the breeze and she followed it. Within minutes, she could look down onto the roof of the cabin. Jed was nowhere to be seen.

She looked up at the sky where white clouds skittered across the blue, blue expanse. She looked out over the valley beyond. It was so beautiful. And for all of these years, Lambert had kept it to himself.

She drew in a deep breath and started up the path again. The distance really wasn't that great. Yet it was still no small hike by the time she reached the grave situated in a narrow passage. There was no way to miss it. Sharp-edged boulders pushed aside. A small patch of freshly turned soil. A flat, rectangular piece of stone planted in the ground at one end, a sheer drop-off from the cliff at the other.

She propped her hands on her hips and looked around, her breath hard and hissing through her teeth. There was no room for a truck or digging equipment. It didn't bear thinking how Jed had performed the task on his own.

Even if he'd been wearing work gloves, it was no wonder his hands had been so beaten up.

She decided the height was no scarier here than it was on that final curve in the road, and edged her way to the marker.

Despite herself, she smiled a little over the inscription. "Well, that says it all, Otis."

Far, far below she finally saw black dots of cattle, grazing in a meadow that ran alongside the hook in a stream she hadn't even known existed. She was almost surprised. Despite the notion that Otis Lambert had been a rancher, she'd wondered whether the cattle existed or not.

The narrow path kept going upward beyond the grave and she followed it for a while. She passed low-growing shrubs. Slipped around trees with trunks more than a foot in diameter. She leaned for a few minutes against a jagged outcrop to catch her breath. Then higher still, through a patch of wildflowers growing on a sunny outcrop.

She finally stopped, standing there in the midst of such beauty. It would be foolhardy to go farther. She couldn't see the summit from here, but she knew it was still covered in snow.

Standing there on Otis Lambert's mountainside, a person could think they were the only ones in the world. And one portion of her mind recognized the pricelessness of that particular sensation.

She shook it off and crouched down, grabbing a handful of wildflowers and worked them loose, roots and all, then started back down.

When she reached Otis's grave, she knelt down and traced the letters on the marker with her finger.

Born here. Died here.

"I think I would have liked to have known you better, Otis." Using her fingers, she scooped out a hole and planted the wildflowers. "I know they're more likely to blow away than take root," she said.

"But there's always hope." She pressed the soil down. The surface was warm from the sun, but the coolness below was still evident. "Thank you for taking care of Jed when he needed it," she whispered.

Then she stood and brushed the dirt from her hands and started back down the path. She reached the small shed first, finally recognizing it was really just a shelter for the horse. There was a water trough. Feed. No sign of the horse at the moment, though. There was no fence, so it wasn't surprising. She splashed water from the trough over her hands and dried them down the sides of her jeans.

The other shed was more substantial. The door was open when she passed and she glanced in, expecting to see the usual kind of farm equipment.

She saw Jed.

Sitting on a footlocker. Head in his hands.

Her heart ached and she stepped quietly into what she realized was really a bunkhouse for one.

"Why haven't you gone?"

"I don't know," she whispered. Then she moved over to him and put her arms around his shoulders. Bent over him and pressed her lips to his head. "Tell me how I can help."

His wide shoulders moved and she felt his arms around her. His fingertips pressed hard against her spine, but then moved away. "April." He looked up at her but his eyes seemed to focus no higher than her mouth.

Heat slipped into her veins, warming her from the inside out.

Her breath was quick like it had been from her hike up and down the hillside, but she knew this time he was the cause. "Tell me," she whispered again.

His eyes darkened.

He slowly reached between them and she went still as he slowly, slowly pulled down the zipper of her jacket. When it was loose, he tugged on the leather, pulling her down until she was at his level, kneeling between his legs.

His gaze searched hers. "Are you sure?"

She knew what he was really asking. Could read the truth of it in his eyes.

She leaned forward slowly, brushing her lips softly, gently across his. "Yes," she whispered, and took his poor, worn hands littered with bandages and drew them around her waist, beneath the jacket. Beneath the stretchy knit fabric of her T-shirt.

Her heart was pounding, but so was his. She could feel it as she slid her fingers under the edges of his striped shirt. Pressed flat against the hard, hot flesh beneath.

She angled her head, running her lips along that square jaw. Down to his neck, where she could feel his pulse throbbing against the tip of her tongue.

She slowly pushed his shirt over his broad, sinewy shoulders. Discovered another small scar. Older than the one on his chin. More jagged.

Thoughts of bar fights and knives were brief, pushed aside by the sheer gentleness in the fingertips he was drawing up her spine.

And then she was shrugging out of the jacket and the shirt. Fitting herself against him was so easy, so perfect. His mouth found hers and she could no more remain closed to him than she could stop breathing.

She was vaguely aware of the constant breeze pushing into the room, curling around them. But she wasn't cold. Could never be cold. Not as long as she was in his arms.

When he drew her to her feet, she went with him. Brushed aside his clothes as he brushed aside hers.

He drew her down to the rough woven blanket covering the narrow bed, and she sighed his name and felt herself melting around him.

He rose over her, threading his fingers through her hair. Spreading it carefully out around her head. "You're too beautiful for this place." His voice was rough. Husky.

She ran her finger over his lower lip. Tears were blurring her vision, and she wasn't even really sure why. "This is what's beautiful," she whispered, and raised up to kiss him. She slid her leg along his, arching into him. Taking him in. Catching her breath at the feel. At the perfect, wondrous feel of him against her.

His breath came harder. His forehead pressing against hers. His thumb rubbing the moisture on her cheek. "I don't want to hurt you."

"You aren't." She twined her arms around him, taking more. "You won't, Jed. I promise you." She found his mouth, only to tear away, gasping with promise as he pressed into her even more deeply. Until there was nothing between them but heartbeats and sighs. Until her blood sang and her name was a rough groan against her ear as he drove them both right off the edge of heaven.

And after, when she lay exhausted in his arms, he brushed the moisture from her cheek yet again. "Stay," he murmured.

Just that simply, she felt her heart being stolen.

She nodded, pressing her head against that curve in his shoulder that seemed designed for her alone. He caught her fingers in his and kissed them.

And then he closed his eyes and exhaled so deeply, it felt like it came from the very center of his soul.

She watched him sleep until the light outside the open door of his little bunkhouse-for-one shifted and darkened.

She wasn't cold. The heat radiating off his body could have heated the world.

When it was fully dark, she finally slid off the

bed, careful not to disturb him. She went to the door and looked out. The sky was ink. The stars brilliant around a white moon.

Her bare skin prickled with chill.

She quietly closed the door and in the moonlight shining through the single window, she went back to the bed.

He didn't wake. Not really. But his arm came around her waist as he murmured something and pulled her close again.

She exhaled carefully, that low, soft murmur ringing through her mind like the sweetest lullaby.

"Forever."

Chapter Nine

When she woke, sunlight was filling the bunk-house.

And despite the blanket tucked tightly around her and the big, shaggy dog curled against her feet as if they'd been lifelong friends, it was *cold*.

She pushed up on her elbow.

You could take in the entirety of the room in one glance. Jed was not there.

She exchanged looks with the dog. "Where is he, Samson?"

The dog licked her hand, then leisurely hopped down from the bed and went to the closed door.

Bemused, she slid off the thin mattress and opened the door for him. There wasn't a lock on the thing. She half suspected the dog could have opened it all on his own if he'd wanted.

She closed the door and went into the bathroom. Equally as empty as the rest of the place.

She used the facilities and washed her hands and face while she looked in the mirror over the sink.

There was no logic to falling for Jed Dalloway.

But she knew she'd gone and done exactly that.

So fully and completely that she marveled why it didn't show in her reflection.

She tugged on the mirror to look behind it and saw the usual stuff on the narrow shelves. Deodorant. Toothpaste. She squeezed some of that onto her finger and did what she could with her teeth. She didn't find a hairbrush, so she had to make do with her fingers there, as well. Goose pimples were breaking out all over by the time she pushed the tube of toothpaste back onto the little shelf.

When she did so, she knocked something off, and she narrowly caught the ring before it could slide down the sink drain.

She held up the wide ring.

Gold metal in a distinctive, chunky weave.

It was large enough to slip all the way down her thumb. She slid it off her thumb and spotted the engraving inside the band. The letters were worn soft, but they were still distinct.

Forever.

She swallowed. A wedding ring, she realized. Sized for a man.

Forever.

It was a simple word.

And it had every singing cell inside her body going silent.

She'd been falling head over heels for him. But he hadn't said that word to April when he'd pulled her next to him in that narrow bed of his.

He'd simply been thinking about his wife.

She pushed the ring back onto the shelf and slammed the mirror door shut.

She felt an immediate and imperative urge to escape.

Fortunately, since the man was nowhere to be seen, she didn't have any problems doing just that.

She pulled on her clothes and jacket and hopped around on one foot as she yanked on her boots.

Five minutes later, she was running down the road to her car.

She couldn't wait to get off the mountain.

And she never wanted to return to it.

"What?"

Three weeks later, April stood in Gage Stanton's high-rise office and stared at him. Alarm was congealing into a hard knot inside her. "I don't want to go back to Weaver. I should never have gone in the first place. Cutting deals is your forte. Not mine."

Gage merely leaned back in his chair and spun it to look out the tall windows at the downtown buildings of Denver. "And there's still one to negotiate."

She flapped her arms. "I don't know with whom! Otis told me he had a will, but none has been filed. If the thing ever really existed, no one is claiming to have seen it. No one who's witnessed it has stepped forward. Lambert didn't associate with anyone in town unless he had to. Archer still checked with every local attorney in case they helped Lambert draw one up and he turned up zip."

Gage spun again to face her. "Snead is in Weaver, asserting he's the rightful heir. The administrator assigned by the court has already determined there are no encumbrances against the property. Even intestate, it's going to be straightforward. The estate should be settled with relative ease within the next few weeks and I want Snead on the hook by then."

April pressed her lips together. She looked at the framed photos placed on his credenza.

His mother, Althea Stanton.

His brother, Noah Locke.

"Otis's interest wasn't in a real estate deal," she said. "It was in *you*. I told you that."

"So?"

She exhaled and twisted her fingers together. "Gage, Otis knew your mother. When he knew he was dying, he reached out to her son. To you. Don't you wonder why?"

"No."

"Maybe he and your mother—" She didn't know how to be delicate about it. "Maybe they had a relationship at some point. You know. Maybe—"

He gave a bark of laughter that was entirely without mirth. "You suggesting Otis Lambert was my father?"

She spread her hands. "Well, couldn't it be possible?"

His lips thinned. "No."

"Are you *sure*? A son would have the first rights of inheritance over a distant cousin! Everyone knows your mother raised you on her own. Isn't it possible that—"

"No." He sighed and shoved his hand through his black hair. "Just because I don't talk about it doesn't mean I don't know exactly who my father was. And it most definitely was *not* a man named Otis Lambert."

The wind whooshed right out of her sails and she flopped down into one of the upholstered chairs fronting his wide desk. "Anyone can make a deal with Snead. You certainly don't need me there to do it. And frankly—" she stared down at her hands, "—I'm not sure I have the stomach for it."

"Why?"

It took no effort whatsoever to summon an image of Jed. There hadn't been a single day since she'd left Weaver that he hadn't been in her thoughts. And Lord knew the man wasn't chasing after her.

Why would he?

April had been nothing more for him than a night of comfort.

She couldn't even blame him for it.

She was the one who'd made more out of their lovemaking than it was.

She was worse than Kenneth; spinning romance out of thin air.

"April," Gage prompted. "What's the problem?"

"It's just, um—" She spread her hands. "I don't want—"

He waited, one eyebrow lifted.

When she still didn't manage to produce any credible argument, he opened a drawer on his desk and pulled out an envelope. "You can deliver this, too." He slid it across to her. "It's a donation—a real donation—to that library thing."

She peeked inside the envelope to see the amount listed on the check, and this time it was her turn to raise her eyebrows. The donation that she'd already made on Stanton's behalf at Vivian's fund-raiser had been just a few hundred dollars.

This donation was in an entirely different class.

She looked up at Gage. "That's a lot of interest in a library thing. In a small town. In another state." It wasn't the typical kind of infrastructure that concerned them. Not unless it was a housing development, and that wasn't Gage's goal at all.

He shrugged. "I've met Vivian," he said as if that explained it all.

And who was April to say that it didn't?

It was Gage's money, after all. It was his choice how he wanted to spend it.

She flicked the envelope in her fingers. "Fine. I'll deliver the check and meet with Snead." She thought about the preliminary proposal they'd prepared for Otis. The one she'd left with Jed a month ago. "Am I putting a proposal to him, then? From everything Archer said about Snead, I think the only thing he'll care about is a dollar figure."

"Straightforward money deal. You know what our range is. Start at the bottom and see how it floats. If he won't agree even at the top, then let me know. I'll decide then if we'll go higher or walk away."

She couldn't help herself. "You'd actually go higher?"

"To own a mountain of undeveloped, pristine wilderness? I might."

She pressed her palms together. "What, uh, what about the ranch house? The cattle and everything?" *What about Jed?*

"The ranch is barely profitable. It's nothing compared with the rest of the mountain."

"It's important, too." The words popped out,

earning a curious look from him. Feeling hot inside, she shrugged. "You could…could have a guest ranch maybe."

"Instead of a resort." He sounded incredulous.

"Or in addition to. The mountain's big enough for both. There are lots of people interested in having that experience. Not just, you know, your usual outdoor—" She broke off when his phone buzzed and he shooed her out with his hand as he reached for it.

End of conversation.

April left his office and returned to her own, which was really just a cubicle in a room full of a dozen identical others. She packed up her laptop and slid it into her briefcase and headed out.

She stopped by her apartment to change out of her work clothes into sandals and a flowered pullover shift. Feeling disgruntled, she threw more clothes into an overnighter and pitched it all into her car. A full tank of gas later, and she was on the road once again back to Wyoming and Weaver.

The drive took nearly eight hours, thanks to road construction on the two-lane highway between Braden and Weaver. With winter finally in the rearview mirror, road repairs and improvements were in full gear.

When Rambling Mountain came into view in the distance, looking purple in the lengthening sunlight, she wanted to turn around and drive another eight hours just to get away.

Of course, she didn't.

She just kept driving toward the mountain, pulling closer and closer until she reached the turnoff for the ranch road.

She hadn't bothered calling ahead to the Double-C. She'd left just as abruptly three weeks ago as she'd be arriving now.

When she drove through the timbered entrance, all she could think about was that kiss the night Jed had followed her from Colbys, and it left such an acute ache inside her that she felt shaky. The feeling hadn't abated even when she finally reached the circle drive at the big house.

She drove around to the side of the house where the usual scattering of ranch vehicles were parked. She parked next to an SUV bearing the Double-C brand on the door, grabbed her belongings from the trunk and pushed her way through the screen door into the mudroom.

She dumped her briefcase and overnighter on the floor next to the enormous washing machine. "I'm back," she announced needlessly as she headed into the kitchen, where she could see supper was in full progress.

A half-dozen surprised faces turned her way.

April saw none of them.

None of them, because Jed was sitting right

there, with her uncle Matthew on one side and her grandmother on the other.

She was glad she'd already set down her bags, because if she hadn't, she was pretty sure she would have dropped them right then and there.

Gloria was the first one to jump up. She gave April a squeeze. "Sweetheart, why didn't you call?"

"Bad cell reception," she lied, trying to keep from staring too obviously at Jed. She closed her hands over the back of the one noticeably empty chair. "Where's Squire? And please don't tell me the two of you are still fighting about Vivian Templeton."

"Council meeting," Gloria provided. "And don't worry. We're speaking again."

"Just not about library projects or anything else to do with Vivian," Matthew said wryly.

April smiled and managed a light laugh, though in truth she was more than a little relieved.

She leaned over her aunts and uncles to give them quick kisses and muttered a hello to Jed only because it would be noticeable if she didn't.

"Sit down, honey. We're all finished, but I'll get you a plate. Been so warm, we've had our first outdoor grilling of the season."

"Actually, I, um…" She looked over her shoulder toward the door. "I just needed to drop off my stuff. There's something I still have to do."

"What?"

"Just, uh, just…stuff." She knew she was flushing but there wasn't a thing she could do about it. She bumped into the doorway as she backed out of the kitchen and nearly tripped over her own suitcase before she managed to push through the screen door again.

The gravel crunched under her sandals as she hurried around the house and to her car.

She didn't have a destination in mind. Only a desire to escape.

"April."

His voice made her flinch. She ignored it and yanked open her car door.

Unfortunately, that was as far as she could go, considering her keys were inside her briefcase.

Which was still in the mudroom.

Jed pulled open the car door and looked down at her. Not saying a word.

Just standing there. Wearing a clean white shirt rolled up to his elbows and untucked over faded blue jeans. Dark brown eyes frowning down at her.

Her nerves were too frayed. "What are you *doing* here?"

"Eating supper."

She wanted to launch out of the car and shove him. She rubbed her hands over the steering wheel, fingers clenching and unclenching. "Don't do that."

"Why?"

"Exactly!" She shot him a look. "*Why?* Why are you *here*?"

"Your uncle's offered me a job."

Her breath wheezed out of her. "But what about the Rambling Rad?"

He propped his arm on the roof of the car, which only stretched his shirt across the flat of his stomach.

She tightened her hands again around the steering wheel just to make sure they didn't go and do something incredibly stupid, like reach out to touch him.

"Otis is gone. It's not my ranch. Remember?"

Her shoulders sank. "How could I forget?" She chewed the inside of her cheek and looked up at him. The last time she'd seen him—before the part in his bunkhouse-for-one—he'd looked as dreadful as a man could after literally burying his friend.

And despite Jed's assertion that he'd only worked for Otis, there was no doubt the man had been his friend.

Now he looked at least more rested. His eyes weren't bloodshot from lack of sleep or whatever.

"How *are* you?"

He pushed his fingers into the front pocket of his jeans. "How do I look?"

Too good for words.

She redirected her gaze upward again somewhere beyond his right ear. "Like you need a haircut." She kept her voice crisp. But then ruined it all because she really did have too short a supply of willpower where he was concerned. Her gaze went back to his. Searching. "You really want to work for the C?"

"You think I shouldn't?" His fingers drummed the roof of the car. "It's your family's ranch. What's wrong with it?"

"Nothing! It's just—" She looked out her car windows at the ranch trucks. The outbuildings. The big house might be pretty modest, but nothing else about the ranch was. "I know it's a cattle ranch, but the Double-C is quite a corporate enterprise now." Everyone in the family held shares. Even her. There were employees who were the typical ranch hand, and there were ones who sat in an office on computers logging this and tracking that. "There is a big difference between working on a ranch like this and running a couple hundred head by yourself on the Rad."

"So?"

"So—" she lifted her shoulders "—I'm not saying you wouldn't be good at anything you want to do, it's just, well you—you don't strike me as being particularly corporate minded."

His lips twisted. "Baby, you have no idea."

"Don't call me baby." Her cheeks went hot. "I, uh, I have a name."

His eyebrow peaked. "From now on, you'll be forever April, then."

He couldn't possibly know what a blow that felt like. He didn't know she'd seen the inscription in his wedding ring.

She should have left well enough alone.

"What're you doing back here?"

Of course he wouldn't expect her to return because of *him*.

She exhaled and looked down at her toes, freshly painted bright blue in honor of sandal season. The color choice might have been a mistake. "Same thing as before. Gage's interest in the mountain hasn't changed. He wants it. Period." She eyed him from beneath her lashes. "H-have you met him? Louis Snead?"

He drummed the roof of the car again. "Everyone in town has probably met the guy by now."

"What do you mean?"

"He's going to inherit everything. Man's no fool. He knows what it is worth. He's been talking to everyone in town."

"Are you still looking after it? The ranch?"

"I told you I would."

"Until someone makes you stop," she remembered.

"From the way things are going, that's going to happen sooner rather than later."

"Has Snead been up to the cabin?"

"He doesn't care about the cabin. Doesn't care about anything except selling it and everything else." Jed's drumming finally stopped. "Right up your alley."

She restlessly pushed him out of her way and climbed out of the car. There was no point in pretending she was heading anywhere. "Don't make it sound like something dirty. If Stanton buys it, the integrity of the land will be respected at least. He wouldn't be mining or drilling." She leaned against the side of the car, arms folded. "You told me once that you disagreed with Otis about what he should have done with the land."

"It doesn't matter anymore, does it."

He hadn't meant it as a question, but she took it as one anyway. "If it *were* up to you."

His eyes turned flat. "But it isn't. Otis and I got what we needed from each other. He got a strong back from me and I got a reason to get up in the morning. Nothing more, nothing less."

"I think having a reason to get up in the morning is quite a lot, actually." The pinging of his chunky gold wedding ring hitting a porcelain sink was sounding inside her head. "Humor me. What do you think Otis should've done with the land?"

He sighed impatiently and took a step, almost as though he was going to walk away from her.

But he didn't.

"It's a natural paradise. It should be protected."

"Wasn't that what Otis was doing in his life? Protecting it from everyone else?"

"You didn't know Otis long enough. Hoarding was more the intent. And protecting doesn't mean it shouldn't be enjoyed." He waved an arm toward the mountain that stood sentinel in the distance. "Everyone around here looks up at that mountain and not a single one enjoys it up close. They can't experience it. They can't hike to the summit where the snow never entirely melts. They can't look down in a lake that is so clear it's unearthly."

"You sound like an environmentalist. What exactly *did* you do before Otis? Before Texas?"

A muscle in his jaw flexed. "Took a lot of money from a lot of people and turned it into a lot more."

"What?"

"I was an investment banker."

If he'd told her he'd been an acrobat in a circus, she wouldn't have been more stunned.

He touched his finger to her chin, making her jump. "Close your mouth, Miss Reed."

She clenched her teeth, swallowing hard. Her cheeks felt positively fiery. She lifted her chin, breaking the contact. "Where?"

"Chicago."

"I meant what company."

He exhaled. "Does it matter?"

She shook her head, still feeling stunned. "How'd you go from investment banking to—" she waved her hand "—to the school of ranching according to Otis?"

He propped his hands on his hips and exhaled.

His profile was sharp against the thinning sunlight. "That is a long story."

It was pathetic how easily she forgot that she needed to keep her distance. To stay objective. "I don't mind a long story."

She knew he wasn't going to say more, though. She could read it in his expression even before he lifted his hand and rubbed his thumb along her chin. "Why'd you disappear that morning?"

Her ears suddenly filled with the rushing sound of nerves. "You were the one who was gone when I woke up."

"I was in the cabin."

She hadn't looked. She hadn't hung around one second longer than it had taken to dress and escape.

It wouldn't have changed anything, though.

She might have fallen for Jed.

But to him, she'd just been a substitute for the wife he lost.

She made herself shrug. "You know how it is." She forced out the light words. "Mornings after are always so awkward." As if she'd ever had a morning after with someone. She was no virgin. But she'd never ever spent an entire night with someone. Never had cared enough to even want to. "It's not like we'll have a repeat. I was doing us both a favor."

Something in his eyes flickered. "Right. No need for things to get awkward. Handy when a girl already gets that."

She forced her smile to stay put as he walked away, heading toward a dusty pickup truck. A truck she recognized, having seen it often enough parked at the roadblock leading up to the Rambling Rad.

The second that truck started to move, wheels crunching over the gravel, her facade dissolved.

She blinked against the tears burning her eyes as she looked toward Otis's mountain.

She wished, yet again, that she'd never met her boss, the old man buried on a mountain, or Jed.

Chapter Ten

The wildflowers had spread. In just three weeks, they had nearly filled in all of the turned-over earth of Otis's grave.

By the time summer ended, Jed knew the only evidence of the grave would be the stone marker.

He poured the water he'd brought up to the ridge over the wildflowers. "Figure this is just the way you wanted it, Otis. Being one with your mountain."

When the metal bucket was empty, he flipped it over and sat down on it.

He knew that April had to have been the one who'd planted the sprig of flowers after Otis died. He'd seen them, looking spindly and frail among the rocky soil that day she'd disappeared on him. It wasn't something he'd have thought to do.

But there they'd been. Heads of purple and red barely hanging on in the constant breeze tugging at them.

He'd brought up water that day. Tamped down the roots again. Added a little more soil and moved some rocks to provide some protection from the wind.

Since there hadn't been any rain, he'd done the same thing every day. And now the wildflowers were taking over all on their own. No longer in need of protection from the wind. Riotous, colorful weeds that would go to seed and sprout up again thicker than ever, finding life among the granite, in a cycle that Jed hoped would never end.

"She came back, Otis." He squinted into the sun, looking down at the creek-side meadow where most of the cows were contained. Babies were dropping regularly, keeping him even busier than usual. Fortunately, there hadn't been any orphans this season. It was a first, though Jed was too practical to expect the luck to continue. "That company of hers still wants your land." He wasn't going to think about anything else where she was concerned. Definitely not the fact that aside from Tanya, April was the only woman he'd ever wanted in his bed come morning.

And even though he'd fallen into the habit of

talking more to Otis now that he was gone than he ever had when he was alive, there was no way Jed would share the fact that, out of all the women he'd been with since his wife died, being with April was the only time he hadn't had a single thought about his past at all.

He pinched his nose to rid himself of the thought.

"Not sure she's gonna get a deal, though," he finally continued aloud. "Snead's already bragging in town that he's got a mining company lined up. You always told me you never wanted to see mining on your mountain."

Jed had heard the cousin showed up a week after Otis died. He wasn't inclined to think much of the guy. He'd never tried to see Otis in the five years Jed had known him. But then Jed supposed he wasn't really in a position to judge another man's character when his own hadn't been anything to write home about.

"Court's sending someone up here from an auction house over in Braden," he went on. "Make an assessment of the place. Your stuff'll go to auction and there's not a damn thing I can do about it. If you've got any power on that side where you're at, it would be helpful if you produced that will you claimed you had. And if it was just a line of bull, then nudge April to the head of the line where Snead's concerned. Otherwise, God knows what's going to happen to this place." A small grave on a high ridge above a few weather-beaten shacks would be easily forgotten.

The sound of a vehicle carried up to the ridge and Jed reluctantly stood. Otis hadn't had much in the way of possessions. But Jed still didn't look forward to a stranger picking and poking through, deciding what sort of value any of it might bring.

He leaned over and tugged a flower away from the marker and tossed it aside. The breeze caught it and carried it over the side of the ridge. "See you tomorrow, old man."

His daily treks up and down the ridge had worn down the long grass even more, making the narrow path easily noticeable from the cabin. When he reached Rufus where he'd left him, ground-tied halfway up, he could see a white sedan parked down at the roadblock. He muttered a curse as he grabbed the reins and swung up in the saddle. He clucked softly and the horse agreeably plodded the rest of the way down.

He was pulling off the saddle when he heard the footsteps on the rocky road. He finished with the horse and headed over to the cabin to find the visitor already poking around inside.

Where was Samson when he needed him? Jed deliberately let the wind slam the door shut just to watch the guy jump.

The skinny man quickly set down Otis's vintage radio. "I didn't realize someone was here."

The guy had a ferret face. No chin. Thin lips mostly hidden by a mustache straight out of the '70s, and a green suit to match. "I didn't realize the auction house sent people who don't know how to knock."

"Auction house." The guy looked like he'd been born with a sneer on his face. "Nothing here worth anything. Always heard Otis was a cheap bastard."

"Let me guess." Jed's voice went flat. "You're Snead. Hate to tell you, pal, but you haven't inherited this place yet."

"Matter of time." Snead headed toward the hallway but Jed stepped in his way.

"Until then, you're trespassing."

Snead was nearly as tall as Jed, but about fifty pounds lighter. His mustache curled. "You're the help, I suppose."

"I'll take being the help over being a relative who only comes out of the woodwork when there's a little money to be had."

"*Little* money." Snead laughed. "You're as stupid as Otis was if you think that small."

Jed grabbed the man's arm and pushed him toward the door.

"Hey!" Snead tried shaking him off. "This is assault."

"Trespassing," Jed reminded. He yanked open the door.

"Oh!" April stood on the other side, her blue eyes

wide. Samson was sitting there beside her, looking like some damn lapdog, flapping his tail against the wood deck. "I was just, ah, just going to knock." She took in Snead and the handful of skinny arm that Jed held.

Some things were inevitable. Her meeting Otis's cousin was one of them. "Snead here was just leaving," Jed said.

Her quick gaze ran over Otis's presumed heir. "Mr. Snead. I just left a message for you at the motel. I'm April Reed." She whipped out a business card so fast that Jed nearly missed it. "Stanton Development."

"Save the business meeting for another time," he advised, and pushed Snead past her. "Preferably when he's not trespassing." He frog-marched the intruder down the steps, ignoring the man's cursing and pitiful attempts to wrestle free.

Samson finally seemed to remember he didn't like strangers and circled around them, teeth baring as he growled around Snead's legs.

Snead kicked out at the dog and missed. "Keep that dog away from me!"

"That's what happens when you trespass. And try to kick him again and see what I do."

"First thing I'm going to do is fire your ass," Snead threatened. "Then we'll see who's trespassing."

Jed didn't release the man until he was within spitting distance of the boulders on the road. "Don't come back until then," he suggested. "Otherwise, the next time I'll give you the Otis treatment and fill you up with birdshot."

Snead had the good sense, at least, not to press his luck. He scurried around the wood barriers, further cementing the whole ferret similarity.

Between April's red car and Otis's old pickup, Snead would have a helluva time maneuvering his car to point down the road.

Jed wasn't sure he cared if the guy went off the edge in the process or not.

He left him to it and whistled to the dog. Samson wagged his tail and shot off ahead of him, back up to the cabin.

When he got there, April was sitting on one of the deck steps the same way she'd done the first time she'd come to see Otis. Only this time her long legs weren't encased in denim and sexy boots. They were bare beneath the hem of the flowered dress she wore. Long and sleek. Toned.

She had a little scar on her right knee. Earned in a bicycle tumble when she was twelve. He knew the shape of it. Knew the taste of it.

The night before, her dress had sported red flowers. Today's version was splashed with yellow.

And it annoyed the hell out of him that all he could think was how easy it would be to push his hands beneath that loose fabric and explore the beauty beneath.

Because one night with her hadn't been nearly enough.

She'd made it clear she wasn't thinking along those lines at all, but even if she were, what good would it do?

She was lovely and ambitious and young and could swing the world by the tail if she wanted.

What did he have to offer?

Not one damn thing.

He had less now than he'd had when he'd fallen for Tanya.

His mood darkened. "Surprised you're not chasing him down to pitch your offer." He stepped around April and the dog who'd made himself right at home at the base of her feet. "Or is that the reason you're up here in the first place? You heard he was coming here?"

She followed him inside and Jed was surprised that Samson didn't come in right on her heels since the dog seemed so enamored.

"No, I didn't know he was up here." She sounded impatient.

"Then what do you want?"

She seemed to deliberately relax. Her eyes half closed for a moment. He heard her breathing. Saw her shoulders wriggle slightly. Saw the edge of lace peek out briefly where the scooped neckline of her dress rested against her breasts.

Then she spread her palms. "I heard about the

auction company," she finally said, sounding carefully calm. "You mentioned it at dinner last night. My grandmother told me about it this morning."

"So?"

Her hands lowered. Smoothed down the sides of her dress. "So I...I thought you might want some help."

"With what? Watching a stranger decide if this—" he lifted an ashtray that could have been an antique or a dime store castoff for all he knew "—is worth being auctioned off or if it should hit the trash pile? Yeah, that's a task sure to wear out anyone."

She looked pained. "God forbid if I suggested that you might need a friend. Moral support."

He dropped the ashtray back onto the dusty table. "Nobody came for moral support when my wife died." He blamed his admission on her blue eyes. Because looking into them was like looking off the side of Rambling Mountain into clear, perfect sky.

He'd gotten over the desire to step off that side a long time ago.

Falling into that abyss of blue looking back at him felt nearly as dangerous.

He was familiar enough with the art of a one-night stand. He'd had enough of them since Tanya. But April Reed, for all her blitheness about sleeping with him, didn't strike him as the type.

"How did she die?"

His jaw felt tight. "Why?"

"You keep bringing her up. Usually a mark of someone who needs to talk about something."

"I don't need to talk about her. It's just this—" he gestured sharply "—this time of year. Otis. All of it."

Feeling hemmed in, he went out onto the porch.

April followed. "Maybe you do need to talk," she suggested quietly. "Bottling things up only makes it worse."

"You're an expert on it, are you?"

Her vibrant hair blew across her face in a sudden gust that also tugged dangerously at the hem of her lightweight dress. "Don't have to be an expert to understand a basic principle." When she finished gathering her hair in one hand, he could see her eyes had darkened. "It's not good to bottle up any kind of emotion."

"What're you bottling?"

Her gaze shifted. "Besides frustration with Otis and his will or nonwill?" She shrugged and let go of her hair to hold her dress down around her thighs instead.

He clenched his teeth and looked away, only to spot another newcomer heading up the road. This one was a woman with gray sausage curls, toting a satchel in one hand and pulling a rolling case behind her on the uneven ground.

"Perfect," he muttered, and whistled for Samson. The dog veered, chasing back behind the house.

The woman had spotted him and was waving the bag. "Mr. Dalloway?"

He heaved a sigh and lifted his hand.

"Oh goodness." She was wheezing a little as she drew nearer to the house. "Didn't think I was ever going to make it up here. I'm Eleanor with—" she paused to yank her rolling case over a bump "—with Braden Auction House. I'm sorry I'm running late for our appointment." She yanked at her case again. "Another accident on that cursed highway from Braden."

As much as he wasn't looking forward to this, he still went down to help her with her load.

"Oh, thank you." She gratefully passed over the handle for the rolling case. "That highway is nearly as bad as the road you've got coming up here." She clucked her tongue. "Felt my life passing on a few of those turns, I don't mind telling you."

He didn't bother trying to roll the case over the rocky path. He just picked it up and carried it under one arm while he took Eleanor's elbow with his other hand. "Watch the steps," he warned. "Have a few bad boards."

"Thank you, dear." She patted his hand with hers. "So nice to meet a gentleman."

He nearly choked and glanced down the mountain toward the meadow. He'd give his right arm to be down checking the mamas rather than up here dealing with the auction house. He'd already been down to the meadow once that morning just after dawn, checking the pregnant cows. It was a trip he was able to make more than once a day, now that he didn't have to stick so close to the cabin for Otis's sake.

Otis was gone. But his calf crop was better than it had ever been. Only Otis would have appreciated the irony of that.

Jed automatically guided Eleanor past the deck board that was splintered all the way through.

"Oh." Eleanor had obviously spotted April standing near the door of the cabin. "You must be Mrs. Dalloway. I'm—"

April's eyes were wide as they caught his and a blush bloomed on her cheeks. "No, I'm…I'm just a friend."

"Ah, well." Eleanor straightened her shoulders and inhaled deeply. "Friends are a welcome thing, too, at times like these." She thrust out her hand. "Eleanor with Braden Auction House."

"April Reed."

"Any relation to Morton Reed?"

April shook her head. "Um, no. Sorry."

"Well, don't be," Eleanor assured. "Pharmacist over in Braden. Died last year. Donated his estate to an ostrich farm out west somewhere even though he had an ex-wife, two grown children and seven grandchildren." She shook her head, clearly thinking the matter unfathomable as she stepped past April through the door.

Jed followed her, setting the case on the brick hearth surrounding the cold woodstove. He was achingly aware of April coming inside, too.

"Thank you, dear." Eleanor opened the bag she'd been carrying and began pulling out ragged-looking catalogs and pads. "I assume you've been in communication with the administrator assigned to Mr. Lambert's estate?"

Jed nodded, impatient to just get on with it. "Guy named Pastore. Told me to keep running things and submit all the ranch records to him until he notifies me otherwise. I sent the ledgers to him already. Otis never trusted computers. Had me recording everything by hand." Now Jed had to send weekly reports to the guy, which necessitated a trip to the post office in town since the mail carriers wouldn't come up the mountain.

"Yes. Mr. Pastore informs me you've been living here on the property, as well." She glanced up, obviously waiting for confirmation.

He nodded. "I use the bunkhouse out back." He slid a look toward April but she was busy adjusting the old radio on the mantel.

"Sure, sure." Eleanor began pulling items out of the rolling case, including a laptop computer that she set out and fired up. "What I have found to be easiest is to walk through the property with you and you can identify anything that isn't part of the estate. After that, I'll just get down to things.

"If you're comfortable leaving me to my work, then feel free to go about doing whatever you need to be doing. If you prefer staying, that's quite all right, too." Her comfortable smile took in both Jed and April. "I can do my part either way. Right now, I'm just getting an inventory prepared for the court. If we get to the point of actually going to auction, I'll make a note of items that are likely to be worth the effort."

"If you do have an auction, how does that work?"

Eleanor looked at April, who'd asked the question, but in Jed's estimation now looked as though she regretted it, considering the way her lips were pressed together and color rode her cheekbones.

"When it's possible, we tend to have auctions right on the property, but considering the difficulty getting up here and everything, whatever ends up going to auction would need to be transported down the mountain. Either to a place here in town or to the auction house in Braden." Eleanor's eyes shifted back to Jed. "But until the court weighs in, we're merely gathering information. Any other questions so far?"

Jed shook his head.

"All right then." Her look was kind. "Tasks like this are never easy. My method is to just jump right in. If you need to stop at any time—"

"I'm fine," he cut her off. "And the only stuff that wouldn't be included is in the bunkhouse out back. Maybe a couple things in the kitchen."

"Well, then. That makes it simple."

"You want to start here or—" He broke off because she was nodding those tight curls.

"That'll be fine. Are there bedrooms?"

"Just one." He gestured toward the short hallway. "Everything in this place was Otis's." There was nothing about the woman that set off alarms the way Snead had. "Give a yell if you need help with anything."

Eleanor gathered up her computer and a notepad and headed off only to return moments later with a stack of library books in her hands. "Judging by the cards inside, these are a tad bit overdue."

Jed grimaced. He hadn't thought about the books in several weeks. Not the ones he'd gotten for Otis—who'd had a liking for mysteries old or new—or the histories that were sitting in his own bunkhouse. He took the stack from her. "Thanks. I'll take care of them."

She smiled and disappeared back down the hall again.

April's gaze skittered away from his. Her hands fluttered toward the books he held. "I can drop them off at the library if you want. I'll need to go into Weaver later anyway."

"Yeah. You still need to get your pitch in to Snead."

"There's no guarantee Snead's going to get the estate."

"With no will, it's a foregone conclusion." He shoved the books onto the mantel next to the radio. "And you still have a job to do."

"I don't need the reminder," she assured him. She rubbed a hand down her bare arm. From the other room, they could hear the faint sounds of Eleanor moving about. "If you want to get out of here, I—I can stay. You know. With Eleanor."

He inhaled and shoved his fingers through his hair. Because he *did* need to check the stock again.

And April obviously recognized it, because she got a set look on her face. "Just go. At least do what you need to do."

"Babies have been dropping," he said, feeling stupid at the strange need to justify himself. "Favorite spot this year seems to be at the hook."

She raised her brows.

"It's a bend in the creek near the spot they've been grazing. Can't see it from here. Has one of the prettiest views you'll ever see."

"I noticed it from up on Otis's ridge. How do you even get down there?"

"Trail. Can't even get the utility truck down it from up here—too narrow. Rufus manages 'cause he's used to it. Once you're down, it's a pretty spot. I could take you there sometime if you want." He damned himself for the words as soon as he spoke them.

But the pleased surprise in her eyes overruled even that. "Really?"

He shrugged. "Long as you're up for a hike," he warned. "Don't know how Rufus would take to being ridden double. Otis used to have another horse, but she died of old age a while back. He wasn't riding anymore, so he didn't bother replacing her."

"I could bring up a ride from the C," she suggested. "Plenty of horses there. Guess you know that."

He shrugged yet again. "Whatever."

He looked past her to see Eleanor move from the bedroom into the bathroom. "I don't think it's going to take her too long." They could hear the squeak of the cupboard door over the washer and dryer being opened. "Here." He grabbed the books again from the mantel and held them out. "If you're serious."

"Is this your subtle way of sending me on my way?"

"Is it working?"

Her lips twitched and she took the books from him.

"There's going to be a fine for them being late. I'll get you—"

"Don't worry about it. Too bad Otis won't be here

to see the new library when it finally gets underway."

"Didn't know one was in the works."

"Mmm." She looked at the spines. "Are you sure this is all of them?"

"I have a couple more out back."

She gestured. "Let's get them, then." She followed him through the kitchen and out the back door. But she stopped there, waiting for him to retrieve his books from the bunkhouse, as if she didn't want to go in herself.

Just as well.

He flipped the woven blanket across the disheveled mattress anyway, then grabbed the books and carried them back to her, adding them to the pile in her arms. "Thanks."

"Glad to help." Her gaze skated across his face. "You're sure you're okay? You know, with all that?" She jerked her red head in the direction of the house behind her.

He actually felt a smile. "Baby, I have survived a lot worse than this. But I appreciate the effort."

She smiled, too, though he thought it looked a little shaky around the edges. "Okay, then." She started down the hill toward the road but looked back at him. Her hair streamed out from behind her and the yellow dress fluttered around her knees. "Be in touch soon."

He wondered if he was going to have that image

of her in his head for the rest of his days. It could keep company with the last words Tanya had ever said to him.

What is the point of you?

He ruthlessly closed off the memory. "If it's to report how things go with Snead, I'll pass."

She squinted a little in the sunlight. "I meant about seeing the creek."

He nodded. Feeling that smile return. "Sure. Yeah."

She hesitated for a moment, then smiled, too, as if relieved, and turned again to head for the road.

He watched until she was out of sight.

Then he looked up toward the ridge. "I hear you laughing, old man."

He heard Eleanor call his name and he turned to go back inside.

But the smile he felt stayed in place.

Chapter Eleven

"The fines total up to $21.50," the library worker told April the next morning.

Twenty-some dollars wasn't going to break her, she knew, but still. The last time she'd paid a library fine, it had been in the neighborhood of three bucks. "How overdue *are* the books?" She unzipped her wallet, pulling out the cash.

The girl sitting behind the desk checked her computer. "Five weeks." She took the money and tucked it in her drawer, returning April's change. "You'd be surprised how many people don't bother paying their fines, though. We have to suspend their borrowing privileges. One of these days, it's going to take a credit check before someone can get a library card." She extended a colorful flyer. "We're having a sale on paperbacks for Memorial Day, if you're interested. Anything we raise goes toward the new building project."

April took the flyer and folded it in half. She still needed to deliver Gage's latest donation. "Do you know how much has been raised yet?"

"Heard they're halfway to the goal." The girl didn't look much older than a teen as she leaned forward conspiratorially. "I bet you that Templeton lady just donates the rest. That's what she did with the hospital, you know. Donated all the money to have it built."

"No, she damn well didn't," a cantankerous voice said loud enough to make April cringe. "We built that hospital through sweat and hard work while that Templeton *lady* was fifteen hundred miles away, sitting in her ivory tower sipping tea and judging everyone who didn't meet her standards."

"Squire," Gloria chastised. "Shh."

His voice didn't get louder, but it got a whole lot colder. "Don't you shush me, woman."

April quickly folded the flyer and shoved it in her purse along with her wallet and smiled apologetically at the library aide before she turned and tucked one arm through each of her grandparents'. She was pretty sure Gloria had suggested they go to the library with her to help prove to Squire how badly a new one was needed.

"Let's just get over to Ruby's," she said as she tried to hurry them toward the door. "You promised me cinnamon rolls and I don't want to get there too late. You know they're almost always all gone by ten."

But neither Gloria nor Squire seemed inclined to cooperate.

They'd needed to be in town anyway—Squire on town council business and Gloria for her volunteer shift at the hospital where she'd once been a nurse. Gloria had suggested breakfast at the diner when they'd learned April was heading to the library.

But now, Squire had planted the tip of his hickory walking stick as though he didn't plan to go another inch.

And Gloria, arms akimbo, was glaring up at him. "You're impossible." Her tone was as hot as the glint in her eyes. "You can't let a simple comment pass without exploding with self-righteousness."

"That woman—"

"Stop! Just stop." Gloria's hand slashed the air. "This fixation you have against Vivian Templeton is out of hand, Squire! It was more than sixty years ago!" She didn't seem to care that they were drawing attention any more than Squire did. "And you behave as though it was just yesterday. I am fed up. You want to work yourself into a stroke or a heart attack? Is that what you want?" She jabbed her finger into his chest. "Well?"

"I want you to stop poking me like I'm that bread dough you make," he said through his teeth. "And I don't give a flying damn how long ago it was. You want to take that woman's side over *mine*? Is that the kind of wife I have?"

"Is that the kind of *husband* I have?" She waved her arms. "I want peace, you stubborn fool. Vivian Templeton is in this town to stay and no amount of you cussing and fussing about it is going to change that."

"Fool, am I?" Squire looked so incensed that April took a concerned step toward him but she froze under the slice of icy blue he cut her way. "Maybe after all these years, you're thinking you want a taste of something different! Someone more your age!"

Gloria reared back. "What is *that* supposed to mean?"

"I know you've been meeting up with Tom Hook. You think I'm blind as well as old?"

Gloria's hand flashed out. The slap she gave Squire sounded loud in the hushed silence of the library.

April inhaled sharply, but no air seemed to come with it.

Her grandparents glared at one another for a moment that seemed to stretch into painful eternity.

Gloria was the first to look away. She shook her head. "Squire, I don't even know what to say to you now." Her voice was husky. "That you could even think—" She broke off again. She looked at April. "I'm sorry, sweetheart."

Then she gave Squire a final angry look and stormed out of the library.

Her grandfather's knuckles were white around his walking stick.

"Squire." She tentatively touched his arm. "Grandpa, you have to go after her."

His eyes were like flint. The imprint of her grandmother's hand looked red against his flexing jaw. "Do I?"

She gaped, feeling helpless.

Then she felt her knees weaken with relief when he strode out of the library, using the walking stick more to whack the door as he went through than as any real support.

She hurried out the door herself and then her knees didn't feel relieved at all.

Because Squire had *not* followed Gloria.

Her grandparents had gone in entirely separate directions.

On the street only fifty feet away, a bus was letting off a horde of chattering preschoolers, who were being ushered toward the library by a handful of adults.

She leaned against the side of the building, shoving her fingers through her hair and closing her eyes. If only she'd told her grandparents that she'd meet them at Ruby's. Or if she'd just come to the library *after* Ruby's. They'd all come in separate vehicles anyway because they were going separate ways after the diner.

Now, *separate* had taken on a whole new meaning.

"April?"

Her eyes flew open and she stared at Jed, who was walking up the sidewalk. "What're you doing here?"

He lifted one hand and she realized he was carrying a book. Another library book. "Found it under Otis's bed. Are you all right? You look like you're about to be sick."

She wiped her hand over her face. She wasn't sure he wasn't right. "M-my—" She had to clear her throat. "My grandparents just had a…a horrible argument."

She bent forward from her waist, lowering her head. All she needed to cap the morning was to vomit her brains out on the grass outside the town library in front of Jed and a bunch of little kids.

His hand touched her shoulder. Slid over her back.

She was grateful that he didn't offer up the usual platitudes.

"She slapped him," she whispered. "I bet she's never slapped anyone in her life. And he, God, he just—" She closed her eyes. Remembering the photograph she'd taken of her grandmother looking like a million dollars, standing and laughing at Vivian's fund-raiser party alongside Tom Hook. Thank God she'd never shown it to Squire.

"Come on." Jed's hand reached her waist just as the first of the kids reached the library door. "Let's get you out of here at least."

She straightened and blew out a long breath. "We were going to go to Ruby's," she told him as they walked around the swirling mass of children. "For breakfast."

He lifted a brow and she immediately shook her head. "No way. Not now."

His hand slid away from her waist but only to wrap around hers. "Somewhere else, then."

She realized he was heading toward his truck, where it was parked on the street. "But your book—"

"It's more than a month overdue. What's another day?"

What *was* another day?

Feeling sick at heart, she climbed up onto the passenger seat after he'd opened the door and shoved aside a pile of clothes. "What's all that," she asked once he'd gotten behind the wheel.

He glanced at the clothes. "Some of Otis's stuff. Taking it to the donation place. Don't know if it's allowed—" he air-quoted the word "—or not and don't care. Eleanor already said none of it would go to auction and I'll be damned if I'll leave it for Snead."

Her heart squeezed. She looked at him. "I should

have asked. How did everything go after I left yesterday?"

His brows pulled together in a quick frown. "Don't worry about it. It was fine." He put the truck in gear and waited for a slow-moving tractor to lumber past before pulling out onto the street. "What'd they argue about?"

She told him. "I've never seen either one of them so angry. They have to get over it, right? I mean they've been together forever. People like them don't...don't—" She couldn't even finish the untenable thought.

His hand squeezed hers.

But then he didn't let go and return his hand to the wheel. He just kept his hand on hers. Right there, atop the console separating his seat from hers.

Her chest ached anew and she looked out the window, not really caring all that much where they went. She wanted to ask him if he'd decided about taking the job at the Double-C. Only she wasn't really sure she was ready to hear the answer. If he did take the job, it meant a possibility of running into him when she visited. If he didn't, then it meant who knew what?

Would he stay in Weaver?

Would he leave altogether?

"Heard that the court will be making a decision on the estate soon."

She startled. "This quickly?"

"He died nearly a month ago. Once Snead inherits, you'd better be ready to act fast."

She chewed the inside of her cheek. "And what about you?"

His hand finally moved back to the wheel as he turned off the main street, slowing to a stop behind a school bus that had its red lights flashing. "I sure as hell don't have the money to buy it." He shook his head. "Maybe once," he murmured as the bus started moving ahead of them. "But those days are long gone."

She gave him a sharp look. "What happened, Jed? Really? Why did you end up here in Weaver at all, when you had a career—"

"And a wife and two babies on the way?"

She inhaled sharply. Babies. She mouthed the word soundlessly.

His hands were wrapped tight around the steering wheel, reminding her too vividly of Squire's grip on his walking stick and he was silent so long she was certain he wouldn't say more.

But then he did. In a flat tone that was all the more wrenching for its lack of emotion. "I had everything. And instead of tending to it all, I worried too much about getting more. And in the end, I lost everything that mattered." His thumb started drumming the steering wheel. His focus straight ahead through the windshield. "It was a car accident. One stupid car accident like a hundred others just like it. She was on her cell phone. Texting."

"Oh, Jed."

His jaw canted. "She was four months along. Didn't know it was twins until the autopsy."

She pressed her lips together, choking down the dismay rising in her.

"Eight years ago last March," he said. "Feels like yesterday sometimes." He turned the wheel again, and she realized he'd pulled into a small strip mall near Shop-World. He found a parking spot but didn't turn off the engine. "She was texting me," he said in that flat, emotionless tone. "Wanting to know why I'd missed her appointment at the obstetrician's." He finally looked at April. "Well?"

It took her a moment to realize the glint in his eyes was challenge. "I'm sorry." Her tongue felt thick. "I'm sorry for all that loss. That pain."

"That's all you have to say?"

She spread her hands. "I don't know what—"

"Working." The word was clipped. "I was working. Trying to redeem myself from a career that was already in the gutter."

"Stop." She closed her hands over the cords standing out in his forearm and squeezed.

"Don't want to hear it was my fault that she died? Maybe you'd rather hear about the kid born and raised on the wrong side of Chicago who dared to set his eye on the daughter of the man who paid his father to keep the hedges clipped and the pool clean—"

She reached across the console and laid her palm against his jaw. "I know you loved her," she said carefully. "And I'm sorry you lost her. Lost that future. And that is *all* I am saying."

She could feel the muscle in his jaw working beneath her palm. His eyes searched hers. "You'd be the first, then."

He exhaled and turned his head and her hand fell away. He gestured at the building in front of them. "Lunch counter in there. Not as good as Ruby's but they've got decent coffee." The corner of his lips jerked in a smile that wasn't a smile, but neither was it a frown. "Maybe it's the same as that egg stuff you made."

She let out a small chuckle and allowed her head to fall weakly for a moment, just a moment, to press against his hard shoulder. God help her, she was just going to keep falling for the man. And there was no hope whatsoever in a contest between her and the ghost he still loved.

She swallowed the knot in her throat and made herself lift her head. Because he'd suffered too many losses already. Because she'd seen him smile once and she was going to make sure he did it again. If only so he wouldn't forget that even in grief, there were still things in the world to smile about.

Even if it only started and ended with a good cup of coffee.

"That sounds really nice to me," she said.

Then she quickly turned away and opened her own car door, taking time to blink hard so he wouldn't see more tears in her eyes.

On a good day, April could make it up the treacherous, winding road to the Rambling Rad from the big house in just under an hour. Driving one of the Double-C trucks with a horse trailer on the hitch, it took her twice that long, particularly when she had to make a stop at Vivian Templeton's house to deliver Gage's check. The woman herself hadn't been there, but the young woman who was her assistant had been so chatty, April could have wasted another half hour if she hadn't managed to pull herself away.

But finally she'd made it to the wooden barricade and she set the brakes and slid out of the truck. She tossed the chucks from the truck bed behind the wheels of the trailer for good measure, then opened the gate to back Daisy down the ramp.

The horse was her grandmother's favorite mount. Reliable. Unfailingly easygoing. She was surefooted and rarely spooked. Which to April felt like the perfect choice to take down a path that was too narrow to accommodate a UTV.

She tied the horse to the trailer while she pulled

out the tack. She was just tightening the cinch when Daisy nickered softly and shifted.

A moment later, Samson ran around them both, giving Daisy's hooves plenty of berth.

"Good-looking horse," Jed said.

April pulled down the stirrup from where she'd tucked it over the saddle horn and patted the horse's gleaming brown coat. "She is. This is Daisy." She finally looked over at Jed. Even prepared, the sight of him caused something in her stomach to flutter around like a caged bird. It was the middle of May and the thermometer had been climbing steadily. He only wore jeans and a white T-shirt that clung to his shoulders. "How'd you know I was here?"

"Sound travels up here. Heard the truck."

Right. She smiled. "I've come for the tour." They hadn't actually gotten around to setting a time. Or a date for that matter. After coffee—which had been particularly good, despite everything—at the little lunch counter he'd taken them to, he'd dropped her off at her car.

They hadn't spoken any more about his wife. Or her grandparents' argument. They hadn't discussed the Rad, or what would happen to it after Snead got his hands on it. They had simply sat there, shoulders brushing because of the close confines of the counter stools, in relatively companionable silence.

Drinking coffee.

She looped the reins in her hand and started toward Jed. "Hope it's not too inconvenient of a time. If it is, say so." She waved her hand toward the cabin and Otis's ridge above it. "Daisy and I will just head up to see Otis."

The sun was already well in the sky, making both his brown hair and brown eyes seem lighter. His gaze was no less piercing, though. It seemed to rove over her like a hound on a scent. "What's wrong?"

If he ever listened to the gossip in Weaver when he got into town, he'd know soon enough. "My grandmother has left the Double-C." Left Squire. The unthinkable had actually happened. "She packed up and went to stay with my aunt and uncle at their ranch." It was hard to get the words out without wanting to bawl.

"Think it'll blow over?"

It was hard to swallow with the knot in her throat. "I don't know how. He's taken himself off to his fishing cabin. She's at my aunt's. They're both refusing to talk, so—" She lifted her hands. "Your guess is as good as mine."

"I'm sorry."

"Aren't we all," she murmured. Daisy nudged her shoulder and she nearly bumped into Jed. "Sorry."

He just steadied her. "Horse likes you. Nothing to apologize for." He called the dog, but Samson was already off chasing something. "Come on." He shoved aside one of the wood barriers so that there'd be more room to walk Daisy through.

"You sure it's not a bad time?"

"It's a perfect time, actually. Any later and I'd have already headed down there. Rufus is already saddled up." He was walking ahead of her, and the leather gloves he'd shoved in his back pocket kept drawing her attention to that whole region.

She was glad he couldn't see her face. She didn't really want to be caught ogling his butt even if it was supremely ogle-worthy.

But if he had caught her, as a pastime it was much preferable to thinking about the state of her grandparents' marriage.

When they reached the top of the road, he whistled and Jed's horse trotted into view. "Need a leg up?"

"I got it." To prove it, she stretched her leg up and tucked the tip of her boot in the stirrup, then swung herself up onto Daisy's back. "Thank goodness for stretchy jeans," she said once she was mounted.

"That's one way of putting it," he said blandly, and her cheeks went hot. She blamed it on the sun and wished she hadn't forgotten her sunglasses inside the truck.

He was smiling faintly as he turned to Rufus. His dun was equally as tall as Daisy, and even though she tried to imagine Jed wearing a suit in some investment bank in Chicago, she just couldn't.

He mounted the horse with ease and she followed him past the cabin, winding around below Otis's ridge until they reached a narrow path that declined sharply through the rocky terrain. He looked back at her. "Doing okay?"

"Yeah." Even though she'd been put on horses since before she could walk, she hadn't been on many trails this rough. "What do you do when it's time for roundup?"

"Drive them down beyond the lake to a meadow near the highway. There're pens and chutes and a place where getting a trailer in isn't a dance with death."

"When you drive them, is the terrain like this?"

"In places. Needless to say, it takes a while. Even with the help we hire."

It boggled the mind. "You know, ranching doesn't *have* to be this hard."

"It does if you were Otis Lambert."

She leaned over Daisy's neck, trying to avoid the scrape of a low branch. From where they were, she could see neither the creek nor the meadow that had been visible from up on the ridge. Which meant she had no idea, either, how far they had to go.

She didn't know if Jed was taking Rufus slower than he would have, but she still appreciated the cautious pace he'd set.

April couldn't tell whether Daisy cared at all, though. The horse plodded along, not seeming bothered by the small rocks skittering out from beneath her hooves or the boulders pressing in on them from both sides.

At one point, April actually had to close her eyes and just trust the man leading them and the horse beneath her.

But at last, they were beyond the path, heading upward again into the clearing that was the grassy meadow. Despite the water rushing in the wide creek nearby, it was measurably warmer than it had been up at the cabin and she pulled the band off her wrist and twisted her hair up off her neck with it before she dismounted. Daisy immediately wanted to head for the water's edge, where Rufus was already drinking, and she let the horse have her way while she stretched the kinks out.

She shaded her eyes with her hand, watching Jed as he cupped water in his hands to sluice over his head. The water dripped off him, wetting his shoulders, his back. His chest.

She looked away and refastened her hair into a tighter knot. Then she pulled off the thin cotton shirt she was wearing over a tank top and walked to the edge of the stream. The water ran over the toes of her boots as she leaned over to douse the shirt in the water. "Oh criminy. That water's like ice!"

"Yep." He straightened and shoved his hair back from his face.

She quickly wrung the water out from the shirt, shook it out, and pulled it back on. The cooling effect was intense and immediate, making her skin ripple with chills that she knew wouldn't last for long.

She propped her hands on her hips and glanced around. The hook of the creek was still some distance away, but it was easy enough to see the cattle. Some were standing right in the water. Some were looking their way. "They're not going to be upset with a stranger in their midst, are they?" She squinted at Jed again.

"Not generally, unless you get between a cow and her new calf. They're pretty protective." He pulled two bottles of water from his saddlebags and tossed one to her. "Need to get a count of calves," he said between gulps of water. "Had three new ones just yesterday." He gestured toward the brush growing between the edge of the meadow and the thick growth of trees. "Most of them are working their way back in there. Fortunately, we've only got a dozen left to drop, but two of them are heifers. God knows why they've decided the maternity ward is up here instead of down by the lake like usual." He'd already emptied the bottle and he crumpled the plastic in his fist and shoved it back in the saddlebag.

Then he snatched the work gloves from his pocket and slapped them against his palm once before he began pulling them on. He released the coil of rope tied to his saddle and slung it over his shoulder. "Find some shade and relax. Shouldn't take me too long."

"I can help."

He gave her a disbelieving look.

She spread her arms. "Come on. Seriously? I've done my share of working cattle. Growing up, I spent a lot of summers at both my grandparents' and my aunt's ranches. I'll bet I'm more comfortable with it than you were when you first came here with Otis!"

In answer, he rummaged in his saddlebag again and came out with another pair of gloves. He flipped them toward her. "They'll be too big, but better than nothing."

She fit her hands into the gloves, wishing that doing so didn't feel as intimate as it did.

It was silly, after all. They were merely a pair of leather gloves. Had no doubt started out yellow, but were now as stained and discolored as the ones he wore. Just because they'd likely gotten to that state while being worn by him didn't mean anything.

Telling herself that was all well and fine. And completely ineffective.

She followed him toward the stand of fir trees and slipped into the shade. Combined with the wet shirt, she immediately felt cooler. She counted off cows. Counted the babies that were so damn cute it was a sharp reminder how she'd always hated leaving at the end of summer and going back to school.

She heard a sudden crashing through the undergrowth, followed by Jed's curse.

Alarmed, she followed the sounds. "Are you—" She broke off when she finally reached him crouched next to a cow that was lying on her side in the middle of a bristly bush. She was clearly laboring.

"Think she's breech," he said, trying to keep the heifer from scrambling to her feet and bolting. He got the rope around her neck. "Can you tie her off if I throw you the rope?"

She motioned for the rope and deftly tied it around a nearby tree

The second he released his weight from the cow, she scrambled to her feet, trying to run away, but the rope around her neck stopped her. Her eyes were wild as she tossed her head. April could see a hoof already protruding from the other end.

"You think the calf's still alive?"

"Gonna find out." He had the taut rope in his fist, slowly working his way toward the cow, though she looked like she was not going to have any of it. "Got straps and gloves in the bags."

"I'll get 'em." She ran back to the horses where they were still plodding around in the cool shallows of the creek. She flipped open Jed's saddlebags and found the pack of OB sleeves. She'd seen calves pulled before, with straps or chains and even mechanical calf pullers. None had ever been breech.

She finally turned up the straps and ran back to him, along with the pack of plastic sleeves.

The cow was off her feet again. He'd shortened the slack in the rope. If she got up again, she wouldn't be going far.

"Hope you didn't have to tackle her." She dropped down onto her knees beside him, forgetting about the plastic sleeves, because he already had his arm stuck up inside the cow's birth canal. The animal was wheezing.

"Wore herself out. At least she didn't choose that damn bush again for her manger." His eyes were nearly closed as he concentrated. "Not all the way turned, but she definitely needs help." He gestured. "Got the straps?"

She shook them out and fashioned the first loop. It was long. Long enough to loop twice over a hoof, pass behind Jed for leverage, and loop twice again over the other hoof.

"Thought this was a two-person job," she said breathlessly as she watched him work. The cow was not trying to fight him anymore. Whether she just wanted to get her baby out or she'd realized he was trying to help didn't really matter when the end result was the same.

"Last time Otis pulled a calf was the second year I was here." He had his boot heels planted in the earth as he worked. "Dammit. Nearly had it." He was sweating. His still-wet hair fell over his forehead. "Come on, baby. Give me that other hoof." He reached farther, then gave a little shout of triumph. "That's it. That's it. Little farther." She could see him feeding the straps. Knew he was looping the second hoof.

Then he was leaning back, using his weight to help ease one hoof forward, then the other, back and forth, slowly, inexorably walking the calf free. When the mama rested, he took up the slack. When she pushed again, he helped, straining as hard as any man could while helping a female bring her child into the world.

Then the calf finally slid free in a rush and he fell back, too, and yanked his T-shirt over his head to rub it over the slick, black little baby. Rubbing its head. Its face.

"Alive?"

"Yeah."

She hooted and laughed as she sank back on her heels. "Yes!" She grinned at him. "Good job, Dalloway. Hero of the day, here."

He looked up at her and seemed to go still for a moment.

She was flushed. From the heat, from the birth. At least he'd never know the fixed way he was looking at her was making her blush. "Want me to let her loose?"

He finally looked away. "Give me a second." He was still cleaning the calf. Checking its sex. "Got ourselves a little boy." As soon as he said the words, the cow was struggling to her feet. April knew that was a good sign.

"Okay. Let her loose now."

She untied the rope and flipped the loosened loop off the cow's neck. As soon as she did, the mama advanced on Jed and he quickly scooted out of the way so she could bond with her newborn.

He scooped up the straps and his soiled T-shirt. "Toss me that bottle of water, would you?"

She tossed him the water. He poured it over his arms, doing the best he could to clean himself up. She figured unless he stretched out flat in that numbingly cold stream, he wouldn't get much cleaner until he was wedged in the small shower inside his bunkhouse-for-one.

And *that* was an image she needed to get out of her head, pronto. He was already half-naked right in front of her. She didn't need to torment herself even more.

"That was pretty impressive work for a city boy."

He gave her a slanted grin. "If the guys back home only knew just how intimate I've been with a cow." Then he actually gave her a quick wink before he was striding back toward the horses.

She dragged her eyes away from that ogle-worthy sight. A sight only improved because of the stretch of naked male back above his worn leather belt.

"You coming or you just gonna stand there admiring the view?" he called over his shoulder.

She hoped to heaven the view he meant was the one lying beyond the mountain.

But the squiggle inside her said otherwise.

She didn't know if she'd made a mistake coming on this horse ride with him, but for now, she wasn't going to worry about it. There'd be plenty of time to worry about it later.

"The view," she called back to him, unable to stop the laugh that came with it.

Then she jogged after him.

Because, just in case he decided to stretch out flat in that crystal clear stream, she didn't want to miss it.

Chapter Twelve

"What's the word on Snead?"

April clutched her cell phone closer to her ear and stepped out of the kitchen, where Jaimie and Matthew and all of his brothers were grousing about Squire's apparent burst of insanity. "I haven't made any progress, Gage," she admitted when she finally reached the heavy front door and went out onto the porch. "I've tried to catch him at his motel more than once but the guy's slippery."

"Then put on some gloves and catch him."

"Rumor has it he's been talking with a mining company. Someplace out of Ohio. Winemeier Mining. Have you heard of them?"

"Not yet. Call me when you've caught Snead."

He hung up in her ear and she sighed, tapping the phone against her lips before dialing again. This time Snead's motel room. She'd called it so often it was on her frequent numbers.

As usual, he didn't answer. But this time her message was as direct as it could be. Just her name and the dollar figure that Gage was prepared to pay.

If that didn't get a response, she didn't know what would.

From inside the house she could hear her uncles' voices rising then falling as they argued over what should be done about their father and Gloria.

As if there were anything that they *could* do.

She looked at her phone, scrolling through the various images she'd taken of Rambling Mountain and the Rad until she found the one of her grandmother at the library fund-raiser.

Her mom and aunt were rallying around their mother, of course. April had spent nearly an hour on the phone with her mom that morning, listening to her rail about the situation.

To a person, everyone seemed to be blaming Squire.

April was shooting more for impartiality.

She brushed her finger over the photo, then nearly jumped out of her skin when the phone vibrated.

Jed's number replaced the picture of her grandmother laughing up at Tom Hook, and she quickly put the phone to her ear again. "Hi." She cringed at her breathy voice. "Pulled any more calves today?"

"Not so far." He sounded grim. "Heard from the estate administrator. Court has ruled on the succession. Snead's getting everything. Lock, stock and barrel. And he wants everything but the mountain itself sold."

Knowing that it had been coming didn't make it any easier to hear. "I'm sorry, Jed."

"Wanted to let you know. Now's your chance to get out your boss's checkbook."

"Not sure he is going to want to measure his checkbook against a mining company's. Are you okay?"

He was silent for a moment. "Got a copy of the list Eleanor prepared. I need to get the stuff packed up for the auction."

"Some people in your position would just walk away."

"I'm not some people."

How well she knew it. "I'll come and help."

"Why?"

Her hand tightened around the phone. "Because I want to."

"Bring boxes."

She nodded even though he couldn't see it. Even though he'd already hung up.

He was like Gage in that respect.

She returned to the kitchen. The men were still

arguing. Jaimie looked miserable. April leaned over her ear. "I'm going out. If I'm not back later—"

Jaimie patted her hand. "I know. You'll be at Belle's."

April didn't feel like explaining that she was not heading to her aunt's, but to help Jed. "I'll check in with you later."

Instead of heading straight to the Rad, she drove into Weaver first on the hunt for boxes. Stops at Ruby's and Colbys had both her trunk and backseat full up with flattened cardboard boxes. Armed with packing tape and a package of chocolate cookies from Shop-World, she drove back through town again and headed up the mountain.

When she reached the barriers, Jed was already there. Sitting on the tail of the four-wheeler.

Another white T-shirt. Another pair of jeans. His eyes were dark and mesmerizing as he headed her way and she couldn't imagine why she'd ever thought he was anything less than beautiful.

A thought that had her insides swimming more than a little. To combat it, she briskly set her parking brake, popped open her trunk and got out to begin unloading the cartons.

"Strapping tape and chocolate," she told him as he hopped off the UTV. "In the backseat."

"Sounds like a teenage boy's fantasy."

One of the boxes slipped from her grasp and it turned, corner over corner as the wind yanked it back down the road, then sent it toppling right off the edge of the mountain.

She tightened her grip. "Strapping tape," she scoffed. "Hate to be that boy's girlfriend." She brushed past him to make for the UTV.

"More the roses and candlelight type?"

She made herself laugh. "Sure. Why not? With Bollinger Champagne and chocolates purchased firsthand in Belgium." She shoved the boxes in the utility box.

They passed each other again—him with the armload of boxes this time. "Expensive type, are you?"

She spread her arms. "The way my daddy raised me," she lied lightly on her way back to the car. The trunk and backseat were empty. She grabbed the plastic bag from Shop-World, headed back to the utility vehicle and slid onto the seat beside him.

"Ever actually been to Belgium?"

"Ten years ago. High school graduation present. Belgium, Luxembourg, France." She grabbed the seat rail when he started up the engine and rumbled speedily around the boulders. "Two weeks from Bruges to Marseille."

"Fancy gift."

She shrugged. "My parents weren't particularly thrilled, but it was from Alex *Senior*. My dad's father," she elaborated at his look. "They had a rocky relationship. Couldn't agree on anything except for the fact that they couldn't agree on anything. In his will, he stipulated a year abroad for me and any other children my dad might have."

The look she got from him that time was speculative. "A year."

She shrugged. "I didn't spend a year in Europe. I chose two weeks in the fall before I started college and dumped the rest of the money into savings. And—" she lifted her hand "—before any latent investment banker cells come surging to the fore, my dad's advisers took over handling the account years ago. They take care of the trust fund, too."

"Who the hell is your dad?"

She shouldn't have been surprised. It wasn't as if she expected everyone in the known universe to know anything at all about her. It smacked of egotism. "Alex Reed. He founded Huffington—"

"Sports Clinics," he finished. He looked at her as if he'd never seen her before. "He's the guy who took Reed Health Systems public."

"Yeah, so?"

"Made a fortune on that RHS stock."

She made a face. "A lot of people did, evidently."

"So what the hell are you doing tramping around small-town USA trying to cut a deal for a developer when you could be doing just about anything else in the world? *Any*where in the world?"

"Just because I have a healthy trust fund doesn't mean I have any desire to live off it." She waggled the Shop-World bag. "That's not the way I was raised. Everyone in my family knows what the value of a dollar is, because we've always had to earn it. Money is never an indicator of quality or worth. And I like paying my own way, thank you very much."

He shook his head and gunned the engine up the last bit of pavement. "Unbelievable," she heard him mutter before he cut the engine and halted the UTV just shy of the cantilevered deck. He grabbed the entire load of boxes and stomped off.

Irritated, she followed him into the cabin, where he dumped the boxes on the floor. "I don't know what's got you so peeved. It's not like I was hiding anything."

"Before he died, Tanya's father was Chief of Staff at RHS Chicago. And I thought *she* was the boss's daughter."

Her breath exhaled in a whoosh. The universe had a strangely twisted sense of humor. "I'm not *your* boss's daughter, so what are you complaining about?" She pulled the large roll of tape from the bag and grabbed a box from the top of the stack to begin assembling it. "If you want my help packing up the stuff, then get over it and get some scissors or a knife. I forgot to bring one and I can't tear that strapping tape with my teeth."

She preferred the look of annoyance that crossed his face to that stunned look he'd had.

He left the room and she heard him rummaging in the kitchen. He came back with an ancient-looking pair of metal scissors.

Old or not, they'd been kept sharp, and they sliced through the filament tape with ease. With the cardboard once more fashioned into a suitable box, she grabbed it in her hand and stood. "What do I pack and where do I start?"

He produced the copy of Eleanor's list. April gave it a thorough look, and then silently went into Otis's bedroom.

He joined her a few minutes later with another carton and they set to work.

Packing up everything took longer than she expected and with each box that she sealed with the sturdy tape, her thoughts returned to her grandmother and Squire.

They finished the bedroom. Jed left for more than two hours to check the stock while she pulled everything out of a closet, sorting, packing. Discarding very little. It was shocking the variety of items that Eleanor had chosen. Everything from the vintage radio—totally expected—to an ugly smoking pipe. Glassware. Flatware. Boxes of old stamps. Boxes of new stamps.

Jed returned while she was working on the kitchen.

They ran out of boxes and got creative. Using the empty drawers from Otis's dresser. Buckets.

An old laundry basket. All stacking up against one side of the cabin.

Finally, they were finished packing anything that fit in a box, and were sitting in the bare kitchen at the table. A half-empty pack of chocolate sandwich cookies sat between them.

"It's going to take a lot of trips getting all of that down the mountain." Even the furniture, what little there was of it, would be going.

He nodded. Rubbed his hand down his face. "Yep."

She chose another cookie, but held it up, studying the simple perfection of it. "I should have brought milk."

He reached out and snatched the cookie from her fingers, downing it in one bite.

"Hey!" She watched him go to the stack of boxes and drawers and buckets, seeming to look for something.

"Ah." He pulled two glasses from the dish towel they'd been wrapped inside and set them on the table in front of her.

"There's no milk in the fridge," she reminded. "There's nothing in the fridge." She knew. She'd cleaned it out, scouring the shelves and the sides, because it was one more thing that was going to be auctioned.

"Got something better." He disappeared out the back door and returned shortly with a bottle. He

unscrewed the cap and tipped it over one glass.
Then the other.

"Not Bollinger, but it'll do the job." He set aside
the bottle and picked up one glass, clinking the base
softly against the rim of the other. "And no. I don't
have a drinking problem."

She lifted the glass, sniffed. Took a cautious sip
and felt the liquor bloom and warm, heating her
throat all the way down. "I thought—"

"I know what you thought." He was studying
the contents of his glass. "It was never the alcohol
that I craved. I stopped drinking when I came here
with Otis. Never found what I wanted in the bottom of a bottle."

She couldn't help but think about the wedding
ring he kept with his toothpaste. "W-what did you
want?" As if she didn't know.

"An end." His lips twisted. "An end that never
came. No matter what I did." He gently swirled
the glass. "First day up here, Otis took me up to
his ridge. Stood there with me right on the edge of
the cliff. Told me if I really wanted to do it, to stop
playing at it and do it right. One step and it would
all be over."

Her hand trembled and she carefully set her glass
back on the table.

"I don't know how many times I made that hike.
Stood right there. Toes of my boots hanging an
inch over. Wondering why the universe couldn't

just make it easy for me. Rockslides happen around here. Small ones. Big ones. You've seen for yourself. But not a single pebble ever slid out from under my feet. Not at that spot." His gaze slid over her. "You believe in God?"

She nodded jerkily. "You?"

"Sadly. The results of a Scotsman father and a Mexican mother." He looked back at his drink. "I finally figured out that neither God nor the Devil wanted me." He stopped swirling the glass and tossed the shot back in one swallow.

"Ever think that God needed you here more? That Otis coming into your life was less happenstance than divine intervention?"

He made a sound. A cross between rusty laugh and something else. "Regardless, here I am."

She knew what he was thinking. That he was here. And Tanya was not. "I should have realized Dalloway was Scottish," she said.

His eyebrow peaked.

"Reed. Go back enough generations it used to be R-E-I-D." She spelled it out.

He made another sound. Less something else. More rusty laugh. "You worried we're cousins or something?"

She picked up the glass again. Took another sip. "And your mom?"

"From Mexico. Crossed the border illegally when she was younger than you were when you were trotting around Belgium. They were both immigrants, but he took the legal route and she didn't. They met working for—"

"Tanya's father," she concluded.

So much for her trying to get him to think of someone else.

"Where my father gardened and my mother cleaned. She was deported when I was nine. I never saw her again."

"Oh, Jed." She couldn't help herself. She caught his hand in hers and squeezed. "I'm so sorry."

He shrugged and reached for the bottle again. Poured another measure for them both, even though she had only taken a few sips. "My dad worked fifteen-hour days making sure I got through school. He never had the means for a proper search for her. Didn't stop him trying. Said he'd love her forever and that's what he did. Cleared my first million when I was twenty-two." He didn't seem to notice her start. "That's when I located her family in Oaxaca. She'd already died. Pneumonia. Dad died a year later. Pretty sure it was a broken heart."

She looked away, dashing a finger under her lashes before she reached for another cookie. She dunked it in the liquor and took a bite. "You're right. Just as good as milk."

He squeezed her hand and let go. "I owe you more than cookies that you brought yourself and a fair-to-middlin' sip of Scotch whisky."

"No you don't."

But he just pulled her out of her chair. "Yes, I do. Dinner at the very least. Steakhouse over in Braden—"

"Good grief, we don't have to drive all the way over to Braden for a decent steak! Colbys is—" She broke off. "Unless you don't want to go somewhere in town. You know. With me."

He gave her a look. "My dad would've called you daft."

Her stomach fluttered. "Let me at least wash up a little. I'm dusty from all the packing."

He waved her off and she quickly went into Otis's bathroom, only to realize she'd forgotten to pack up the cupboard above the washer and dryer. She darted back to the kitchen to grab one of the big black bags they'd been using for the stuff that needed to be hauled off to the trash. "Forgot to empty the stuff over the washer."

"It can wait."

"It'll only take a few minutes, and then it'll be done." She grabbed the copy of Eleanor's list that was sitting on the counter and took it with her.

Jed followed, reaching above her head to pull down the items crammed on the highest shelf. Like her, he set everything on the top of the dryer. "This is all trash. Just hold open the bag." With his arm, he swept everything into the bag.

"Hold on." She rescued an amber-colored ashtray. "It's on the list."

"He was a smoker, that's for sure," Jed muttered. He cleared the next lower shelf. "Always had a pipe stuck in the corner of his mouth when I met him. Didn't stop until last year. Said he wasn't gonna get better, so why stop one of his remaining joys. Only reason he quit was because it hurt too much to continue."

"Not that one, either." She snatched the silver box that had contained the bandages and set it aside. "It's a jewelry box." She looked at the list. "Circa 1800."

He let out a short laugh. "I swear, the only thing that old man didn't keep above the washer and dryer was actual laundry supplies." He tossed her the can of peanut brittle. "Nuts."

She took the can and shook it. Figuring it would rattle. Surprised when it didn't. She turned it upside down. Looked at the lid. "Oh, this is one of those novelty things. You open up the can but instead of the treats, one of those springy snakes flies out." She twisted the top. "See?"

But the snake didn't pop out.

"Terrifying," he said dryly.

"Guess they have a shelf life." She poked her fingertip at the paper curled inside. Then looked more closely and drew it out. It wasn't a snake. It was a small white envelope, yellowing around the edges. Holding a perpetual curl from being stored inside a narrow round can.

"Hold the bag again." He was waiting to push more garbage inside.

"Wait a second." Excitement curled inside her as she slowly uncurled the envelope. There was nothing written on the outside of it, but she knew. She waved it at him and started jumping around like some silly schoolgirl. "This is it! I know it is. Otis's will."

He angled his head closer to her, looking at the envelope. "Nah."

She waved the can at him with its colorful peanut brittle image. "He even told me! Called it his sweet will." She shoved aside all of the stuff on the dryer so she could flatten out the small envelope. "I don't know if we should open it."

"If we don't, how are we going to prove to you that it isn't his will?"

"Don't be such a pessimist." She lifted her head. "We need to call Archer. He'll know what to do."

"The estate's been settled, April."

She swatted him with the envelope. "Well they can *un*settle it!" She closed her hand around his. "Come on. We have to go."

"Thought you wanted to call Archer."

She grabbed her hair in both hands and yanked. "Are you trying to make me crazy?"

His eyes suddenly crinkled. He yanked her

close and pressed a fast kiss on her lips. "Seems fair enough to me," he said when he let her go, just as quickly.

If he noticed that she swayed a little, he didn't say.

"If it *is* his will," he told her over his shoulder, "it doesn't necessarily follow that you'll like what it says. He might not be leaving it to your boss." He snatched up the receiver. "What's the number?"

She went still. "I don't think that. Gage certainly doesn't."

"What about Otis being your boss's father?"

She shook her head. "Gage sounded certain that he wasn't. The only logical person for Otis to leave the ranch to is *you.*"

He shook his head. "No. I was only his—"

"—friend." She went over to him, taking his face between her hands. She searched his eyes. "You were his friend. And from everything that I've seen and heard, his *only* friend."

His gaze lowered and her mouth ran dry.

She swallowed and took a step back, holding up Archer's number on her cell phone screen. "What are you waiting for? Start dialing. Probably going to take you at least five minutes on that old rotary dial."

"April."

Her chest felt tight. Her stomach shivery. If anyone else described the feeling, she'd suggest they were coming down with something.

But the only thing she was afflicted with was him.

"Look at it this way. It didn't sound to me like he wanted to leave things to Snead. Now, are you going to call, or do I have to?"

He exhaled sharply.

Then began dialing.

Chapter Thirteen

The envelope *did* contain Otis Lambert's will.

Written out entirely by him. By hand.

It was dated.

It was signed.

But what else it specifically said was going to have to wait.

April sat in the courtroom gallery along with Jed and Archer Templeton while Judge Fernandez conferred with Martin Pastore, who was the lawyer the court had appointed as the estate administrator.

Accompanying Pastore—a middle-aged man who looked to April as if he routinely kicked kittens for entertainment—was a young woman who kept consulting the laptop open in front of her. She wore a severely tailored gray suit that seemed entirely at odds with her riotously curling brown hair.

There were only three rows in the gallery. Wooden benches that seemed more suited to a church than a courtroom, but since April hadn't spent a lot of time in courtrooms, she didn't have a lot of experience to draw upon.

She leaned toward Jed, whispering as if they were in church. "Surprised that Snead isn't here. Do you think he got word?"

"I know he did," Archer assured quietly. He was sitting on the other side of Jed. "Notified him myself when I turned the envelope over to the judge."

That had been Friday.

Now it was Monday afternoon. And the powers that be were trying to decide how to proceed.

The uptight Mr. Pastore strode from the judge's bench back to the table where his associate was busily tapping away on her computer. He bent near her, murmuring something that they couldn't hear, then strode back to talk to the judge again. The curly-haired brunette sneaked a look in their direction, but quickly turned back to her computer when she saw April noticing.

She leaned again. "Archer, they have to accept the will, don't they? Even if Otis did something crazy like leave it all to Dogcatchers of the West?"

"It's a holographic will," Archer murmured. "Entirely handwritten. We just have to prove that it was Otis's hand that did it."

"Otis kept all his books by hand," Jed said. "Only change in the last seventy-some years was when I took over a few years ago." He gestured toward the lawyers. "They've already got the ledgers. Half-dozen boxes worth of proof to match his handwriting."

"It should be a straightforward matter," Archer agreed. His gaze was following the same path as the brunette with the computer. Going from the courtroom doorway and back again. "Who's Nell watching for?" he wondered aloud.

"You know her?"

"You might say that. Cornelia Brewster." He looked like he'd swallowed something bitter. "My stepsister's best friend."

April leaned forward. Lowered her voice again. "This isn't a conflict of interest, right?"

Irony shoved aside the bitter as he smiled. "Plenty of conflict, doll, but not in this situation."

She rolled her eyes. "Don't call me doll."

"It's so much fun to yank her chain," Archer said to Jed. "Oh, *hello*." The courtroom doors had flown open and Snead walked in, strutting like he was very much lord of the manor.

The overlong hair had been groomed. The mustache tamed.

Gone was the vile green suit. In its place was a

charcoal gray one that smacked of being custom-made. She knew. Her father had a preference for them.

She realized she far preferred Jed's style. Clean jeans. White button-down shirt. He'd tucked it in this time, in deference to the courthouse.

Jed leaned close to her ear. "He still looks like a ferret."

She closed her hand over his. She agreed. But she was less concerned with Louis Snead's new uptown look than she was with the entourage following him into the courtroom.

And Archer's grimace didn't help any.

Snead and his party arranged themselves across from them in the gallery and Pastore headed back to his table. He didn't seem surprised by the late arrivals. But then he'd probably had plenty of dealings with Snead already. He sat down beside Cornelia. The brunette didn't send Archer any more sideways looks. Nor did she keep looking toward the door.

The ones she'd been watching for had arrived.

Judge Fernandez was an unsmiling woman whom April didn't know. She was from the district court, and Archer had told her and Jed they were lucky to slip into the docket last minute since she traveled among several municipalities. From Weaver or not, she at least didn't seem particularly delighted by the latecomers. "We're not turning this into a circus," she warned before calling the session to order. "It's already quitting time, and I want to keep this brief. We're here today for one purpose only. This." She lifted a clear bag containing the familiar yellowing envelope between her fingers. "While it appears this document is the last will and testament of Otis Jerome Lambert, the estate in question is obviously one of significant importance. Therefore, I'm going to allow a reasonable period for proof."

Snead jumped to his feet, despite the tugging on his sleeves he earned from his companions. "Your Honor, I've already been recognized as my dear cousin's only heir. That man—" he pointed toward Jed "—had undue influence over Otis. We're supposed to believe he only just now found the will? I don't—"

The judge gave him an annoyed glare. "Sit down, Mr. Snead. I'm well aware that until his death, you had no interactions with your dear cousin whatsoever. This is not a hearing for you to air your opinions."

He grudgingly sat.

"Mr. Pastore." Judge Fernandez looked over her rimless glasses at the attorney. "You will work out a time for our next meeting with my clerk at which point I'll rule on the validity of the will. Two weeks from now should be sufficient to work into the schedule." She lifted her palm toward Snead's direction. "And before you bother again, your opinion on the matter is noted for the court."

"Two weeks!" Snead hopped up again despite her warning. "I can't wait that long. I have a right to know what it says!"

"Mr. Snead, you can wait as long as I say you can wait and so can your new friends there from Winemeier Mining. I know you're all salivating over the prospect of mining Rambling Mountain."

"Your Honor." Mr. Pastore popped out of his seat. "With respect, Mr. Snead's business interests are hardly relevant."

"That's right!" Snead shouted. "What I do with my land is my business!"

The judge sent them all a quelling look. "And if you interrupt one more time, I'll hold you in contempt." Her eyes swept across the room. "If or when the document is proven, it will be entered and the contents will become public record. Adjourned." She slapped her gavel, rose from the bench and strode out of the room.

"And the games will begin," Archer murmured. He gestured and they followed him from the courtroom, past Snead, who was huddled with his entourage, waving his arms around and looking frantic.

As the double doors swung closed behind them, April saw Pastore approaching Snead's trio.

"Mr. Pastore doesn't have anything to gain, does he? Regardless of what happens with the will?"

"I have no love for Martin Pastore," Archer admitted, "but even he has some respect for the rule of law." He gave them an encouraging smile. "Keep in mind that the judge could have denied the will out of hand, but she didn't. Now, we just need to make sure the thing is deemed valid."

"It's certainly not fraudulent," April said quickly.

"I know," Archer soothed. "This is just going to add to the length of the probate, which never moves quickly anyway."

"So what is Jed supposed to do in the meantime?"

"Continue following the stipulations that Pastore has already assigned where the ranch is concerned. It's not to anyone's benefit that the livestock suffers or the ranch falls into disrepair." He eyed Jed. "I know you're receiving compensation for your care-taking duties, but you do have a choice."

Jed's eyes slid toward Snead. His lips twisted. "Do I?"

"So now what?"

They'd parted company with Archer at the courthouse and somehow ended up walking to the park. To the gazebo.

It was a late Monday afternoon. They could hear the children from the schoolyard not far away, where a baseball game was in full play. The park itself, though, was quiet.

April chewed the inside of her cheek, studying Jed's face. "Well? Now what? Archer *was* right. I know you don't necessarily agree, but you really do have a choice. You don't have to keep working the Rad."

"Who else is going to? I promised Otis." He sat down on the edge of the raised deck of the gazebo. "This thing needs to be painted."

"Winters are hard on it. It probably needs painting every year. Pastore could hire someone else to tend the stock."

"Leaving me to take your uncle's offer? Work at the Double-C?"

"That's not what I meant." She sat beside him. He was right. When she closed her hand over the wood beside her, the paint was chipping and ragged. "In a few weeks, when Otis's will is accepted—"

"—I'll need to find work. If not there, then somewhere else. And the days of me working in finance are done."

It shook her to think that he might leave Weaver. "B-because you're not interested in finance anymore?"

His lips twisted. "Because *it* isn't interested in me."

"I don't understand."

His arm brushed hers when he gripped the edge of the wood the same way she was. "The firm I worked for was Hampton-Tiggs."

Even though she tried, she couldn't squelch her shock.

And he obviously recognized it.

"Yeah." He gave her one look and grimaced. "*That* Hampton-Tiggs."

The once-prestigious financial institution had made the news all around the country when the company's two principals—Macarthur Hampton and Veronica Tiggs—were arrested for fraud, theft and money laundering. "I was in college when all that hit. Nearly ten years ago, wasn't it?"

"Eight." He looked her way again. "Go ahead and ask. Everyone else did."

"Sorry?"

"If I knew." His lips thinned. "I didn't. A lot of us didn't. But it took a six-month criminal investigation to convince anyone. Didn't matter that we were cleared. Guilt by association was enough to end a lot of careers. Not just mine."

Eight years ago. He'd told her his wife had died eight years ago, too. She couldn't help wondering if it had been before or after.

But what did it matter, anyway?

She looked down. They were both cupping the edge of the wood. Only a few inches separated her hand from his.

She stretched out her pinkie finger and touched him. "I'm sorry. That was a really awful year for you." Followed by several more. Before he and Otis had encountered one another. "What happened to the others?"

"No idea. There's some bull notion that people going through the same crisis will band together. But they don't. We spent eighty-hour weeks working together, but when the scandal hit, we couldn't get away from each other fast enough. Rats on a sinking ship."

"Hardly rats. You just said you didn't know what was happening."

"Should have. Right under our noses."

"I think you're too hard on yourself. And before you start to argue with me, you keep making assumptions about what Otis wrote in his will."

"And you don't?"

She had to give him that point. "Well, it's only two weeks and you'll know." She hopped down and dusted her hands together. "We'll all know. You have only one thing you have to decide right now."

"What's that?"

"Where you're taking me for that steak you promised me."

"That was three days ago."

She lifted her hands. "A promise is a promise."

His gaze ran from her head to her toes and back up again. Unlike Jed, she had worn a suit to court. "You're overdressed for Colbys."

The warmth running inside her had nothing to do with the warm day and everything to do with that look of his. She slipped out of her suit jacket, leaving the black slacks and thin gray tank. "Better?"

He shook his head regretfully. "Still over-dressed."

She huffed and looked down at herself. There was no regular dress code at Colbys. Pretty much anything went, as long as it included clothing. "I am not."

His eyes suddenly glinted. "For what I have in mind?"

Shivers skidded along her spine. Somehow, she managed to ignore them and gave him a smirk. "Tempting as you think that might be, let's just stick to being friends."

A smile was flirting around the corners of his mouth, making that little scar look more like a dimple. "Friends can—"

"*Clothed* friends," she said blithely. "Not that you're not…sort of cute and all." A description for him that couldn't have been further from the truth. Jed Dalloway was definitely attractive. But most definitely not in a cute, harmless sort of way. "Nevertheless, you know, better that we don't—" She waved her hand. "You know."

He stood, too. Sort of rose up, like a lion who was leisurely waking up from a nap in the sun. "You know?"

Her mouth felt dry. She took a step back, only to feel her high heel sink into the grass. She wobbled slightly, adjusting her footing. "Don't play dumb."

His hand clasped her arm. "You don't seem real steady there."

"It's the grass." She tugged her arm free. "I can be your friend, Jed. But I…I can't be your friend with benefits. I'm not made that way."

His eyes narrowed slightly. "I see."

"Do you?" She stepped back again. Sank into the grass again and heaved out a sigh. "Wish I did," she muttered, finally just stepping out of the high-heeled pumps and leaning down to pull them free from the grass.

"You're not in Weaver for the long haul."

She straightened slowly.

"You're here because of Rambling Mountain."

What he was saying was true. And so, so far from the truth.

She dangled her shoes from her fingers. She was tired of talking about the matter. No matter what happened with the will, she felt certain her boss was destined for disappointment, and she was hard-pressed to feel regret. Not when she felt so strongly that Otis would have left everything to Jed. "Where's that steak?"

His dark eyes studied her for a moment. Then his head dipped slightly and he gestured. "Across the street."

She forced a friendly smile and started off across the grass in her bare feet.

After a moment, he followed. When she reached

the sidewalk, she stopped to slip on her shoes once more, and then they crossed the street, aiming for the grill.

The place wasn't quite as busy as it usually was, and they took a small high-top table near the window overlooking the street. April hung her jacket over the back of her chair when Jed pulled it out for her before sitting. When they were both seated, his knees brushed against hers.

"Sorry," he murmured.

Privately, she didn't think he really looked it and she was painfully grateful when a perky-faced waitress came by to deliver tall glasses of ice water.

"Special from the grill tonight is lasagna." The waitress handed them their menus. "Get you started on something from the bar?"

April shook her head. The last thing she needed was alcohol. "Just the water, thanks." She set aside the menu without needing to even open it. "I'll have the rib eye. Medium rare. No onions or mushrooms. Baked potato with all the fixings."

"Same," Jed said when the waitress turned her attention to him. He shifted in his seat, glancing toward the bar and his knee brushed April's again. "Plus whatever seasonal you have on tap."

"You bet." The waitress scooped up the unnecessary menus and headed off.

His knee was still pressed against April's.

She lifted her water and took a long drink, but it did little to calm the rattling going on inside her.

"So what do you hear from Loverboy?"

She nearly choked on the water and quickly set it aside. "Kenneth?"

"You have more than one lover boy?"

"He's not my lover boy. He never was. And I haven't seen him since, well, you know."

"Not even when you went back to Denver?"

"Not even."

The waitress returned with Jed's frosty glass of beer and when she left again, April rested her forearms on the table, clasping her hands together. "How old are you?"

His brows quirked. "Why?"

She shrugged. "Curious."

"Thirty-two."

She hid her shock. He looked older. Considering everything he'd gone through, she shouldn't have felt so surprised. He'd lost his wife and his career eight years ago. Which meant he'd been just twenty-four.

"You're still young," she said. "When the Rad is yours, is that how you want to live out your life? Ranching the hard way on the side of a mountain?"

"It won't end up mine."

"*Why* are you so certain of that? I would have sworn that you loved the ranch. Loved the mountain itself. Do you just not want it?"

"Nothing I've ever loved has lasted."

An ache filled her chest. "That doesn't mean this wouldn't. You told me you believed the mountain should be shared. You could retain the ranch. Sell the rest."

"To your boss."

"Well, certainly not to Winemeier Mining!"

"Is that what this has all been about?"

"What do you mean?"

"Hedging your bets? The whole *friend* routine? Just in case that old man leaves me the mountain?"

"Wow." Stung, she sat back and had to fight the urge to get up and walk away. "That came out of left field. You really are cynical."

"Realistic. You're here to strike a deal. With someone. You wouldn't be the first woman to sleep—"

Fire shot through her veins, incinerating anything as mild as *stung*. "Don't even go there," she cut him off. "I didn't sleep with you for a bloody deal. I slept with you because I—" She managed to put the skids on her hot tongue and slid off the stool. "You know what? If you know me so little by now, it doesn't even matter."

She grabbed her jacket and spun on her heel. She'd never seen red before. But she saw it now. It actually hazed her vision as she strode toward the exit and shoved through the door so hard it bounced back against the wall.

Outside on the sidewalk, she immediately turned and kept right on walking, her heels snapping out angrily on the cement.

She'd reached the end of the block before she even realized it. Her car was still parked at the courthouse. In the opposite direction.

She cursed under her breath and turned around to start walking back. Her ears were still buzzing. "Impossible. Impossible—" She couldn't think of a word vilifying enough. *"Man."*

"Whoa there, doll."

She glared up at Archer. "Where the hell did you come from?"

"Sheriff's Office."

It was almost directly across the street.

"What's got you in such a lather?"

"Who says I'm in a lather?"

His hands went up peaceably. "The snarl?"

"Well, I have a whole lot more where they come from," she assured, and stepped around him. "And don't call me *doll*!"

Through the window, Jed watched April stomp across the street. Her long red hair was bouncing against her back. Less than a minute later, Archer Templeton had pushed through the door of Colbys and his gaze landed on Jed.

The other man looked wryly amused as he approached. "Where's the date?" He nodded toward the two steak dinners on the table.

"On her way back to Denver, no doubt."

"A certain testy redhead?"

"She's not testy. She's just facing reality." Jed gestured with his empty glass. "Want a steak?"

Archer pulled out the chair, angling it so he had more legroom. "Looks as excellent as the steaks always are here, but I'll pass."

He gestured to the waitress and pointed at Jed's beer. He held up two fingers.

She nodded and headed to the bar.

"Doesn't look like you're in the mood to eat, either," the other man pointed out. "What reality?"

"Once a bastard, always a bastard."

"Speaking personally, or about our friend Snead?"

"Either applies."

The cheerful waitress veered to their table, delivered the drinks and after learning that Archer didn't want a menu, headed off again.

"Pretty girl," the lawyer commented.

"Didn't notice." Jed stabbed at his steak once and set down his fork. He picked up the fresh beer, but didn't drink that, either.

"You should go after her."

Jed knew the guy didn't mean the waitress.

"That's an attorney for you. Always handing out the advice." He waited a beat. "Wanted or not."

Archer smiled faintly. "We have that tendency." He took a long drink. "Too bad I never take my own." He looked back at Jed. "I know who you are. John Edward Dalloway."

Jed went still. He looked past the attorney, out the window. Seeing the past more than the street outside. It was like looking down a long hallway. One that didn't hold the pain that it once did, but one that would always be there. Reminding him.

"That was a long time ago," he said finally.

The other man was drumming the table in a deceptively leisurely way. "Not going to ask why I know who you are?"

Jed toyed with the beer. "You're representing her boss. The developer. Pays to know who all the players are at the table."

"Are you *at* the table?"

Jed grimaced. "Not by choice. None of us knows what that will contains yet, but it would have been easier if April hadn't found it."

"Even though it would have meant Snead getting it all."

"He still might."

"True."

"She'll be able to keep him from selling to the mining company."

"How do you know?" Archer raised an eyebrow.

"You're not the only one who can do his research. Winemeier isn't as stable as they appear." He saw the glint in the attorney's eyes. "Surprise, surprise."

Archer sat forward, resting his arms on the table. "Neither is Snead. He's in debt up to his eyeballs."

"Not like Winemeier is. Family owned. And there's a power struggle going on between them all. They'll take too long structuring the deal. Stanton just needs to move quickly."

Archer looked curious. "Aside from wondering how you know all that—"

"Library has adequate internet."

He smiled. "Not according to my grandmother, Vivian." Then his smile died, but evidently his curiosity didn't. "Most people wouldn't give away a second chance at a fortune. But it sounds like you might."

"You know who I am, then you know the first fortune didn't get me anywhere."

"I know you didn't have to give yours away to put into a fund benefitting the victims of Hampton-Tiggs."

"On that, you and my late wife would have agreed." Jed pulled out his worn leather wallet and extracted enough cash for the untouched meals plus tip. "Otis didn't want his land going to a developer.

April's best chance of getting her deal is with Snead." He tossed the cash on the table and stood. "Or anyone else, for that matter. Anyone other than me."

Chapter Fourteen

"I think you should stay."

April looked away from her grandmother's concerned face, pretending an interest in the scrambled eggs on her plate. "I need to get back to Denver. Toss out the houseplants I've left dying."

Belle refilled April's coffee cup, then sat down at the table and tucked her dark hair behind her ear. "What about Lambert's will?"

April continued rearranging her eggs. Rather than return to the Double-C after she'd walked out on Jed the previous day, she'd gone to her aunt and uncle's ranch. Mostly because she'd gained a painful understanding for her grandmother making that stand against Squire.

She was as furious with Jed over his insinuation as she'd ever been in her life, and they'd only known one another a matter of months.

What was it like for Gloria? She'd married Squire when April's mom and aunt were just teenagers. Shouldn't a couple be safe after so long together?

She realized her aunt was still waiting for an answer and lifted her shoulder. "The judge said she'll rule in a couple weeks. If Gage wants to pursue it then, that'll be his choice. For me, I'm done. He doesn't need me to make this deal." She gave up on the eggs and lifted her cup, burying her nose in it.

"I still think you should stay," Gloria repeated. She rose and tightened the belt on her flowered robe before she whisked away April's nearly untouched plate. "And not because of Rambling Mountain." She scraped the plate into the trash. "Your breakfast has been cold for an hour."

"I guess I wasn't hungry."

She saw the look that passed between her aunt and grandmother.

"You're always hungry," Belle pointed out gently, as if it were stunning news. "What about Jed?"

April's throat tightened. "What about him?"

Again, a look passed between Belle and Gloria.

"Honey…" Gloria sounded vaguely chiding. "One look at your face tells us how much you care for him. You're in love with him."

"You can't love someone you've barely met two months ago."

Her aunt and grandmother gave her twin looks of "are you kidding me?"

Gloria was the first to speak. "Sweetheart, I fell in love with Squire two hours into meeting that damn man. Not that I was going to admit it to him, of course."

"And here you are." April waved her hand, encompassing Belle and Cage's kitchen at the Lazy-B.

"That is because your grandfather needs to get his head out of his hind end. Not because I don't still love him. Instead of living in the here and now, he's twisting about something that happened long ago when he was just a young man."

She snatched up the bowl that had held the scrambled eggs and went back to the sink. But April had seen the way Gloria's eyes glistened, which was an alarming rarity.

Dishes clattered in the sink. "He's not a young man now. Not even a middle-aged one, despite what he may think inside that hard head of his." She sniffed. "I'm well aware that Sarah was the love of his life, but I have stood by him and been his partner for more than thirty years. I don't think it's too much to want him enjoying *our* life and the time we have left without him always getting sidetracked about the distant past."

Belle looked like she was ready to cry. She got up

and went to her mother, hugging her. April wiped her eyes with her crumpled napkin.

"I loved your daddy, Belle," Gloria choked. "But—" She broke off.

"I know, Mom. It's all right. You and Squire are meant to be together." Belle lifted her head and gave April a wet wink. "He'll come to his senses and show up here to haul you right back where you belong," she assured bracingly. "You know he will."

Gloria made a sound, half-tearful, half-wry. "Yes, well, frankly, I wish he'd get on about it before I lose my willpower and just go on home, myself." She patted her daughter's shoulder, dashed her cheek and tightened her robe again, once more in control, even though her eyes still looked damp.

She moved briskly back to the table to clear a few more plates. "Good lesson to learn, April." She gave her a direct look. "Age doesn't matter a speck when it comes to love." She pointed toward her with the stack of plates. "You love that man. Or you'd have negotiated a deal with that Snead fellow as soon as the wind turned his direction weeks ago, instead of hanging around helping Jed. Finding that will."

"Finding the will was an accident. Turning it in was the right thing to do."

"Of course it was. And I still think you should stay."

"For what?" She shoved her chair back and stood. "He accused me of sleeping with him over *business*!"

Her cheeks heated at the admission but she was too far gone to care. "He does not know me at all. And why would he care to? He's not over his wife. And I must've missed inheriting that strong gene of yours, Grandma. This isn't like you and Squire back in the day. I can't hang around here, hoping that one day he'll want to move on, or that when that day comes, he'll want to move on with *me*."

"Because your life in Denver is so perfect?"

"Because it hurts too much!"

Gloria's eyes softened. "Well, at least you're admitting it."

The pressure in her chest grew. "Yes, well, I'll get over it." If she said it often enough, maybe there was an actual chance of it one day coming true.

"Are you sure you want to?"

She pressed her fingertips to the pain in her forehead. "I told you. He's not over his wife. Frankly, I don't think he ever will be."

"He's told you that?"

"Some things don't have to be said." And the thing that he *had* said was going to burn inside her for a good long while. Because her chest felt like a vise was squeezing it, she pushed away from the table. "I need to go back to the big house and get my things."

"Are you going to see Piper before you go?"

April felt an entirely different stab. She hadn't talked with her friend even once since coming back to Weaver. "She's at school." She brushed a kiss over her aunt's cheek. "Thanks for letting me crash. And tell Cage thanks for the loan." She plucked at the oversize black T-shirt she'd slept in. She knew he'd been out working cattle since dawn.

"You could stay and tell him yourself. He'll be in for lunch in a few hours."

She knew what Belle was trying to do. Thinking if April stayed a little longer, the two of them would convince her not to go. They'd probably get her mom on the phone, too, so that Nikki could add her well-intended pressure. "It's a long drive back to Denver." Her throat was tight. She gave her grandmother a hug. "Love you."

Gloria squeezed her. "Will you still come back for the barbecue next week on Memorial Day?"

Every year the Double-C hosted a huge barbecue for the holiday. April usually tried to make it. "We'll see." She straightened and gave her grandmother a close look. "Will you?"

Gloria's lips lifted slightly. "We'll see," she returned. "Squire will miss you terribly if you don't."

"Play dirty, why don't you?"

Gloria's smile grew. "We use what tools we have." She patted April's shoulder. "It's okay, sweetheart. You do what you need to do. As long as you stay honest with yourself."

On that oh-so-delightful note, April slunk back

to the guest room and changed once more into her clothes from the day before.

Turmoil whirled in her head as she drove back to the ranch.

The house was empty when she got there, which was some small relief, since it meant not having to explain herself to anyone else. She showered quickly, and then packed up. She hadn't brought a lot of clothes with her, so it didn't take long. She left a note on the kitchen table that she'd gone back to Denver and went out to her car.

Try as she might, she couldn't stop herself from looking toward Rambling Mountain. From imagining Jed and Rufus picking their way from that weathered shack down to that creek-side meadow.

The acute ache inside her was still mired in fury. So much so that she still couldn't tell which was worse.

Get over it, April.

She tossed her suitcase into the trunk, slammed it shut loudly and got behind the wheel. "You'll be home by supper," she told herself as she drove away from the big house.

A combine was lumbering down the highway when she reached it and she waited for it to pass. Her gaze kept straying to the mountain.

"Hurry up," she muttered to the tractor. Which was about as effective as spitting into the wind.

Finally, it was past and she pulled out onto the highway, the mountain in her rearview mirror.

She made it nearly to Weaver, before she suddenly pulled around in a U-turn and started back. Her pulse thrumming in her ears, she drove past the ranch entrance. Caught up to the combine and passed it, too, while the mountain loomed larger and larger until she turned off onto the private road that wound its way up the side. The pickup truck was gone when she finally reached the barricades and the UTV was parked on the other side of the boulders.

Jed wasn't there. And that was just as well.

She pulled out her pen and quickly scrawled on the back of a business card. Then she walked up the rest of the way, bypassed the weathered cabin, and pushed open the door of Jed's bunkhouse. She already knew it had no lock.

She didn't linger. Didn't want to allow the sight of the plaid blanket on the bed to remind her. She placed the business card squarely on the top of the blanket and turned around.

Samson was sitting in the doorway, flopping his tail. The teeth that could look so ferocious now curved as if in a happy grin.

She crouched down next to the dog and wrapped her arms around his neck. "Take care of him," she said against that thick gray hair.

Then she stood and walked away.

Not even the constant wind was enough to dry her cheeks.

* * *

Muddy and tired from a day of wrangling cows for a man who wasn't even around anymore to care, Jed let himself and Samson into the bunkhouse.

He noticed the small white rectangle sitting on his bed almost immediately and knew in his bones that it was from April.

He gave the bed as wide a berth as the dinky place allowed and threw off his filthy clothes in the bathroom. "Come on, dog."

Samson whined. But he was as muddy as Jed was and finally the dog stepped under the shower that Jed didn't bother trying to heat.

He scrubbed over the dog until he was clean enough to let run free and then he just stood there alone, head bowed under the beat of the icy spray until the water pooling around his feet ran clear.

He shut off the water. Got out and sluiced the moisture from his face and raked his hair out of his eyes with his fingers. His grim face stared back at him from the mirror on the medicine chest and he yanked it open, pulling out the bottle of aspirin. He swallowed one dry, then went out to pick up the business card she'd left.

The message was brief. Written in the same neatly slanting hand that had graced her note for Otis that first day.

A dollar sign. Followed by a whole lot of commas and zeros and the words "Top offer."

It was a helluva lot of money. But not as much as he knew the land was really worth.

The aspirin was stuck somewhere midway down. He rubbed the pain it was causing in his chest and set the card, dollar signs and zeros facing down, on the counter.

When Samson suddenly stopped trying to shake his coat dry and growled softly, Jed's nerves tightened all over again.

The dog took off like a shot when Jed opened the door. He followed more slowly after dashing himself with a towel and yanking on his jeans and boots.

The cause of the growl was apparent as soon as Jed rounded the cabin.

Samson was on his haunches, teeth bared.

Jed knew it wasn't the horse that had the dog's hair standing up, but the rider.

He finished pulling on the shirt he'd grabbed and eyed the man. Below the tan Stetson was a shock of iron-gray hair. Below that, a steady look from blue eyes so pale they seemed almost white.

If Squire Clay was wary about the hackles Samson was displaying, it didn't show.

"You ride all the way up here from the Double-C, Mr. Clay?" It would have taken him half the day or more.

His visitor's lined face creased even more. "Not the first time I've done it. But no. Left the trailer about ten miles down the hill." Squire's uncompromising gaze switched from Jed's face to look up at the cabin, then out over the view. "Every ten years or so, I'd come up here, trying to deal with Lambert. He ever tell you that?"

Jed smiled slightly. "A time or two."

The elderly man grunted. "Easier coming up on horseback than having to walk that last stretch of road after the slide. Might need to bury me, too, if I tried." He nudged his hat back a few inches and rested his crossed wrists on the saddle horn. "Any news about that will?"

Jed shook his head. "Not yet."

Squire sucked air between his teeth. His saddle creaked softly again.

"Nice-looking horse."

The old man nodded and ran a hand over the palomino's neck. "Clays breed some mighty fine horses. My son tells me you turned him down on the job."

Jed nodded once. He wasn't inclined to explain himself.

Squire crossed his wrists again. "Figure my chances of getting those acres I want are dwindling by the day. But the offer still stands. Fair market value."

"You should be telling that to Snead."

"I 'spect I'll be talking with that twit before long."

Jed considered *twit* a mild term where Snead was

concerned. "Thought you wouldn't try to negotiate against your granddaughter."

"She's gone."

Knowing it would happen didn't stop his stomach from turning hollow.

"Since I'm up here, might as well tell you that I have a fair interest in the herd, too." He squinted off into the distance. "Figure Lambert's rolling around in his grave now, laughin' hard about me admitting it. He and I never did see much eye to eye."

Jed couldn't deny that. "Otis is probably laughing about a hell of a lot these days."

Squire harrumphed. "He did like spiking people's guns."

"Pretty certain he's not the only one."

Squire gave a sharp crack of laughter and a herd of wrens shot from the grass into the air. "True enough." He looked out beyond the cliffs. "Always was a damn pretty view up here. Been in this land as long as Otis was. I started with nothing. He started with a mountain."

"Now you have one of the most profitable cattle companies in the western United States. And the Rad probably hasn't changed in the last fifty years."

"I know you started with nothing, too."

Jed listened to the buzz of insects. Felt the breeze pull at his shirt. For five years, he'd lived there with nobody but Otis knowing his past. Now, in the span of two days, it'd turned into a trending topic. He kept his voice expressionless. "Thought you and Otis weren't on that good of terms."

"Otis didn't say squat. But you've been keeping company with my granddaughter. And I make it a point to know the company my family's keeping."

She's not keeping company here when she's gone back to her life in Denver. He kept the thought to himself. "Is that the real reason you came up here? To tell me I'm not good enough for her?"

"Are you?"

"No."

Squire settled his hat more squarely on his head. "I wasn't good enough for my wife, either."

"Which one?"

A corner of his stern lips lifted. "Both." Then he thumbed his hat back an inch again and leaned forward. His gaze was penetrating. "But a man changes, son. When he finds a treasure worth it."

"Man still has to have something to offer. And I've got as much nothing now as I ever had." He regretted the admission, even though he figured it was an obvious one. "I'll convey your interest to Martin Pastore," he said abruptly. "He's the one in charge of the estate."

"Lawyers." Squire's lip curled almost as much as it had when he'd mentioned Snead. "Heard of Pastore. Usually sticks down in Cheyenne." He waved an all-encompassing arm. "Figures he'd get himself involved in a thing like this." His gaze sharpened on Jed again as he gathered up his reins. "You think about what I said."

"I'm not the one to talk to about a deal, Mr. Clay."

"Wasn't talking about the mountain," Squire said evenly. "Mind if I give Birdie here a water before I head back? I know where the trough is."

In answer, Jed shoved his hands down his front pockets and turned sideways.

Squire clucked softly and the horse swished her white-blond tail and angled beyond the cabin.

Jed was still standing there when they reappeared a short while later. Squire nodded his head once as he passed and Jed watched him ride away.

When the soft clip-clop of hooves on rough road finally faded away, he went to the cabin.

The boxes that April had helped him pack were still sitting there. Finding the will had put a halt on everything, including sending it all off to the auction house. He walked through to the bathroom and grabbed his clothes out of the dryer.

If he'd had a choice, he wouldn't go in the cabin at all. But he had to get his clothes clean somehow.

Bunching everything under one arm, he went out through the kitchen.

The bottle of scotch was still sitting on the table, where it had been since the day she'd helped him pack.

In his bunkhouse, he dumped the clothes on a

chair, then went out and filled a bucket with water and trudged it on foot all the way up to Otis's ridge.

He dumped the water over the riotous flowers then turned his gaze out.

"Gonna miss this place, Otis." The knowledge sat under his breastbone, a deeper ache than he ever would have expected. It provided a good strong base for the slice he felt whenever he thought about April. "I'm doing what I can for you. And for this place. But day's going to be here before long when I won't have that choice anymore. Figure you knew that, though."

He dropped his boot on the bucket to keep it from blowing away. "Don't know where things'll take me." Streaming red hair and a fluttering yellow dress swam in his mind and he closed it off, but not well enough to stop the throb of missing her. "Just know it won't be like before, when you pulled me up. God knows why I'm still on this earth, but I'll stick around until he's done with me. Know that's not something you ever concerned yourself with too much." He studied the flat headstone. "If I was here, I was here. If I decided to step off the cliff, you'd have kept right on being the same as ever."

His shirt flapped. The flowers bobbed and swayed.

Some things stayed constant.

The mountain. The wind.

The fact that Tanya's last words to him still applied.

What is the point of you?

He leaned over to grab the bucket handle. Briefly pressed his hand against the marker. "Rest easy, old man."

Then he straightened and went back down to the bunkhouse that was still his home.

At least for the next few weeks.

Chapter Fifteen

"Quite a crowd," Gage said two weeks later when he and April arrived at the Weaver courthouse.

They'd flown up from Denver by charter that morning, making quick work of the trip, even including flying over Rambling Mountain. It was handy that April's uncle Tristan happened to have a private airstrip outside of town. Gage's ex-wife, Jane, had arranged an SUV to be there waiting for their use.

"Mmm." Even though she'd spent the past three days—ever since they'd gotten word from Archer about the court schedule—mentally girding herself, she couldn't stop searching the people gathered there for Jed.

But she didn't see him.

Pastore and his associate were there. Snead, of course. Wearing one of his uptown suits, though it looked to her like it was hanging on his skinnier-than-ever frame, and the entourage who'd accompanied him last time was missing. She saw the mayor, who did have an entourage. A suited woman she recognized from the state Senate. Even Vivian Templeton's chatty assistant, who'd taken Gage's check that day.

"Sure you want to do this?" Gage asked. "You're really willing to invest your trust fund?"

They'd had the conversation more than once. Ever since she'd proposed the idea of adding her trust fund to his investment and becoming a silent, minority partner. "If the will's not accepted, together we'll be able to outbid Winemeier for certain." They knew it for a fact, since Archer had managed to find out just how deep the mining company's pockets actually were.

"If the will is accepted?"

"Then it's moot, because Jed'll inherit."

"Nobody knows that, yet," Gage cautioned.

"Then you'll get the mountain from whoever does." She spotted Squire about the same time he spotted her and waved. "There's my grandfather, so remember all that is just between you and me." Despite what Gloria had said that day at the Lazy-B, she was still staying there. Still hadn't returned to the Double-C. June had arrived and Squire wasn't hauling, nor was Gloria returning under her own steam. "I'll introduce you."

"Look a lot like your mama," Squire greeted as he leaned down to give her a hug. "She always used to wear suits like this when she was working for your dad."

April smiled and gestured. "This is my boss, Gage Stanton. Gage, my grandfather, Squire Clay."

Squire shifted his walking stick to his other hand in order to shake Gage's hand. "Lot of curious folks turning out today," he observed. "There's not a room *in* this courthouse big enough to fit 'em all."

Gage was just as tall as Squire. Black-haired against iron-gray. "You here as a council member or because of your own interest?"

Squire gave a chuckle. "Both. They're gonna have a stampede on their hands if they don't open the courtroom door soon."

"Archer's here," April said, watching the attorney work his way toward them. If she'd expected Jed to be with him for some reason, she would have been disappointed again.

"Place is a zoo," the attorney said when he reached them. He gave a nod toward Squire. "Good to see you."

Fortunately, despite Squire's antipathy toward Vivian, he didn't extend it to her grandchildren and he returned the greeting in a friendly enough way.

"Any luck finding out how she intends to rule?"

Archer shook his head at Gage's question. "Not even Pastore knows." His gaze strayed toward the opposing team. "At least that's what Nell told me yesterday. If it's true, at least we're all in the same boat."

The courtroom doors swung open as he spoke, and the crowd surged inside. She wasn't sure if it was simply determination or some well-placed blocks by Squire's walking stick, but the four of them managed to get a place in the front row of the gallery. Unfortunately, Louis Snead also slid in next to her, taking up the last of the space.

"Thought about raising that top offer?"

She had to work hard not to shudder. The man was positively oily. "We can discuss that if there turns out to actually be a reason to discuss it with *you*."

"I'm confident."

The chewed-off nails on his fingers implied otherwise. Either that or he had a terrifically bad habit.

She couldn't help herself. She looked over her shoulder. Scanned the faces in the gallery seats. The ones crowded behind them. The senator was directly behind Squire and kept leaning forward over his shoulder to talk to him.

April faced forward again to see the judge had entered the courtroom and was now sitting behind the bench.

"Standing room only," Squire murmured across Gage. "Figured I'd see Jed here."

She didn't reply. So had she.

The hearing was called to order and the judge looked over the top of her glasses. "This will be brief, and since we have a few more laypeople here than usual—" her dry statement earned a smattering of laughter "—I'll speak plainly. The holographic will dated November 2 of last year written by Otis Lambert has been duly authenticated—" she raised her voice over the swell of comments, including the noisy cursing coming from Snead "—to the court's satisfaction and probate is adjusted accordingly, effective immediately."

She nodded to her court clerk, who rose and carried a document over to Pastore, where he sat at the table in front of the bar. "Mr. Pastore, as administrator of the estate, you're receiving a copy, but to save everyone's time, I'll summarize the pertinent portions *if* y'all will shut your traps!"

It was more effective than a gavel. April's neck prickled in the abrupt silence and she looked back again.

Jed was standing against the closed courtroom doors and he looked so good to her that it hurt.

His eyes met hers.

Her breath felt hard.

"The area known as Rambling Mountain," the judge continued, "excluding the boundaries known as Rambling Rad Ranch, is to be titled to the state of Wyoming for the purpose of establishing a state park." The statement earned another rash of commentary that she only quelled after several bangs of her gavel, and April was vaguely aware of the senator once more leaning in toward Squire.

When the courtroom was silent again, Judge Fernandez continued. "If the state is unwilling or unable to establish said park, the property passes to the Town of Weaver, again with the stipulation that the area is to be protected yet remain of public use. I'll forgo the legal land description, but in general he's referring to the mountain from somewhere just above the lake all the way down to the highway."

April saw Jed's eyes close.

She blinked hard. If Otis had made a point of separating out the ranch, he'd *had* to have planned for Jed to have it.

The judge's gavel pounded a few more times and she finally turned back around.

Snead had buried his face in his hands and she had the strong suspicion he was trying not to sob too loudly.

The judge continued. "The real property defined as the Rambling Rad Ranch—essentially from the lake to the summit—including all buildings and improvements and physical property—are to be sold forthwith." The words earned another whack of the gavel to silence the brooding eruption.

April, however, could barely fathom the words. She looked at Gage, who had a speculative look on his face.

"Preferably to the highest damn bidder." Judge Fernandez looked over her glasses again. "That's a quote, by the way. All proceeds from the sale go to Mr. John Edward Dalloway." She lifted her gavel yet again, then grimaced, as if realizing it was pointless. Her courtroom was in chaos. She leaned over her microphone again. "There are a few additional comments for Mr. Dalloway that I see no need to mention in this setting, and that's it."

"But I'm his *relative*!" Snead gathered himself enough to protest.

"That's it," the judge repeated loudly. "Mr. Pastore, I assume the auction of personal property that was stayed is still ready to proceed?"

"Yes, Your Honor."

"Good. Then I expect you to wrap things up quickly on that end. I'm sure you'll be busy entertaining offers on the real property soon enough. Adjourned." She stood up as the courtroom went wild and walked out.

When April looked again, Jed was gone. And she didn't even know if he'd stayed there long enough to hear it all or not.

Along with everyone else, she stood. Squire was thick in conversation with the senator and April looked up at her boss. She kept her voice as low as she could. "Get the ranch."

"April—"

"I know you think its value is minor compared to the rest of the mountain," she cut him off. "I don't care if it takes every penny I have. Just keep it under the company name like we'd planned before. Only this time it won't cost you a dime."

Gage looked pained. "You're really serious about that. A *guest* ranch?"

"Run by Jed, if he's willing. You offer it to him."

"Why would he keep working the Rad if he gets the money from the sale?"

"Just offer. Are we partners or not?"

His lips compressed. Then he nodded.

Satisfied, she worked her way around Snead, who'd become a sad slump in his seat, to push her way through the crowd and out into the corridor. There was no sign of Jed.

She hurried to the stairs leading down to the main floor and still couldn't spot him. When she made it outside to the sidewalk surrounding the building and still hadn't caught him, she leaned back against the stone wall, heaving a sigh of defeat.

She was still there when the stream of people exiting the courthouse dwindled. Her grandfather was one of the last.

"Never would have expected it of Lambert," he said when he stopped next to her. "Man never shared anything he didn't have to." His gaze was penetrating. "Your Jed's going to be a rich fella."

"He's not my Jed and he's not going to care about the money any more than I do. It's just giving him a bigger reason to leave." She could only hope that she was right and the ranch meant more to him. "What were you and the senator looking so thick about?"

"Lambert wouldn't deal on that pass I wanted, but state land is a different matter."

"Of course." Squire was always Squire. She pushed away from the wall. "I need to find Gage." It was an excuse. Her boss was probably already getting in the offer to Pastore. "We're flying back to Denver later this afternoon."

"Hmm." He tipped up her chin. "Try and see your grandma before you go. You missed the do on Memorial Day and she misses you."

April made a face. "She misses *you* and I wish the two of you would just end this stupid standoff!" Then, because no matter how frustrated she was with him, she loved him beyond measure, she pulled his head down to kiss his leathery cheek. "I'll be back for July 4 for sure," she promised thickly. "I expect to see both my grandparents there."

She hurried back inside the courthouse.

There was an elevator, albeit aging and slow, but she took the stairs again to the upper level, where most of the courtrooms were located, and as she'd hoped, she found her boss and Archer in deep conversation with Pastore and his curly-haired associate.

Aside from them, the courtroom had emptied.

Gage certainly didn't need her. She pushed through the doors and felt her knees actually go weak. "Jed."

He was standing in the corridor, a paper coffee cup in his hand. If he was surprised to find her still there or if he even cared at all was anyone's guess. His dark brown eyes were as unfathomable as ever.

She clutched the leather strap of her skinny briefcase. "You left the courtroom. Did you hear—"

"I heard."

She exhaled, feeling even shakier inside. "Otis was full of surprises, wasn't he? Turning around and doing what you said he'd never do? Leaving it for public use?"

"Yeah."

"You weren't entirely right about the rest. He might not have left you the Rad, but he did leave you what it's worth." She chewed the inside of her cheek. "Several million at the very least. You'll be able to go where you want. Do what you want."

"Appears so."

Her chest was aching and she fell silent. Looked back at the courtroom. "I don't want to keep you if you were going back in there. Nobody has more of a vested interest in what's being discussed in there than you. Pastore's got a copy of the will, too." She made her legs move, aiming for the staircase again. "You can see what else Otis had to say to you."

"Already know what he put in the will. Just came from talking to the judge." He pulled a folded sheet of paper from his back pocket. "Have my own copy now."

"Oh, well right." Her head bobbed mechanically. "Good." As anxious as she'd been to find Jed after the hearing was adjourned, she was even more anxious to escape now. She edged farther toward the stairs. "That's really good. Considering how old the envelope it was in, the will turned out to be pretty recent." It was an utterly inane observation.

"You saw for yourself. He kept everything in that cabinet. Apparently, even old envelopes. Why the hell he hid it away like he did is just one more Otis mystery."

She managed a genuine smile at that. But holding it for long was too hard. "I'm glad it's not going to drag on for you. The Rad won't languish on the market, that's for sure."

"Your boss not interested anymore?"

She managed to lift her shoulders. "He's got something up his sleeve. He's in there now with Pastore, making an offer. You should go talk with him." She gestured vaguely. "I think Squire's downstairs waiting for me." It was an outright lie and the tips of her ears burned even more because of it.

His voice followed her when she made for the stairs. "Don't you want to know what else he said?"

She sent him a look. "It's none of my business."

"It concerns you."

She stopped at that. "Since Otis wrote his will months before we even met, I know that's not true."

He closed the distance between them and held out the folded copy. "Take a look for yourself."

She obviously wasn't going to get out of there without a fresh new layer of torture. She took the paper from him, annoyed that she shivered when their fingers brushed, and slowly unfolded it.

It was brief. Just a few paragraphs, really. In handwriting that was shaky, but not so badly as to be illegible. The judge had gone in order, she realized, as Otis's first bequest dealt with the state park matter. The second, the sale of the ranch.

The last paragraph, though, obviously included the additional comments the judge had mentioned.

Ain't leaving the ranch to you, Jed, though I thought about it plenty. Don't want to see you end up like me. Too easy to hide away from things that matter when you're holed up on the side of a mountain. You were right about the Rambling needing sharing. I'm right about this. Take the money even though I know how you'll feel about it. You can give it all away like before, but I'm hoping you won't. The point of you is to go back out there and live a life worth living. Ain't nothing served by having your only companion be a past that's dead and buried. I should know.

Her vision blurred as she read the last line. "Your friend, Otis." She sniffed and handed the copy back to him. She forced a smile. "Told you that he was your friend." A movement behind them caught her eyes.

Gage and the others had come out of the courtroom. Archer and her boss spotted them immediately and headed their way. "A slightly unexpected twist," he greeted, quickly introducing Jed and Gage.

She avoided the glance that Gage flicked her way. "You all have things to discuss. I'm going to—" she waved her hand "—find the restroom." Before any of them could comment, she practically jogged away. Her heels sounded loud on the stairs. She was lucky she didn't land on her face, considering the way she raced down them.

The restroom was as much an excuse as finding Squire had been and she went straight out the exit.

Gage was her ride, but this was Weaver. Everything downtown was in walking distance.

The sun felt hot and she pulled off her jacket as she headed down the block. It didn't really matter where she went, as long as it was away from Jed. Eventually, she'd have to see him if Gage secured the ranch. But that would still take time.

She realized she'd reached Colbys when she walked right past it.

She backed up and went inside, going straight to one of the stools at the bar. She tossed her briefcase and jacket on the empty stool beside her and rested her forehead on her hand.

"I can serve you," Jane said, "but frankly, most of the folks coming in to drink this early in the day don't tend to look as classy as you. Hearing over?" she asked when April looked up at her.

She nodded. "Surprised the news hasn't already made its way in here. And I'll take whatever cola you have." She watched the other woman fill a glass with ice. "Nice of you to arrange the SUV for Gage."

Jane smiled. "Easy to be nice to Gage now we're not married." She set the filled glass on the bar top. "How'd it go?"

April told her the gist of the will.

"And Gage really wants to buy the Rad." Jane shook her head slightly as if it were hard to believe. Which, of course it was. "Well, knowing him, he'll make a success out of it like he does everything else."

"Probably so." April was glad when a sizable group of women came in, chattering like magpies and pushing tables together, because it meant a distraction for Jane.

She pulled out her phone and sent a text to Gage

so he'd know where she was and dropped it back into her briefcase. She closed her eyes, rubbing her temples.

"You look like you've been pulled through a knothole."

April opened her eyes to see Piper standing there wearing summer shorts and a sympathetic look.

She got up and hugged her friend. "You said you were going to be in California with the youth group from your dad's church."

"They didn't need me as a chaperone, after all." Piper squeezed her hard. "Last thing I want to do now that school is out is herd a bunch of thirteen-year-olds seeing the beach for the first time in their lives." She pulled back to search April's face. "I heard about the hearing. How's Jed?"

April blinked hard and slid back onto the bar-stool. "Who knows?" Her voice was thick.

Piper sat beside her and bumped her shoulder companionably. "Everything's going to work out. Just because Jed is going to get the money instead of the ranch doesn't mean he'll just disappear or something."

"Turning into an optimist now?"

Piper smiled. "For the summer."

Jane was at the far side of the bar filling drink orders and April lowered her voice. "Gage is making an offer on the Rad."

"That guest ranch idea of yours?"

She nodded and quietly told her the rest and when she was done, Piper sat back.

"You don't look as surprised as I thought you would."

Piper gave her a look. "That you've found something you care about that much? What's surprising about that? Whether or not you think he'll never get over his wife, you're in love with Jed. When it comes to people you love, you'll do most anything. And I know that trust fund of yours is hefty, but won't turning the Rad into a guest ranch involve even more money?"

"Yes."

They both startled at the deep voice.

Piper pressed her lips together and widened her eyes at April. "Gotta go," she said suddenly, and hopped off the barstool to brush past Jed, hurrying through the breezeway that led from the bar to the family restaurant on the other side.

Which left April alone.

With him.

"You going to look at me or not?"

She did. Through the safety of the long narrow mirror on the wall opposite them. She felt hot all over, but her face looked pale. And unfortunately, even in the reflection, his gaze trapped hers. "How long have you been standing there?"

"Long enough."

Which told her absolutely nothing. She finally

managed to look away and lifted her glass, taking a gulp. "Did you talk to Gage?"

"He presented his idea."

Her hands felt shaky and she set the glass back down before she dropped it altogether. "And?"

"And it bears some thought. What are *your* plans'?"

Confused and still wary, she frowned. "About what?"

"Going to go back to Denver? Plan your next development deal with Stanton?"

"*For* Stanton," she corrected, feeling even more wary. "It's my job. So—"

"Not planning to be involved in morphing a hundred-year-old cabin into a viable guest ranch if Stanton succeeds in buying the ranch?"

"Not really my forte." Her hands were tight as knots but she managed to keep her tone more or less calm. "Unless you're planning to head off for easier conditions with the money you'll be getting, you could still be the one running the Rad." She steeled herself. "Nobody would blame you if you washed your hands of ranching the hard way."

"I'm not still in love with my wife."

Her eyes snapped back to the mirror. Oh, she definitely had her answer now about how long he'd been standing there.

The women at the pushed-together tables were

laughing riotously about something and his brown eyes shifted away toward them for a moment.

She swiveled around to face him. Her chest was tight. "I don't believe you."

His lips compressed. Then he gestured at the bar. "That paid for?" He didn't wait for an answer, but whipped out his wallet and tossed a few dollars on the bar top. "Come with me." He wrapped his hand around her upper arm, seeming oblivious to the jerk she couldn't quite hide.

She barely had the presence of mind to grab her briefcase as he pulled her out of the grill. His grip didn't ease when he paused briefly at the curb, and then jaywalked across the street.

She had to skip a few times for the rest of her body to keep up with her arm. They were aiming for the park. "Jed—"

"Don't talk right now, April."

Despite the turbulence inside her, she huffed. "I *beg* your pardon?"

They'd reached grass and he stopped abruptly, finally releasing her. "Have I ever lied to you?"

Her mouth opened. Closed. She shook her head.

"Then why think I'm lying about that?"

Her throat tightened. She held the briefcase in both hands in front of her. It was paltry protection against the pull of him. "You still have your wedding ring," she finally said.

His brows yanked together as he squinted at her. "What?"

She looked over his shoulder toward Rambling Mountain. Toward the Rad and his bunkhouse-for-one and that thick gold band in his bathroom with *Forever* etched inside. "Your wedding ring," she repeated thinly. "I know you still have it. I saw it right next to your toothpaste the morning after we…we—"

He swore under his breath and rubbed his hand down his face. When he looked at her again, his eyes were soft.

So soft, they made hers burn.

"Come on." Instead of shackling her arm, he took her briefcase from her and closed his hand around hers.

Resisting him took more willpower than she possessed and she walked with him across the grass. Around a young couple and their baby spread on a blanket and past a gaggle of teenagers tossing a Frisbee. He didn't stop until they reached the empty gazebo. He set her briefcase on the weathered wood and nudged her down to sit, though he didn't.

"I need to tell you about Tanya."

There was no hope of squelching her tremble. "No, you don't have—"

"I do." He propped his hands on his hips and studied her. "From the first time I saw Tanya, I wanted her. I was like the peasant—"

"You're not a peasant."

"Trust you to say that. You don't think anyone is." His eyebrows were lifted slightly. "Going to let me finish?"

She clamped her lips together.

"She was like the princess in the tower. We were the same age, but she was private schools and exotic summer vacations and I was public school and sweating alongside my dad all summer."

She sucked in her cheek between her teeth. Great. A fairy-tale love.

"I was ten when she kissed me. The fact that she'd done it on a dare by her friends only made me more determined to get her." He spread his hands, then dropped them. "And I did, but not until I'd scraped my way up from peasant to a position with Hampton-Tiggs and was pulling down seven figures. Until then, I was still the kid with dirt under my nails." His lips twisted. "Just because I loved her didn't mean I was blind to her. We were twenty-three when we married in the biggest damn wedding—" He broke off, shaking his head. "She liked playing the princess to the hilt and I was ambitious and driven." His eyes roved over her face. "We were already crumbling when everything hit the fan at Hampton-Tiggs a year later. There were months of investigations. Every time I turned around there was another deposition. Another hearing. I started working with the investigators, putting as much time in with them as I'd ever done with the firm. She wanted me to go to another investment bank. Then when I put all my money into a fund benefitting the victims, she moved out. But she was pregnant, and—"

She reached out, her fingertips grazing him. "You don't have to do this."

He closed his hand around her fingers and pressed them to his chest. "I may not have loved the princess the way I should have, but I loved the baby." His eyes flickered. "Babies. You already know she was texting me when she had the accident. What is the point of you? That was the last thing she ever said to me."

Her heart felt like it was cracking. *The point of you is to go back out there and live a life worth living.* Otis had said it in his will. "I'm so sorry. Nobody should say such a thing."

He bent his head and kissed her fingers. "Nobody should. It doesn't change the fact that if I had been at that appointment, she wouldn't have been driving and texting me about it. She wouldn't have died. There was no way we would have made it together, married." The look in his eyes was heartbreaking. "But losing two babies before we even knew there were two." The scar on his chin looked whiter. "That broke me."

Her vision glazed.

"Three years later, I met Otis. He was in Texas

because someone there had died. Maybe a relative of Snead's. Maybe someone more important to him. I don't know. He never said. But I do know he kept me alive that night when he didn't have any reason to do so. Maybe he recognized someone more miserable than he was. When he bailed me out after the bar fight, he said I could come and work at the Rad. And you know the rest." He tugged her to her feet and touched her chin, nudging it upward. "That wedding ring I keep was not mine. It was my father's. He said he'd love my mother forever, and he did."

She blinked and a tear spilled over.

He thumbed it away, smiling faintly. "Such a softy."

She sniffed. "I thought—"

"I know." His gaze still on hers, he lowered his mouth to hers. Kissed her softly.

Her knees went weak and her fingers somehow ended up looped in his belt loops.

He cradled her face. "Why're you staking Stanton's deal?"

She sagged. "He wasn't supposed to tell you!"

"Too bad. Why?"

It was too hard to pretend anymore. Not with his eyes searching hers, seeming to reach down into the very heart of her. "Because I love you," she said huskily. "And you need the Rad."

"Oh, baby." He exhaled slowly and pressed his

mouth against hers until she was quaking. "I don't need the Rad. I *need* you, April. You're *my forever*."

She sucked in a shaking breath. Her heart was falling wide.

He threaded back her hair. "It's still going to take a while for the court to decide on the sale of the Rad and I don't want to wait a while for you. I'm not that same kid who crawled his way up a princess's tower, but that doesn't erase who I was. Even though I know you deserve better—"

"Stop."

He ignored her. "I'll follow you if you go back to Denver. And I'll keep following until you stop and let me catch you."

She let out a choked laugh. "Oh, Jed." She traced her finger down his jaw. Running it slowly over his scar. Then his lower lip. "You caught me weeks ago."

His arms tightened and she could feel his heart beating just as hard as hers. "Then you'll stay?"

"I'll stay."

"If you get the sale, the money goes back into the Rad. We'll make it work together or not at all."

She moistened her lips. "Partners."

"Wouldn't you agree that's what a husband and wife should be?"

She went still and stared up at him. "Are you proposing?"

"At the risk of committing good ol' Ken's error—"

She cut him off with a fervent kiss. "You're not Kenneth," she assured thickly.

"Damn straight." He smiled slightly. "Reed and Dalloway. Rad. What do you say?"

His chocolate eyes seemed lit from behind and everything she'd ever wanted was there for the taking. All she had to do was reach.

The Rambling Rad had stood for nearly a hundred years.

And so would they.

"I say *yes*, Jed Dalloway." She slowly pulled his head down to hers, tumbling willingly into whatever their future would hold. "Because you're *my* forever, too.

* * * * *

MILLS & BOON

Coming next month

ONE NIGHT WITH HER MILLIONAIRE BOSS
Kandy Shepherd

The rain was coming down so hard it had driven channels into the gravel, forming small gushing streams. The path was well lit, but it was getting more difficult to avoid the streams and save her shoes and she found herself jumping from side to side as if in a game of aquatic hopscotch. She cursed out loud when the umbrella suddenly turned completely inside out. She was left with only a light jacket over her dress for protection against the elements.

Then Ned was there. 'Seems like you could do with some help,' he said. He was sensibly encased in a long oilskin raincoat and held aloft an enormous black umbrella.

'This darn umbrella is useless,' she spluttered and threw it on the ground.

'Don't tell me—you chose it because it was purple.'

'It was the first one I saw,' she fibbed. Of course she'd been attracted to the pattern of purple iris. The possible sturdiness of the umbrella hadn't been a consideration.

'Come here,' he said.

Ned pulled her to him and under the shelter of his umbrella. Suddenly the stinging onslaught of the rain on her face stopped, but she was far too distracted by Ned's closeness to care. She was dry. She was warm. *He was hot.*

'It's great to get rain. We need it. Trouble is when it all comes down like this at once, so much of it runs off.'

'Hopefully it will ease off,' she said.

His chest was a wall of solid muscle. As he led her towards the house, steering her through the channels, she leaned in closer. Just, of course, to make sure she was completely under the shelter of his umbrella.

'We're almost there or I'd pick you up and carry you,' he said.

'*What!*'

'You're a little thing. Nowhere as heavy as a full-grown sheep to sling over my shoulder.'

Before she had a chance to reply, they reached the house. In one fluid movement, Ned ditched his umbrella, put his hands under her armpits, lifted her off the ground and up the steps, depositing her on the veranda. Freya was back on her feet, out of the rain, before she had time to protest.

'Did you just compare me to a sheep?' she said, mock glaring up at him, a smile twitching at the corners of her mouth. His hair was dark with damp and fat drops of water sat on his cheeks. He grinned. Her heart gave that curious lurch of recognition—she didn't know where it came from.

'A ewe, if I'm to be precise,' he said.

'I'm glad you at least amended that to be a lady sheep.' She couldn't resist his grin and responded with one of her own. 'Do you really lift and haul sheep around the place?' If so, no wonder the man was made of muscle.

'If needs be,' he said. 'I grew up learning to do everything that needed to be done with sheep. Rescue them, shear them, sometimes birth them. So yeah, I've had to haul around the odd sheep or two over the years. No special treatment for the boss.'

He sounded so laconic, so laidback, so *manly* she leaned up on tiptoe and kissed him on the cheek. 'Thank you, for rescuing me like a stray sheep caught in the rain.' She froze. *Why did she do that?*

Her lips tingled from the connection to his skin, cool with raindrops. For a crazy moment she'd wanted to taste them, taste *him*. Her gaze connected with his for a long, still moment.

Continue reading
ONE NIGHT WITH HER MILLIONAIRE BOSS
Kandy Shepherd

Available next month
www.millsandboon.co.uk

MILLS & BOON
MEDICAL
Pulse-Racing Passion

Set your pulse racing with dedicated, delectable doctors in the high-pressure world of medicine, where emotions run high and passion, comfort and love are the best medicine.

JOIN US ON SOCIAL MEDIA!

Stay up to date with our latest releases, author news and gossip, special offers and discounts, and all the behind-the-scenes action from Mills & Boon...

 millsandboon

 millsandboonuk

 millsandboon

It might just be true love...